RED MONKEY

w w goss

Disclaimer

Red Monkey is a work of fiction. Names and characters presented in the work are products of the author's imagination. Locations and events may be loosely based on actual places and events.

Cover

From an image created by Javier Alberich, Basel, Switzerland

wwgoss.com

Acknowledgments

Javier, thank you for sharing your time and formidable talent in support of this unknown writer. Thank you Holly Lorincz, my tough-love editor. You stuck with me and that meant the world to me. Thank you Jay Zebrowski, my steadfast friend and patient grammarian. And most of all, thank you Marie, my wonderful and supportive wife, for letting me run with this obsession to write a good sentence and for reining me in when I got out of control.

For Marie

The Dolder Grand

Max Stonecrop was neither unaccomplished nor anti-social. He liked peace and quiet and routine: a morning latte at Café Stehli, a few deliveries for the boss, a sunset run in the Zürich foothills, and dinner at his studio apartment in the Niederdorf. This afternoon, the not-quite-yet familiar routine was interrupted by the presence of a sealed envelope taped to his apartment postbox. The directions neatly printed on the envelope read: *A SURPRISE! Deliver to G. Ratzow at 19:15 today, Carezza Suite, The Dolder Grand Hotel.*

Stonecrop slipped the envelope into the jacket pocket of his running suit and headed out the door. The uphill jog to the Dolder took less than half-an-hour and in five minutes more he found his way to the Carezza Suite. It was seven p.m. Close enough.

His boss, Gregor Ratzow, greeted him at the open door, took the envelope, gave it a cursory inspection, and shoved it into his pocket. Whatever was on Ratzow's mind—and something was bothering him —it had nothing to do with the note Stonecrop had just handed him. As Stonecrop turned to leave, Ratzow grabbed him by the arm, and spun him around. He strong-armed Stonecrop through the doorway and paraded him into the room.

They made an odd pair. Stonecrop was thirty-five and six-two, and didn't carry an ounce of fat. The short man with the vice-grip on his arm was nearly twice the age and twice the weight. Ratzow's five-o-clock shadow rubbed Stonecrop's ear. "Stay," the boss ordered in a tone was as harsh as the stubble on his chin.

"Really?" Stonecrop smiled but held his breath to avoid the odors of cigar and cologne, odors befitting an East European thug out of a C-grade movie.

Before he saw the guests in the flesh, Stonecrop caught and noted their reflections in the suite's floor-to-ceiling windows. Two drawn curtains and two earth-toned de Sede sofas bracketed a dining table that had been strategically positioned to capture the view. The Giacometti-style table was set for a party of seven.

In the distance and well beyond their reflections—Stonecrop's joining them as he entered the room—the graceful arc of the Albis foothills stretched southward and merged with the horizon. The Mönch, Sustenhorn, and the Tödi rose above and behind the silhouette of the Zürcher Hausberge—the local foothills. Below, in the growing darkness, a crescent of city lights limned the edge of the Zürisee.

The conversation among the guests seemed casual but anticipatory. The four men and two women were clad in business attire. Stonecrop's orange running suit with its reflective Adidas striping suggested a prison uniform.

The winding two-and-a-half-kilometer jog from the Niederdorf, the old town below and on the same side of the Limmat river as the Dolder, had not been enough for Stonecrop to break a sweat.   He keen to turn around and return to his apartment.

"Why?" Stonecrop challenged has master.

Ratzow snapped back: "To sit in this seat! That's why." He pointed at a chair and Stonecrop sat. Then Ratzow turned to the group: "I introduce Mr. Max Stonecrop, my man who does errands. He is fastest man in Zürich. Olympic medal winner. He *brrrings* me this!" Thinking his Bulgarian accent charming, Ratzow over-trilled the "r." He retrieved the envelope Stonecrop had given him. "*Soooprrrise* it says! For me! I read later. Now, we talk, eat, and thank our host, Mr. Alexander, who pay for dinner with number-one view in all Zürrrrich!" Another "r" flourish wrapped up the announcement. The unopened envelope disappeared into a trouser pocket.

It was futile to challenge Ratzow's hyperbole. Stonecrop was not an Olympic medalist, although he had been invited to join the U.S. Biathlon Team. He let the exaggeration pass but found it curious that Ratzow was aware of this detail from his past. They had never spoken about it.

Ratzow reached an arm around Stonecrop's back and shoulders, "Where is my daughter?"

Stonecrop shrugged and sat like an obedient Labrador that was confused by his master's question. He fixated on Ratzow's watch-faced Bucherer cufflink. Was it a functional timepiece or a decorative artifact? It read 7:35 p.m. That was about right. Federica should have finished work. He usually received a text from her as she left the hospital.

Ratzow's question hung in the air. He clearly expected his daughter to be here. In a failed attempt to appear at ease, he stepped behind Stonecrop and squeezed his shoulders. "If she calls, you take car. Get her."

"Gregor," Stonecrop twisted in his seat to face Ratzow, "I'll wait in the lobby."

His boss laughed stiffly and attracted the attention of several guests. He flashed a smile. When the gazes drifted elsewhere so did the smile. "Stay, please," he said. "I need you stay."

Ratzow was anxious for good reason. The chatter around the room was about a project that Federica had asked the attendees to support, a project intended to provide medical services to remote communities in Africa. Her absence was an insult to their host.

Ratzow glared at the door, willing Federica to appear and letting Stonecrop know there was to be no escape until she showed.

Over the last six months, Stonecrop had couriered items to and from every member of Ratzow's team. They were not a friendly bunch. When he had been hired, they had written him off as a short-termer; he was too old and over-qualified for this sort of work, he kept to himself too much, he wasn't Swiss. They had been dismissive. Yet, six months had passed and here he was, sitting next to Ratzow, who had told them all to go to hell. Today, these people still knew as little about Max Stonecrop as the day Ratzow had hired him.

"You okay?" The words were spoken by their host, the large African American man seated across the table and to the left of Ratzow.

Stonecrop had been rubbing his hands together. They were cold from the post-dusk run in the November air. "I'm fine, thank you." He looked for an excuse for his distracted state, and finding none, extended a hand, "Max Stonecrop."

"Dante, Dante Alexander. CEO, Potomac Defense." Two enormous and toasty warm hands swallowed the one Stonecrop had offered. Alexander, like Ratzow, probably weighed in at close to three hundred, mostly bone and muscle in his case. His scalp was clean-shaven and starred with beads of perspiration. "I've been working with Frau Doktor Ratzow. I assume you're acquainted."

"Gregor's expecting her. He wants me to pick her up if she needs a ride."

"Did you run here? Do you need a car? I can ask the concierge."

"Gregor has one. But thank you."

"Gregor said you're a courier—something like that?"

The offer to help and the tone of Alexander's voice put Stonecrop at ease. The small kindness was a break from the snooty treatment he usually got from Ratzow's minions. Alexander was nobody's minion.

Alexander ignored Stonecrop's silence and repeated his earlier statement, this time as a question: "So, you are acquainted?" When he smiled or spoke, Alexander flashed a set of near-perfect teeth, the exception being a distracting gold-capped canine on the upper right, his right.

Stonecrop didn't sport a gold tooth but he did have a crooked one—a front tooth, the one on the top right. The angle of the tooth created a narrow, triangular gap, the wider part being at the gum line. The asymmetry was offset—balanced, really—by a second asymmetry, a nose that tilted slightly in the opposite direction. The anomalies coarsened his features and gave them a certain angularity and hardness, even cruelty.

During a pause in which neither man spoke, Stonecrop continued his examination of Alexander, noting the muffler of black flesh that in places draped over a Cuban chain around his neck.

"Not work, but yes, we're friends."

"A remarkable woman," Alexander said, and then, as if correcting the statement, "A remarkable *person*, I should say."

Stonecrop waited in silence.

"Look, you don't have to talk, *dat's bon-bon, mon*. I don't want to make you feel uncomfortable. Hey, I'm surprised at the turn-out," he said, continuing the one-sided conversation. Something made him chuckle and triggered a tremor through his torso. "I thought it would be just the three of us: Gregor, Dr. Ratzow, and me," he said. "I had to ask the concierge to up the headcount."

"Yeah, Lenz. He's a good man. You know, I've never been in this part of the hotel," Stonecrop veered to a neutral topic. "Can't beat the view. We're on the outside tip of the Spa wing. The other wing is called the Golf wing. For once," Stonecrop smiled, "Gregor is not exaggerating; the view *is* extraordinary."

"You've been here before?"

"In another lifetime, different job. Used one of the breakout rooms for a couple meetings." He paused, and then continued, "I remember they were pricey. Can't imagine—well, I can guess—what the Carezza costs."

Dante laughed, "One of the perks of being a defense contractor."

His firm had to be paying ten thousand Swiss for the suite.

"No judgement intended," Stonecrop said. "Have you seen the spa?"

"Not yet, but tempted."

"You can reserve a room where it bloody snows on demand," Stonecrop reported.

Ulrich "Uli" Geissner, executive vice president of Ratzow's company, GR Group, AG, slid into the chair next to Stonecrop. He didn't look at Stonecrop but adjusted his wire-rim glasses by pushing up the bridge-piece with his middle finger, the gesture symbolic of Geissner's attitude toward most of humanity.

Geissner wiped his brow with a silk pocket square. He refolded the material so the dampened portion would be on an inner layer, and returned the square to its home. The man was fastidious. He was Swiss, but somehow the truly endearing Swiss qualities had bypassed Geissner. There was none of the likable craziness, modesty, and self-deprecatory humor.

Geissner inserted himself into the conversations, listening rather than joining. As a long-time resident of Zürich, a city where one-third of the population hail from someplace other than Switzerland, Geissner prided himself on his ability to identify the origin or nationality of people's accents.

Alexander's Caribbean heritage was obvious. Geissner addressed his wife, Uta: "I hear a splash of something else, a little *salsa*."

Uta, seated beside him, joined the game. "So?" she asked, pronouncing the first letter of the word like a 'Z.'

"*Karibisch, vielleicht Puerto Rico, . . .*" he declared. Stonecrop couldn't hear the rest of their conversation.

Seated farthest from Stonecrop and on Alexander's side of the table were Ratzow's administrative tag-team, his acolytes Henrietta Reeb and Meyer Pfaff. They sat quietly as Geissner transitioned into a stump speech about GR Group.

Stonecrop checked his phone for a text or email from Federica. Finding nothing, he fired off a note, and, for no reason, wrote in German, <MS: *Wo bist du?*>

Geissner droned on, "I want to reiterate. Group has no intention of changing the terms of the agreement prepared by your investment bank. Tonight, we make a friendly meet and greet. Next week, we post the LC. Remind me, what bank?"

"Moretti & Cie, Banquiers," Alexander supplied the name, speaking mechanically, making it obvious that he knew that Geissner knew what bank. Alexander's body language told the real message: stop stalling, damn it.

The acolytes bobbed their heads in chorus to Geissner's spiel. On cue, they spoke. Meyer was first: "As Uli was saying, the lawyers need to take one more pass. Group will expedite Canton filings." Reeb, strutted out and botched an English colloquialism, "a stamp-rubber affair."

The confluence of banker, accountant, and Ratzow's number one, Uli Geissner, conferred gravitas to the gathering—a gravitas that, in light of Federica's absence, came up short. As they all knew, Federica Ratzow, though artless by nature, was the force and reason for their gathering. The leadership vacuum amplified the significance of her truancy.

Stonecrop felt it too: This was her deal; she ought to be here. His concern compounded as he considered for the first time that her absence might not be work related.

He withdrew from the table talk and nursed the drink Ratzow had ordered for him, a Stoli on the rocks with lime. Despite making one or two deliveries a week for Group, he knew little about its affairs. He suspected irregularities, and that suspicion contributed to a reluctance to learn more. *What* do *I know?* he thought to himself. Group was domiciled in Zug, a tax-friendly Canton an hour south of Zürich. The types of filings he delivered to the Cantonal Tax Office suggested Group was primarily a holding company, administering investments in companies which do not conduct business in Switzerland.

His courier work was not limited to Zürich and environs. Every other month he traveled to Valletta, Malta, where he handed over a briefcase to one Francis de Bruyn, a South African staffer in Group's office. Ratzow referred to Francis as "the Clerk," though the Clerk didn't come across as a pencil pusher; he was more a rocket-propelled grenade kind of guy. The Clerk, and a dozen others in the Valletta office, seemed to manage whatever it was that Group did.

Ratzow himself traveled frequently and was obsessed with security. In Zürich, Ratzow lived and worked out of Hotel Storchen—pricey digs for a home office. By contrast, Federica's little non-profit, Aide Direct, was housed in an inexpensive, urban office space on the backside of Löwenstrasse. The office exhibited the crowded chaos common to every young, volunteer-based organizations. Photos taped to the walls depicted medical personnel working at sites of natural or man-made disasters. The geographic focus was Southeast Africa.

The AD office overlooked a seedy section of the Schanzengraben moat, part of an old Baroque fortification and hangout central for teens. The area was littered with discarded plastic bottles, cigarette butts, and paper trash. And, of course, drug paraphernalia. The City must have decided to let the area go to hell to demonstrate that Zürich was not entirely antiseptic and soulless. As one neared the mouth of the Zürichsee, the moat became progressively cleaner and vintage motorboats, like charms on a bracelet, dangled off moorings along its eastern bank.

"Max, that's quite impressive, yes!" Pfaff said, directing the comment at Stonecrop and catching him lost in his own thoughts.

"I'm sorry, I missed what you said."

"Our guest, Dante, graduated from Rensselaer Polytechnic Institute and Stanford! Robotics and computer science degrees, and an MBA!" Pfaff went on, "Quite an achievement. Imagine, Dante was born in the Bahamas and home-schooled until he was twelve."

"Yes, very impressive," Stonecrop agreed, interested, though having nothing to add and only after-the-fact realizing that Pfaff's compliment could be interpreted as condescending.

The patter fizzed out as it became clear that Federica was likely a no-show. The meeting tonight had a purpose. These were busy people and they wanted to get on with things—with or without her.

Gregor Ratzow was animated one minute and withdrawn the next, frequently asking Stonecrop about Federica, or gesturing by raising one shaggy eyebrow. The see-saw feat, when Federica and Stonecrop had a go at it, always ended in hilarious failure. At one point, when speaking privately with Stonecrop, Ratzow referred to his daughter by her family nickname, "Fede".

Alessia Federica Ratzow had not answered, and perhaps had not even received, the texts or calls from her father or Stonecrop. She was more likely to contact Stonecrop first, a fact Ratzow grudgingly accepted, and no doubt the reason for his keeping Stonecrop joined to his hip tonight.

"Gregor," Stonecrop leaned over and spoke quietly, "Why don't I swing by the Spital? If she's not there I'll check Ott's and AD. It must be something urgent."

Stonecrop used the Swiss German word for hospital. It was less of mouthful than *Universitätsspital Zürich* and was pronounced "Shpital."

The short-on-patience Ratzow leaned across Stonecrop and

addressed Geissner, "I don't know what is going on with Federica. No text, no call. We eat." Then he turned to Stonecrop and once again gave him the doggie treatment, "Sit." Stonecrop wanted to ask for a treat but knew better.

Geissner, an effete substitute for the absent woman of honor, took the stage. Defying Ratzow's directive to move things along, Geissner prattled on, expounding upon how Potomac Defense technology would enhance Aide Direct's capacity for rapid-response aid. Geissner had only back-of-the-envelope knowledge about Aide Direct but came across as reasonably savvy about the technology Potomac was offering.

Alexander got the picture. Without Federica, they were all going through a charade. Alexander made a statement that was short and to the point—he was honored to be able to contribute to the good work being done by Aide Direct, had enormous respect for Dr. Ratzow, and regretted that she was not present.

Others spoke. The delays frustrated Ratzow. He fidgeted and opened and closed his hands into a fists. He bent back the neck of a fork and that seemed to make him feel better.

The waiter stationed at the sideboard/bar—as keen for progress as the guests—took their orders. He replaced the fork Ratzow had maimed. Stonecrop picked up on Ratzow's stress. He gave the menu a cursory look and ordered the tuna tartar with citrus vinaigrette, to be followed by Balik salmon with cream sauce, a Dolder specialty. Having limited tolerance for the affectations of the culinary elite, his choice was determined by price. If these people were going to make him suffer through a business dinner, then the least Stonecrop could do was make them pay through the nose—the spirited act was a nod to Stonecrop's venture capital pedigree. He chose a pricey Montrachet Chardonnay to pair with the salmon.

Ratzow was unmoved by the extravagant order. The non-reaction bothered Stonecrop. He fired off another text to Federica: <MS: Gregor flipping out. Where are you?>

The dinner schlepped on, following the trajectory of all such occasions, wherein the parties invite or deliver worn narratives related to their vocations and life-altering but self-flattering experiences. The hackneyed drill bored Stonecrop. He focused on his phone and food. The meal was—as always at the Dolder—exceptional.

It soon became apparent that Ratzow had little interest in prolonging the torture. Group would execute the guarantee. She was his daughter and Ratzow couldn't care less about the size or terms of the credit support. Ratzow had an instinct for people. He had sized up Alexander ten minutes after they had met.

Ratzow put away his fifth vodka, a chaser to the dinner he had wolfed down and already forgotten. He indecorously belched, then dug out and opened the envelope in his pocket. He extracted the notecard and read it.

His face tightened. Without a word, he rose and walked away from the table. He crammed the crushed card and envelope back into his pocket.

Stonecrop was about to follow when his attention was distracted by a question from Uta and directed at Alexander, asking Alexander how he and Federica had met.

"In Mozambique, last year. We were working on different projects, both connected to the Somali crisis. I was consulting to a team of U.S. Military advisors; Miss Ratzow's organization was providing support at a refugee camp. Her 'brother' ran the camp—not her actual brother, but that's how she referred to him."

"Very different agendas, I would think. What brought you together?" she asked, and then added, "Is it common for a company like Potomac to engage in humanitarian work?"

Alexander smiled, "I don't know. But the answer to your first question is obvious—Federica. I mean, Dr. Ratzow—"

"We *all* call her Federica." Uta tilted forward to avoid speaking over other conversations at the table. "If you know her at all, you know she's not one for formalities."

"She's professional and persistent as a bulldog! I respect that. And I respect her organization's commitments. The people she serves are desperate. Seeing the conflict first-hand, I appreciate the challenges." He gave one of his roly-poly laughs as a lead-in, "And she *is* a charmer!"

"How interesting," Uta added a flirtatious cant to the statement. "It seems you were under her spell!"

"Guilty!" Alexander replied. "Hey, I'm *here*. Doing *this*! It is a first for Potomac, to provide services to an NGO. I'm excited and it feels right." He paused to address the uncomfortable and obvious issue, "A shame Federica's not here to celebrate our collaboration. I'm sure there's a good reason."

As the dinner wound down, Ratzow returned to the table. He stood at his seat, hands on the back of the chair. "I just receive text from my hard-working daughter. She work four jobs. She is sorry. She apologizes, especially, she apologizes to Dante, who travels far and pays for big dinner! Was good dinner, da!"

The dinner comment earned an upbeat approval from the crowd.

"Emergency at hospital. She works all night." Ratzow frowned, "Message was sent one hour ago. Only now on phone." He raised the phone overhead and glared at it, "Technology shit!"

In a calmer voice, Ratzow asked the group to move to the terrace to take in the city lights and stars and enjoy a digestif.

On the terrace, even under the wall-mounted warming lamps, the chill prickled the flesh. A white wafer-shaped cloud hung over the lake and was lit from below by city lights and from above by a gibbous moon. Stonecrop wondered what stage the tide would be at in Palma, Mallorca. *Once a sailor, always a sailor.*

Ratzow nodded in his direction: time to go. Stonecrop made the rounds, making goodbyes and walking up to Ratzow last.

"One moment, Max. Read." Ratzow took the crumpled note from his pocket and unfolded it. Moving to a quiet corner away from the others and under a deck light, he held the note so Stonecrop could read it. The words were clear enough: —*Papà. please do what they ask. no police, no problems. ti amo. FR*

At the bottom of the note there was a spiral symbol, in red.

"The text? You said you got a text. She was at the hospital." Stonecrop asked but knew the answer.

"Only this shit, no text." Ratzow turned his head to the side and spat.

"Let me see it again." Stonecrop held the note closer to the light. He reacted the way he always reacted when something to be feared presented itself. An internal switch regulated his breath, dampened his pulse, and put his senses on alert. The air was dry and still; the night overly clear.

"Federica didn't write this," he continued. "But whoever did was familiar with her handwriting." He felt the warmth from the lamplight on his palm and for no rational reason imagined Federica's hands, with their long, deft physician's fingers, swollen and shaking from the cold. He felt and then discarded a rising anger. Anger was an infantile antidote to fear. "Who is it, Gregor? What's with the spiral? It's like one of those targets you piss on at an airport urinal!"

"You piss on this one, you lose dick," Ratzow flatly stated.

Stonecrop replayed how the note had come to him. It had been delivered and taped to the outside of his apartment postbox. Generic evidence. Certainly wasn't Swiss Post. The note was made to look like a personal announcement or invitation from one of Ratzow's friends.

Ratzow asked, "Where and how?" His eyes were feral, momentarily accusing Stonecrop, then scrutinizing the guests—all of whom were admiring the view but cold and preparing to call it a night. The temperature was dropping fast. "Not time to fuck with Potomac," Ratzow said.

Ratzow's English, normally fair to good, worsened. Stonecrop had noticed the trait before. Under stress, or when he intentionally played dumb, Ratzow would forget common expressions and mix up verb order and tenses. His hostility was in free-fall, sucking in the energy around him.

Stonecrop felt caught in the backwash. He gripped Ratzow's shoulder and squeezed hard enough that there could be a bruise in the morning. Once again, he inhaled the aroma of the man. Their heads touched.

"Maybe that's why," Stonecrop said.

"What you mean *why*?"

"Potomac. The people who wrote this message don't want you to fuck with Potomac." Stonecrop repeated Ratzow's words back to him.

"Think about it," Stonecrop added. "Only someone very close to you and to this deal would know your whereabouts and hers—and mine and Dante's. There's gotta be a connection."

"Not close. Federica would say Babbo, not Papà. I *know* who this is," Ratzow said. The words trembled, hiding their thunder. "If she harmed, one hair on her head, I kill the people who take her. Hell, I fucking kill them anyway." There was no hyperbole in the threat. Nothing but deadly certitude. "Go home," Ratzow continued. His tone of voice was venomous. "Gregor fix. You wait. Do nothing. Understand? Do nothing."

Stonecrop didn't move. "Do nothing" was not in his DNA. Not for something like this.

"Get out!" Ratzow yelled.

The guests turned toward them. Alexander focused on Stonecrop. Their eyes connected.

"Let go," Ratzow said, "you brrrrreak arm?"

Stonecrop released his grip; Ratzow massaged the shoulder. Nothing more transpired between them.

The air thickened with moisture and grew colder as Stonecrop descended and neared the lake. Rime coated the cobblestones at the entry to his apartment building. In the foyer, he stared at the bank of mailboxes and slammed the bottom of his fist on the box where the message had been taped. He immediately felt stupid about the outburst and thought about how Federica would have chided him. The thought made him smile and remember the first word she had spoken to him, seven years ago, in the dining car on the overnight express to Venice: *Khairete.*

Khaìrete

"Khaìrete!" the young, female voice from behind greeted him. "Can I join you?"

He sensed her hands resting on the suit coat tossed over the back of his chair. At first, he wasn't sure if she was addressing him. But then, of course, who else could she be speaking to. Leaving his elbow on the table and hand buried in his unkempt thicket of hair, he twisted his head to the left, then the right. Each time she stepped just out of sight. He closed the book he was reading, Homer's Odyssey, a Greek-only edition. The book had been his companion for the past three months as he'd traveled from one money center to another, visiting private banks, pension funds, monied individuals, and wealth management companies in a campaign to raise funds for COLS IV, Colorado Life Sciences' fourth venture fund and the second COLS fund in which he would have a modest associate's carry.

The dining car bustled. All the tables were taken, several by single travelers like himself. The hide-and-seek game ended. The body belonging to the voice took one long, playful stride to the opposite side of his table. Before him, arms akimbo, stood a scraggly girl, eighteen or nineteen, tall, maybe five-ten, and dressed in the universal uniform of an American teen—distressed jeans, oversized hoodie, no socks, and floppy converse sneakers. The neck opening for the hoodie had been stretched to overlarge and straps from a tank top or camisole were visible. A toe peeked out of a hole in one shoe. Her flaxen hair was an unruly affair, a match for his own thatch and a feature that immediately made him like her. The asymmetric cut reached the bottom of one ear and on the opposite side grazed the top of the other ear. The sloppy image did not comport with the other data point about the girl—a fact that commanded his attention—namely, that she had quite clearly and distinctly said "good evening" to him in ancient Greek.

"My favorite book! Are you a pious man?" she looked to him for confirmation. He did not provide it and she asked again, "Well, are you or aren't you? You can't be inhospitable to a stranger *and* slog through *The Odyssey*? That would be, like, so totally untrue to yourself!"

The in-your-face interrogation floored him. She shifted her weight from one leg to the other. Her hips followed, as did the heads of onlookers. There was something ridiculous in the pendular synchronicity of the watchers' heads tilting whatever direction she was tilting.

"Well? I'm like super hungry and they close in an hour!" Diners fidgeted in their chairs, ready to offer her a seat at their respective tables. She'd been in the dining car less than two minutes and she owned the place. And she had picked him.

"Of course, yes. Please, sit." Stonecrop motioned to the empty chair across the table. He wiped his hands on a napkin and rose to shake her hand. But before he had finished standing, she took her seat and reached for a *grissino*—a breadstick—from the breadbasket, handing him a smile in lieu of the hand. "Oops, sorry!"

The offered hand hung in space; Stonecrop raised it to brush back a swath of hair that had fallen across his forehead.

"No worry. Dig in. I'm Max."

"Federica," she shot back, and held the wine bottle over an empty water glass she had turned upright. "May I?"

"Why not," he replied.

Without fanfare she filled the glass half-full and took a sip, nodding approvingly. "Good." It was a short, clipped "good," barely aspirated, lips hardly moving. A Chicago native?

"Do you—" Federica stopped mid-sentence and looked past his shoulder. "*Scusi!*" She hailed the waiter and ordered *polenta e cinghiale*. Polenta and wild boar, one of Stonecrop's favorites. The waiter's demeanor, at first registering offense from the public summons, melted as she added in flawless Italian a plea to hurry. She was dying of hunger—*morendo di fame*! There would be no dying on his watch, the *cameriere* assured her. He, personally, would care for her like he would his own daughter!

"You're Italian?" Stonecrop said, surprised and expecting confirmation of his presumption that she was Italian and had learned

English in Chicago.

"Nope. From Plovdiv. That's in Bulgaria, two hours north of the Greek border. See, I had a jump on the Greek."

"And home is still Plovdiv." He supplied the answer, expecting it to be incorrect.

"Papà travels tons. Suitcase in one hand, me in the other. I grew up like everywhere!"

Stonecrop interrupted, "You say "papà," is *he* Italian?"

"No. I prefer papà." *Tatko's* okay, too—that's a Bulgarian papà. I call him Babbo when I need something."

She was cheerful and talkative. And Stonecrop was bored and in the mood to listen.

"Go on, please. I'm curious. So, where is everywhere?"

"Papà's office is in Malta. But now Zürich. I like Zürich. I'll move back when school's over." Federica looked up at nothing, then responded to his question. "Yes, absolutely, everywhere! Nobody believes me. You wouldn't believe me if I told you."

"Try me. I shall believe every word!" He laughed and crossed his heart.

"Again! Cross it!" she ordered. Nearby diners overheard the directive and Stonecrop could have sworn some of them crossed themselves.

In a single breath, she rattled off a list of cities like she was reading destinations off the departures board: "Zürich, Paris, Valleta, Rome, Kiev, Moscow, Kigali, Nairobi, Maputo, Mexico City, and Tokyo—love Tokyo." She laughed and exhaled, "He yanks my arm and I go when I can." To demonstrate she tugged at the shoulder of her hoodie, rolled her eyes and stuck out her tongue. Several diners wiggled in their chairs; her animation was infectious.

"You live in the States now?" he asked.

"Yup," she answered, "as of last summer. Sort of. I was an exchange student for a year in middle school, like ages and ages ago."

"Yes, I'm sure it was long, long ago." For the young, a year is an eternity and three days somewhere is long enough to call it home.

"I'm not in love with diacopes, truly I'm not."

Stonecrop only half-understood the joke. His expression asked for a clarification.

"That's repeating words, like 'Bond, James Bond'," she matter-of-factly stated. "At university now." She took hold of the bottom of her sweatshirt and straightened her arms to stretch the fabric so he could read the name printed on the front. Though faded and stained, the *University of Chicago* was legible. "I work for Papà when I'm not in school. I'm his interpreter," she said proudly. "We're working tomorrow."

Stonecrop poured wine for himself. She slid her empty glass toward him. He poured, less than before. "That's an impressive responsibility," Stonecrop said. The sentence was stuffy and sounded like it. Really, he asked himself, who are you trying to impress? "And your studies," he looked upward and then closed his eyes. "I'd guess freshman art major, a minor in classics or history—Italian Renaissance."

Federica neither confirmed nor rejected his statement. Instead, squaring off with him, she asked, "By what powers of observation do we make this deduction, Mr. Max?"

"Boarding school in Europe. Because many have basic Greek. Not the public schools so much. Your English is American." He looked at her sweatshirt, "The paint stains say art."

She gave him a regal smile along with the royal wave, rotating at the waist to one side her chair and then to the other and making eye contact with diners to the front and rear of the diner car. Her response was in received pronunciation, the hallmark of privilege in Britain. "Really now, Mr. Max. Basic! Bollocks! And, as for *basic* Greek, shall I recite the first ten lines of *The Odyssey* for you, or forty, or a hundred?"

Stonecrop laughed. Her Queen's English recitation rang true to his not so true ear. A half-dozen co-diners good-naturedly waved back to her.

"My money's on private school in Switzerland. Of course, there could be an exceptional ex-pat school in Plovdiv. I wouldn't know."

She smiled again and winked at him. Had he been correct? Or was she luring him down a false path? He pressed on. "The throaty Italian was Florentine. You were a student in Firenze," he asserted, "and you love anything and everything Italian."

"Good try! Yes, I was once one of *those*," she said wistfully, and then obliterated half of a second grissino, chewing as she spoke, "an angst-filled teen, struggling to chew gum and read Dante at the same time. *Hardly!*" she scolded him.

"Well, alright. Enlighten me!"

"Not yet," she returned to American English. "You're doing well, Mr. Max." She waved the remaining half-grissino in the air, like a conductor cuing the first violin. "I *like* the attention. Please, continue and . . ." She slurped her wine. Her chin moved back to its perch above the glass on the table, "we'll see how *wrong* you can be." Federica laughed and propped her elbows on the table, chin now in one hand. Her head bobbed up and down as she munched on the doomed grissino.

To himself, Stonecrop replayed her order to the waiter. The Italian was too natural. It had to be native. "Mom. She's Italian, right? And English."

Her attention drifted. When it returned, the smile was gone and eyes were empty. The connection—rapport, antipathy, or whatever it was between them—felt visceral.

He apologized, not knowing why, "I'm sorry." You're an adult, he told himself, be kind.

"It's okay," she said, this in an even tone. She was determined to run with this thing they had—whatever it was—and make it to endgame. "Go on, please do."

"Sure . . ." He agreed, though unprepared for the shift in tone. "Well, you and your dad, traveling together, is kind of endearing. I see your dad as this peripatetic McKinsey-type."

"Warmer, getting warmer," Federica answered, less shaky than a minute ago. She drew lines on the tablecloth with a grissino—a lucky grissino singled out for survival by virtue of that utility. "Is that it?"

Stonecrop didn't point out the "warmer, getting warmer." He wasn't a gotcha kind of guy. "Your dad's gotta be a nice guy. I think I'd like him if I met him." Stonecrop showed his palms, signifying his open interest in perhaps meeting the father.

"For the record, Mr. Max, my father can be one very, very cruel S.O.B. It's better you don't meet him. You do *not* want to get on his bad side. I'm not kidding. Truly, I'm not."

After delivering the warning, Federica redirected the conversation. "Do *I* frighten you?"

She didn't. The reminder of how cruel a father can be did. Stonecrop's father had been a mixed bag. Though never really loving, he had been supportive. He had also been hard on his children. Fairly or not, Stonecrop blamed his father for his own violent tendencies.

A hiatus in their conversation arose naturally. Their audience took advantage of the intermezzo to resume eating dinners that had cooled during Federica's performance. Stonecrop and Federica stared at the darkened window beside the table.

The November night kept the stars to itself. Power poles flickered by as the train snaked through a blanket of black. Its belly clung to the rails and the crossbow-shaped pantograph slithered under silver catenaries that arced unpredictably and generated evanescent after-images of the berm beside the track.

Stonecrop stared at her reflection. She held the wineglass in her hand, elbow on the table. Their reflections swayed in unison to the rhythm of the train as it consumed meter after meter of track.

The food arrived quickly by European standards and the two travelers found silent refuge in eating their meals. Stonecrop's redoubt was steak-frites with mustard. Federica caught his eye and poached a clump of frites. She dipped them in mustard before downing the lot. Stonecrop wiped a dribble of mustard from her lip. He had two daughters and felt comfortable, even warmed, but the parental act. Neither of them spoke as they ate.

When the cameriere paraded the dessert tray through the restaurant car the respite ended. Federica fussed. Stonecrop could not follow the Italian. Roughly, he got that they were hunting for the largest square of tiramisu on the platter. The sympathetic waiter added a rotto—a broken piece—to her plate. The wine bottle sat empty. Stonecrop ordered an espresso, and Federica followed. "*Due caffè.*"

"So much for *la bella figura!*" she laughed and stuck her tummy our and patted it. "*Stai attento*—look out, it's my turn!"

She examined his watch, a Concord, purchased in Geneva. "Swiss, gold, not a macho Rolex or Omega. Feminine, a woman's watch. I *like* it." Her finger moved clockwise on the face of the watch, as if the watch were wakening and sharing secrets with her. "Your wife picked it out."

He nodded back in the affirmative.

"She comes from money." The statement was followed with a huge spoonful of tiramisu.

The observation pricked Stonecrop's attention. Indeed, his wife had purchased the watch for him as a present when he had completed his International MBA. Again, he nodded in the affirmative, and then took a sip of his caffè, the way an American does, not an Italian, who would have raised the cup to his lips and drained it.

She peeked under the table. "Hmmm, Ferragamo shoes." Then she rose, and reached across to lift the napkin off his lap. Stonecrop started. "Gucci belt. Ugh, *brutto!* Ugly and expensive, label-crazy tourists' shit. You should've let wifey buy the belt!" Continuing the wardrobe examination, she looked behind his shoulder.

A strand of flaxen hair fell across his cheek and like a trembling wing hovered against his skin. He inhaled her warm odor and once again thought about his family.

"Zegna, yes, I thought it was Zegna. The suit would be good on you. I mean, it's an athletic cut and you're . . . an athlete."

"Married, as we already know." She placed a finger and thumb on his wedding band and rotated it in half-circles. "Mamma used to say married men ripen well under a woman's care. It sounds better in Italian."

The animation in Federica's face diminished, then revived. "You're easy with women; and I think not only attractive women you meet on trains." She flirted, and then rephrased the claim to defang it of sexual innuendo. "I mean, you're comfortable around women, like you grew up with sisters? Or have a daughter?"

"Maybe." He had two daughters, a brother, and a half-sister he hardly knew.

Her head hung down and the long part of her hair swept the tabletop. A snorting laugh emerged from under the semi-veil.

"Okay." He put his phone on the table and panned through a few photos, quickly finding a picture of his daughters. "Seven and five. Nothing but trouble. I adore them. Sarah and Jenny."

"They are, Mr. Max, adorable. Look," she pointed at the younger girl in the photo, using two fingers to zoom in, "It's hard to make out, but her eyes are like yours, which, if you haven't noticed, are *exactly*, like mine—hazel, kind of brown in the middle and shifting to green. On the outside a thin black ring. See . . ."

Stonecrop, who had superb vision, could not make out the details in the photo. She was inside of him, making him see what she wanted him to see; he didn't fight it.

"We have lovely eyes," she continued with the dramatics, "dangerous, like the eyes of a predator!"

A mound of tiramisu disappeared into her mouth. "I have determined your profession," she announced through masticated cream and cake. "You're a stockbroker." She swallowed and followed up. "The rich in-laws gave you a fat trading account which you churn like a hamster at the wheel; the commissions pay for the Porsche and country club and the second home where you *summer*." She poked fun at the verb. "Maybe a sailboat. I'm on a sailing team. At university. Not very good, though." She clarified the statement, "Me, not the club."

Alright, in the photo his girls wore life jackets and were aboard a turnabout dingy at the East Sound yacht club. Turnabouts are the staple of yacht clubs for instructing young sailors-to-be. She got the in-laws right, too. He was not a stockbroker, but he was a venture capitalist—close enough. And the family connections unquestionably had advanced his career. A deer-in-the-headlights look on his face fueled her enthusiasm.

"I'm right! I know it!" Federica bounced up and down in her chair and clapped her hands. Every head in the dining car turned to witness the celebration, ready to clap with her.

"I concede to the woman with the cocoa powder on her nose! A-minus. I'm an associate with a life-sciences venture fund in Boulder, Colorado. We have offices in the Mid-Atlantic region and Bay Area. I'm setting up the Zürich office. And yes, my wife, bless her heart, is loaded and the family chipped in on the latest fund. Well done, Watson!"

"Hey, I'm the Sherlock," she shot back while wiping off the cocoa—there was only a spec. She took both of his hands in hers and turned them upward to examine the palms. "See that?"

"My love line?"

"It's a *heart* line, not a *love* line. And no, hardly, Mr. Max! I *am* a materialist! See them there callouses." She flipped his hands. "Healing blisters, cracked skin at the nails, scar tissue on the knuckles." With an air of authority, she pronounced, "A climber, if ever I've saw one. Look," she pointed to the inside of his long finger, the second pad, "here's where a big flapper tore off. A total giveaway." She continued to hold his hands.

It's true, he thought. Spend an hour or two hanging off plastic holds in a climbing gym and you get blisters. A blister tears and you end up with flapper and cut it off.

"Creepy," he said.

"Come on! Ninety percent of the population of Boulder climbs. God, you *are* a slug!"

Stonecrop didn't respond, uncertain of what was next. His look said as much, a look which no doubt encouraged her.

"You got to be all fucked-up if you're a climber. I know my climbers. You got that quiet brave. I kinda like that. You're a tough guy. Maybe it's the tooth. Love that crooked tooth, Mr. Max. Just love it."

Stonecrop never thought of himself as a tough guy. The opposite. He knew a few tough guys and felt he didn't stack up.

"Yeah, I climb," he laughed, still bowled over by her sleuthing. Federica was on a roll; she was animated, and other diners were following the action like gawkers at the roulette table.

She released his hands and with fingertips of both hands raised her cup. The coffee was long gone. "More?" she asked.

"Sure." They both knew she wasn't referring to coffee.

"You're lonely. That Homer's beat-up. You don't scribble vocab in the margins . . . impressive. I truly mean that."

Her words lulled him into a surreal state. He was still thinking about climbing, and that it had been—maybe it still was—an important part of who he was. She had nailed him.

"Too much?" she asked.

"No, sorry. Distracted."

"Am I boring you?"

"Not at all, Federica, not at all," his tone of voice skirted the edge of intimacy, intimacy in a nice way.

She put her fingers on top of the backs of his hands and let her thumbs rest within his palms, and then closed his hands around her thumbs and bent forward. Puffs of breath touched his face and carried aromas of chocolate and espresso, and something else. She needed to brush her teeth. The confirmation of her humanity was oddly comforting.

They sat in silence. Stonecrop tried to withdraw his hands. She refused to release them. He looked downward and noticed light-colored scars on the backs of her hands. "Finished?" he said and looked up for the answer.

Her expression said No; she spoke softly and tightened her grip. "I know that feeling. You're talking with somebody, and then, kapow! They're like right inside your head."

The non sequitur disoriented Stonecrop. As did the idea that the heart of an adult, his heart, was in the hands of this wildly precocious, eighteen-year-old girl he had randomly met and with whom he was sharing a table in the dining car on the night train to Venice. Stonecrop had been enduring a quiet but persistent hell in his personal life. Time apart from his wife had become the norm. He missed her; he missed his daughters; and he missed the easy intimacy of family. He was using Federica as a surrogate, recreating something to fill the void, and he felt badly about it—like he was taking advantage of her. Be thoughtful, Stonecrop told himself. Something's stirring up the insides of this young woman across the table. Listen.

"How was the cinghiali?" he asked.

She released his hands and flopped back in her chair. She laughed,

"Honestly, not even close to Mamma's." Tears gathered, released, and streaked down both cheeks. "Sorry." She slipped a hand inside the sleeve of the hoodie and wiped her face. Game-time was over.

Stonecrop waited.

Federica explained, "Yeah, finished. Sorry. There's a tradition in Firenze, Saturday mornings, they hunt boar. Mamma was special. The men adored her. She hunted with them, with the men. Trust me, that's not normal in Italy.

"Mamma *was* Italian. Classics professor. Worked at the Villa I Tatti in Firenze."

Stonecrop nodded in acknowledgement, more concerned about her feelings, not about his earlier assessment having been correct. I Tatti was Harvard's center for Renaissance studies in Florence. He had spent time there and might have met Federica's mother. He didn't want to interrupt Federica's track, so he said nothing.

"She died in August; it was hot in August. Insanely, super climate-change hot. The grass around her grave was shriveled and brittle, the dirt had cracks like dry, empty veins. So greedy for my tears." She was in another world. The last words, spoken to herself, were barely audible.

"Federica." Stonecrop's tone softened. "I'm sorry." What eavesdroppers remained in the dining car, out of politeness, turned away. Others, making a respectful exodus, offered a sympathetic good-bye nod or understanding smile.

"It's okay." She sniffled and wiped her nose. "This is good. Talking with you. Fuck, I don't know what I'm saying. I'm just babbling. I usually don't talk so much—you don't believe that for minute, do you?" She laughed and looked out the window. Streaks from tears had marked her cheeks and marked a pathway for those that followed. The eyes didn't know they were supposed to cease weeping.

Stonecrop flagged the waiter and asked for *il conto*, and a small bottle of grappa. When both arrived, he put the requisite cash on the table.

"You get a B-minus," Federica suddenly rallied. She ignored the tears, one of which was suspended on the tip of her chin, and for a second time presented her sweatshirt to him. "These stains—this," she pointed at a series of dark red splotches, "is iodine. I spilled it dying slides. This one," she grabbed a handful of sweatshirt with holes in it, "is some nasty-shit organic polymer."

They both laughed, grateful for the release. He pointed at a stain right under her chin, "That?"

"Ah." With effort, she was just able to see the place he had pointed to, giving herself a double chin; the chin tear left a stain where it touched the sweatshirt. "Caffè," she sniffled. "Here's the most impressive." The young woman twisted to reveal a series of small holes in the side of her hoody. They could have been cigarette burns. "Sulfuric acid." She smiled proudly. "I'm like a disaster in the lab, nobody wants to be my partner. It's pre-med, not art . . . But maybe I should switch to art!"

The tears stopped; her nose was still running. A baggy sleeve did double duty, wiping both nose and eyes.

Stonecrop gave Federica a napkin and a hug as they stood up. "I hope I wasn't," he fished for the right word, "insensitive."

"No, you're a kind man. I like you, I like you a lot." Federica paused, "Can I ask a favor?"

"Of course," Stonecrop responded.

"Will you read to me?" She put a hand on his Homer. "Mamma and I used to read together."

"Now? It's late?" he asked.

"Just a little. Your cabina, if it's not too small. I'm like majorly claustrophobic . . . oh, crap," she said, a thought suddenly coming to her. "There are probably other people in your cabina. We can use ours. Papà sleeps through anything. He snores like a team of horses . . . and he farts like a team of horses."

"A better venue for *The Iliad*," Stonecrop quipped and got a huge smile in return. He gave his report: "Well, my cabin has four berths—quite spacious, and a private bath. I'm the sole occupant."

Federica took his arm and pressed against him. "Perfect! What book are you reading?" she asked.

"Book Ten."

"*Who art thou among men, and from whence? Where is thy city, and where thy parents? Amazement holds me that thou hast drunk this charm and wast in no wise bewitched.*" It was a quote from the passage where Odysseus first meets Kirke in Book Ten.

Stonecrop was nonplussed, Who art thou, he said to himself, who art thou? She was not a child. But tonight she needed to be one. Yes, of course he would read to her. He would die to read to her.

"Call me Fede. Mamma calls me Fede. Called me Fede."

"Fede it is. And my name is Stonecrop, Max Stonecrop."

"Like the flower?" she asked.

"Yes, like the flower," he gently replied.

"Good." It was the clipped "good" again. Federica's eyes locked onto his, as open and wide as if she were standing before a mirror and staring into her own.

Stonecrop stole a line his classics professor had used to start every class: "Let's read some Greek."

Mozambique Drill

A naked and half-conscious Stonecrop curled up in the fetal position on the tiled floor. He dreamt. The repetitive throb in his head synced with the sway of the memory of the sleeper car when he and Federica spent much of the night reading passages from *The Odyssey* They had recited the first lines of each new chapter together—him reading and Federica by memory, her eyes closed—until at one point her lips had stopped shaping words and she fell asleep, leaning against his shoulder and lightly snoring. For whatever reason, maybe to preserve the tender perfection of the memory, they had not seen or spoken to each other since that night.

The air was warm. Still, the tiled surface sucked the heat from his body. He had survived another night. The beating yesterday, like the day before, had been more numbing than painful.

There was the hurt, but, as far as he could tell, no broken bones and no missing teeth. He was dehydrated and well-past hunger. His jailers threatened to set dogs on him. That nightmare played, rewound, and played again. He imagined canine teeth tearing his flesh and had a macabre curiosity over what part of his body would they would go for first. Once subdued, which tasty organ would he serve up—intestines, liver? Cheer up, he told himself, it was an organic way to go, red in tooth and claw. And maybe, the dogs would just sniff him, lick the salt on his skin, and decide that a thirty-four-year-old, extra-lean human was more trouble than it was worth.

In some respects, the nightmare was a break from the regrets recycling in his head. The descent to penury and torture had taken five years. The descent had commenced with the transfer to Zürich as a newly minted partner of COLS's latest venture round. After the fact he had learned that COLS had gotten tangled up with a less-than-ethical portfolio company that tested and unloaded unmarketable pharmaceuticals in Mozambique. Every attempt he had made to clean up the mess COLS had created had been thwarted.

His most recent misstep—initiated a year ago—had been to personally bring the drug merchants to justice on the ground floor in Africa. This altruistic misadventure had cost him his career, his marriage, and now, probably would cost him his life.

Through a hole in the roof Caravaggio-like light painted warmth on his upper back and head. A droplet of sweat trickled from the nape of his neck, followed the line of the jaw, threaded its way through a week's stubble and lost itself in the viscous scum on the floor. A malodorous concoction of blood, urine, feces, and wet dog thickened the air.

The guard unbolted and cracked open the door. Stonecrop rolled to a crouch with his arms wrapped as if he were hugging himself. The dog's snout banged at the door. Staccato pants, no barking. Was it muzzled? Stonecrop had a plan. Not so much a plan; more a movement. He'd visualized and mentally rehearsed the choreography to the point of obsession.

The guard kicked open the door. The Rottweiler—explosive, unmuzzled, and malevolent—snarled once and leapt. Stonecrop made the body do what the inner coach had prescribed. He offered and raised the left hand and wrist as bait. The animal's jaw rose upward. Stonecrop unwound his torso and with his weight behind the blow slashed the dog's throat with a half-fist of his right hand. The Rottweiler choked on a gargled snarl and crawled away on its belly.

Dog dispatched, now the handler. The guard strode into the holding cell, swore in Portuguese, and reached down to inspect the whimpering dog. He was a big man, two-hundred-pounds plus, taller than Stonecrop and black as night. He had a muzzle and leash in one hand and a Louisville slugger aluminum baseball bat in the other. The dog twitched and heaved for air. The distraction gave Stonecrop time to deliver a sideways blow to the guard's knee. Cartilage popped and the leg collapsed inward at a satisfyingly unnatural angle. A swinging bat grazed Stonecrop's head and sang as it connected with the wall. The guard grabbed Stonecrop by the ankle, but both the ankle and the hand were sweat-covered. Stonecrop kicked free, stepped out the cell, and slammed the steel latch in place.

The adjacent room was a makeshift office. In a kennel in the corner a second Rottweiler quivered on three legs and glared at him. One forepaw was bundled with a ball of dirty, gnawed upon gauze. The dog fidgeted with excitement and weighted and unweighted the injured foot. Saliva dripped from the edges of its muzzled snout.

Stonecrop looked for his clothes. Keys hung off a magnetic hook stuck to a narrow tall metal cabinet. A mobile phone with a leather case and strap lay on the desk. A second leash and a faded Day-Glo green safety vest were draped over the back of a wooden desk chair. On the seat was white, safety hardhat. *Crap, where are my clothes.* He searched in the cabinet, then pulled open the desk drawers. No clothes.

A worn, thinly woven throw rug lay between the desk and a visitor's chair. *So be it.* Stonecrop wrapped the rug around his waist and tied it in place with the leash. He attached the phone and keys to the swivel hook on the leash then slipped into the vest and put on the overlarge hardhat. The new worker, an embarrassed because by his ill-fitting skirt, stepped into the blindingly quiet, bright outdoors. He looked ridiculous and felt ridiculous.

Stonecrop inventoried the surroundings. Judging by the sun, it was late morning. Parked in tidy rows over two acres of dried red earth were a half-dozen light-duty white panel trucks, several semi-trailers —also white—and one flat-bed truck. In a garage at the opposite end of the yard someone was crawling around under a tow truck on raised jacks. *Must be Sunday, or a holiday.* On the right were storage units. A dirty white Nissan Datsun pickup was parked in front of the office, presumably the guard's car. A cement table and two sun-bleached canvas chairs commandeered the shade from twin fig trees, gaunt survivors of years of neglect. A layer of rust-colored dust covered everything in sight.

"Lovely!" A soft and playful voice said to him. Delirious and surprised by what at first he mistook for a talking tree, Stonecrop froze. From behind the tree, a woman stepped into view. Her gaze worked its way from his filthy feet to the makeshift shirt, the vest, the hardhat plopped over mop of matted hair, and then resettled back to the skirt. "Lovely," she repeated. No concern in the eyes, no surprise. Seemed she'd seen worse.

Stonecrop dropped his hands to his sides. He gave an honest assessment. "Doesn't flatter the hips . . ."

The woman laughed. She stepped toward him. She was in her forties, rail-thin and barefoot, and wore a colorfully patterned *capulana,* a one-by-two-meter printed dress common in rural Mozambique. The verdant zoomorphic pattern, a frail bloom, clashed with the sere grounds.

"Did you kill him? If no, Koko surely kill you." The cadence of the words, the deliberate enunciation, their sing-song certainty, gave them an Orphic credence.

"No such luck."

"You shake the dog, you shake the owner."

"Yeah, well, I shook the fucking dog, alright. You live here?"

"You mean here?" Atop an overly long neck, her head swiveled as her gaze stretched across the compound. She moved slowly, a flower pursuing the sun. "Five years," she said. "Now ten years in Maputo. I am from Kampala. I know why they take *us*, us women folk. But you . . ." Her voice had risen as she rescanned him from head to toe. She squinted. The crows' feet narrowed, then came a hint of a smile. Her voice trembled. The breeze jostled stubborn leaves, ". . . why a man, a man like you?"

"The boss-men. Where are they?"

"I bring them tea. You want tea?" From atop a stump behind the tree where she she had been standing, she retrieved an ornately decorated silver tray. The tray would have been heavy even without the pitcher of iced tea and two glasses; the mass burdened her boney frame. She drooped forward and then gracefully twisted her head toward the larger of two sun-bleached, blue clapboard buildings to his left. She must have exited from the side door of the smaller one, a guest house.

He'd not noticed the buildings at first, not until he had gone a few steps from the doorway. His confusion and fear must have been apparent. Stonecrop approached and carefully lifted the pitcher off the tray. He drank the first liquid he'd had in two days, maybe three.

"Koko's gun is in the glovie." She whispered. A puckered smile spread wrinkles from the corners of her mouth. Did she intend for him to use the deadly information or not? Was she mad?

"Thank you," he said, feeling like a little boy thanking gran for a cookie.

Stonecrop crept around the back of the truck, reached through the open passenger window, and retrieved the handgun from the glovebox. He deposited the hard hat on the bench seat. The Browning Hi Power was old, but serviceable. A simple enough weapon. It typically held a clip with thirteen cartridges. He inspected the clip— nine remained—and flipped the safety to off and made sure a round was chambered. He rejoined her. "Max, my name is Max." He followed about ten steps behind as she carried the tray toward the door of the larger structure. The liquid had quenched his thirst, the sugar and caffeine were fixing the ache in his head.

His plan was to have no plan. For months, he'd been playing cat and mouse with Alves and Henrique "Hennie" Couto. They were always a step ahead. Supported by two local police he had marched into the Coutos' Maputo office and expected to see them arrested. It turned out to be a happy reunion between the police and the Coutos. Then the lights went out. Later, no idea how much later, he had woken up with a lump on his head and in Koko's cell room. The brothers had wanted to know who had sent him. He assumed that was the reason he was still alive.

Alves had run the interrogations with the guard at his side and he referred to the questioning sessions as lessons. "Have you learned your lesson?" He'd hammer Stonecrop with the question and Stonecrop would stare back and ask for water. The accent was Portuguese, from Portugal, not Mozambique. Alves had warned him that exposing irregularities in the drug trade had consequences. He was sorry, he said, but at least the prisoner would be offered the luxury of a pleasant death if he would tell them who he worked for. Stonecrop had made up names of people and agencies, all bullshit and Aves would grin and tell him so. *"Issue é tetra, mate."*

The woman's elongated neck swung the head to the side as she looked over her shoulder to respond to him. "My name is Chloë."

She opened the screen door to the main house by hooking her big toe on a corner where the screen had separated from the door frame. Another dog? On the shaded porch and next to the door were two ten-liter jerry cans of petrol, two shrink-wrapped cases of bottled water, and a pallet of wooden framed boxes with stick-on labels—Hoffmann-La Roche Ltd, Merck & Co Inc, Bayer AG.

Through the screen mesh he saw the two men seated in wicker chairs before a low, glass-covered wicker table. Two shoulder holsters with handguns sprawled atop the table. One man was unfolding a large map and holding it close to his face, trying to make out some detail. The other held a laptop in one hand and pointed to something on the screen. They were comparing the map to the screen. Neither man noticed Stonecrop.

"On the sideboard," one of them ordered without looking up.

The pencil skirt was slipping off. Stonecrop hiked the rug up, fiddling with his fingers and almost dropping the handgun. Men in skirts are badass, he told himself. Think Highland Scots, the Greeks at

Thermopylae. He slipped in behind Chloë and let the closing door close the way it would have without his interference. He thought about staying behind her but opted to move to the side to keep her out of the line of fire.

The Browning rose—he held it with both hands— and loosed two rounds. Light streamed out of two small holes, an inch apart, on the map in Henrique's hands. Alves had caught the movement before the shots had been fired and had reached, too late, for his handgun on the table. The rounds hit Henrique in the torso and sent him flying backward over his chair. Alves yelled, "Hennie," and lunged at Stonecrop. He struggled to free the Glock from its holster.

Stonecrop stepped forward, gave an awkward tuck-up to his rug-cum-skirt, and this time using one hand, fired twice. Alves chest, like the map, displayed a pair of holes an inch apart. He slumped sideways across the chair, gripping the holster with one hand and pressing the other to his chest.

Stonecrop walked around Alves to check on Hennie. He lay motionless. Stonecrop stared at the carnage. He had not wanted to kill the men, not before. He really wasn't sure what he had wanted, other than to stay alive. The experience had felt like some abstract training exercise, just another combat pistol competition as part of his cross-training for biathlon.

Except it wasn't. He'd had a choice. He could have tried to slip away. That decision was on him. Their deaths were on him. Two men, put down like rabid dogs.

The odor of gasoline cut short the second thoughts. Chloë was dousing the floor and furnishings. He turned, prepared to yell at her to stop, but then decided to say nothing. Let'em burn, burn in hell. She dropped the Jerry Can, passed Stonecrop and then returned from the kitchenette with a matchbox.

Petrol flooded the room. Stonecrop turned the can upright, then heard a groan. He whirled around. Hennie lay face down in a pool of blood and petrol. The sound had come from Hennie. Browning at the ready he approached.

Behind him, a match struck. The petrol ignited with a whump and a wall of heat slapped his face.

"Chloë!"

The next sound was a sickening thwack. A flash of color flitted across the periphery of his field of vision. He looked up and saw Chlöe's body fly across the room like some ungainly tropical bird. The serving tray tipped off the sideboard and crashed to the floor. Flying shards of glass sowed the inferno.

Chloë had not seen the blow coming. The baseball bat had caught her in the side of the head.

Koko, a colossus with a makeshift splint duct-taped to his knee, blocked the door. Stonecrop stared in the man's eyes. He wanted give him a few seconds to appreciate the fact that death was imminent. The first two rounds, practically in the same hole, drilled a tunnel in Koko's heart and precipitated back-to-back shudders. The next round hit mid-face and exited through the occipital bone. Mozambique Drill, that's what it's called—two to the chest and one to the head. Still have two rounds.

"Fuck you, asshole," Stonecrop swore. No reflection this time; fuck remorse.

Chloë lay face down on the floor. Her skull was cracked open and bleeding. A pinkish, membraned mass the size of a golf ball bulged out from under crushed bone. She was breathing. Stonecrop, still undecided about Hennie's condition, skirted the flames to reach Chloë. He tucked the Browning in his skirt and did his best to pack the protruding cerebral material into her skull and secure it by repositioning bone and tying together blood-soaked braids of hair.

Koko's injured leg was within arm's reach. Stonecrop peeled off a strip of duct tape and wrapped the wound. Then, cradling her head with his left hand, he gently slid his right arm under her belly and scooped her up. He had hoped to grab the Glocks, a pair of pants and the map, but it was too late. The kindling-dry walls had caught fire; the heat and flames were driving him out.

At the back of the room, Hennie crawled toward the kitchen. His clothes were in flames. Let him burn or not? The uncertainty ended when a sensor set off the fire-alarm.

The mechanic had to have heard the alarm and gunshots. Stonecrop strapped Chloë into the passenger seat and unclipped the car keys from the leash. As Stonecrop turned the ignition, the mechanic ran in front of the truck, waving one hand and reaching for a sidearm with the other. It took two tries to start the engine, by which time the mechanic had drawn his weapon and started firing.

A bullet deflected from the rim of the windshield lodged in Stonecrop's ribs. He ignored it, shoved the gearshift into first and stomped on the gas. The suspension groaned twice as the pickup bounced over the mechanic's body. Stonecrop drove toward the compound's gated entrance and punched a red button on the fob attached to the car keys. The iron fence groaned and rolled to the side and revealed the shanty town beyond the compound.

There must be a clinic nearby. He'd drop off Chloë, ditch the pickup, and disappear.

She was trying to talk. He put his ear close to her lips, incredulous that she could speak.

"Até já." Stonecrop didn't understand the words.

He steered with one hand and with the other gently brushed a glass shard off her cheek and another away from her eyebrow. Self-loathing, nausea, a longing for kindness—it had been too much. Stonecrop cried —no tears, he was too dehydrated—but in heaves as dry as parched dirt.

Toblerone

One consequence of a tent-less, sleepless bivouac on a ledge fifty meters below the summit of Sustenhorn was painful, stiff muscles and joints like a rusty erector set. It was worth it. The week of hiking and scrambling across rugged, unpopulated mountain terrain, had been the perfect prescription for mental health. Stonecrop had, on his first day back in Switzerland, gone directly from the airport to Bächli Bergsport. He maxed out his credit card on a change of wardrobe, boots, anorak, ice tools, a forty-meter rope, water bottle, a pack and six bars of Toblerone chocolate. He hadn't had enough for a bivouac sack or stove. He changed clothes at the store, discarding his travel clothes, and then hit the underground COOP for food basics and caught a train to the Göschenen valley trailhead.

Post Maputo Stonecrop had spent six months adrift in Africa. He had lived in constant fear of imprisonment or retribution and couldn't shake off the memory of Chloë, crazy Chloë—the wispy, the tragic arsonist. The "Lovely" wouldn't leave his head. Had she survived? Probably not. And Hennie Couto? Shit, he'd been burned alive. Christ, what a mess he'd made of things.

These second thoughts came to a sudden and dramatic end when a fist-sized rock slammed into the top of his backpack. The *thwack*, akin to a hundred-mile-per-hour fastball kissing the catcher's mitt, buckled his knees. The rock had nestled in a crater-like depression in the pack flap. Pay attention, he scolded himself. As the day warmed and the ice melted the couloir was turning into a shooting gallery.

Four points of steel attached Stonecrop to the ice. Fortunately, the ice was *plastique*—that perfect balance of soft and firm, like liquid Styrofoam. The front-points of his crampons sank into the ice as he leaned on the heels of his boots. His hand tools, a couple of used, old-school droop-picked alpine ice axes he'd found at Bächli, held little of his weight. One tool had an adze opposite the pick, the other a hammer. He'd sharpened the blades and tips. On sixty-degree ice they tools were used only for balance. A gentle tap was all it took for the ice to swallow an inch of the carbon-steel beak. Too forceful a swing resulted in a exhausting struggle to extract the pick.

A short traverse along the lip of a twenty-meter escarpment lead to a second couloir, this one in the shadows and filled with soft snow in which he could safely plunge-step or glissade the last hundred meters to Kelenalphütte, his objective for the night and the end of his tour. The air was dead still. An indecisive tendril of smoke drifted upward from the chimney of the refuge and promised his first coffee and first warm meal in week.

A second rock, this one the size and shape of an elongated dinner plate, fell edgewise across the blades of both of his ice tools and walloped him square in the chest. Two parallel scars in the ice marked where the tools ripped out. He cartwheeled backwards through space, entirely too aware of his situation and perversely grateful for one last view, albeit an upside down one, of the surrounding Alps. A fusillade of stones flumped into the snow. His own impact, he cheerfully observed, hadn't been fatal. He continued to tumble down the couloir, out of control and gaining speed until he careened headfirst into a rocky outcrop and the world went black.

Universitätsspital Zürich

The patient tried to speak. Nothing came out. His lips were sunbaked leather; his tongue a sanding block wedged in his throat. He grunted. The sound was inflected, as if he were asking a question. People shuffled around, moving things, and moving him. Someone fussed with a needle in his forearm. The cannula abraded his nostrils. Oxygen-thick air stung the back of dry nasal passages. Everything hurt. Neck and head were immobilized. The pain in his head was accompanied by a constant thrum. He couldn't move either arm. He grunted again and got a reply.

"Universitätsspital, der Intensivstation," a man's voice answered, then made the switch to English. He'd correctly pegged Stonecrop's grunt as an English one. "University Hospital, Intensive Care Unit. What's your name?"

Stonecrop tried again. "Wha—?"

A cheerful female voice behind him chimed in, "His name is Stonecrop, Max Stonecrop. Mr. Stonecrop recently had a scenic heli-ride, compliments of REGA." The words were spoken rapidly and confused Stonecrop; he recognized REGA as Swiss Air-Rescue. And that voice, he had never forgotten. He wanted to say something or sit up. That wasn't about to happen.

Stonecrop replayed the last week, or what he thought was the last week. He'd been soloing along a ridge, some traverse in the Göschenertal. The weather had gone to shit. Rain and hail one day, cloudless skies and sun the next. The climbing had been dicey. Mentally, he had been trying to re-center, to sort out the shit that had gone down in Africa. He remembered being in a couloir, an escarpment, stones whistling by, thinking about baseball and justice, a hot meal . . .

When he re-awoke, he had no clue about how long he had slept—it could have been hours, it could have been days. He did remember where he was and noted the clean, crisply sheeted bed. A transparent tube, like the tentacle of a jellyfish, dangled from a sack of fluid and converged with a second, shorter tube at a vein in his left arm. A pulse-ox meter held his index finger in its jaws. Someone had removed the nasal cannula. The neck brace was gone. A floor-to-ceiling curtain surrounded an area just large enough for his bed, a bed stand, and a single chrome-frame chair. The curtain blocked the view but not the sound of activity in room.

A hand, cuffed in medical garb, parted the curtain and hesitated, as if debating about whether or not to reveal the body to which it was attached. When the curtain did part, Stonecrop could not see her face. Her head was turned away from him—she was speaking to one of her colleagues. Again, he instantly recognized the voice.

"Fede?"

"Hi Max! Long time no see! You look like shit." She approached the bed and took hold of his wrist to check his pulse. It was a moot act; the monitor above his bed was continually recording heartbeat, oxygen level, and blood pressure. Periodically the cuff affixed to his upper arm inflated and deflated. It annoyed the crap out of him.

Her touch was deft, efficient, and electrifying. "Follow my finger."

He couldn't take his eyes off her face.

"Max, the finger . . ." she repeated.

"Yeah." He complied and remained silent as she conducted the brief physical assessment.

Stonecrop was spellbound and confused. He remembered the gangly teen, gawked at the woman before him, and wondered at the transformation. The flaxen hair hung long and rolled over the shoulder and down her back. He recognized the familiar constellation of blemishes and freckles and the birthmark on her neck under her right ear.

On the overnight to Venice, suspended between the rhythm of her breath and the clack of the rails, he'd woken early and, not wanting to disturb her, watched the dawn light play across her face. The memory evinced a sense of calm and comfort and made him want to believe that their connection had endured. Common sense reminded him that a lot can happen in seven years. He was living—emphasis on the word *living*—proof of it.

"My shift's over at two. I've only got a few minutes before the tram."

"I kinda lost track of time." The sounds he made were thick, groggy, as if he were new to the act of speaking and trying to find the right register. "Have I been here long? Where were you?"

"Less than a week. I saw you when REGA brought you in. Doktor Weller's caring for you—he's the department head. I had to leave for a conference in Milano right after you arrived. You're in good hands with Weller."

He was waking up, getting his bearings, though their conversation was so preposterously normal. Maybe he was dreaming. "Is it really you?"

"In the flesh." She squeezed his hand. "I'm really happy to see you."

This was too formal—the doctor and her patient going through the motions—and, in those roles, vaguely disappointing.

"Did I fall?" Stonecrop asked.

"Hard to say. There was rockfall. That's what the medics said."

"Where? I remember a couloir—"

"The one next to the arete running down from Sustenhorn to Kelenalphütte. Were you going to the hut?"

"I was. Yeah, now I remember. In the morning, there was shitload of lightning. I was trying to get off the arete. Crossing this little patch of ice."

"They found you about fifty meters downhill from an area where there had been rockfall. Your helmet was cracked. You were transient—in and out of consciousness, confused, repeating words, and bleeding from the head. Max, it wasn't good. I'm sure Doktor Weller explained."

"He might have. I remember . . . nothing."

"A big bonk on the head—subarachnoid hemorrhage."

"And a wicked bad headache."

"Wicked bad—I remember you liking that expression. Wicked enough REGA did a fly-by of the local clinic. They ferried you straight to the me. You'll need regular CT scans and a neurologist to watch for intracranial bleeding."

"Head still attached to the body?"

"Mostly, yup," she said, and straightened up, pushing the gown aside and putting hands on her hips, the posture she had assumed when they had first met. The professional mien fled; the impish girl returned. "Mr. Max, you about broke that lovely neck of yours."

"Ah, so that's what the chart says!"

"Verbatim. I don't know why there's a BP-monitor." She uncoupled him from the blood-pressure cuff and switched off the device.

"They just put it on."

"Damned thing is annoying."

"I was just thinking that…"

Fede smiled and shook her head. Underneath her gown he noticed her shirt collar. She saw him looking at it.

"You missed a button," he said, and raised his hand to his own neck. She mimicked him and confirmed his observation.

"Ah, so I did." She shrugged it off.

Same old Fede.

"You have a slight fever," she dropped back into medical mode, "an infection. Not serious, but we need to keep an eye on it.

"I've missed you," she said. Fede took his hand. Stonecrop felt his pulse quicken. Did she notice? "I followed you for a while, online. Then got wrapped up in my own world."

"You stalked me!"

"Yes, that's me, stalker Ratzow." She tightened her hold on his hand, "I gotcha now."

"I missed you too. Thought it might be weird to stay in touch." Stonecrop was unable to find the words he really wanted to say.

"You really remember me?" she leaned closer than professionally called for.

"Like yesterday. C'mon."

Her forehead touched and rested just over his ear. "Good," she whispered.

The Chicago accented "good" zinged him good.

The tease a success, she went back to business. "And do we know where we are?"

He followed her lead. "Well, we remember things before the couloir. Foggy after that. It comes and goes. Yeah, now is fine. Universitätsspital, right?"

"Gold star. And how long have you been here?"

"A day or so?"

"I'm gonna take back the star—"

"A week. Can you find out about my discharge?"

"*Già fatto.* Already done, sir. You're free to go." Fede sat on the bed, at his feet. "Where are you staying? Friends, family?"

"None of the above," he said.

"Your wife? Mattie—that was her name. Is she here? Have you called her?"

"No. Divorced. Fairly recently. A friendly divorce as divorces go. We're in touch and everything. I don't want to worry her." Stonecrop noted how canned the qualifications sounded. "I've been staying in hostels, or huts when I'm in the mountains. I'll try the Rössli. I like the Niederdorf. And the art in the hotel."

"You shouldn't bullshit me, Max. Someone's got to keep an eye on you. The head injury is no joke. Can't release you unless there's someone—family, hired nurse. That's the deal."

Fede furrowed her brow, then brightened. She leaned over him, hands on the bed to either side of his hips. Again, her face was inches from his. He vividly remembered the asymmetric cut of her hair, and when the hair, the long side, had brushed against his cheek. He remembered her tiramisu breath.

"Problem solved! You're staying with me. Cheap rent and way good art, too," she laughed, "like living in a gallery. Here's the plan," she ordered. "You rest. I'm gonna run home, get the car. I'll be back at five."

"Fede, I don't want to be ungrateful, but I don't want to impose. I am feeling better. Thank you, truly—"

"Nonsense!" She cut him off. "You're terribly weak. You look like shit and need a shave. And a bath! I'll see the nurses run you through the car wash."

"There's a car wash?" Stonecrop said, drugged enough to imagine himself on the gurney going through the sprayers.

"*Zitti! Zitti!*" she said, using the word Italian teachers use to order a class of unruly students to be quiet. "See you at five!" She rose abruptly and with a swoosh of the curtain, like a magician, she disappeared.

From the Moon

A punctual as the S-Bahn Federica reappeared at five p.m. At first Stonecrop thought she was wearing work scrubs. As she approached, he recognized the *Mammut* mammoth logo on the baggy, cotton, fire-engine red climbing pants. Topside, she wore a loose, white tee with an aqua camisole underneath. There was a small hole in one armpit of the T-shirt. A black sweater was tied around her shoulders.

"I signed your release and have come to abscond with you," Federica cheerfully announced.

"Can we get something to eat?"

"Yeah, *hausgemacht* Jell-O." She pulled down the blanket covering him. "Or, if you behave, I'll hustle up some chicken broth!"

"You mean 'rustle' up."

"See, I need you." Federica feigned exasperation. "My English sucks."

"Right," Stonecrop smiled. He didn't care what language she spoke or how well she spoke it or what words she said. Her presence was taming the monsters in his head. He rose on his elbows. The effort made him dizzy. The IV was gone. The nurses had given him a sponge bath.

Federica put an arm under his and helped him sit up and swing his legs to the floor. He was still wearing a patient gown. With her other arm, she grabbed a pair of pants from a bag on the chair. They were not the wind pants he had been wearing on his climb.

"These should fit. Wrong size for me, too baggy."

It was a second pair of climbing pants. These were bright green. Next, she extracted a white polo shirt, Ralph Loren. It was a men's XXL. He had noticed the label as she had pulled it over his head. The sleeves reached his elbows.

"My fiancé's." She looked him over and grimaced. Stonecrop was swimming in the shirt. "Shit, you're *flaco*. You skinny boy. Last real meal?"

"Just before I set out. Lots of chocolate though, Swiss, the best. Kind of sick of it now."

"Dumb. You don't even have climber fat . . . What's that from?" Fede touched a scar on the left side of his rib cage. She traced where stitches had been, probing slightly, openly curious. One probe went too deep and he jumped.

"I forget. Old wound."

"Bullshit." She continued examining the wound, making faces at the crude medical work. An aide had cleaned and dressed the wound at the clinic where he had dropped off Chlöe. She had been the focus of attention. He had been a side-show and had had only a couple of minutes to spare.

He said nothing more. Fede let it go.

With some fanfare Federica tossed a pair of Adidas flip-flops on the floor and helped him pull on the pants. She paused halfway through the process, when he had one leg in and one out. "Forgot undies, sorry."

"We're like an Italian flag."

Federica took charge. He was clearly not able to manage on his own. Nor was he was embarrassed by her caring for him, the way men can sometimes be. First, she was a physician; second, she was a climber—something he'd surmised from the combo of strong shoulders and the climbing garb. Climbers don't give a rat's ass about modesty. Mostly, she was just Fede.

His academic mentor and Greek philosophy professor had instilled in Stonecrop and his fellow students a sense of something quasi-sacred about reading Greek together. Stonecrop had stayed connected with several of his college peers. He told himself that the connection he felt with Federica came from that, from reading together. The kindness and tenderness had not been diluted by time and separation. Is that why he had returned to Zürich? He remembered Fede mentioning that her father had an office in Zürich and that she would return to the city after university.

She helped him into a wheelchair and efficiently rolled him through the discharge process, out the automated doors, and up to a 1990 red Alfa Romeo Spider. The paint was faded, the body a saga of scrapes and dents. The lines, however, were an enduring tribute to good automotive design and took Stonecrop back in time, to the young boy with grease under his nails and working in Dad's shop where his father tricked out Audis for the pro rally circuit. His dad occasionally took in an Alfa the way a household would take in a stray cat. He'd patch it up and then send it back into the cold. The cars were an accident-in-the-making on ice and snow.

Federica had parked the vehicle outside the building exit. She tossed his bursting-at-the-seams personal effects bag from the back of the wheelchair to the back seat of the Alfa, giving no thought to the crampon points and the spiked tips of ice axes. Not so with Stonecrop, whom she eased into the passenger seat, carefully guiding his bandaged head to avoid the low-profile convertible top. An aide took away the wheelchair.

"Fede, is this going to be awkward? I don't want to impose on you and your fiancé."

"Not an imposition, Max. We don't live together, not even close. Andreas is off doing whatever Mexican playboys do in their spare time —which is all the time. Andreas and I have seen each other maybe once in the last month, and that was a bust of a dinner party where dear Papà pilloried him after Andreas pitched some cockamamie business idea. The privileged don't like being told they're dumb. Anyway, I got a backup!"

"Me?"

Federica gave him a playful punch in the shoulder, trying and failing to hold back from laughing. "Why does every man always think it's about him!"

"Playboy number two?"

"There are two backups! I'm being silly. They're friends. My god, I'm babbling like a teenager. It's funny, that first night we met, I felt more adult then, then I do now. I was such a cocky little shit—not like that now—I hope." She winked at him. "Seven years. *Merde.* You're sitting here next to me! It's like we're starting right where we left off. Strangely pleasant and natural, like floating . . ."

"It is," he agreed, not only to be agreeable but because he genuinely felt the same way. Floating was a good way to describe it.

"Aren't playboy and fiancé mutually exclusive?" Stonecrop asked.

Federica avoided the question and chattered away, keeping up the conversation for the two of them. Stonecrop was fading. The throbbing in his head had not abated; if anything, it was worse. Federica the physician understood, as did Federica the person. The banter distracted from the pain.

Stonecrop attended to traffic. Any driver he rode with, unless they'd had hours of track time, made him uneasy.

The Alfa wound up Gloriastrasse to Krähbühlstrasse. Shortly before the crest of the hill they turned north on Susenbergstrasse. The homes on Susenbergstrasse formed a terraced ring around the hillside below the Zoo and Zürichberg city park. Old Zürich money lived on Susenbergstrasse. The pricey location rewarded the inhabitants with a glorious panorama of the university, city, and lake and mountains.

A couple intersection later she guided the Alfa through a narrow slot in a two-meter-tall wood-slatted fence facing the street. The house behind the fence resembled a three-story Rubik's cube with the eight corner pieces removed. The street-side profile was a cross in the same proportions as the Swiss flag. The back side of the house, the side with the views to the west and the lake, was entirely glass. The exterior walls of the other elevations were gray and surfaced in concrete that had been imbedded with river stone. There were few windows on the non-westerly elevations, and the ones that were there were beveled and vertical, like arrow slits on a medieval fortification. Diamond-paned windows were tucked in the shadows of the eighteen-inch-thick walls.

Cement Barragan stairs led downward to yard level. With Fede in the lead they brushed aside stalks of timber bamboo and descended. At the foot of the stairs and in the narrow space between the house and the wall of bamboo lay a failed attempt at a Japanese garden. Moss-covered pavers led to the entry to Federica's bottom level apartment. A cement bench, a pitcher, broken clay pots, and a bucket of gardening tools implied work in progress that had been abandoned. A corner of the bench had broken off. No water flowed from the oxidized copper pipe of a mossed-in fountain. The basin held water from a recent storm and was littered with leaves and small branches. A sparrow, unperturbed by their approach, drank, looked at them, and drank again.

The attack, unprovoked and unannounced, came from under a low-limbed Japanese pine. A pointy snout full of pointy teeth lunged at him. Federica yelled, *"Lass!"* just as the dachshund's teeth reached their intended target. The animal's muzzle wrapped around Stonecrop's ankle, the teeth not quite breaking the skin.

Stonecrop dropped to his knees and grabbed a trowel from the bucket. The trowel quivered in his hand; he was quite prepared to disembowel his attacker. The size of the animal didn't matter. Any dog attack was enough to send his mind skittering back to the cell in Mozambique.

"*Platz!*" The tan-red, long-haired dachshund, its bravado diminished more by Federica's command than Stonecrop's trowel, obeyed and sat. "*Braver Hund! Bleib*, stay. *Gut!*

"Max," she took his arm and helped him stand, "What the fuck? You okay? You scared the shit out of me. And Rosie."

"Bit of a story. Sorry." Stonecrop stared at Rosie, knowing she was a dachshund, but seeing a Rottweiler ready to rip out his throat.

"What say we try again. Max, meet Rosie. She—yes, Rosie, you—is queen of the household. She lives upstairs with Frau Ott." Federica put her finger on Rosie's snout. "Or I should say Frau Ott lives with Rosie!" She scratched Rosie on top of the head. Rosie's tail wagged. Rosie appeared to have forgotten the intruder she had, a minute ago, intended to maim.

Federica's apartment was on the floor below the home's main living quarters. Floor-to-ceiling windows and glass doors on the west wall of the apartment opened to a good-sized backyard comprising a vegetable patch and a grassy plot partly shaded by a large, gnarled plane tree. Along the north and south edges, planting, with graceful abandon, boxed in the yard. To the west, the hill dropped from sight. Underneath the plane tree a one-meter-tall cement statue of the meditating Buddha accumulated moss. Next to the Buddha and under an umbrella of boughs hung a hammock that had seen better days. The wooden bench at the west edge of the yard, the part just before the ground fell away, overlooked the homes on the hillside below and the Zürichsee. In the distant horizon the jagged ridge of the Bernese Oberland divided earth and sky.

Stonecrop, expecting no one else to be at the apartment, was again caught off-guard.

"Max, Alicia. Alicia's my dear friend and off-and-on roomie. We were spoiled boarding-school kids in Leysin. She's from the States; works here now. Well, not here in Zürich, but in London."

"Now we're spoiled adults," Alicia said by way of greeting and held out a hand.

Stonecrop mustered a "Hello." Then his legs gave out. The activity had been too much. Federica and Alicia caught him before he collapsed to the floor. They helped him to Federica's room and onto the bed. The flip-flops dangled off his feet. Federica used the bedsheet to wipe Rosie's saliva from of his ankle.

"You need to rest. I'm sorry about Rosie," Federica said.

"It's okay," Stonecrop said. "Doggie's doing her job." It exhausted Stonecrop to talk.

"Yes," she said distractedly as she checked Stonecrop's pulse, and then his forehead. Federica turned to Alicia. "He really should rest."

"A patient?"

"A special one." Federica replied. In a subdued and serious tone she added, "This one is very special to me. We're from the Moon, you see —ἀλλήλων."

Alicia missed the allusion, "Huh, all alone?"—which is what it sounded like in English.

Federica didn't bother to explain.

Stonecrop, even in his spent state, got the reference. The ancient Greek word means "of one another" and refers to Aristophanes exegesis on love in Plato's Symposium. Love arises when globules from the Moon, once separated by Zeus, find each other. Fede's fingers had not left his wrist.

Susenbergstrasse

They lay back-to-back with bodies fused and leaden. The shallow unstrained cadence of her breathing lulled Stonecrop into a suspended state. He was neither asleep nor awake; he was incapable of movement.

An hour passed and he still hadn't stirred. Coming from the kitchen, fragments of conversation drifted in and out of hearing range. Federica gently withdrew her arm from under his neck. She rested on her elbow; the mass of her leg pinned his in place.

The first voice he distinctly identified was Federica's father's. He'd heard the man speak only once before and then only for seconds. He had been three-quarters asleep at that time as well. The other voice was a woman's. Hers was brittle and saccharine.

Déjà vu. *I'm back on the train.*

Her father was searching for something in the kitchen. He disrupted space, like a gravitational mass telegraphing information about its location and direction. The door to Federica's bedroom opened. Stonecrop, eyes shut, visualized Herr Ratzow watching his pajama clad daughter untangle her limbs from the naked stranger sharing her bed. Said stranger remained immobile. She drew the flower-print Christian Fischbacher bedsheet over his waist, then the shoulders. The boney flesh transformed into a snowy hillock.

"Shh!" A finger to her lips.

"What is that?" Ratzow asked as if the body were an inanimate object. His voice was only marginally less than full.

"Quiet Papà! He's the man from the train to Venice, remember, the nice man who read to me. You probably forgot."

Stonecrop opened one eye and saw the intruder's reflection in both the mirror leaning against the wall and the glass of the partially opened window on the wall opposite the bedroom door. The reflection expressed disbelief. One furry eyebrow rose dramatically higher than the other. Stonecrop feigned sleep. The smile over Ratzow's facial antic came and went undetected.

"Honest. It is truly the same man." She shooed him out of the bedroom. Before she reached the door, another face, this one with bulging eyes bracketed by thick tortoiseshell glasses, peered in. She too was visible in the mirror.

"My, my, *zu dünn*—too thin for me." She fiddled with her glasses to see better. Had she seen him before Fede covered him? "Taking in strays, are we?"

"Nice to see you, too, Claudia," Federica brusquely shoved the woman out of the doorway. Stonecrop noted the name.

Federica returned to bed briefly, leaned over Stonecrop and whispered to him. "Don't get up. It's only Papà and Claudia. She's his advisor."

From the hallway and speaking loudly, as though it were her duty, Claudia asked: "Who *is* our sleeping beauty?"

Federica ignored the question walked past her, speaking instead to her father, "Max is resting, Papà. He's very weak."

Though the throbbing had subsided Stonecrop had no desire to engage in conversation. He was sweating, working through the infection. Clammy, damp skin stuck to the sheets.

The reflection captured through the partially opened door showed the three bodies milling about the kitchen.

Ratzow place two baguettes on the butcher-block table. The aroma of freshly baked bread wafted into the bedroom. Stonecrop was instantly ravenous.

"Strange, no? A second time I walk in and you are in arms of this American. Is crazy, da? I never, not once, hear one word with this man, not one word!"

"I swear I've not seen him since the train, Papà. Not until last week." Federica eased the bedroom door closed; as she walked away, it creaked back open, the gap not as large as before. He could still see her in the mirror and hear their conversation. She added to her explanation: "He was airlifted to the hospital from Kelenalphütte."

"I don't know this kennel-help."

"A mountain hut, in the central Voralpen, about fifteen kilometers west of Göschenen. I was there last summer on an overnight with friends from Poly."

"By Andermatt, da?"

"*Genau!*" The broadly used Swiss German expression can mean anything from exactly, to *just, very, sure*, or, in this case, *right*. Max was climbing on Sustenhorns and fell. At least that's what it looks like; he doesn't remember. Hikers found him at the bottom of the couloir. His helmet was split in two. They thought he was dead. The hutkeepers radioed REGA."

"Why was your sweetie risking life and limb? To what purpose?" Claudia's tone of voice questioned and condemned.

"Sometimes climbers fall."

"Does he know, dearie, how risky it is to sleep with Gregor's daughter?"

Federica gave her a nasty look. "He was discharged yesterday and had no place to go. I brought him home."

"And you slept with him, dearie? Is he your pet from the pound?"

"Yup, I did. He had a mighty shitty night: Nightmares, sweating, chills. And terrified about something. I was worried—because of the head injury. So I woke him up and we talked. I held him and he calmed down." Federica shrugged her shoulders, "We fell asleep."

"This man who reads to you falls out of sky and my Fede like angel catches him! He is lucky man," Ratzow smiled. He was more curious than upset. He went to the refrigerator and returned with a plate with a square of Gruyère cheese on it. The aroma made its way to the bedroom and Stonecrop's stomach growled. He heard Federica get a knife from the dish rack on the counter and wondered if Rosie, with her superior hearing, could, from the floor above in Frau Ott's quarters, pick up the sound. Maybe I am a pet. Please, a treat for me and Rosie!

"*Credo di sì*," she said, smiling back at her father. "Hey, the bed beats the sofa. And Alicia snores worse than you. She's here, in the other bedroom. She leaves tomorrow."

"No judgement, my dear." Claudia pursued the conversation with Federica and tried to make peace. "What do we know about the wounded stray?"

"*We* know very little about him, my dear, and *we* prefer to respect his privacy," Federica mocked Claudia, fed up with her nosiness. "And since I've slept with him before, he's not exactly a stranger, is he!" Federica turned her back on Claudia. She broke off le croûton and took a bite, speaking while chewing, "Thank you for the bread, Papà. It's yummy."

"Da, from bakery by Kino Stüssihof."

Ratzow broke off a piece and added a thick slice of cheese.

"He has quite a package!" Claudia pursed her lips. Neither Ratzow nor Federica responded. Unfazed by the silent treatment, she explained herself, "The Blue Knight at Stüssihof, not lover boy. Or does he as well?"

Stonecrop, still watching their reflections in the mirror, saw Claudia put her hands on the table and leaned forward. The act suggested she and Federica were confidants, "Come now, pet, I can't stand it. You simply must tell me more about the man in your bedroom!"

Claudia wasn't going to let Federica off the hook. Federica, a head taller, looked down at her as she spoke, "His ancient Greek is fair—not as good as Mamma's—but still, pretty good. He is kind, intelligent, and fun. American. Speaks passable German and French, understands Italian. Two children—a well-to-do family. He works in finance and likes to climb and sail. There, how's that?"

Ratzow re-joined. "Da, better," he said, expressing satisfaction over the bread and cheese and likely not commenting on the summary Federica had just delivered.

"Remember, that was seven years ago, right after before my birthday."

"Fede, you're Papà is confused," Ratzow said, and then took another bite of bread and cheese. "You're engaged to dipshit. You don't sleep with him. You don't know married man. But him you like sleep with?"

"Papà, don't talk with your mouth full." Her tone wasn't angry. "He is divorced or separated. Well, I think he is . . ."

On the surface Ratzow's words had been critical, but the underlying message had been one of concern. Fede and her father loved and trusted each other. That had been the case on the train seven years ago. It was no different today.

Claudia adjusted the squelch in her voice to modulate her inherent and unbridled curiosity, "Tell me this, dear, *why* was he on the train— the first time you met him?"

Federica busied herself with the coffee grinder as she addressed Claudia's question. "He was going to Venice. He had a Swiss *torta*—a cake to bring to a friend, an art restorer, for his birthday. A silly tradition they had. It was right after Mamma died." The racket from the grinder forced a hiatus on the conversation. Then Federica resumed, "I said that already, about Mamma, didn't I."

"Intercity stalker bearing torta returns! What fodder for *Zwanzig Minuten!*"

Stonecrop overheard and felt an urge to get up and throw her out the door.

"Yup. Happens to me all the time." Federica had had it with the grilling. She packed six scoops of finely ground coffee in the Bialetti Moka Express, assembled it, and placed it on the stovetop. "You two. Out! Papà, I love you. I gotta be at work in an hour. And heat up broth for Max. I'll call later."

If there was anything else they had come for, it had been forgotten. Ratzow and Claudia made their good-byes and left Federica to her chores. The departing visitors stood briefly in the garden area, a short distance from the partially opened bedroom window. Stonecrop eavesdropped.

"Shall I check him out, love?" Claudia said. "Never keen on coincidence, you know."

"No." Ratzow replied. "He is harmless."

Rosie

He lost the food war. The reentry to everyday living had been on Federica's terms. Having to put in long shifts at work Federica designated Frau Ott as her stand-in. As Federica's majordomo and Swiss to the core, Frau Ott brooked zero deviation from der Plan. The first two days Stonecrop had slept much of the time—first in Federica's room, since Alicia was still in the extra bedroom, then in Alicia's room after she had returned to London. He learned that Alicia stayed at Federica's out of choice, not necessity. It was an opportunity for two friends, maybe more than friends, both career-driven women, to spend time together.

Stonecrop's diet had been clear liquids and Zweibach crackers. On day four, Frau Ott had appeared, bearing a tray with juice, a pot of coffee and two brioches. Stonecrop had proposed to her on the spot; and she had politely declined, saying he was too young and inexperienced. Post-breakfast and endowed with super-powers, he had managed an afternoon walk through the Zürichberg woods. From inside the Ott residence, Rosie had yelped annoyingly at his departure and arrival.

Frau Ott had yet to let Rosie out of the upstairs apartment in the presence of Stonecrop. Today, day five, was different. Stonecrop sat at the garden table, nursing a coffee. The plane tree shaded him from the midday sun. He had been contemplating an afternoon walk/jog, a gentle one, when Frau Ott approached. Rosie led—leashed and snarling. The doggie tugged and Frau Ott resisted. Her extended arms clung to the leash and her head, torso and legs were ruler straight, like the Leaning Tower. Stonecrop struggled to keep a straight face.

"Herr Stonecrop, I believe your fit of illness—Rosie halt!—is past. You show visible improvement in health and in spirit. Rosieeeee—"

Although Stonecrop's German was solid, Frau Ott stubbornly clung to her tortured, Austenesque English.

"Frau Ott, good morning. I am much better, thank you. And thank you for the care, and for letting me stay. The art in the apartment is extraordinary. The gigantic Jean Dubuffet, wow! I'll be out of your hair soon, promise."

"Ah, yes, my blowsy hair. Your stay is no matter. I want for company, as Federica is often at casualty." She and Rosie had achieved a ceasefire. Frau Ott relaxed the death grip on the leash, though not on the English language. "Dear me, how shall I word this? I own a request."

"Sure," Stonecrop had no choice but to agree.

"Between Rosie and me, that is, Rosie and I have discussed—yes, I know she doesn't truly speak—"

At "speak" Rosie barked at the sky.

"Ah, Rosie's bilingual!" Stonecrop joked. Frau Ott did not react.

"Yes, I was saying, about her behavior towards strangers and obedience quite generally. We've met success with 'Sit' and 'Stay'—she is learning some English commands, you see! What distresses most, is that she does *do* inside what she ought *do* outside." She trumpeted each *do* at Rosie.

"May I prevail upon you, as I've noticed you regularly indulge the wide air, to take Rosie with? Air and exercise—en plein air, as it were, rather than pas de plein air—I believe, will afford—"

"Frau Ott," Stonecrop interrupted, saving Frau Ott additional linguistic angst. "If you mean 'take Rosie for a walk so she can do her business,' well, sure, no problem. Love to."

"Yes, that's it exactly! No problem!" She enunciated the last two words as Stonecrop had spoken them. "Only," she went on, "if it does not signify." Stonecrop figured it didn't signify, whatever the hell that meant.

Since he had not responded, Frau Ott pressed on: "Now, regarding the course: exertion in proportion to need, to the Zoo and back will suffice. If you cross some beast intending harm, hold Rosie thus—" Frau Ott demonstrated by picking up Rosie in both arms and holding her tightly to her bosom, "You must support the spine, thus."

She spoke to Rosie, repeating much of what she had said to Stonecrop. Rosie clung to every word.

At the conclusion of the conversation between human and canine, Frau Ott plopped Rosie and leash on Stonecrop's lap. Neither man nor dog knew quite what to make of the unexpected intimacy. Last encounter, Stonecrop was about to disembowel Rosie with a trowel. Both knew better than to defy Frau Ott. Rosie trembled; a trickle of warm doggy pee wetted Stonecrop's running suit.

"Return in one hour, at which time I shall remunerate you the sum of one hundred francs—not to be reported to the tax authorities." Frau Ott winked and then spoke, nose-to-nose with Rosie, "And you shall receive a treat! That will be all." She spun on her heels and marched back to the house.

Stonecrop gently lifted Rosie, as he had been instructed, and placed her on the patio stone. She neither barked nor snarled. They both hankered for the plein air.

Hammock

On day six, after a lunch of celery soup, bread and bresaola, Stonecrop rallied in earnest. His maintenance workout consisted of a five-kilometer run, twenty pull-ups, forty push-ups, and sixty sit-ups—climber staples. Stonecrop gave his all at exercise stations along the trail; he failed to complete any one routine in a single go. The pounding in his head came and went. Federica had ordered a follow-up scan. The headaches, they learned, were a result of strained muscles in the neck and upper back. There was no evidence of intracranial bleeding.

His legs wobbled as he schlepped the last hundred meters to the house. *Not in shape, not even close.* Rosie greeted him at the gate and was at his heels as the two of them made their way to the plane tree. Stonecrop stripped off shoes and socks and collapsed into the hammock.

. . . .

"Yo, lazybones; it's almost six!"

He was aboard Zaca—that is, he was day-dreaming that he was aboard Zaca—in the port berth, being tossed by the waves. The reality was that the forty-four-foot Swan sloop was being stored—on the hard, as they say—in Formentera, the most southerly island of the Balearic Islands. She'd been parked there for three years and likely impounded for past-due rent. The thought of losing her depressed him; he opened his eyes.

Fede's upside-down face looked two-dimensional, like it had been pinned to the underbelly of the plane tree. The face swung in and out of view. Her ponytail swatted him. He grabbed for it and missed, "Yo yourself, I'm seasick!"

"Heaving to!"

The hammock shuddered to a stop. Fede stepped out of her clogs. "Comin' aboard, make way, mate!" She flopped into the hammock beside him. They lay head to toe. The coarsely woven fabric of the hammock groaned. Tree limbs overhead held fast.

"I'm pooped. I say that every day after work. Sometimes ten patients an hour; that's insane. God, I'm boring. I used to be interesting." Fede hung her head to the side and stuck out her tongue.

"You look like Rosie!" Stonecrop said. "But her tongue's a healthy pink. Yours is gross! How about a few Swiss Energy Pets. Rosie loves them."

Fede elbowed him in the thigh. Her look said you're about to walk the plank! The commotion annoyed Rosie, who barked once, turned in a circle three times, and resettled in the cool dirt.

Stonecrop dropped a leg off to the side. His toes touched the ground, enough to gently rock them. "Permission to ask a question, Capt'n."

"Out with it, mate!" Fede wrestled free an orange that had been in her pocket and wedged between them. She rested an elbow between Stonecrop's shins. Orange peels mounted in a pile on her tummy. She gave Stonecrop a segment and plopped the next one in her mouth.

He finished his before speaking, "Here goes . . ." He put his arm behind his head. His fingers bumped into her foot; he lightly took hold of her toe.

"Well."

"Okay. How many languages do you speak?"

"I don't know, a dozen, maybe more—I mean, some are dead, right. Read only."

"I've never seen you study. Not once. Your ancient Greek's as good —hell, way better— than any professor I've had. Italian and Bulgarian are from your parents. Med school and a year in Chicago were in English. You're fluent in German and French, both of which I get by in, but don't speak like a native. You do."

A minute went by before Fede realized Stonecrop was waiting for her to say something.

"I can explain. Nothing special, really. Modern Greek was in my bones. Papà has family in Kavala. We went there on weekends, to be by the sea. Ancient Greek, of course, is a different animal. Brutal structure, studying it is like weightlifting, even for me. Mamma read

Aesop's Fables to me, in the old Greek, from as long as I can remember. I get that that sounds totally weird. When I was little, we sort of talked to each other in ancient Greek—it was our special, secret language."

"You're kidding, you actually *spoke* the language first?"

"Well, the fables, like Homer, are an oral tradition. So, yeah, we did."

"That's crazy. Mind-blowing . . ."

"I piggy-backed on Bulgarian, too. If you speak Bulgarian, you've got a shot at Serbian, Macedonian, Croatian, and even Russian . . . well, maybe not so much Russian. A lot of the words are the same, and the Cyrillic alphabet, but the structure and pronunciation are dissimilar. More like Old Church Slavonic. I've been told Bulgarian's the best language for love." She winked, took another piece of orange, and tossed it to Stonecrop. "I am *mysterrrious* woman, yes?" Fede laid down a Gregor worthy thicket of r's. She batted her eyelashes.

"Spanish; I heard you on the phone."

"Any Italian speaks Spanish. My fiancé's from Chihuahua, Mexico. Lupita's his cousin. We're friends—I love love love Lupita! You'll have to meet her."

"More?" Behind his head, his hand felt the hem of her slacks and a place where the hem had come unstitched. He made a mental note to find a sewing kit—being a climber and a sailor, Stonecrop could sew.

Fede ignored his question and closed her eyes; she *was* tired. Her body exuded exhaustion. The circles under her eyes were darker than the day before.

Stonecrop pinched her pinky toe. "Don't be a shit," she said, "I'm so wiped out! Between us?" She handed him an orange segment as she spoke, and then took another for herself. Her fingers were sticky. "I usually don't talk about how freaky I am with languages, okay? It's fun, don't get me wrong. But I don't make a big deal out of it."

Stonecrop thought she was finished. She wasn't. "I know more than a little Russian. I'm fluent in Swahili, Portuguese and Japanese—lived with Papà two years in Tokyo." This claim, she must have thought, required further explanation. "Mamma was ill. The first signs of pancreatic cancer. She didn't tell us, and much of the time when I was in Japan, she was in Firenze and Milano for treatments. When she wasn't with us in Japan, a Japanese family cared for me—easier for Papà to work and travel around Asia."

"And Swahili?" he asked.

Fede obliged again, "Two years in Mozambique. Picked up

Portuguese—accented—and Swahili. Again, Papà worked, and Mamma stayed in Italy. She wasn't up to caring for me or living abroad. And she didn't like Africa. Like I said, she hid the cancer from me, and Papà kept me close, to watch me, and to keep me out of her hair. For the longest time I thought Mamma was mad at me, like I'd done something horribly wrong and she didn't want to see me."

"What was Africa like?" Stonecrop's almost two-year stint had been bloody and horrific.

"My family there is . . . they were poor and did chores for Papà. Stuff like cooking and cleaning. When he left town for travel—which, again, was a lot—I stayed with my adopted family. You see the pattern.

"My family's house had a dirt floor; but it was clean. It's hard to explain. What I hated, though, was when they cooked. They used earthenware pots and burned charcoal or wood. The air inside the house was acrid, from the smoke." She squinched her eyes, reliving the memory.

Stonecrop didn't press her, but Fede continued, either revived by the snack or motivated by the topic. "One of the things we do at Aide Direct," she said, "is supply pellet stoves to households. The stoves are free, and the families can barter brush and wood for pellets. Pellets use ten percent of the biomass for the same BTU output, and there's no *HAP*—household air pollution. HAP kills two million women and girls a year."

"Did you feel safe with the adopted family?"

"I was always accompanied by older brothers or sisters. Everyone in the village looked out for me—I obviously stood out."

"Sounds unhealthy, and dangerous," he said.

"Not so!" She rallied to defend herself. "It was cozy. The countryside is lovely. So varied. Mozambique is larger than France! *I* loved it, and I was maybe never so carefree." She exhaled a deep, grounding breath. "People are the same," she declared. "Once you're family, and help with dinners and diapers, people are just people."

"A romantic notion," Stonecrop said, "a nice one." He didn't want to appear bitter. "How old were you?" he asked and immediately felt badly for dumping another question on her. "Fede, I'm sorry. You're tired."

Fede thoughts were were lost in the tangled limbs overhead, "I don't mind, if you don't mind a tired girl."

Stonecrop gave her toe a gentle squeeze and smiled.

"Seven and eight." Her body grew heavy. Tension left her face.

"You weren't kidding, were you? You remember, on the train, when I asked where you had grown up? You looked up, like you are now, and said 'everywhere.'"

She returned to his original query, "Arabic. I read classical Arabic and speak passable street Arabic."

"No way—like eighth-century Qur'anic script?"

"Exactly, but only the few works I've studied and translated. The calligraphy is exquisite. You gotta dial in the scrivener's style." Fede spoke as if she were saying sure, anybody can read that stuff.

"Mamma's academic specialty was hermeneutics—theories of interpretation, specifically, the impact Islamic translators had on how the Christian West came to understand the Neoplatonists. Shit, I'm lecturing? I forget you're a philosophy guy."

"Go on, I'm interested. And the philosopher in me is curious."

"Yeah. So, the Arabic and Greek commentaries were her meat and potatoes. We went ever day to the Biblioteca Nazionale—she called it 'home school' . . . I revere that library, the setting on the Arno. We worked in the rare books room. Have you been there?"

"The library, of course. Rare books room, never." Stonecrop shook his head, mesmerized by her voice and drawn into her remembrances.

"The chairs are so heavy. When I was little, I couldn't *move* one by myself. They line up at this long table, a sort of community desk, made of thick, blackened planks of wood." Fede spread her thumb and index finger four or five inches apart to indicate the dimension. "'Stained from the toils and tears of scholars,' Mamma would say.

"You had to request a book from the librarian. I loved the velvet worms they gave us, to hold the pages open. The librarian made a special one for me! It was orange; my *carotina*—my little carrot—she called it. The books, some of them were *so* huge they had to be supported by these foam beds," she held her hands in a V to demonstrate the size and angle, "to keep the spines from splitting."

He thought about her reflection in the windowpane from their dinner on the train. She had lulled him into a dream world again. He drifted freely between her thoughts and his own, and realized that the day, this day, had passed without nightmares of Maputo, without fear of being hunted, without fear of the uncertain world.

"At first," Fede went on, "I just watched her work. Mamma's health had improved, the cancer was in remission. The translation work was invigorating; the script is so much, so much more than simple writing. It's easy to believe it's divine. I helped her—it became my playtime. In time, I was translating. A colleague from Verona, Italian but Arabic speaking, noticed. He was the one who insisted I be tested." Fede distributed the last of the orange.

"Tested? Do you have a photographic memory?" he asked, coming back to the conversation and wondering if he had already asked the question.

"No one has a photographic memory. That's a myth. But I am, like I said, a freak. The testing came up with something different. Mamma's friend, *zio* Marco—uncle Marco—called it kinesthetic memory. Actively touching, talking, turning the pages, all of it—*engagement*—is what triggers my ability to recall linguistic stuff like really, super well. Zio Marco said my brain tricks a semantic memory and turns it into an episodic one. Those are easy to remember. Anybody can do that. I do both naturally."

"Incredible," he said. "Christ, I can forget anything."

The musky aroma of narcissus washed over them. A wisp of hair drifted across Fede's cheek and stuck to her lip. She puffed it aside.

"Smell that?" he asked.

She closed her eyes. Stonecrop raised his foot and brushed the underside of her chin with his bare, dirty toes. Sticky fingers brushed the foot aside. "*Grrrrross!*"

Fede rolled out of the hammock, spilling the orange peels onto Rosie, miraculously not waking her.

"Dinner time," Fede had returned to here and now. "I picked up pizza. Ah, there's the timer!"

The timer's chime, the mention of pizza, or both, roused Rosie. Her head shot up like a periscope on a submarine. She scanned the horizon for Stonecrop. An orange peel that had landed on her head stayed in place, a doggy beret atop the stalwart scout.

Linguine con Vongole

Stonecrop did not leave his station at the stove to greet Fede. A little over a full week had gone by since his arrival at Susenbergstrasse and he had felt well enough to take the Number 5 tram downtown to shop for dinner at the Coop market in Bellevue.

The 'Coop'—the Swiss pronounce it with a long 'o', as in 'hope'—is, as the name suggests, a cooperative. Coop stores are ubiquitous and account for much of the organic food and everyday household items sold in Switzerland. Stonecrop liked the convenience and quality of the stores but bristled at the near oligopoly status that Coop and their one major competitor, Migros, had achieved in Switzerland.

From the kitchen, he heard the door close behind Federica. He heard her send her clogs clunking against the hallway wall. Sweater and bag flew to the corner chair. The bag made it. The sweater fell short—a sleeve reached up from the pile on the floor to the seat of the chair. She ignored the disarray accompanying her arrival. "Ahhh,' she let a long breath out and then inhaled deeply, "It smells so good in here!"

"*Linguine alle vongole,*" he answered. He had just cleaned the clams —they were the small Adriatic variety—and was heating olive oil and garlic in a red enameled Le Creuset skillet.

"*Bianco o rosso?*" Fede asked.

"Bianco, for my Tuscan girl." Max knew both recipes. The rosso is made with tomatoes and is more common in the south.

"Apparently, the man can cook! Fede gave Max a hug from behind.

"Easy dish. Don't like complicated food—or women. Ah, I used up the rest of the white swill in the fridge."

"Ah-huh. You're a sexist pig. But for food, we'll give it a pass. Do I have time for a shower? Tough day; tough week; glad it's over. I'd really like to wash my hair."

"Go for it. Absolutely no rush." Stonecrop looked up from the stove. Dark semi-circles under the eyes seemed the norm. "You left at eight and it's what, almost ten? I didn't think you were coming home . . . Good you texted."

Fede charged off to the bathroom and missed what he had said. She didn't bother to close the door. The toilet flushed. A minute later water hammered the shower floor.

Stonecrop loved to cook. The family dinner had been one of the few rituals he had vigorously enforced as a parent. The kids could invite home as many friends as they wanted, but his kids had to be at home for dinner and had to help cook. He missed the happy chaos of it all, and hoped his girls would, when they were older, keep the dinners-at-home tradition.

Cooking had clear objectives: no career crap, no quixotic righting of wrongs, no psychodrama, no anything with women or relationships. Just a good meal. This night, he vowed, would mark the beginning of a quiet, mentally healthy, and simple existence. His ex and daughters would be fine. He would Skype with the daughters weekly. His old firm would stay in business. The trouble he had caused would mark him as a whistle-blower, making it hard to return to work in finance. So be it. The sun would still come up. He would ski and climb. He assigned no timetable to his mediation with the recent past, and resolved to be wary of anything that smacked of commitment.

Stonecrop covered the skillet to let the clams open and release their juices. While they steamed, he put napkins and silverware in a pile on the table, plus an extra bowl for shells. He lit candles—the soft light was restful. His intent was not to create a romantic setting. He and Fede were not lovers. He had been staying in Alicia's room and he hoped to find an apartment directly. With five months remaining on his visa, there was more than enough time to find some sort of undemanding work that was *not* venture capital, his former métier.

The bowls warmed in the oven. Max used a slotted spoon to move the clams to a separate bowl, and then fished out a strand of linguine to test. *Perfetto*! The verdict—*al dente*.

He added a half-cup of the pasta water to the skillet. As the liquids came to a boil, he drained the pasta and tossed it in the skillet to soak up the sauce and then mixed in the clams and juice. The final touch was parsley, salt, pepper, and red pepper flakes.

"*Voilà!*" he announced to a barefoot Fede re-entering the room. She wore a cozy Calida flower-print cotton nightshirt. The non-outfit was topped off by a white towel wrapped like a turban to hold her wet hair in place.

"I am a so frickin" starved!" she announced.

"We're ready—don't want a cranky girl."

"Speaking of cranky, how are the headaches?"

"Off and on, better every day."

"What a good *Mann* he is! He cares for the girl. You wanna stick around, big boy?" Holding her turban in place, she tossed a playful look his way and kissed him on the cheek.

Fede took a seat at the table and poured out local, twelve-franc-a-bottle Pinot Grigio. Stonecrop served up pasta. Baguette and oil were on the table. The baguette was local and hearty, not the typical Italian cardboard excuse for bread.

"Tell me about the tough day," he said, as they both methodically extracted clam meat and chucked gutted shells into the bowl mid-table. The bowl clinked when a shell hit the sides.

"It's not the hours," she said, taking a bite of pasta. "I haven't been a doc for long. I am *not* thick-skinned, and I am not used to losing someone. Maybe I'll always be like that; fuck if I know." Fede lowered her gaze, spun her fork against the side of the pasta bowl and gathered a coil of pasta. "I'm gonna try to be cheery. My colleagues and I tried everything to save this young woman. She was adorable—smiling and spunky, despite feeling horrible. Her eyes are still in my head." Federica paused, held her fork in the air, and looked directly at Stonecrop. "We failed."

"Tell me more."

"Her case was straightforward. She came in with flu symptoms. We kept her in observation in the ICU for a couple hours, medicated her, put her on an IV, and stabilized her. She was one hundred percent ready for discharge—chatty, breathing, heart, blood-pressure, temp, everything was fine—when we released her. Then, an hour-and-a-half later, the EMT's brought her back. She was in a coma. We lost her. It was so fast. Morbidity review is Wednesday." Fede ceased speaking. She downed most of her wine and refilled the glass. They sat in silence.

"I'm sorry, Fede. Is the review a normal thing?"

"Yeah, it's routine. Max, she was so young, so full of life. Everything to live for. What did we miss?"

Max thought of his own daughters and the unbearable emptiness he would feel were he to lose one of them. Even worse, feel responsible for the loss.

Fede needed to talk. Stonecrop went with it. "I wonder what I'm doing. Like, if maybe the work is too much for me."

"The job's not a lark. Life and death, every day. One thing I am sure of, you're a really good doc."

"Yeah, I hope so. Her name was Elena. I don't know if she was married. She or someone else had removed a ring. I saw a white band where the ring had been."

"Hey, you're saving lives. *I* am grateful for what you and your colleagues do."

"You gonna cheer me up?"

"You don't need me for that. C'mon, you're engaged. Friends and family love you. You're damned smart; have a great career; and live in Zürich. That's a pretty good hand you're holding."

Fede got out of her chair. She slurped up the remainder of a linguine dangling from her mouth and inadvertently flicked oil on her nightshirt. It reminded him of the stains on her hoodie when they had first met. "Be right back," she said.

She returned shortly and took her place. She used one hand to resume twirling pasta with her fork. With the other, she plunked an engagement ring on the table in front of Max. "Speaking of rings, this is *the* ring, *my* ring. A recent addition to the jewelry box."

Stonecrop picked it up and held it close to the candle's flame. As he rotated the ring light refracted through the diamond and splattered the wall and ceiling with a jittery, confetti-like carousel of color. "You don't wear it?"

"Of course not!" she said, as though the answer were obvious.

"This is a Gibraltar-sized rock. Is it real?" he asked.

"It is indeed—the isthmus to marriage, and Andreas has a *Ferrari* to match!" She paused to shovel in a coil of noodles secured in place by a clam skewered at the end of the fork.

They ate in silence for a few minutes, removing meat from newly found clams buried under linguine. Stonecrop discarded an unopened clam.

"Think about it," she said.

Max did. "It's big," he astutely observed.

"Brilliant! No really, how do I get a latex glove over this?" She took the ring with both hands, examining it. Her elbows rested on the table.

"I see what you mean." Max got it, the prong setting would get in the way. "Why not just take it off for work?"

"Yeah. Off and on, off and on. I'd lose the damned thing in a week.

Anytime I work, or climb and ski. Hell, I fix toilettes. Before you know it—*oops*— down the drain! This thing, this ring and me, we got a serious lifestyle compatibility problem." Fede slid the ring on her finger and then off, overdoing the struggle at the knuckle.

"Plumbing skills, cool!"

"Not just the ring," she said, "Andreas."

The statement puzzled Stonecrop. Other than the name and the fact that "playboy" wore an extra-large polo shirt and drove a Ferrari; he knew nothing about her fiancé. "He's not the right guy, not for me."

Using both hands, Fede unwound the towel from her head and dropped it to the floor as she simultaneously slurped up a suspended linguina hanging in limbo from her lips. Stonecrop found her artlessness as endearing tonight as he had on the first day they had met.

"The sex is—I don't know how to say it—well, there hasn't been much."

There are times, Stonecrop knew, when a man should say nothing. This was one of those times.

"He wants people to think he's engaged to a Frau Doktor," she said, filling the space in the dialogue. "It's a status thing."

Stonecrop flip-flopped. Curiosity got the better of good sense and tact. "The sex . . ."

Federica finished what she had started. "It ended almost before it began. He got very . . . physical and hurtful. Then the ring showed up —like a peace offering. We haven't been together since the weirdness and ring episode."

She poured wine, inhaled, burped loudly—and burst out laughing, spilling a little wine. The tension broke; he laughed with her, eager to drop the topic.

"Par*don*. Golly, how fucking lady-like, huh. This is fantastic linguini. I mean it. I need a—what do they call them—personal man? Like Hollywood stars have."

"Personal assistant. As you wish!" He delivered the words as a nod to *Princess Bride*.

"*Westley Stonecrop*, what a yummy name! I could just eat up somebody named Westley Stonecrop."

"Too soft and stuffy, no thanks."

"No?" she said, "Maybe I'll talk you into it." Fede tore off a chunk from the baguette, and then tore off a small piece of it to dip in the sauce and popped it in her mouth. "Or maybe you're right. My steely-eyed, hardened, and . . . and other macho adjectives I can't come up with now because my brain is fried . . ." Federica tapped a knuckle to her head.

Stonecrop leaned back and smiled. "Truth is, I'm the hubby invited to the wives' only luncheons, the luncheons *verboten* to the other husbands. I play with kids, cook, do laundry, clean house. I never watch the game and never owned a Lazy-boy."

"Ah, so that's what women do! I've always wondered." She closed one eye and pretend-glared at him with the other. "You're losing ground, Max."

"Touché!"

They ate in silence, a silence as easy-going as their conversation had been.

After a while, Max reengaged, "How long you been climbing?"

"Seven or eight years, not consistently though. I started in earnest right before we met. A few trips with the Chicago Mountaineering Club—crazy to start in the Midwest, at Devil's Lake. I grew up with the Dolomiti in my back yard. I enjoy climbing."

"Me too; at it since I was twelve. Sometime—when you get a break in the nutso schedule—you want to grab some plastic?" he asked, a reference to the holds on the walls of indoor climbing gyms.

"Did you just ask me out for a date, whoa! Very exciting, I accept!" They clinked clamshells together. "Yikes, I forgot! I'm so self-involved tonight, sorry." She put her fork down to deliver the news. "I talked to Papà. *You* have a job! Remember how you said you wanted something super simple, brainless, no commitments—"

"I meant it. I gotta work. Zürich's pricey."

"The health insurance," she added, "not cheap."

"Insurance, yes, an arm and a leg."

Fede was excited to tell him the news. "Right, so I told Papà. And, he said he will hire you. You get to be *the* official courier for GR Group, AG! Papà needs someone to deliver and pick up things in town. I don't know for sure, but I assume Group will take care of health insurance and the visa. I didn't ask." Fede spent a few minutes adding detail, explaining what she thought the job would entail. A part of his responsibilities would be the delivery of confidential documents to and from one or two locations abroad.

"Why on earth would your father trust me? He doesn't know me from Adam. And you gotta admit, our relationship—between your dad and me—is kinda whacky."

"He has to! I said you were the most trustworthy man I'd ever met!" She clapped her hands to make the point, a magician who had just performed a wondrous trick. "Oh yeah, and you gotta cook for me once a week—that's my commission."

"You'd sell dad down the river for a good meal."

"Is that recognized as a racial slur?"

"Don't know. But seriously, thank you. I'd very much like to thank him in person."

The dinner was finished, the wine as well. Fede left the table and returned with a bottle of Vin Santo di Chianti, two small water glasses instead of wine glasses, and a plate with a half-dozen biscotti. Without asking she poured and handed him a glass.

"That was so scrumptious! Oh, happy tummy!" She stuck out and patted her stomach, then sat down and immediately bobbed back up. "Can we hit the sofa; been on my feet all day. I need to sprawl."

They migrated to the sofa, which was an inexpensive, boxy Ikea love seat with high sides and back and room for cushions, the two of them, and not much else. Fede plopped down at one end, almost spilling her Vin Santo. She placed the bottle on the floor between them, precariously leaving it at a tilt, half of its base on the floor and the other half on a Persian area rug, another IKEA purchase. She faced Stonecrop and tucked her feet up under her nightshirt, cross-legged. He put the plate of biscotti next to the wine, righted the bottle, and took a seat on the other end of the sofa. She worked on a biscotti as Tuscan's do, dipping it in Vin Santo before each bite.

"I like Ferraris." The statement came out of nowhere. "*Scusi, sono brillo.*" She translated, "I'm a little tipsy. It feels good."

"Yes, it does," he agreed. Stonecrop rearranged himself, adjusting his legs to sit cross-legged. He faced her, feeling relaxed and at ease.

Fede continued, "There once was another man I loved, Max. Not a lover, but like an uncle. He had a Ferrari too."

"Okay," he laughed, not getting why the talk of lovers and their cars. The explanation came forthwith.

"Marco Manucci, di Verona. Know him?" She asked him in earnest and waited for a response.

"You had mentioned him before. He was your mother's colleague. I don't know the name. Should I?"

"Maybe. You'd know him if you had you had taken your degree in Europe instead of the U.S. He was well-known for his work in logic, and translations of John Philoponus. JP's one of my favorite neoplatonists."

"I'm vaguely familiar with the commentary on Aristotle's theory of impetus."

"Zio Marco had one hell of a library—one of the largest private collection of neo-platonists works. The library had its own wing in the house. And the house wasn't just a house. It was this take-your-breath-away palazzo, close the Arena di Verona. In the summer you can hear the singers from the balcony. Can you imagine!" As she spoke Fede closed her eyes, visualizing—Stonecrop assumed—the palazzo, or maybe replaying an aria she had heard from the balcony. "He had a full-time librarian. We all borrowed books. He was always generous with his collection and his knowledge. Zio Marco helped me with Greek, along with Mamma. They were peers, and co-published. They worked together—a lot. You understand?"

"I do," he answered, although he didn't. She had spoken about Zio Marco before, but not in this tone of voice. After a minute of reflection, he got it. He understood and was as surprised by the revelation as by the admission.

"Look at me. Do I look like Papà?" She lifted her head, offering her profile on one side, and then the other.

"Hmm, I dunno," he scrutinized her face and the shape of her head. "One ear's lower than the other."

Her hands shot up to touch her earlobes, lightly pulling them downward and letting her fingers slip off, the way a hair-stylist would to measure the length of hair on each side of a person's face. She spilled wine in the process. Max looked aside, smiling.

His gaze returned in time to see a curl of her flaxen hair drop into the Vin Santo. Fede had not noticed. He traced the graceful line running from her chin to the base of her ear. Wisps of hair shimmered in the candlelight.

"Well?" She queried, impatient for a response.

Stonecrop had been so lost in her features that he had forgotten her question. "Well, what?"

"Do I look like Gregor?" she repeated.

"You betcha! The big nose seals it."

Federica took a fake swing at him. He ducked back and asked, "Of course, Gregor knows."

"I think not. He believed everything Mamma told him. Just like he believes whatever I tell him. It's his Achilles heel. Well, he has two, no three fallibilities—Mamma, me, and his own fantasy about how the world is."

"If you believe that, you're the one who's naïve!"

"No one knows. That is, I've never told anyone, not even Alicia."

"Why are you telling *me*?" Stonecrop was genuinely shocked and confused about why he was chosen to be the honored confidant.

"I don't know. I like your legs!" The flip reply was her way of not replying, or maybe of saying she really didn't know why. She abandoned the paternity talk and distracted him by tugging at the sock on his foot. She pulled it off, switched her wine to her other hand and, with the free hand, pulled off the other sock.

"Okay. I like yours, too." He laughed quietly. The conversation and her intentions were adrift.

"What's next, my soon-to-be-gainfully-employed courier? More alpine adventures?" Fede returned to safe ground; the shunt toward intimacy closed.

"Nope. That was dumb, a sorta grand finale to the divorce and my career blowing up. I'm lucky to not be dead or locked up in some makeshift prison in Africa. I did things I shouldn't have done. Things I deeply regret." Stonecrop was surprised by his own candor. It was the same candor he had experienced with her seven years before.

"Uh huh." Her expression softened, and her voice, "Max, we aren't born good. We all have blood on our hands." She was inside him . . . again. Fede paused, as if she were debating—to add or not add to what she had said. Her decision, he could tell, was not now, not this night.

Unexpectedly, she perked up, ignited by some inner realization. "You've inspired me. I'm gonna dump Andreas, for real. In my heart, it's been a dead deal since . . . you know . . . *Corragio!*" Fede laughed to herself and pounded her hand against her chest. Her hand became a fist and over her heart and then slowly and deliberately dragged downwards, stretching the nightshirt tightly across her breasts, until it came to rest in the hollow between her legs.

Where did that come from, Fede?

She read the surprise on his face, "Relax, Max. Honestly, I want to know, do you like *my* legs?" she asked, and didn't wait for an answer, "I do."

"Of course," he said, speaking at the same time as she had.

She wiggled her toes, admiring them, and then threw her head back and laughed, "No regrets, we are not going to wallow in fucking regrets!"

He waited, fascinated, and curious about what was next. He

wondered whether to reintroduce the question, to retrace the half-serious piece of their conversation—the topic she had circled back to. "That's a big decision, to separate."

Fede didn't skip a beat. "It's Frau Ott's to blame! She's so keen to marry me off. Her helpfulness borders on desperation. According to Frau Ott, which means to paraphrase Jane Austen, her singular provenance of any thought or word in English," Fede was back to playful, slipped into RP English, and drew upon that fathomless memory, "'. . . a single man in possession of a good fortune, must be in want of a wife.'

"Frau Ott encouraged me. And I, in turn, let Andreas make a flirtation into more than it deserved to be. Practical fool that I am, I, like Henry, found engagement 'convenient.' In truth, I didn't want this stupid ring; and I don't want him."

She broke off for a sip of vin santo, then shrugged her shoulders and tilted her head to the side. "Though I didn't mind jetting off for a weekend ski! He keeps a jet in St. Moritz! There, the onus is on me. Fun at the time grew into something more to him and way less to me. We never talk."

"Hey, I got a beat-up old boat in Ibiza." Then he corrected himself, "Actually not that beat-up and on a little island south of Ibiza. And not mine anymore—"

"Ibiza," she interrupted, localizing his pronunciation and making the "z" a "th" sound.

With little to justify it, Stonecrop felt some sympathy for Andreas. The man was being pilloried with no opportunity to defend himself. "But still, he's there for you."

"No, it's the other way around. I'm there for him—another fancy car in the garage to take out for a spin when he comes to town. It's gotta end. And his temper, well that my friend, is a bona fide deal-breaker." She lowered her voice and her head. "He scared me once, Max. And now, Papà loathes him. Papà said he'd break Andreas's legs or cut off his balls if Andreas got outta line again. He said 'your say, I do.' "

Stonecrop now regretted revisiting Andreas. He wanted to lighten things up, but didn't know what to say.

Fede pouted, "Papà was serious." Then she smiled, close-mouthed and feigning contrition over the mood change. *"Basta così.* You know the expression, *that's enough!"*

She helped herself to another half-glass of vin santo and inclined forward toward Stonecrop. The nightshirt hung loosely. He caught sight of her breasts as she stabilized herself on one arm, concentrating on holding the bottle to refill his glass and trying not to spill. Her hand trembled. He checked his own hand and glass—steady, they were steady. After what he had been through the last few days, he ought to have been shakier. He exhaled slowly, then tried and failed to count to ten.

Fede rocked back against the armrest. She replaced the bottle on the floor beside the sofa, once again atilt and half on the rug. Her nightshirt, which had covered her legs as she sat cross-legged on the sofa, slid up and over her knees as she repositioned herself. She adjusted the nighty—not modestly covering herself as he had expected but lifting the nightshirt. Her undies were cotton, a pink and gray print. Stonecrop turned away in a half-assed attempt at modesty. His actual reaction was visceral. Marriage, children, divorce, revenge, self-destruction, pride and principles—all of it, all of it, was erased by this one act of desire.

"Cute, huh?" Her voice had a whimsical lilt.

Stonecrop had been holding his breath. Denial worked its mojo and he offered a non-committal compliment. "Yeah, very nice." The words were a thin veneer for the desire he felt.

In the silence that followed, he listened for her breath and, for no reason, matched it. Without taking her eyes from his, Fede slowly and carefully set her glass on the floor. With the same deliberation, and still holding his gaze, she uncrossed her legs and planted her feet flat on the sofa. She slid down in her seat, settling in a slouched squat with her back resting against the tall arm of the sofa. Her toes slid up to and rested against his feet and triggered another frisson of desire. Fede hiked up the nightshirt, tucking in the sides behind her to keep them in place. Her breasts were half-covered. With each breath, two scalloped shadows rose and fell across her bare abdomen.

She broke the spell with a short soliloquy, "'Stand and face me, my love, and scatter the grace in your eyes . . .'" The words were material. Like stones, they had texture and weight, enough to shatter misgivings and doubts. The words connoted values they shared: beauty, dignity, respect, decency, honesty . . . and exaltation of love. Lastly, those words were from a world they shared. "Sappho," she said softly. Stonecrop was transfixed.

Fede slowly and deliberately let her knees unfold, one falling to one side, the other falling against the backrest of the loveseat. From the movement, a faint bilabial separation sounded like a soft kiss suspended in the air, an audible manifestation of her arousal. One corner of her mouth twitched briefly, a further indication of continence in retreat. Max turned away. Then, she drew him back. As surely as if she held his head in her hands, her eyes took hold of his and guided his line of sight downward to settle upon her sex.

She put the tips of two fingers to her lips for a dab of saliva. The curved fingers cupped the saliva and descended to the damp shadow between her thighs. No detail was lost on Max. A minute passed, and another. Her other hand rested atop the two fingers below, arrhythmically moving side to side, shoving aside the flesh of each thigh in turn, and resting only long enough to allow the two fingers a more exacting and pleasurable purchase.

"Fede, I adore you. I do, but—"

Her response was unhurried, whispered and dream-like, "Good. I want you to adore me."

The *good* got to him, like it had on day one. But differently. Then, she had been a pre-adult. He had been chastely comforting her. Not so now; he was insanely aroused.

"It's been a really, really long time. I mean, a relationship should—"

"*Shhhh*, it's okay," she gently interrupted.

Fede rocked forward on her hands and knees and in one awkward motion slipped off her undies, leaving them to dangle from her ankle. Her hands went to Stonecrop's stomach, then dropped to his baggy climber pants, undid the waist button, and unzipped the fly.

She tossed him the playful smile of a woman on a mission.

"Don't know if I'm ready—" he tried to speak.

Her eyes brightened and drank in his aroused state. She grasped his cock in both hands. Her breath was short, irregular. Her forehead pressed against his own; her lips brushed against his lips and prevented him from speaking. "Oh, you're ready. I'm a doctor, I know ready."

She shoved him inside her sex and slammed against him, locking him between her loins with the ferocity of a Serengeti lioness. She held him there. His face was lost in her hair, his lips resting just above her ear. In his teeth, a lock of her hair tasted of vin santo. They breathed in unison and came, awash in an exuberant torrent. He smelled her breath, the wine, the garlic from dinner; and on her body the musky redolence of sweat and the heady odor of her sex. At the core of the intoxicating olio of aroma and emotion lay, like the eye of a hurricane, the simple act of holding her and being held.

"Golly," Stonecrop whispered the words, afraid to undo the moment.

"Yeah, golly," Fede softly repeated back to him.

The sexual tension, so commanding and intense moments before, had waned and been replaced by a tender calm. Still bound with him, Fede rocked slightly to one side. "*Un peu de vent, pardon.*" They erupted in goofy laughter. "We're silly creatures," Fede said, giving a kind of snorting laugh about her own awkwardness. "That, Max, was just for you. Girl's gotta mark her turf!" She disengaged, reclined on her elbows, staring at the wet pool between them, on their bodies, Max's clothes, and the sofa.

"Silly is good." Max laughed. It was impossible to hold back the stupid grin on his face.

"Can we keep this just between us? I'd really prefer that."

"Me, too."

Stonecrop had considered suggesting the same. To proclaim a relationship is to invite a host of expectations. He wasn't ready. Fede probably had picked that up and saved him from an uncomfortable moment.

"What say we let the dishes go," Fede said. "Come to bed; I'm spent. It's night, my love, time to tuck in this flower delirious from the light of day."

Max cradled her head on his shoulder. "Sappho fragment?" he asked.

"Nope," she half-laughed, half-snorted again. "Nope, tipsy me fragment. Jesus, how could you think that was Sappho? You're such a dolt," she scolded.

Fede was cratering for real. Holding her securely in his arms, Max swung his feet to the floor and rose. She mumbled to him as he carried her to the bedroom, "Stay with me. In the morning, wake me, fuck me. No talk, just fuck me. Wake me like that. Promise?"

"Promise, and double promise," Stonecrop said, surprisingly ready to make good on the vow well ahead of schedule. But he would wait.

"How's the headache?" she asked out of the blue.

"What headache?"

"Good." The word was a mere breath. Her eyes closed. She fell asleep in his arms.

Bruxelles

"Why am I here?" Stonecrop asked. He'd never been to Brussels and since their arrival had been trying to get his bearings.

"Moral support for your girl," Federica put her hand over her heart, "because you love me *soooo* much."

"You drag my butt to Brussels for moral support?"

"I'm not used to talking with investment bankers. You are."

"They're amoral animals. Feed 'em money and they're happy."

"And I don't want to bother Papà. This is Aide Direct business, not his."

Three months had gone by since that first week at Federica's, the week during which he had recovered from his accident on the Sustenhorn, a week during which Federica and Stonecrop had rediscovered each other as adults and become lovers. Since then, he had found a small but clean apartment on Münstergasse in the Niederdorf, the lively old town section of Zürich on the east side of the Limmat River. His apartment was above a florist and across the street from his favorite coffee house, Café Stehli.

The courier work he did for Ratzow's company was exactly the sort of no-stress employment he had wanted. He supplemented that income with part-time work for a well-established art gallery. Initially, he had simply made deliveries and pickups, however after the owner and Stonecrop had gotten to know each other, and after the owner, Herr Bachman, learned that Stonecrop's ex-wife owned the prestigious Holstein-Scherer gallery in Aspen, he had hired Stonecrop to help with two exhibitions.

And, of course, Stonecrop still walked Rosie. The chore was anything but, however he had been unable to convince Frau Ott to *not* compensate him. Stonecrop tried to make up for taking the money by helping Frau Ott around house, including cooking, which, in truth, was another non-chore chore.

"You remember my promise?" she asked.

"I do *not* remember your promise," he replied, honestly having no idea what she was talking about.

"Baloney. I said I was going to do it, remember, that first night, well technically *third* night we were together, and I *am* going to do it."

They were to meet their two guests at Wesh Rhey, a new, hip café near the city center with outdoor seating and an Afro-French cuisine. They adjusted their chairs to take advantage of the afternoon Indian summer sun. The air was chilly and had driven other patrons indoors. Stonecrop breathed in the odors of wet leaves on the ground and fresh bread from the kitchen. When the café doors opened, he smelled moules frites being served inside, not this café's specialty, but ubiquitous in Bruxelles. He was starved.

"I can't wait for these guys. Can we order."

"Fair enough," Fede replied. She efficiently flagged the waiter and placed their orders. Last minute Stonecrop switched to his regular, bifteck frites. Fede skipped the menu. Trusting her nose, she went with the moules frites. They chose to ignore the African specialties.

"Did you tell me? I'm sorry, who are we meeting?" Stonecrop asked. She was supposed to bring him up to speed on the flight from Zürich, but instead the conversation had been all small talk. It was the nature of their relationship, the little things mattered, especially little things that were fun.

"Hitoshi Sato. He's the investment banker. He's about my age and works for New Horizons. He has a client that I met in Africa, whose company has this nifty drone technology we can use to support AD sites in Mozambique. The last cyclone the flooding made it impossible to resupply our medical team. The drones can do that and do it safely." Federica added another point of information. "I checked Sato's profile. Academically, he's a rock-star."

"Yeah, well, keep in mind he might be an idiot when it comes to actual business and not finance. And the other one—man or woman?"

"Man. These dicks, they're everywhere."

"The other dick is?"

"Andreas Reyes Castro."

"Ah, he *is* a dick. *The* Andreas! I shouldn't judge. I remember now, you told me he's the brother of your friend in Dardin, Lupita?"

"No, thank god! A cousin. They're complete opposites. But they come from the same money—scrap steel and aluminum business in Chihuahua and Monterey."

"Have you even seen him in the last few months? I mean, since we —"

"Maybe." She looked up and to the left. Stonecrop didn't remember which it was, right or left. One or the other indicated you were lying.

"Yeah, well. We'll leave it at maybe."

"I love you." She took his hand.

"I know." Stonecrop reassured her and smiled. He was not the jealous type. Or so he told himself. "Why Andreas?" He asked the question in reference to their lunch meeting, not their relationship. Federica took it as such.

"He's AD's biggest funder by like three digits. Seven million U.S. I have to play nice."

"That's real money. So he's the pooh-bah—"

Federica did not have a chance to respond. Hitoshi Sato, erect in posture, thin and tall—almost imperial—with jet black hair to his shoulders and eyes that seemed to be constantly looking at something behind you, approached the table. Although meeting Federica for the first time, he seemed to recognize her. He shook hands with each man in turn and then took a seat.

"We just ordered. I'm having mussels. Same for you?" she asked Hitoshi.

"No! I'm vegetarian, green tea is fine. Environmentally, if you're going to eat meat, mussels are an excellent choice! I live only a few blocks from here. The food is good. Our offices are nearby."

Federica rose to get the waiter as Stonecrop and Hitoshi sized each other up. Cave man meat-eater versus enlightened vegetarian. The conversation with the waiter, which should have taken seconds, took longer and switched from French to Italian—something about the waiter being from Greve in Chianti, a small town south of Firenze and well-known to Federica.

Hitoshi broke the ice. "Are you an attorney for Aide Direct?"

"Not at all," he laughed, "I'm a friend."

"I see. And what do you think of Brussels? You're American, correct?"

"Never spent time here."

"I hope you have a chance to explore the city," Hitoshi said, as he craned his head over one shoulder and then the other, looking for Federica.

"Not this trip."

The stilted non-conversation ended at Federica's reappearance. Although she had not met Hitoshi in person, she had had a number of conversations with him about the transaction in question and seemed at ease with him.

"Hitoshi, can I brag about you? You never talk about yourself." She had disarmed him. He leaned back in chair, a sign that he did not object and would set aside his modestly.

"When Hitoshi was in college, he decided he would dedicate his life to good works. He completed a physics degree at Chicago, a fellowship grant, same time I was there. It's a big school, we never met —"

"My nose was in the books!" Hitoshi added.

"Then a doctorate at MIT—in what, three years? After graduation, correct me if I'm wrong, you blew off research offers and went to work for Greenpeace, the World Bank, and then New Order."

"I was a lowly intern at those institutions."

"Yes, but New Order loved you, paid for an MBA at Wharton, and brought you in-house to head-up the technology transfer and socially responsible business development teams. Have I got it right?"

"My very own—minuscule—fiefdoms." As he spoke Hitoshi turned his head to the side, looking off somewhere for something. Stonecrop followed his gaze and saw nothing.

The waiter set two beers and the tea on the table. The glasses were like oversized wine glasses. Federica took too big a drink and unceremoniously burped before continuing. It amazed Stonecrop how she could be so herself, and not have that behavior in any way diminish the authority and respect she commanded from others.

"There's more." She winked at Hitoshi. "He got this brilliant idea to use defense technologies—where they could be used—to advance work done by social benefit companies and non-profits like AD."

Hitoshi filled in. "The benefit to New Order is that it expanded their client base to include the defense sector, i.e., big-fee clients. In return, the recast technologies generated great PR for the tech provider, and, potentially, fresh commercial opportunities."

"Are you a partner?" Stonecrop asked.

"A lowly associate."

"Still, very impressive." Stonecrop complimented him; the admiration was genuine. "And, what's the deal with AD?"

Hitoshi's hands, like his facial features, were flawless, clean, and slender. He rested those perfect hands together, immaculate fingertip to immaculate fingertip.

"The goal is an arrangement for Dr. Ratzow's foundation, Aide Direct, wherein AD shall have use of a certain class of drones, designed and manufactured by Potomac Defense, to support the foundation's medical teams at remote medical service sites. Potential locations include sites serving people impacted by the drought in Namibia, floods in Mozambique, refugee camps in Sudan—"

"These are the same drones used to kill people, like in Afghanistan?" Stonecrop interrupted.

"No. These particular drones are smaller, fixed-wing vertical-take-off-and-landing aircraft with significant load-carrying capacity. Of course, they can be fitted with offensive weaponry and stealth technology." Hitoshi went on to explain other technical differences between conventional combat drones and the Potomac Defense drones.

"Very cool," Stonecrop said, nostalgic for his once career as a venture capitalist and the excitement that came with learning about nascent technologies. "And what are the hurdles?" As he knew, every deal had issues.

"Yes," Hitoshi nodded agreeably, "there are a number of challenges. Well, in this case, two: First, the technology cannot be exported or released without authorization by the appropriate department at the Pentagon. Second, AD needs funds to pay Potomac."

"So," Stonecrop replied, "scrub the tech and lease the drones. Get a relief org with deeper pockets to pick up the tab for AD."

"Very good, Mr. Stonecrop!" Hitoshi complimented him. "But easier said than done."

The deal structure talk continued until it was interrupted on two fronts: The waiter wheeled over a cart with Stonecrop's bifteck and steak knife, individual buckets of steaming moules, and a mountain of frites with mayo on the side. Stonecrop and Federica simultaneously asked for mustard, confusing the waiter because the request had been in two different languages. Stonecrop, forgetting he was in Brussels, had spoken German.

The second interruption, the more noticeable of the two, was the arrival of a half-million-euro red Ferrari. The driver parked the automobile practically in the middle of the street and a meter from their table. A tall, swarthy, and undeniably handsome man wearing a white XXL Ralph Lauren Polo shirt squeezed out of *la macchina*. Out of nowhere a passel of kids oohed and ahed the vehicle. The local traffic cop working a nearby intersection swooped in to personally re-route traffic around the gleaming red machine perched like the sun in the middle of the street. Andreas Reyes Castro, clean shaven and cologned to high heaven, his bristled, black hair well-gelled, posed before them. The self-appointed fiancé to Federica Ratzow said nothing as he stepped over the slack chain separating the street from the al fresco dining patio. He looked strong. With Gucci man-purse in hand, wearing hand-stitched, black, Ferragamo Gancini driver shoes, sans socks, the man could have been a male model. Stonecrop disliked the sockless loafer look. It reminded him of real estate agents sucking up to well-to-do clients.

Castro settled into the remaining aluminum chair at the table. He sat to Stonecrop's left. The table was small and he had no need to lean forward for his arm to reach halfway across the table to shake hands with Hitoshi, and then Stonecrop. A Patek Philippe watch dangled loosely from his wrist and clanged against the metal tabletop. He looked at Federica but said nothing.

From inside the man-purse, he extracted and displayed a framed photograph of himself shaking hands with the director of UNICEF. "For funding Aide Direct. A little thing for the office," he announced to the table in a tone of a superior speaking to underlings.

Hitoshi appeared rapt, as impressed by the award as by the Ferrari. A friendly but competitive conversation followed between Castro and Hitoshi about Ferrari specs, followed by a second, shorter conversation, wherein Hitoshi fanned Castro's ego regarding his support for good causes.

An unusually reticent Federica said nothing and picked at her moules frites. At one point, Stonecrop leaned over and whispered to her, "A bloody love fest." He too focused on the food in front of him and ate Euro style—armed for the meal with fork in left hand and knife in the right.

Hitoshi was an investment banker, Stonecrop reflected. As such, his antennas were always on the hunt for potential clients. Andreas Reyes Castro oozed money, power, and connections. To boot, Hitoshi's prey was a philanthropist!

The car and save-the-world talk petered out, with both Hitoshi and Castro looking to Federica for direction. Uncharacteristically, she lowered her gaze.

Her indifference upset Castro, who pouted like a child from not getting the attention he deserved. A sudden revelation seemed to broadsided Castro.

"You're not serious? Come now, my little Federica." he laughed too loudly; he was chiding a disobedient minion.

"I am," she responded in dead flat tone that must have felt like a roar to Castro.

"*En serio*, this is it?" His face reddened; his gaze bore into Federica.

"Si, *perdóname*," she said. The Spanish softened the apology.

In the dark as much as Stonecrop, Hitoshi said nothing. Federica reached into the pocket of her jeans, extracted the engagement ring— the one she had before, over linguine con vongole, shown to Stonecrop. She took Andreas's hand, a hand that was soft and twice the size of her own, carefully placed the ring in it, and closed his fingers around it.

She's keeping her word, and she wanted me to see it. Or is there something else, like physical fear?

Castro clamped his hand around hers and pinned her wrist to the table, obviously hurting her. "You ask me here to guarantee a loan and then you break up with me? Just like that? Here!" He did a one-eighty scan of the public surroundings. A vein in his forehead pulsed. He practically spit out the words: "Who the fuck do you think you are?"

"I'm sorry, Andreas."

"You fucking whore. You used me. You used me!"

Stonecrop was shocked by the violent outburst and uncertain about what to do about it. He tested the shape and grip of the handle of the steak knife.

"No, I didn't—" Federica turned away from Castro. He abruptly stood and raised a hand as if to strike her.

Without thinking, Stonecrop rose with him, stepped behind him, and pressed the tip of the knife into the flesh under Castro's ribs. With his left arm he reached around Castro's waist and pulled the man's torso against the blade. Stonecrop grinned a not-a-care-in-the-world grin. *A bro-hug, dude.* The embrace was marginally successful at concealing the knife. Either that, or onlookers thought it best to say nothing.

Castro released her hand. He had been holding his breath. He didn't move as air whistled in and out of his nostrils and flared them, like a bull staring at the muleta.

Imitating the old-fashioned gotcha handshake, Castro brushed his hair back with the raised hand and faked a laugh. The other hand dropped the ring to the table. Stonecrop eased back to his chair, knife in hand. A spot of blood, or, more likely juice from the steak, showed on Castro's shirt where the point of blade had been. Stonecrop had not been gentle with him.

"Sorry about that," Castro said. The apology was directed at Hitoshi and Hitoshi alone. Castro pointed a thick finger at Stonecrop, "You're a fucking crazy man!" The accusation drew no reaction.

Hitoshi, worried and eager to defuse the situation, forced a warm smile—a physical effort to will away what he had just witnessed, "Can I drive your car? I've looked at one, a similar model. I think maybe a year or two older . . ."

Castro played along, grateful for the exit Hitoshi had created, an exit with dignity. "Of course! Excellent suggestion. It would be better to talk someplace quiet, away from this madman."

Hitoshi turned to Federica for permission. His expression implied he still had a job to do and that he had worked with assholes before. It also implied uncertainty about which was the greater threat, Andreas or Stonecrop. Her look was one of relief: *thank you for getting rid of the jerk.*

Her freed hand reached out; the fingers curled around the blade of the steak knife. Stonecrop wouldn't be able withdraw the knife without cutting her.

"Brilliant, great! Let's do this," Hitoshi said, as if he were agreeing to some exciting adventure Castro had suggested.

Castro wiped his mouth and hands with a napkin. He took a drink from his water glass and then dipped his napkin in the glass and used the napkin to dab at the stain on his shirt. It was blood. With man purse in hand, Castro stepped over the slack chain and circled around to driver's side of the car. He addressed Hitoshi: "I'll get us out of city, then you drive. Fair enough?"

"Fair enough, yes!" Hitoshi cheerfully replied. He made brief, polite good-byes to Stonecrop and Federica.

The passenger door opened and Hitoshi took his seat. The policeman, who had missed the altercation between Castro and Stonecrop, came to life as the Ferrari did the same. Overly animated—did he expect a tip?—he fanned aside pedestrians, both imaginary and real, in the macchina's runway.

"That went well," Stonecrop dryly observed. "You okay?"

Federica cleaned her hand on the napkin on her lap. "Don't you ever, ever, pull a stunt like that again."

Stonecrop knew that if he spoke, she would leave the table. He didn't want her to be alone, not after what had just transpired.

"Were you really going to stab him?" she asked. She kept looking back and forth between Stonecrop's face and the napkin.

Stonecrop examined the blade of the knife. "Rather dull. But yeah, I might have had a go."

"What the fuck is it with men. Are you all so insecure about your precious masculinity? You're as bad as Papà."

"You're welcome." He ignored the reproach. "I've kinda worked up an appetite. Can we finish eating?"

He reached across to her bowl, took a mussel in a half shell and slurped it down. Stonecrop raised his beer in the air. A hesitant Federica, on automatic, did the same.

"I'll behave. And, congratulations. That took guts," he said.

"Ah, the adult returns. Thank you," Federica said. "And—"

"Oh, oh."

"Pass the mustard."

On the table the ring and the glass from the framed picture reflected the hard afternoon light.

Polybahn/Starbucks

A lone gull strutted along the water's edge, looking for whatever gulls look for. Stonecrop watched it wander back and forth over the same narrow stretch of wind and wave lapped sand. His thoughts too wandered back and forth. He replayed conversations from the dinner at the Dolder Grand last night, visualizing for the thousandth time the ransom note and listening Ratzow's *I know who this is* echo in his head. He replayed re-meeting Federica at Universitäts-Spital. He smiled at the memory of the first time they had made love. And he was discomfited and still regretted, though it had been several months ago, his behavior in Brussels with Andreas. He had hoped that after Africa the violence in his heart would have dissipated and become a clouded remembrance, as had his visions of the men whom he had shot and killed. But the familiar and unwelcome feeling had returned in force. Contrary to before, when Fede's presence and the passage of time had tempered those feelings, there was no Fede and time was now the enemy. Her sudden and unexplained disappearance had ignited and fueled a violence inside that was seeking expression. Fede had remarked that he was like her papà. Stonecrop hoped that that was not the case.

He'd given up on sleep last night and in the pre-dawn light had meandered along the lakefront and made it as far as Seefeld and the beach at Strandbad Tiefenbrunner, a popular after-work gathering place for Zürchers in the summer months. The air was cold and still; light skipped across the top of Mount Tödi.

A quarter hour passed. The seagull and Stonecrop lost interest in watching each other. Walking back in the direction of the Niederdorf he tried to focus on positive things. He had had a fulfilling relationship with Federica; he'd moved into a modest apartment in the Niederdorf;

the job with Group was stress-free and left him time to train and re-hone his shooting skills. His life, at last, had been trending toward normality. En route to Central Square Stonecrop kept to the boardwalk —a direct route—and arrived fifteen minutes early for the eight-thirty meeting at Starbucks.

The sun beat him there. He stood near the curb and about ten meters from Starbucks, positioning himself so the sun's rays struck and warmed his face. Adjacent to Starbucks and sharing the building façade was the entrance to the Polybahn funicular station. Commuters entered the red door on the right and exited the red door on the left. He remembered Federica arriving and greeting him with a smile as bright and warm the light on his face.

Every three minutes the ebb and flow of people announced the arrival and departure of the funicular. Two fire-engine-red railcars shared the main track—slipping by each other midway on a short passing track—and took turns ferrying university personnel, tourists, and incidental riders up and down the twenty-three percent grade between the Central Square and ETH—*Eidgenössiche Technische Hochschule*, Zürich's science and technology university and home to twenty-plus Nobel laureates. The original name for ETH was *Eidgenössische Polytechnische Schule*—Federal Polytechnic School—and locally the school was still referred to as Poly. Hence the name— Polybahn. The ride took one hundred seconds.

ETH was the reason Stonecrop had come to Zürich in the first place. The University's technology transfer program was a bold one. The firm he'd worked for specialized in commercializing university-originated life-science research. He was to set up a branch office in Zürich. That had been seven years ago. For five years, all had gone well—six investments, even one successful exit. Then, his world had turned upside down. Naively, he had plunged into business irregularities in one of the portfolio companies. His attempts to unravel and mitigate what had transpired had failed.

What had followed was a year-and-a-half-long misadventure in Africa—a period he and Federica recently had dubbed "the Fall"—and a desperate escape and retreat to Zürich and the subsequent and totally unexpected re-connection with Federica. News of his escapades had spread, and had had ramifications. His former firm had been forced to close up shop when ETH had cancelled their agreements.

Stonecrop was now a whistle-blowing pariah in the investment community. The last six months, working for Gregor, had given him a chance to get back on his feet. Federica had given him a reason to do so.

Stonecrop regularly walked Frau Doktor Ratzow to the Polybahn. They would stand outside the entrance, near where he was standing right now, and say goodbye, giving each other the customary Zürcher air-kiss on each cheek. Then she would enter the red door, the one on the right. That was the last place he had seen her.

. . . .

Stonecrop stepped through the door at Starbucks at exactly eight-thirty. The café was bustling with students, workers from the Niederdorf, and tourists. Three construction workers wearing hard hats waited in the line at the counter.

He found Ratzow and Ratzow's tablemate; they already had drinks. The woman, familiar to Stonecrop from his first night at Fede's, was approximately the same age and build as Ratzow. She was taking notes. Stonecrop stood beside their table, debating with himself—join the queue or not.

"Max, you meet Claudia? Claudia Knight. I call her last night. Anything from my little girl?"

The way Ratzow posed the question grated, though there was no real reason why.

"Nothing."

Stonecrop had crossed paths with Claudia and didn't need the introduction. Ratzow, in his own world, pressed on with the reintroduction. "Claudia is a partner at G24/7. Risk management company."

"And crisis support," she said, completing the replay of the last time he had met Claudia.

"She was big spy for America, the best!"

"Gregor, cut the bullshit," Claudia interjected.

Ratzow, for once being the good client, took her advice, "Max, we are in discussion about options before I see Kommissar Vormittag." That name *was* new to Stonecrop. He looked at Claudia, then at Ratzow, deciding Ratzow was the person from whom he should expect a clarification.

"Vittore Vormittag is Kommissar in Stadtpolizei; and works in Kantonspolizei. What is word, Claudia?"

"He *liaises* between the agencies."

"Da, two jobs for one. Is good deal for everyone except him! I know him long time. Claudia, too. I told Claudia about dinner."

Stonecrop nodded to Claudia. He'd get coffee later.

Ratzow resumed where he had left off with Claudia, "Where is she?"

"I have no idea, dear. Playing hide and seek! You've heard nothing in what, twelve hours?" Claudia smiled, *"La donna e mobile."*

From *Rigoletto*, Stonecrop remembered: a woman is fickle!

Clearly Ratzow had not shown her the letter. From her limited perspective, his concern over Federica's absence was unwarranted.

"Did you talk to Federica Tuesday?" Claudia asked.

"No," Ratzow said, "Sometimes we don't talk for week, or more! But this one," he tilted his head toward Stonecrop, "Every day: talk, talk, talk."

"Well?" she asked, turning toward Stonecrop, who had since found an unused chair and brought it to the table.

"We keep in touch. Meet up with friends at the climbing gym, very informal, once or twice a week. Sometimes a run in the park, if she has time—which is almost never." Stonecrop would ride with Ratzow's story, for a time. And downplay his relationship with Federica.

"Facebook?" she asked, "Does Federica post on Facebook?"

Stonecrop answered: "Think so, but not much. She keeps in touch with her friends."

"You last heard from her when?"

"Yesterday," he said. "She had a packed day; no time to climb. But we met for breakfast and I walked her to the Poly."

"That's it?"

"That's it."

Federica had texted him later that morning. She had to attend to a few things at work, and was going to see if she could get free for a weekend in Bäretswil, an hour from Zürich and where she owned a small, country house. Stonecrop figured the planned weekend getaway wasn't relevant to the topic at hand.

"Uh huh," Claudia said, sensing some omission in Stonecrop's report. "Did you work yesterday?"

"Walked Frau Ott's dachshund. Delivered a print for Bachman. Nothing for Group, except the letter." He delivered the response in a monotone.

"And you had spoken with both Frau Ott and Herr Bachman. I assume they could attest to your having done these things?" she asked.

Stonecrop gave her a puzzled look, so Claudia elaborated, "Sorry to grill you, dear. But if there is a problem—as Gregor supposes there will be or *I* wouldn't be here—then *someone*, a someone who's not so friendly, will be asking these questions."

"Sure," he said, regretting the decision to put off coffee. He hadn't slept and needed caffeine.

"And this letter? What's that about?" Claudia asked. "Gregor, you jumped—" Claudia's antennae were up. Her radar was constantly sweeping the room. She probably had counted and catalogued every person there. Stonecrop looked around and started his own count, forgetting her question and attempting to classify the inhabitants by age, sex and likely occupation. The pussyfooting was driving him crazy.

Before Stonecrop regrouped to respond, Ratzow stepped in. "Max, I haven't told Claudia about the note, not yet."

"Ah, I'm missing a card. This is how you treat your Claudia. After all these years!"

"Da," Ratzow said, "is game. And I pay for game."

"Unfair," Claudia said with faux resignation and a sigh, "but I shall do my best." Stonecrop didn't understand what Ratzow hoped to gain by withholding information. Claudia, as if she were reading Stonecrop's mind, answered the question. "You want to know what Vormittag will do if you don't mention this mystery letter. This is clearly something you do not wish to share with the inquisitive Kommissar." Ratzow remained silent, effectively confirming her observation. She pressed on. "Fine. I'll play, dearie, but don't test my patience."

Claudia resumed, "I assume you've checked her house and work. Does she work today?"

"I called her boss, Herr Doktor Weller. He said she is off today, and the weekend. No one's home. She worked yesterday."

"Max, are you worried?" she asked.

"I am," he spoke truthfully; he'd been up all night worrying. "I really am."

"Ah, you're *both* in the know!"

"Where is she, Claudia?" Ratzow pressed.

"You've given me crumbs, dear, nothing but crumbs. I will go off on the only real *lie* I've been told today." She twisted in her chair to face Stonecrop, "You're lying—which is fine. It's a start." Claudia sipped her tea, "I want to back up. Remind me again, when did you and

Federica first meet? Gregor recalls it being six or seven years ago. Anyway, it was before that time I saw you at Frau Ott's—looking for all the world like baby Jesus. You were a mess then, love, I hate to tell you. Bit of a fanatic, weren't we? Still like that? Gregor swore I needn't fret over you."

She scrunched up her face, "Tell me, *do* I have to worry about you?"

He had been looking away from her, gauging the length of the queue and only half-listening to what she had said. He turned to face her and lied matter-of-factly, "I think not." *I'm worried about me, why the fuck shouldn't you be!*

Claudia backed off, recalibrating her internal polygraph, and asked again about what had transpired when Federica had first met Stonecrop. Clearly, her curiosity had been smoldering for some time; she wasn't going to miss an opportunity to learn more.

"Well?" she said, impatient over his reticence.

He offered a tepid response, "C'mon Claudia, this is not new, not to you. Seven years ago, the train to Venice. Not that it's relevant."

"Gregor told me he considered throttling you the first time he saw you. And the second!" She thought this amusing, and presented a U-shaped smile. The middle portion of her lips remained in a compressed horizontal line as the corners turned upward. A sparse moustache, dyed to be less visible, shaded the upper lip.

Stonecrop was distracted by the bustle at Starbucks, by his own train of thought, and his sleep-deprived and caffeine-deprived physical state. He forced himself to re-engage, "I don't know what Gregor thought. I can understand why he'd be upset. I have two daughters, teens, in the States, with my ex." He stood up abruptly, "Excuse me. Gotta get coffee."

The line had grown to reach their table. Stonecrop took his place in the line, still within earshot of the conversation between Ratzow and Claudia.

It was hard to believe Ratzow had not already told the story to Claudia. If he had, and if he was repeating it, Claudia was willing to hear the story again. He couldn't imagine how the retelling would turn up anything useful, something she could link to the matter at hand.

"Is morning. I wake up in cabina, and no Fede! Text says she is fine and sleeping in Cabina 6. She says I snore too much! I am mad; I am thinking she is with a man and she is—shit I forget, yes—eighteen years! I go to Cabina 6. I wear bathrobe, no shoes. I remember, no shoes; the metal floor is cold. Is November, almost December. The door is unlocked on Cabina 6.

"I go in, prepared. If a man is there, I choke him. I find them. Together—not like that together." He made some obscene Italian or Bulgarian hand gesture whose meaning was obvious and caught the attention of bystanders in the line with Stonecrop. Ratzow lowered his head and his voice, "They are dressed—is good, yes. She sleeps on the long seat, her feet under blanket, an angel. Her head is on his hand like pillow." To demonstrate, Ratzow tilted his head against his own paw-like palm. A sweet gesture, if any gesture from Ratzow could be considered sweet. "This one," he nods toward Stonecrop, "sleeps in corner, half-sitting with legs on the table and book on lap. His head is wedged in corner. I say 'Good Morning,' loud! They both wake up—not surprised, like this happens every day—and move full of sleep. No one cares Papà is there! They both have hair like this." He put his hands next to his head with fingers spread and extending toward the ceiling. "Like roosters. When they look at each other, they laugh like crazy!

"Federica, she drooled on Max sleeve. He didn't care. He is a rock, this one, nothing bothers him, not drool, not angry father, nothing. He grins stupid grin." Ratzow glanced at Stonecrop, "Rock with big smile. My little girl, she wipes her mouth off on his shirt. Can you believe! She says, 'Papà, this is Mr. Stonecrop.' She tries not to laugh, so hard she tries she can't talk. 'He's a really nice man,' she spits out at last. 'He read to me like Mamma did.'" Ratzow's eyes moistened, "I almost cry, my little girl is like sunshine! 'Max reads to his daughters, he misses them,' she says. Then she says she is sorry. 'I fell asleep,' she says. My Federica is safe. She is happy. The man is not ogre. I don't kill him. I go back to cabina. Go back sleep. We never talk again about man in Cabina 6."

"Why, Maxie," Claudia twisted toward Stonecrop, who had hardly moved in the line, "How terribly sweet and innocent. Is that it?"

"Pretty much," he replied. "She'd recently lost her mother. Reading together was good, it was good for both of us."

"Gregor says you're not a talker. Humor me, please. Try talking with me. It might help me find her if I understood more. Obviously, you were quite chatty with Federica when you two met on the train. You were chatty with her yesterday, weren't you?"

"Coffee first," he said, annoyed at having to keep up a conversation as he inched forward in line. Claudia remained as she was, twisted in his direction and staring at him. He relented, too tired to resist.

"Philosophy, we talked philosophy." Knowing she would ask more, he gave her more. "She can quote, in English or ancient Greek, a passage from every chapter of *The Odyssey*. And much of *The Republic*, and the tragedies. She's brilliant, just flat out brilliant. I was awed. Still am."

She motioned for him to come closer, to step out of the line. He did as she wished. Instead of bending forward to listen, he squatted down beside her, keeping one hand on the back of her chair for balance.

"You care for her," she whispered. "You would never, ever, hurt her, right? You've done crazy shit before—we know, don't we darling—and she *likes* crazy." She said this as if it were a secret they shared. The hushed talk caught the attention of the people in line near Stonecrop, and, if anything, prompted them to listen in. "Later in that day, after you saw her off. What did you talk about?"

"The weekend, getting away for the weekend. That's it. Happy now?"

He had had enough of the inquisition. Stonecrop rose and stepped back in line. Others in the queue politely let him return to his original place. He focused on the drink menu scribbled on the blackboard above and behind the serving counter.

. . . .

When he returned to the table, latte in hand, they were discussing Federica missing the dinner at the Dolder.

"Accept it, Gregor. She blew off the meeting—cold feet, maybe? She's not a child. And she is hard to read, and—excuse me for saying this—she has an *interesting* history with men. Maybe there was something between them. Maybe she didn't want to see this Alexander?" Claudia looked briefly at Stonecrop, but it was unclear if he was included in the interesting history. The statement drew an exasperated look from Ratzow.

Ratzow's head hung down as if he were talking to himself. "Don't be stupid, Claudia. She does not say one thing and do another; she does not lie. I know. Every day I work with liars and thieves." He looked at Stonecrop, "She is not thief either."

Ratzow sipped his tea—he and Claudia were tea drinkers—and continued, "And why? Last night, meeting was for her and for me to meet this man who helps Aide Direct. He is CEO of Potomac Defense, a tech company. He is patient man; I like him. I bring my team; to make sure is no last-minute screw-up. I try to help. Maybe I butt in too much. She would be a upset about others—Uli and wife, Reeb and Pfaff. Closing is next week. But Federica would tell me. Not say nothing and then not come."

"Is the deal important to *you*?"

"No, don't give shit. Do I care for a little money? I do for her, like good father does for daughter. Papà is, what's expression Max—" He turned to Stonecrop and held his hand up and wiggled the little finger.

Claudia giggled, referencing and demonstrating a similar Italian gesture. "Love, that means you have a small penis!"

Stonecrop smiled and provided the intended English expression. "Wrapped around her little finger."

Claudia clung to the idea of Federica being the agent of her own disappearance. "Gentlemen, consider the following: She is young, attractive, *and* impulsive. She knows she'll get what she wants, gala or no gala at the Dolder. Maybe work got the best of her. Her job *is* stressful. She was thinking about leaving town with Max darling. Maybe she was fed up with the lot of you!" Claudia tilted her cup on its saucer and read the tea leaves. "And—this is the real reason I think she's okay— I can't believe anyone would have the cojones to kidnap her, right under your nose, in bloody Switzerland!"

Ratzow was letting her run with the information he had supplied, ostensibly to get an indication of where the same information might lead Vittore Vormittag. It was Ratzow's modus operandi, to always hold something back. Stonecrop had seen it before; as, no doubt, had Claudia. She cooperated, asking questions—it almost didn't matter what questions. The process was second nature to her. Dance around the problem, look at it from here, pick at it from there. Chip away the unnecessary, a Michelangelo working a slab of marble with hammer and chisel. The process was tedious and tiring. No matter: she was indefatigable.

Claudia turned toward Stonecrop and adjusted her over-sized tortoise-shell eyeglasses. Enlarged eyeballs rolled around in the lenses. She looked like a venomous toad tracking a juicy fly. Her stare was his cue to speak.

"Claudia, she's not off on some lark."

"Are you a suitor, my bad boy? Did you spook her?" she flung the non-sequitur at him. It was an obvious attempt to flush out a reaction.

Stonecrop responded too evenly, "We're friends, Claudia, just friends." Too late, he realized Claudia had gotten what she had wanted.

"Uh-huh," she said, certain he had lied again. She started doodling on the newspaper. "Boys, Federica did tell Herr Doktor Weller she would be gone for the weekend, meaning she might have left last night. And she must have been upset with Daddy-dear for lording over what should have been her cozy show-and-tell. Plus, her *friend* here," she glanced at Stonecrop, "no offense dear, could be yet another male she'd rather not deal with. On the surface, nothing nefarious."

"Good, Claudia, very good," Ratzow stated with finality. He had raised his voice, momentarily halting conversations at nearby tables. He removed the note from his pocket, the one Stonecrop had delivered to him, and slammed it face down on the table. The noise drew offended looks from a few customers and curious smiles from others.

Claudia did not look at the note. She continued doodling on the newspaper—*Zwanzig Minuten*, Zürich's lowbrow tabloid and daily dose of gossip. She drew a sailboat, the way a child would draw it—a banana shaped hull, vertical mast, and a triangle for a sail. She used a flattened "M" above the boat for birds, and a flattened "W" below for waves. From the seat opposite her, the boat was sailing upside-down in the sky. To Stonecrop, the world was topsy-turvy. His dream of leading the simple life in Zürich had become just that, a wishful dream.

She stopped drawing, her thoughts settled. Both men looked up, having been momentarily mesmerized by the doodling.

"Enough," Ratzow said. It was unclear whether he meant their meeting was over, or he was ordering Claudia to stop drawing. He repeated, "Enough," and turned over the crumpled and sweat-stained note. His thick fingers pressed flat and spread the piece of paper. She bent forward to read the words, her goggly-glasses slipped down her nose and she had to catch them.

"Well, *fuck* me," Claudia placed her fingers on her forehead, rubbing at a wrinkle in her brow. A theatrical pose but a real enough. "Gregor, I don't believe it, after all these years?"

Ratzow shrugged his shoulders, displaying no regret about having delayed showing her the note.

She admonished him, "Dearie, foolish man! You should have told me straight-away, last night."

"No. Better my way."

The endpoints of Claudia's mouth drooped; her whole body sagged. She was shaking her head. Stonecrop had no idea what little secret she and Ratzow were keeping from him.

"Well, shit," she said. "Let's do the drill." She straightened up, inhaled deeply, and coughed. "Start here, in Zürich. Tell me about the letter."

Stonecrop succinctly described how he had come by the note and delivered it to the Dolder. Claudia, as always, took notes in her spiral notebook.

"Who do I talk to next?" she asked Ratzow.

Gregor returned the note to his pocket. He proceeded to touch a different pudgy finger for each name he proffered.

"First, call Marion Cook, she is part-time housekeeper for Federica. Used to be nanny. Marion is like family. She worked for us in Firenze; she moves here to help Federica. I keep small apartment for her. Is pension. Marion is old, seventy. She won't return to U.S. Too long in Europe. Hard to say who cares for who. They are very close. I have number."

"She's U.S., ex-pat?"

"Da, Boston."

He moved to the next finger.

"Herr Professor Doktor Weller. We spoke this morning. Call again. He is German, her *chef*—boss, head of emergency department. Federica works eight or nine times in a month." He looked for and found the word in English, "Shifts, eight or nine shifts, crazy doctor times. And write papers. Federica must tell the staff if she takes time off to fart. She has two jobs. The other one is different than the first, she treats people without hands—that is wrong—without using her hands to touch bodies."

Stonecrop, having rejected the Starbucks coffee after the first tongue searing sip, desperately needed a replacement. Impatient for progress, he put on his venture capital hat. It was a persona he usually kept in check, "Let me explain, Gregor. What she does is an international emergency medicine specialty called Tele-trauma care. She and a team of specialists work with personnel at the scene of mass casualty situations, usually at remote locations. Field-based intensive care units and small robotics installations let physicians in Zürich remotely assess, direct care, and execute minor procedures."

Claudia squinted at Stonecrop, broadsided by his polished delivery. "My, Maxie, what the hell!" she exclaimed. The pause and waffled brow indicated that she had generated a plethora of questions for later.

"Da. That's what she does. Is very hi-tech." Ratzow ratified what Stonecrop had described and went on to the ring finger. "Alicia Gilli.

She is Federica's friend. Like sisters, Alessia and Alicia! Ex-pat from States. Long-time friends. Alicia works in London. She stay with Federica when she comes to Zürich, two, sometimes three times a month."

"More, please."

"She and Federica are friends a long time," he repeated. "They went to expensive boarding school in Leysin. School lasted only a few months for Federica—bored. By herself, she took train home to Firenze. Back to Mamma. Federica and Alicia stay friends, even after Gilli family goes back to Chicago. Federica was at school a year with them. And another time, they lived together. Federica went one-year pre-med in U.S., before Royal College of Physicians in Dublin. Enough?"

"Thank you," Claudia nodded. "Others?"

Ratzow went for the pinky. "Yes, Aide direct admin, Rachel. Use my name when you call." Ratzow hesitated, and then came forward with another tidbit for Claudia.

"Federica has off-on engagement with the burro-brained Mexican, Andreas Reyes Castro." He waited for Claudia to comment. She didn't. "She says thing with Castroias kaput. I hope is true." Ratzow paused and added, "Find him. He comes from Chihuahua; pisses away money in Cap-Ferrat. Family has scrap-metal business, big company, very rich. He flies here. Comes in jet and off they go—Seychelles, Paris. Things rich people do to show how rich they are! He gives big money for her charity business."

"Aide Direct?"

Ratzow nodded in the affirmative. "He has cousin, Lupita. She is sweet girl in Graubünden. She is real friend to Fede. But him— dogshit."

Claudia interrupted. "Last time they were in touch?"

Ratzow didn't listen. He suddenly needed to vent. "He is vain, spoiled," Ratzow said, and then qualified his statement. "But not useless, not for Federica. She used him. She wears ring to scare off men! He is always traveling. Convenient for her, work comes first. Convenient for him, dick comes first."

"He's a little like you, when—"

Ratzow snapped back, "I was not arrogant playboy. I was not screwing other women. I work." He sat still, quietly deliberating, and then loudly announced, "I don't hit women!" Seeing people turn toward him, Ratzow toned it down and then backed up his assertion,

"Federica never tell me. But once she called Kantonspolizei. Vormittag, he tells me."

It was unclear if the warning from the police had been to alert Ratzow to what had happened to Federica, or to warn him to lay off Castro. Stonecrop, knowing Ratzow's violent temper, presumed the latter. Ratzow immediately confirmed the suspicion.

"This country is backwards," Ratzow said. "In Bulgaria, the police would give me knife to cut off his balls."

"We'll run playboy to ground, thank you." Claudia said, tickled to have a fresh target for her unrelenting inquisitiveness.

Ratzow, trying to not sound like the tough guy he actually was, had one last comment. "I told playboy he was *cacasotto*—chickenshit. Not enough man for my daughter."

Stonecrop had been half-listening to the conversation. He had had little to contribute. Claudia was wrangling strays. He, on the other hand, was drawn to the image of the man with the golden tooth, Alexander. Stonecrop spoke: "I think there must be a connection with Potomac Defense, though Gregor disagrees. For me it's about the timing, given that the transaction's about to close. It could be coincidental, like Gregor says. Though, in my venture capital days, I've seen people go to crazy extremes to kill or make a deal."

Unlike Ratzow, Claudia listened well. "I agree, dearie. No specific motive, but yes, it certainly could be the case."

Claudia queried Ratzow. "Gregor, other thoughts?" One of her toad-eyes twitched as she asked the question.

"You mean, other than what we talk about later?"

"Yes, other than that," she said.

Why are you leaving me in the dark, you douchebags? Stonecrop was angry: Had he spoken those words or just thought them?

Ratzow picked up where he left off, "Dante Alexander flies back to Brussels tonight." He addressed Stonecrop, "I will call Uli. You go with him and see him. Maybe we miss something with Dante and you are right. Maybe not. You understand?" Stonecrop nodded.

The queue was gone. As the need for caffeine overcame loyalty to his preferred coffee haunt, Café Stehli, Stonecrop excused himself to try for a second coffee. He had tasted and rejected the first one; too hot, and the milk had been re-steamed.

Claudia pressed Ratzow for more detail on the Dolder meeting and Alexander.

* * *

. . . .

When Stonecrop returned with a new triple latte in hand, Ratzow was sitting at attention. Claudia repeatedly drew circles around a short article at the bottom of the front page of the paper upon which she had been doodling.

"What's that?" Stonecrop asked. He had been planning to make Claudia and Ratzow come clean about their little secret. He tilted his head toward the paper.

"Love, do you think there is more than one Marion Cook in Zürich?" Claudia asked.

"No," Stonecrop replied.

"According to this article," she paraphrased, "an unnamed source told a *Zwanzig Minuten* reporter that last night a woman, later identified as Zürich resident Marion Cook—our Nanny, dearies—tumbled into the Sihl canal. She survived a fall from Stauffacherbrücke and made it to the embankment. Or possibly, someone rescued her."

Stonecrop took a sip of his latte, burning his tongue a second time. "Dammit!" He regrouped to ask about Cook. "Is she okay? There's hardly any water in the Sihl, only a couple of feet. It's a good five meters from the bridge to the water."

"From what the article says, she suffered injuries from the fall and almost drowned. The reporter said the police said nothing more, no details."

The article was Claudia's clarion call. "My boys, we do the same. We provide no details, to anybody, until I learn more. I'll take care of Vormittag. You do the other thing, Gregor. Max, you're on the Potomac connection."

"A fall like that is deadly for someone her age," Stonecrop said, understanding but not acknowledging Claudia's directives. And not at all happy to be on the outside. He and Marion lived only a few blocks from each other. Once a month or so, he and Federica would get together with Marion for dinner and a movie. Her passion was old movies. Half the time, Stonecrop would fall asleep. Nobody seemed to mind.

Claudia continued to draw. Ratzow put his hand atop hers, immobilizing the hand, the one making circles. "Nothing about Federica in paper. I don't want risk Federica hurt. And I don't want my face on front page of little paper or *Die Zeitung*. I will go to Marion right away. Poor woman!"

"I shall be discreet, dearie, quite discreet."

Claudia offered Ratzow an amphibian smile and sidled her bulk against his bulk. She placed her other hand atop Ratzow's. The tangle of chunky, bejeweled fingers could have been mistaken for table centerpiece. "I'm sorry about Marion."

It was time to go, to get food, to be with good people, to walk the dog, and to figure out what *he* was going to do about Fede *and* Marion. With no attempt at goodbyes, Stonecrop rose and walked to the door. He pitched his latte into the trash and headed up Niederdorfstrasse toward Café Stehli.

Black Rebel

"What do you do at embassy? Why does embassy talk to me?" The man Ratzow addressed was attired head-to-toe in black motorcycle leathers. He was a half-hour late for their meeting.

Ratzow liked to appear to be a busy man. Today, as Stonecrop knew, he had indeed been a busy man. He had made calls to medical staff regarding Marion's condition, and he had had a series of meetings with Claudia. No doubt those meetings had been about issues they had been reluctant to discuss in his presence—specifically, the significance of the curious red spiral. Ratzow also mentioned that he had met with Geissner to follow up on the suggestion about seeing Alexander before his flight tonight.

All of this had transpired while Stonecrop had showered, glanced at *Die Zeitung* to see if there was anything more about Marion, and grabbed a latte and calorie-packed power muffin at Stehli. His plan was twofold: First, to check out the scene at Stauffacherbrücke—not that the Kantonspolizei had missed anything. He just wanted a look-see. And second, to force Ratzow to explain the note. He didn't like being in the dark, not where Federica's safety was concerned.

Ratzow had just texted him to leave directly to join a meeting at his "office," the exposed and unheated riverside patio at the entrance to Hotel Zum Storchen. Ratzow claimed the patio wasn't bugged. The outdoor service area was an on-again-off-again affair with the hotel. This week was an "on" week. The hotel provided blankets, furs, and warm drinks to patrons and guests willing to brave the chill.

"Harry Chum," the man in leathers introduced himself. He extended a hand to Stonecrop. Stonecrop reciprocated and was surprised at Chum next word, "Ah, I know you." Chum clung to Stonecrop's hand. "Or rather *of* you. U.S. Olympic trials. Biathlon, where you shoot and ski?"

"Well, yes. Didn't make the Olympics, though."

"But you qualified. My younger sister was an amateur competitor. I read about you in the club newsletter or maybe it was some alumni publication, I don't recall which. Why didn't you go? You qualified, right?" Chum said.

"Bad timing. Death in the family." *My brother Charley, my loveable cross-dressing brother, my smiling never-hurt-a-flea brother, had OD'd on heroin.* "I can't believe you recognized my name. That was over ten years ago." The unexpected notoriety made Stonecrop uncomfortable. And the reminder of his brother was like a punch in the gut. They had been close.

"Yes, I remember the story now. I'm very sorry about your brother. It's an honor to meet you. Do you still compete?"

"Nope. Coaching junior competitors here, fun stuff," Stonecrop answered. He was relieved when Chum released his hand and turned to face Ratzow.

The reminder of his brother's suicide brought up feelings of failure and guilt. Zürich was to be a place where Stonecrop was to have no past—no survivor's guilt, no bullshit from Africa, no divorce. When the percolated up to the surface, as it had just then, he grew confused, angry, and tormented by regrets.

The unease seemed to have brushed off on Ratzow; his paranoia about publicity gnawed at him. He dissembled, making it increasingly difficult to know what he was thinking. He poured it on thick for his new acquaintance. "You must to me speak real slow, my English is no good. What brings you here from lovely Bern to my humble table? You like their food, yes? I will order something for us."

"No, thank you. Very kind of you. We tried to reach you by phone, but your receptionist said you would only meet in person. So, voilà!" The man in leathers spread his arms apart, looking like a goth IKEA greeter.

Stonecrop's experience aligned with Chum's comment. As Ratzow's aide-de-camp, he had often carried simple messages in person, messages which could have easily been conveyed in a short phone call. Ratzow had a challenging relationship with the telephone—sometimes he trusted it, other times he hated it. His phones in Bulgaria had been tapped, so why not in Switzerland?

Both Ratzow and Stonecrop were lost in their own worlds. Chum brought them back. "I'm here to speak with you about Mrs. Marion

Cook. I understand you employ her as a part-time housekeeper. You are aware of her accident?"

"Yes. Is in paper. I called. I go soon today, to visit. When we finish. A quick meeting, then I go," Ratzow said.

"What do you know about the accident?" Chum asked.

"Should I get the paper for you? Max, can you get a paper for Mr. . . ." Ratzow hesitated, "Tell me again, your name?"

"Harry Chum." This time he added a title: "U.S. Embassy, Community Liaison Officer." Chum handed his card to Ratzow, who in turn gave it to Stonecrop. "Please, don't bother with the paper. I just met with Kommissar Vormittag at the Kantonspolizei."

"Ah, good man, yes, very good," Ratzow said. As he spoke, he pushed his lips forward slightly, like a half-kiss. His head bobbed up and down.

Stonecrop didn't know if Ratzow was referring to Vormittag, or Chum for having spoken with him.

"Now, you tell *me* what happened," Ratzow asked. "Tell me, too, why Community Liaison Officer for the U.S. Embassy dresses like one of those motorcycle people, like Marlon Brando." He laughed, pleased with himself and unaware of how inappropriate his levity was. "Hah, I remember movie. What are they called, the gang, Max? Hell's Angels?" Ratzow asked for an answer from Stonecrop, but Chum supplied it.

"*Black Rebels*," Chum said.

"Da, are you a Black Rebel, Mr. Chum?"

Chum's smile was as fake as Ratzow's. "I belong to a club. We are not Hell's Angels or Black Rebels. We're awfully dull professionals— dentists, attorneys, bankers, diplomats. Men *and* women. We ride together once a month. Today's the last ride of the year. First snow is around the corner. I was on the road to St. Gallen when I got the call from the embassy."

Stonecrop watched Ratzow, Chum, the waiter, the maître d'. Everyone wore a smiley-mask. It was surreal.

"And the leathers," Chum added air quotes around the word leathers, "are lightweight synthetics." He offered a sleeve to Ratzow to touch. "They keep you warm and dry. Not the real thing, not at all. The jacket and pants have Kevlar armor in the lining."

"And what did the caller say?" Ratzow fished for information.

"Mrs. Cook, although she has lived in Italy and Switzerland for some time, is still a U.S. citizen. Naturally, we get involved anytime something untoward happens to a U.S. citizen."

"Naturally," Ratzow mimicked the pronunciation. "What is untoward? I'm not understanding?" Ratzow had reversed the direction of questioning; he had taken charge of the interrogation.

"Something unfortunate," Chum explained. "The attempt on her life." Chum paused to rephrase what he had said. "I'm sorry—I misspoke. Her *accident*, it was unusual. She almost died. She is unable to speak, though not in a coma, either. There are cognitive complications."

"She fell in river, da."

"Yes, but not exactly. Two witnesses reported that she was *thrown* into the river."

"Mr. Chum, are you serious! This is Zürich, not Moscow."

"I'm sorry to tell you this. It does appear as if someone tried to abduct, and then harmed Mrs. Cook."

"She is old woman? Why? Impossible—*unmöglich*!" Ratzow slipped in the German word for impossible, which can be translated as "not making any sense whatsoever." Stonecrop agreed, although he said nothing.

"Explain, please. I am extremely upset," Ratzow said, the levity seeming quite distant, a lifetime ago.

"At approximately 6:00 p.m., two men, alleged methamphetamine users who were camping under the Stauffacherstrasse bridge, pulled Mrs. Cook out of the Sihl river. They claim they saw a dark shape fall from the bridge, and next heard a loud splash and flopping in the water. 'Like a big fish,' they said.

"When the Polizei and medics arrived, they found a loop of duct tape dangling from her ankle. That foot still had a shoe. The other shoe was on the bridge, by the curb, some distance from cement railing. The sidewalk is wide. They think she escaped from a vehicle and was running away from somebody. Her mouth had been taped. There were bruises on her body and abrasions on the wrists, like they'd been tied with tape. Her hands were free, however.

"She's in her late sixties. The struggle or fall—even her extraction— any of it could have resulted in serious injury. It's unclear if her hands had come free before or after she had landed in the water. No tape has been found."

"What do the doctors say?" Ratzow asked.

"The medical examiner from the Polizei said there were serious head and neck injuries. He has a theory, a theory that the tape across her mouth kept her from ingesting too much water. The other side of that coin is she suffered some asphyxiation; there's brain damage. They're doing tests."

"And how is it drug people save her?" Ratzow asked.

"The two men waded into the water and hauled her out. They did not immediately remove the tape from her mouth. One of them ran up to the street to get help. The other, the more drugged-up of the two, tried to talk to Mrs. Cook. He reported having been frustrated that she wouldn't answer him, which, of course, was impossible—her mouth had been taped shut and she was semi-conscious. The Polizei unbound her. They successfully revived her. She began breathing normally, could see and hear, but didn't speak. Nor did she respond to questions." Chum added his own opinion, "Quite understandably she was in shock."

"Do the Polizei know who did this awful thing?" Ratzow asked.

"Apparently not. Or they were unwilling to share that information with me."

Ratzow noted the qualification, then asked, "What can I do to help, Mr. Chum?"

"The Kantonspolizei will want to talk to you. I suggest you call them as soon as possible. Cooperate, answer their questions. And, if you're acquainted with family members and friends, contact them or give me their names. I can help. It's my job to manage these sorts of things. I would also suggest you let me handle inquiries from the media. What I have told you is, for the time being, confidential."

Ratzow nodded as Chum spoke, indicating he would act as requested.

Chum had more. "If anything comes to mind that might be helpful, or if you have any questions, please contact my office." Chum passed a card to Ratzow and then to Stonecrop, forgetting or ignoring the fact that he had already given them one card. "The embassy can help with travel, visas, and lodging for the family."

"She is very close to us," Ratzow said. "We know her family. They are in the States, New England. My associate, Claudia Knight, will call you today, and she will speak with Kommissar Vormittag." He paused. "I have another meeting in a few minutes, Mr. Chum. Then I visit Marion. Is that all?" Ratzow's voice tightened as he spoke. The emotion was not feigned.

"Yes, thank you. I'm terribly sorry about Mrs. Cook," Chum said, sounding as if he meant it. "Again, call if I can be of service." Chum shook hands with Ratzow and gave a friendly goodbye nod to

Stonecrop. He rose, stretching and zipping up his faux-leather jacket. Two steps later, he turned and addressed Ratzow. "Just a thought. You haven't ever come to one of our *Welcome to Switzerland* affairs, have you? They're monthly, the embassy hosts U.S. companies new to Switzerland. Very informal affairs."

"Group is Swiss domicile."

"That's the point, to introduce locals and newcomers to each other. GR Group's name came up last month, and the month before in conjunction with two different companies—Potomac Defense and their investment bank, New Order Investments. I had the pleasure of meeting Potomac's CEO, Mr. Alexander. He's an imposing fellow. I believe you've met him?"

"Yes, the man that is like American football player."

"That's him alright. And the banker, a wonderfully bright young man, is Hitoshi Sato. He's Japanese, tall and with long black hair? Do you know him?"

Ratzow searched his memory and the darkening clouds for clues. He answered, "No." He offered no specifics, nor did not contribute anything about having just met Alexander.

"Mr. Sato mentioned that he had working with your daughter—spending a lot of time with her, actually—on something or another for her foundation. She sounds impressive as well, bright, and with challenging opinions. Mr. Sato and I argued about the politics of climate change." Ratzow ignored the attempted congeniality and yawned. Stonecrop was curious but said nothing.

Without invitation Chum volunteered additional information. "Between us, there were a few curiosities with young Mr. Sato. He had been an activist trouble-maker in college—a mix up with some eco-group. I'm sure it's nothing and, from what we know now, he seems to have settled down. Let's keep in touch about Mrs. Cook; please let me know if there is anything where the embassy can be of service." Chum turned and waddled away, looking like the Terminator out for a stroll.

Even before Chum was out of earshot, Ratzow commented, "He is funny man, yes?"

"Chum?"

"Our visitor with calling cards coming out his ass," Ratzow replied.

"Funny? Not particularly," Stonecrop stated. Years ago, pre-Chum, he had been to the embassy in Bern, when his firm had considered opening an office in Zürich. The commerce section of the embassy had hosted a luncheon for the new arrivals. The affair had been unremarkable.

"Chum is the 'Minister of Fiestas.' He is social director for embassy; he is also resident CIA. Where's Claudia? We need to talk. They always know more than they should, these Fiesta people."

Stonecrop nodded in agreement. "That was a load of maybe confidential information, Gregor. Why share all that?"

Ratzow asked, for the hundredth time, "Anything?" meaning anything from Federica.

"Nothing," Stonecrop said. He wanted to press Ratzow about why he hadn't said more to Chum.

"Not good. Not good at all. Is what Claudia always says, ha!"

"Gregor, I have questions."

"Da. I see Marion now. Later, we talk. After you and Uli meet Mr. Alexander."

Ratzow rose and walked away. Stonecrop watched Ratzow's back as it disappeared into the shadowed foyer of the Storchen. He considered following him and then cornering him someplace where he couldn't walk away. Instead, he rose and headed in the direction of Stauffacherstrasse.

Flughafen

Alexander was waiting for them at Bàcaro II, a café in a quiet corner of the Public Zone at Flughafen Zürich. He had a window of time before clearing security for his flight to Brussels for a five-day FAA conference on air transport safety. Geissner and Stonecrop sat in silence as Alexander finished scheduling a post-conference flight to Reagan National and a ride to his home near Potomac Defense's office in Fort Washington, Maryland.

Uli Geissner's body language spoke for him. He was an impatient and an important man and endowed with the right to gripe. Gestures accompanied the carping: The meeting at the Carezza Suite had been an unproductive charade, Federica was irresponsible and he was tire of picking up after her, Ratzow was impossible to work with because one never knew what he was really doing. The belly-aching reinforced Stonecrop's pre-disposition to dislike Geissner.

Ratzow had instructed Stonecrop to say nothing about the note or Cook's accident to either Geissner or Alexander. Probably neither of them reads *Zwanzig Minuten*. Geissner, Ratzow had said, would be brought up to speed when it was time. For this meeting, Geissner's marching orders were to dig into the technology. Ostensively, Stonecrop was there to pick up a package for Group at Execujet, a private Fixed Base Operation at the Zürich airport. Ratzow had no compunction about using Geissner as a distraction while Stonecrop fished around for a connection between the abduction and Alexander.

"Thank you for agreeing to meet again, and on such short notice," Geissner said with typical formality.

The dress code was the reverse of last night's, with the majority—Alexander and Stonecrop—in Nike running suits. Geissner was attired as usual in his well-tailored gray suit, Swiss made.

The Cuban chain moved as Alexander spoke, "I don't have a lot of time before my flight. What can I do for you gentlemen?"

Geissner began, "I'm afraid we haven't heard anything new from Miss Ratzow today. I'm sure we will soon. On the letter of credit, we're fine. Gregor still had a few questions related to the technology."

"Uli, you could have called and saved yourself the drive," Dante's tone made it clear he was going out of his way to accommodate Geissner and his colleague. The gold tooth flashed. Stonecrop wondered if the tooth would ever cease to be a distraction.

"We are not technology people. I'm sorry. Would you mind if we quickly ran through this one more time?"

Geissner and Alexander passed the next forty-five minutes covering the same material they had covered the night before, albeit this time in slightly more detail. It took Geissner some time to grasp how a "devkit Sat" drone could autonomously wander the skies on its own for weeks at a time, recharging at remote, unmanned AWOS–like stations.

After hearing it a second time, it had become clearer. The drones were in fact sophisticated airborne robots, and the Automated Weather Observing Systems did a heck of a lot more than provide weather stats.

Alexander took another fifteen minutes to explain how Aide Direct would use the technology. He wrapped up the explanation with a description of the first application—a plan to regularly resupply three teams of medics at mobile refugee aid stations in Mozambique.

"Very good. Yes, an excellent enhancement of AD's first responder capability. And it dovetails nicely with her remote medical services work."

Geissner had made a similar statement last night.

"Is there an issue with security at the AWOS? They're stationary, yes?" Geissner asked.

"Correct. We intentionally diminish the value of AWOS components to make them less attractive to theft."

"I'm curious. You've been at this for over ten years. I suppose the technology is well-protected."

"Three hundred patents and counting. Some of the work is classified and patents applications have been deferred. The only organization using the full-on system right now is one I can't even say the name of."

"Will AD be using a classified technology?"

Dante put his hand to his chin, as if, recently, he had sported a goatee and was still in the habit of stroking it. "You hit the nail on the head. Biggest challenge, and it's an expensive one," he laughed good-naturedly. "We dusted off and reconfigured several prototypes, one-off or dumbed down units which we then had cleared for non-military ops. The AD configuration lacks many features of the military version. Still, they're mighty sexy and probably could be reverse engineered to some degree of lethality.

"Understand," Alexander continued, "Potomac does not need non-military, commercial business. I can say *that* with authority—the board got its pound of flesh out me for advocating the AD program."

Stonecrop was bored. Geissner and Alexander rehashed the terms of the letter of credit's indemnification clauses and an ancillary tech-support agreement to be provided by Potomac. *High powered venture capitalists these guys are not. And why are we even talking about this crap when somewhere, somehow, someone has taken Federica.* Geissner unsuccessfully prodded Alexander for more detail on the differences between the military and civilian systems. The conversation ended with Alexander suggesting Geissner follow up with Mr. Sato and visit Potomac offices in Maryland.

The mention of the name, Sato, sparked interest from Stonecrop. "Uli, do you know Sato?"

At first, Geissner misunderstood the question. "Sato is a common name in Japan, like Smith in the U.K." After the know-it-all moment passed, Geissner responded to the actual question Stonecrop had asked, "If you are referring to Hitoshi Sato at New Order, then of course I know him. He's red-lined every document in the deal." Geissner looked to Alexander for confirmation. "He's a partner at New Order, yes? Or an associate. Whatever he is, he's competent."

Alexander had had enough of "polite." He was tired of replaying the conversation they had had the night before; and their meeting so far had been anything but quick. "Gentlemen, can we wrap this up?"

Geissner wasn't quite finished. "I've heard—I believe it was from Miss Ratzow—about something called the Echo system. Will this feature be included in AD's system?"

Stonecrop sensed or imagined a shift in Alexander's demeanor.

"Gentlemen," Alexander repeated, his tone marked the termination of their discussion, "I have to go to my gate." He nodded to them, "A pleasure. Please convey my good wishes to Gregor and Miss Ratzow. I regret we didn't have the opportunity of her company last night."

"Yes, I must be going as well." Geissner checked his Omega, the frown on his face implying he had more important business elsewhere.

"I assure you. We'll complete our arrangement as planned. Safe travels, Dante. And thank you for taking the time to meet today."

Stonecrop made his goodbye to Geissner, saying he would catch the train back to town, freeing Geissner to drive directly to his "important" meeting. He joined Alexander as they headed toward the security checkpoint.

Alexander walked briskly at first, and then stopped. He took hold of Stonecrop's arm and faced him, "He's really a stiff, isn't he?"

Stonecrop halted, cracked a smile, and responded, "Yes, he is."

"And a toady," Alexander said, matter-of-factly.

"I'm not arguing with you."

"Do you work for him?"

Had Alexander abandoned the idea of making his flight?

"I'm the errand boy, although not Geissner's. Like I said last night, I do little chores for Gregor, Federica, a handful of other folks in Zürich, a couple galleries. I'm sort of taking a break and enjoying the simple life."

"Horsefeathers, Max. Horsefeathers!" Alexander took hold of Stonecrop's elbow and pinned him in place. "You're close to Federica, so close Gregor wouldn't let you out of his sight last night. He was damned nervous. Everybody, me included, was walking on eggshells."

"Federica and I *are* friends," Stonecrop conceded. "We met when she was eighteen. We share an interest in academics and sports, nothing related to her professional or volunteer work. We climb at the local gym."

"I see." Alexander pulled Stonecrop closer. He wasn't bullying but his physical presence, three hundred pounds of it, could be interpreted as intimidating. Stonecrop didn't know why, but he felt the opposite of intimidation. Something more like protection.

What was also clear was that Alexander was done with charades. "Max, you're a better man than Uli, but you're still full of shit. What the hell's going on? Last night. Just now. Something be fishy, mon. I get it. Gregor's outfit is sketchy. Federica never brought up Group until Potomac asked for the guarantee. She tried to get backing from some wealthy associate—one of Aide Direct's funders. That fizzled." Alexander hesitated, as if he were arguing with himself. "And Geissner knows more than he lets on. I don't like that."

Alexander didn't wait for Stonecrop to comment. "Either New Order violated our confidentiality agreements, or Federica talked out of turn. Either way, like I said, I don't like it. And I don't like the way

Geissner was pumping me. That was more than due diligence."

"Federica's a rock. She would not share confidential information. She's a trained doctor. Anyway, it's just not in her DNA." Stonecrop spoke honestly, and then, going with his gut, let it out. "Dante," Stonecrop put his own arm through Alexander's trunk-like arm as he guided them away from the security area entrance, "Federica is missing."

He let the statement sink in before he continued. "We don't know where she is. She was not detained at the hospital last night." After gauging Alexander's reaction—deep concern and shock—he expanded on what he had said. "I was ordered to keep mum. I believe the only people who are aware of her disappearance are Gregor, his security consultant Claudia Knight, and me. I don't know what Geissner knows; he seemed convincingly ignorant. Claudia is coordinating things with the authorities." Stonecrop took a breath before he went on. "Federica has vanished. No calls, no texts, nothing since yesterday morning. There's reason to believe she's been kidnapped."

That news hit Alexander hard. His body tensed. He spoke with deliberation. "You're not gonna get fired for talking to me. What do *you* think is going on?"

Stonecrop was direct, "A couple things: First, he kidnapping—if that's what it is—was timed to happen at exactly when we were meeting at the Dolder. Someone knew every move of everyone involved, including you and me. Second, I don't buy the deal between Potomac and AD. You're sharing military technology with a loosey-goosey aid organization? Get real, this deal is a nightmare and you know it. And, somehow, it's connected to the kidnapping." Stonecrop was aware he had slipped into business mode. "And you, personally, are pushing it. Why?"

"You're the errand boy, huh?" Alexander seemed both pleased and puzzled. Certainly not threatened.

They were walking past the Fernweh Bar. "Grappa?" Alexander asked.

"Love one. I'll take mine in an espresso. Workers call it a *caffè corretto*."

They ordered coffees, corrected, and a basket of breakfast croissants that, judging by their flat appearance, were already stale.

Alexander spoke first. "What the hell," he exhaled. "Here's the backstory. I met Federica at the Matemwe Lodge. That's on the northeast coast of Zanzibar, about an hour by car from Stonetown. You probably don't know where it is, but it doesn't matter—"

Stonecrop interrupted. "I know exactly where it is. Great bar. But that's neither here nor there. Please, continue."

Alexander was curious and surprised by Stonecrop's comment.

"I went there to decompress after a nerve-racking drone test in Somalia. It got ugly and I ended up flying my drones in an actual, active combat role but without any official title or operational clearance. Authorization arrived after the fact. In the end, the so-called test was a success. Stressed me out, and let me tell you I'm a hard guy to stress out."

Stonecrop didn't doubt it. "And?"

Alexander downed a glass of water. "Federica was at the Matemwe for a not dissimilar reason—she needed a mental break. Unlike me, she'd been trying to save people, not kill them. Her experience had been all frustration and failure. AD had two operations going. In the first, they tried to reach survivors in this small township in Galguduud. That's in central Somalia and impossible to get to. Rebels had ravaged the place and AD lost a couple staffers—a husband and wife team—who had been trucking in medical supplies and food. An IED killed the husband. A machete ended the life of his wife, but not until after she had been raped. The second operation and incident was related to flood relief in Mozambique; I don't recall the specifics, but it didn't go well."

"Idealists caught in the crossfire. Not the first time."

"Not the first time, Max. And not the last. Like I said, our stays at Matemwe overlapped. We shared our experiences." He raised his left hand, showing the wedding band in anticipation of the question from Stonecrop. "No monkey business. She is an attractive woman. Incredible linguist. I swear she spoke Swahili like a native. Refused to talk about how that was. And she's engaged, as you no doubt know." Alexander sat back in his chair. "Are you the guy? I mean the guy she's engaged to?"

"Hardly," Stonecrop responded a little too quickly.

Alexander, who missed nothing, let it drop. "For the record, I'm married, four kids. Federica and I talked mostly about her work, and I mine. I learned about Aide Direct. For her it was personal, righting wrongs as if she had been the wrongdoer. That didn't make sense to me, but I didn't press her. Actually, I was the one who had the idea to make a system for AD, one that was not as expensive and feature packed as our military version. I did *not* disclose the real cost of the modified system—to her, or to Uli and company. The simplified AD pack cost is a significant multiple of what's stated in the lease agreement."

Alexander reached across the table toward Stonecrop's glass of water. "May I?" Stonecrop pushed the glass closer to him. "Maybe," Alexander spoke after downing the water in one go, "this is my way of balancing the scales."

Stonecrop listened, and thought: *We're all doing that, balancing the scales.*

"Can you tell me more about your side of the deal?"

Alexander accommodated. "I had a hell of a fight on my hands in Maryland. Private equity, the Pentagon, and our IB held my feet to the fire. We use the investment bank for acquisitions support, technology transfer matters, compliance, and cover. I got folks to accept a watered-down agreement with AD provided Potomac retain full ownership and day-to-day control of the technology—we can do this remotely. Equity insisted we charge something. There was no goddamned good reason for it but I lost the argument. Potomac has, like I said, zip interest in the non-military market. This AD unit is a one-off, and it's for Federica. If she leaves AD, we repossess the system, immediately. We can do this real-time if there's a problem and should be able to destroy critical components so they can't be re-used or copied."

"Got it," Stonecrop said. Federica was not a key man, in the typical sense. AD could function quite well without her. "It's about trust," Stonecrop said.

"Exactly," Alexander agreed, and then added, "Max, I prefer we not share our present conversation with Uli." The statement wasn't a question and Stonecrop didn't take it as one.

Alexander consumed another croissant. In his giant hands it looked like a canapé. "Now, what can I do to help?"

Stonecrop sipped his espresso and took his time before speaking. "I don't know. I still don't know enough about what's going on. Do you have a private number?" Alexander pulled out his mobile. Stonecrop did the same and they exchanged numbers. "Who else is aware of the details of the deal, specifically the Dolder meeting, and the technology exchange?"

"A handful of New Order employees, a couple attorneys. Of course, the team running the deal in-house. Maybe a dozen people if you include tech." Another croissant vanished before Stonecrop's eyes, like the last, in two bites.

"I knew a lot of IBs, never heard of New Order."

"Boutique firm, eight partners. My go-to guy is Hitoshi Sato. Young, intense, wicked-smart."

"Oddly, him I've met. A couple months ago, I joined Federica for a lunch in Brussels with Hitoshi and Andreas Castro. Castro is the founder who backed out of providing the credit support for the deal. That's why Federica had to ask her father for help. Castro is also the ex-fiancé. She dumped him, then and there, in front of Hitoshi and me. Castro went crazy. The guy's vain, got a temper. He left in a huff with Hitoshi at his side. Hitoshi realized what was going on and gave Castro an out, so Castro wouldn't do something he would really regret. Smart move by Hitoshi."

"Interesting. I never heard about it. Hitoshi's an enigma. Tech nerd for sure. He flip-flopped on this deal. All gung-ho at first—out to save the world from the forces of evil, which fits, roughly, with New Order's mission—'business for a better world.' But after my investors brought up the LC and Group entered the picture, Hitoshi tried to kill it. I overrode him." The third and last croissant went down the hatch before Alexander continued. "To say the connection with GR Group 'upset' him would be an understatement. In this business, hell, I work with companies whose histories and capital are anything but transparent. Shit, half my backers have obscure foreign addresses no one can find. Sato was always okay with that. I thought his reaction to Group was hypocritical bullshit; I told him as much."

"Hitoshi's hard to read," Stonecrop agreed. "That's my impression based upon the minimal interaction I've had with him. But Federica genuinely likes him."

"So, who'd you work for? Wall Street, a Sand Hill Road shop?" Sand Hill Road in Palo Alto and Menlo Park, as everyone knows, was the home of venture capital in the Bay Area.

"Mid-way. Boulder Biotech, a small life-sciences VC, four hundred million under management, based, obviously, in Boulder, Colorado."

"Ah," Dante spread his hands out on the table, "Ratzow's gopher, huh? What bullshit. Seems neither of us is quite whom we appear to be."

The statement made Stonecrop wonder what it was that he didn't know about the man across the table.

Alexander rose and excused himself to check the ticket counter for the next flight to Brussels. Stonecrop ordered a second caffè. He had not noticed Dante's gold tooth.

The Fall

On the ten-minute ride on the S-Bahn from the airport to the Hauptbahnhof Stonecrop had sat next to the window, riding backwards, and looking at the past. Upon arrival he had swung by the Hauptbahnhof ShopVille, a subterranean mall with multiple markets. The unpacked bags sat on the table. He had no appetite and no desire to cook. Nothing made sense to him: not the last twenty-four hours, not the last twenty-four months. Certainly, the last six-months' self-imposed exile and life of denial had not gone as expected. Normal life, a life that was peaceful and routine, had eluded him. *Fuck it*, he scolded himself. *Deal with it*.

The meeting at Flughafen Zürich had been productive. He'd made an ally of sorts, a person he trusted at least as much as anyone on Ratzow's team. For the hundredth time he considered going to the police. And for the hundredth time he shelved the idea. The last time he had appealed to the authorities for help two results had ensued: First, he, Stonecrop, had become the target of the investigation; and second, the outcome he had sought to achieve had failed to materialize. In the case of Federica's disappearance, an outcome of the second sort was unacceptable.

He checked his phone. Nothing from Federica. Her phone had to have been turned off, destroyed, or its settings modified. They shared locations—something they did only with each other. And there was nothing new about Marion's condition. Ratzow had promised he would call if there were any change. The two events, the kidnapping and the assault on Marion, obviously had a common origin.

Why had he not told Alexander about Marion? He should have; he just didn't have his wits about him. Stonecrop was tortured by a recurring image of Federica's body, bound with duct tape, writhing in a convulsive struggle to breath, and then lifelessly drifting to the bottom of the Zürichsee. *The divers would find her*. The city used divers to scour the lake bottom for trash. It would be hard to miss her body and its flaxen hair waving like golden kelp.

The text from Claudia had said they were to meet at the Rathaus Café on Limmatquai at 22:00 hours, giving him time to make dinner—if he could muster the energy for it—and catch up on work email. He would cancel whatever he had scheduled over the next few days. He needed rest but rest could wait.

The Rathaus Café was less than five minutes by foot from his apartment. Named after the nearby historic Rathaus—the Zürich Town Hall—the café was built to lure tourists to its al fresco tables alongside the Limmat river and on inclement days to shelter them within wood-paneled walls and a warmly-lit interior. The food was tourist fare. When he arrived Claudia was at a table and seated in front of two glasses of house red. She hovered over the glasses of wine as if the three of them were having a conversation.

She looked over the rims of her glasses to greet Stonecrop. "My darling, how are you? Trying day. I know." Claudia's demeanor was unchanged from the morning. She appeared unwearied by the day's events.

"Getting by. What's up?" Stonecrop took a seat across from Claudia.

"Alexander?" She asked.

"Nothing new." Technically, he hadn't lied and Claudia seemed inclined to believe him.

"We had an off-the-record conversation with Kommissar Vormittag. He believes it's possible, but unlikely, that Federica was kidnapped. Much the same as my initial, uninformed reaction. He says we'll know soon enough. Bad guy kidnaps daughter of rich guy. Ransom request to follow. Quite straightforward, you see. As Gregor requested, I did not show the note to the good Kommissar. However, our expectation is the same as the Kommissar's. If it's a straightforward extortion play and if the ask comes, we pay; there'll be no fuss. Vormittag is treating the assault on Marion as a stand-alone incident. He has his reasons."

"I don't get it, Claudia. Who knows what-the-fuck the kidnappers are doing with Federica, and we're sitting on our hands. The Kantonspolizei are not amateurs. They need to be in the loop. Time matters; resources matter. I don't know Vormittag; but I think I don't like the guy." Stonecrop brushed away a swath of hair. He wondered if he looked as ragged as he felt.

"We will put him to work, but not quite yet, dearie. He is a good man, even if he is Polizei. He and Gregor have known each other a long time. Trust me," she responded.

Stonecrop did not trust her. His head fell forward and again the mop of hair fell across his face. He slouched in the chair and combed the hair back with his fingers, intertwining them behind his head to pin the hair in place. He moved his head in a circle—clockwise, then counter-clockwise. His neck ached, a reminder of his tumble on Sustenhorn. Marion, his thoughts zeroed in on Marion. What could she feel? Did her neck ache? Had she been up all night like he had been, but unable to complain or tell anyone?

"And Marion?" He said the words while looking up at the ceiling and picturing her being pitched off the bridge.

"The same—stable, but unresponsive." She reached out with her hand. He ignored the consoling gesture, leaving her hand extended in space and stubborn pinky aloft. She withdrew the hand and offered consoling words instead: "I'm sorry. She's receiving the best of care."

Claudia shifted the conversation back to the kidnapping, "We're talking to other resources, an alternative to the dauntless Kommissar Vormittag who, despite the German name, was raised in Palermo and is a lot more street savvy than he lets on. For now, love, bear with me. I need a few minutes with you for a bit of housekeeping."

Why does she do that? Stonecrop wondered. *Couldn't Vormittag just be Vormittag?* Why did he have to be the "good Kommissar," or "dauntless Kommissar." And it's always "we this" and "we that." There was little Claudia said or did that didn't rub Stonecrop the wrong way. She probably felt the same about him.

He stretched back, head in his hands, and examined details of the wood-paneled ceiling and the hemispheric mirror-ball chandelier, and then shut his eyes to see if he could retain what he had seen—counting countless slats, estimating the weight of the glass pendants and the iron ring the pendants hung from. *I am so exhausted.*

Claudia stayed on task, "Gregor adores you, dear, and I don't want you to take this the wrong way." She expected him to say something. When he didn't, she continued. "You went to work for Group six months back, that was . . ." Stonecrop closed his eyes as she flipped through pages in her notebook, "Yes, in the spring. Shortly after a week of R&R at Susenbergstrasse, and after sweet Federica, who had brought you home like a soggy stray, talked to Daddy. You remember, of course, she had implored her father to find work to accommodate your . . ." she hunted for an inoffensive expression, "your mental state. Seems you thought the sky was falling."

Claudia helped herself to a drink of wine; he heard glass being taken from the table and the gulp as she swallowed. "Over the last half-year, you've behaved and done an exemplary job. You keep to yourself. I'm not to worry, he's shy, Federica says. *Shy* is not a word *I* would use to describe you, but what do I know? Your unnerving remove, my dear, always has me guessing. Is that intentional? Or is it, as sweet Federica suggests, you're a timid man?"

Don't test me, Claudia.

"And Gregor, bless his heart, goes along, believing every word." Claudia took another drink and noisily cleared her throat, as if she were afraid of Stonecrop falling asleep in front of her. Stonecrop didn't stir and went back to the architectural details of the woodwork on the ceiling.

"Now my job," she continued her monologue, "at the time you joined the company, was to vet you like I vet any new hire. We're having this tête-à-tête because I had not done it—my job, that is. Frankly, I didn't think you'd last a week. I was busy and Gregor was lax. I simply never got around to it. And, too, one mustn't pick a fight with sweet daughter."

Stonecrop didn't rise to the bait—to defend Federica, or himself. However, the last comment managed to get his attention. Claudia was pleased. "Since then, I have gotten to know you. I too am fond of you, dearie, you do know that I hope. You're dependable and you're discreet. And you're not unhandsome in rugged sort of way." She delivered the last remark with a wink.

Stonecrop read the clock on the wall. The Rathaus would close in fifteen minutes, and he would be done with her. He was being a jerk but he didn't care. That this was what she was doing to help Federica was ludicrous.

Claudia refueled on wine. Her mannerisms drove Stonecrop nuts. When she held a glass or a cup that ring-bedecked and double-jointed pinky made a right angle to the back of her hand.

Poke your eye out if you're not carefully, dearie.

"Since I *am* so fond you, I'm going to run my update by you before I pass it on to Gregor. We are worried, my dear. You and Federica are close; how close is anybody's guess. You're both so bloody . . . Whatever.

"So, let's begin: You do deliveries for everyone in Group and never complain. And when Federica has time off from work, you two . . ." she consulted her little black spiral binder, "hike in the park and climb at Gaswerk Schlieren. And you do little chores or cook for her, and, off and on, for the addled—is that too strong?—Frau Ott." Claudia paused to adjust her coke-bottle glasses and glanced again at the notebook; she never used a tablet or phone for notes. "Your forte is hearty Italian— why haven't you invited me to dinner, ducky? I've heard you're a wonder in the kitchen. I suppose I shouldn't be jealous, those women on Susenbergstrasse did nurse you back from the dead, from something called *the Fall*. That's the name for it, right, the name you use? Not that accident on the mountain top. The other one, the accident in Africa. Quite dramatic, the name, don't you think!"

"Anyone can slip and fall, Claudia, anyone," he said, reengaged and hoping the statement was not taken as a threat. Claudia was unmoved, happy it seemed, that she had successfully baited him.

"And the off-again-on-again business with Andreas? Does the competition stir you? Or that other one, the Japanese boy?"

"I'd say it's proof Fede has a sense of humor," he offered. They both smiled.

"Gregor trusts you—a rare and generous thing, his trust. He is always, always, awfully concerned about Federica. The thing bothering him, love, unlikely as it may seem to you, is this: He fears someone from *your* past might be a link to what happened to her. We don't *really* think so, but it would be dandy to officially cross it off the list."

"Claudia, you're wasting your time. I am not some poohbah worth exploiting," he blandly reported.

"Exploitation is good, though sweet revenge can lead to the same mischief. The jealous ex-wife, who knows? Let's run with it, shall we?" Claudia was warming up, her face animated. "When you tried to walk yourself to death—it was what, a week or ten days—and you ended up on the doorstep of some unpronounceable mountain chalet, I understand that you had recently learned that you had been booted out of your marriage of many years to a wealthy celebrity sort. What was her name?"

"Kelenalphütte—that's the chalet. And it's Matina. Matti for short."

"Yes, Matina, nee Matina Holstein-Scherer. She slapped you over the head with a divorce, and you, you dutifully signed on the dotted line and walked away from a small fortune. Well, not *that* small, something in the range a 100 million U.S. Odd, isn't it, you're doing that, unless she really had something on you—like you having your way with the nanny or the granny on the kitchen table in front of the kiddos. I hear you rolled over, put up zero fight for your share of the treasure. You even turned down money she willfully offered. You 'had to breathe.' A direct quote from the celebrity blogs. Did you really say those words? Sounds like something out of a bloody soap. Quite a good read, these blogs about the rich and famous, if you like that sort of thing. And I *eat* it up.

"You are an unusual man, Max. Other than your net worth being less than her next objet d'art, the celeb sheets say what pushed the ex over the edge was the infamy following your business suicide. What was the snooty work wifey did?"

"Still does." Stonecrop didn't know why he bothered to answer, but he did anyway. "Private gallery, in Aspen, mostly museum-to-museum sales. And a handful of non-institutional clients—fellow celebrities, Saudi princes, and the like."

"Ah, yes, the Holstein-Scherer Gallery. And you engineered some clever practice so buyers could lend out newly acquired works for six months or more, for which the gallery was paid a handsome rental fee and said buyer could avoid those annoying state sales taxes. The rich only get richer, don't they? It's rumored your African antics spooked a couple fat buyers, some of whom also happened to be investors in that fund you were a part of—"

Stonecrop cut her off. He couldn't listen anymore, "Your suggestion regarding my ex-wife harming Federica out of anger or jealousy is preposterous. Marriages fail. Happens every day; it's always sad. Matti was and is a good person, and a good mother. Nothing but respect, both ways. As far as the art patrons and investors, we're talking small change. Rounded errors in their balance sheets. Don't waste your time —or mine."

"So civil! I'm impressed." She was unflinching, unsympathetic, and definitely not impressed. "Between us," she spoke as if he were a co-conspirator, "I understand. It's so tiresome entertaining rich muckety-mucks, their mooning over meaningless squiggles on canvas." Claudia was in her Claudia zone. "Am I missing anything?"

Stonecrop said nothing as she droned on, reporting a life story he already knew too well and parts of which he wanted to forget. He felt powerless, except for his silence. He imagined wringing her neck. Bit of the old self coming to life, but not the self he cared for. And he thought about his childhood and his brother and forgot where he was . . .

Stonecrop snapped awake. Had he missed something important? Why wasn't she tired? Her face revealed no hint of fatigue. He must not have slept for long or she would have said something.

"I'm told you had been leading the good life of the venture capitalist —it was bio-tech—when you learned one of your portfolio companies contracted with a less-than-reputable outfit to flog drugs in some third-world cesspool. You had the temerity to go public with their transgressions and the firm threw you out on your ear. That right?" Stonecrop watched the bartender wipe down the bar, wash the last of the glasses, and put away several bottles of liquor. He saw the bartender watching the two of them in the mirror behind the bar.

"Must have been your young and stupid phase. Let's see . . . You didn't take the hint and knocked on the door of the International Trade Administration. The Feds ignored you, which is what happens when you buck monster pharmas with pols in their pockets. So, you, my little pit bull, checked the do-it-yourself box and, my dear, things really went to the crapper."

She scanned pages in her notebook, "According to my jottings, after a year of chatting up a slew of official agencies, you jetted off to Mali or Mozambique, something that starts with 'M,' or maybe it was an 'L', and you hunted down the offenders on their own turf—really a shame you didn't know Gregor then—and after a month of having as much success there as you had Stateside—after all, money is money, and works its magic everywhere—you lost it."

She sought confirmation from him and got nothing. He stared at the clock. Claudia was in her own world, busily reconstructing his. "The boss of the sales shop in that M-place, a little-respected local, ended up beaten to within an inch of his life and had been threatened by someone—now who could that have been?—to do his boy-scout best to avoid the pharma trade forevermore. Then that someone—that's you dearie—moved up—or was it down?—the food chain. Whatever it was, it seems you got more than you bargained for." Claudia drained the rest of her wine. She smiled at him. "Gregor has good reason to be pissed about that. Or a little bit proud."

He cocked his head at her and smiled. "Claudia, oh Claudia. Either you are making up stories or wasting my time and yours telling me what I know. No comment."

She seemed to have not heard. "Now this is the missing piece," she said. "And I confess it's a worry, pet, and something I don't *have* to mention to Gregor. As I said before, even if you don't take believe me, I *am* fond of you." Claudia reached for her wine glass and raised it in the air before realizing it was empty. Her pinky finger remained erect, as if aroused by her very own discourse. "You were nowhere to be found for the next three months. Not a bad idea, you get credit for that, sweet. Then, lucky us, you pop up in Zürich! Meanwhile, in the backwaters of Mozambique—or was it Lesotho—the scuttlebutt is that two men, crooked execs who managed dozens of worthless shits like the crony whose career you rearranged, well, these two gentlemen vanished from the face of the earth. That was the same period you were MIA. Funny, huh. Have I got it right? No judgement on my part, just curious. Anything to add? Rumors of revenge, that sort of thing?"

He rose, needing movement like a prisoner in a cell and circling the room. Hysteria, anger, beyond tired, finding his predicament humorous one moment, insane the next. Faces—dead and alive— stampeded for an exit from his mind. The worried bartender, Claudia, and Stonecrop filled a room that was more confining for its emptiness. The apartment, the Rathaus, the train, everywhere Stonecrop turned was empty space.

"Please, love, sit down. You're making me nervous. I'm not going to chase you around the table." She turned her head awkwardly to the side to see him.

A violent image of twisting her head off surfaced. It frightened him enough to do as she had requested. He sat and clasped his hands together on the table. He faced her. "Claudia, sometimes I need to get away. Go for a walk. It's my therapy. I took a stroll in the Giants Castle —that's in KwaZulu-Natal, nine hours southwest of Maputo—for days and days. I don't know how long. Same at Kelenalphütte. It's a climber thing. We go off-grid. Don't read too much into it."

The bartender stood silently at the door.

The half-truth fell short, so Stonecrop expanded upon what he had said, hoping to satisfy her and conclude their meeting. "I was devastated by what my firm had condoned. I tried and failed to change things. There was nothing I could do to undo the deaths from counterfeit and misdirected meds and goods, and god knows what else. The two people you referred to, if it's who I think it is, well, they had a lot of enemies. It was a difficult time. Things happen in Maputo that no one on the outside would understand. I don't talk about it. And I don't want to hear any half-baked theories, not from you or anybody. Whatever went down in Africa had nothing, absolutely nothing, to do with what happened to Federica."

"She was there, same time. A short stint of work. A coincidence?"

That caught him off guard. But then, where hadn't she traveled, either with Gregor or on her own, or with Aide Direct. And Africa is enormous. The U.S. lower forty-eight would fit in the Sahara.

Claudia went on, "I don't believe in coincidence, love—"

"Claudia," Stonecrop tried to not appear as upset and threatened as he felt, "this has been quite entertaining, but we're done."

"Just listen, muffy, just listen. This is between us . . . for now." Claudia paused for dramatic effect, or perhaps, at this point, to intentionally piss off the bartender who had returned to the bar and was clanking glasses. "Those two lovelies you offed . . . Well, they worked for Gregor. I'm not planning to bring it up with him."

The lights above the bar went dark. No one moved. The barman's fingers reached for the light switch for the chandelier. Two still bodies locked onto each other's gaze at the table. One glass of wine lay untouched, brimming with blood-colored wine; the other was the empty, dregs drying at the bottom.

Stonecrop broke the silence. "You're wrong, Claudia, in so many ways I don't know where to start. None of this is any of your goddamn business. Mozambique, my relationship with my ex-wife, my relationship with Federica. Tell Gregor whatever you want. If he doesn't like it, he can go to hell."

Stonecrop rose. He cracked a hard and unpleasant smile and panned the room. "So can you."

Zürichberg

Impatient for a morning walk and upset with her walker being late for the chore, Rosie enthusiastically heralded Stonecrop's approach before he knocked at the door. The barking alerted Frau Ott, who, wearing a red and richly embroidered silk robe, unlocked the door and greeted him. With leash in hand, Frau Ott positioned herself to block Rosie's escape.

"*Rosieee, ruhig!*—quiet!" Rosie stopped yapping.

The ruse commenced. Stonecrop took the leash, tethered Rosie, and bade goodbye to Frau Ott. He had expected Frau Ott to have noticed and to ask about Federica's absence, but she made no mention of it.

With Rosie in the lead the actors set off at a moderate pace, passing the community gardens to reach Zürichberg, the massive, wooded park dominating the skyline east of the city. At the pole gate meant to keep autos from accidentally driving up the fire road, Rosie came to a halt. Stonecrop kneeled. He gently placed his hand under Rosie's snout.

"You know the deal, Rosie. I call. You come. *Capeesh?*"

Rosie twitched in anticipation. He unfastened the leash, and the pair began their one-hour jog. Stonecrop counted steps in sets of eight, a numeric mantra synced with his breathing.

Cold air cleared his lungs. Limbs of trees, sere and skeletal, reached skyward. He remembered his first walk with Rosie and smiled. It had not gone smoothly.

Stonecrop had taken on Rosie-walking as a way to repay Frau Ott for her kindness and generosity. That first walk, at the trailhead, she had slipped out of her collar and bolted for the trees. He had followed her by following the telltale shaking of the brush as she tunneled through the undergrowth. Whenever he closed in, she took off. At one

121

point, she had tumbled into a walled rock pit with no exit save a thigh-high step. With admirable grit, Rosie had perched on her hind legs and clawed at the top of the step until she had gained sufficient purchase to heave her wurst-like torso over the top. Stonecrop dove and missed. At the top she had unwound like a slinky and leapt into space, ears in the air like a cape. Stonecrop lost it. He abandoned the chase and collapsed in laughter on a bed of grass. The victorious Rosie circled back. She licked him on the chin, reclined against him, and rolled over for a tummy scratch.

Frau Ott had been waiting for them when they had returned to Susenbergstrasse. Nothing had escaped her scrutiny—not the burrs in Rosie's fur and Stonecrop's socks, not the scratches crisscrossing the backs of his arms from scrambling through the brambles.

The reprimand had been sharp and steely, "You were off-*piste*! Take care this does not happen again." Rosie and Stonecrop exchanged a guilty look. But—an important but—Rosie never did her "business" in the house again.

Today, Rosie detoured from the path to lap water from a trough hewn out of a tree-trunk. Stonecrop took a drink from the jet of water coming out of the pipe above the trough. The water was cold, delicious and, like all of Zürich's public fountains, giardia-free. He sat on the edge of the log and scratched Rosie behind the ears. In a start, she began gnawing at something on her paw.

Stonecrop thought about Claudia's revelation connecting him to Gregor's African business dealings. He had done his homework before going to Maputo and did not remember come across either Gregor's name or Group's. If there had been a connection, it had to have been a tangential one. Maybe the Coutos had worked for some third party.

Federica would never accept her father pushing counterfeit drugs in Africa or anywhere. It was antithetical to everything she and her foundation stood for. Or, he reflected, is that why she had created AD? To compensate for his misdeeds. He back-burnered the matter, along with Claudia's disparaging insinuations about Mattie, his ex. What mattered was getting Federica back. He was getting nowhere, and he was going nuts.

"Rosie," Stonecrop said, "any ideas?" Hearing her name, her head popped up briefly before returning to the paw. People and dogs look at each other's expressions. Do we do that with any other species?

There was a thorn in one of her pads. Rosie let him hold and steady the paw. He found a twig and dragged it across the pad a few times to coax out the thorn.

"Who the fuck can I trust—Dante? Alicia?" he asked Rosie.

She licked the back of his hand as he rubbed the pad. He released her paw and she sprung to her feet. When Stonecrop stood, Rosie froze, prepared to launch in whatever direction he went. "We'll get her back." Rosie wagged her tail. The two of them loped back on the fire road toward Susenbergstrasse, determination in their gaits.

The next step in Stonecrop's plan-in-process was standing in front of him talking on the phone in the backyard at Susenbergstrasse. He'd already decided to call Alicia. She was Federica's closest friend and knew the family.

Alicia greeted him with a curt nod. They stood apart from each other to give her privacy for the call. With Rosie in tow, he walked to the bench at the west side of the backyard and stretched his calves, hamstrings, and hips. Alicia watched him as she carried on her conversation. Rosie curled up in the shade under the bench.

The usual hillside breeze was absent, but the air felt clean and clear. He had an uninterrupted view of the foothills on the opposite side of the lake and of the tallest point, the Uetliberg tower. Above the tower four picture book clouds were pasted to the sky like construction paper cutouts. In a neighbor's garden a short distance downhill lay fallow the remains of tomatoes, squash, and a trellis veiled in a tangle of dried vines, enough for a half-case of wine. He wondered what grapes they had planted—had to be something suitable for the cold climate. His Swiss favorites were from a temperate region, the eponymously named pinot noirs from a string of wineries in the Graubünden and southeast of the Walensee.

Alicia approached him from behind. Ignoring his post-run sweat she gave him a warm hug. She was an attractive woman. Unlike Fede, her breasts were large and fleshy. The arms were shorter and the fingers and hands holding his torso were compact—better for boxing than Fede's surgeon-slender digits. Stonecrop recalled Fede joking about Alicia as her bodyguard. In the Gilli household, a family night out had meant a workout at the local dojo. Both parents were black belts, one in Judo and the other Karate.

"Hey stranger!" she cheerfully greeted him.

"Alicia, good to see you," he said, and spun, like a dancer, within her arms so he could face her and offer a proper hug.

"You must be a wreck. I was in London. Came as soon as I heard about Marion. I thought I'd be consoling Federica. Now I learn she's missing! What the hell?"

"What the hell is right," he said.

"I saw Marion this morning. Gregor told me she was in a coma, but she's not. She's not exactly responsive, either. Every exhale she moans aloud, like a child, this plaintive sound. It's so sad. The doctor, his name was Weller, said there was brain damage from the fall or asphyxiation. That's about it. Now it's just wait and see. Marion didn't recognize me. She's been in my life a long time, you know."

She had more to say but took a moment to gather her thoughts.

"I ran into Kommissar Vormittag," she continued. "We talked shop. He said a traffic cam at the east side of the bridge from where Marion fell showed a car with two men in the front and one passenger, possibly a woman, in the back. A second traffic cam a short distance from the other side of the bridge recorded the same car. It picked up only the two passengers in the front seats. Could've been the angle of the cam. They're trying to identify the vehicle. Vormittag wants to question Federica, and he said Gregor hadn't gotten back to him yet."

"Alicia, thanks for coming." Stonecrop said, and then paused to properly phrase the question he asked next. "What did you mean by 'you talked shop'?"

Alicia tilted her head to the side, "Ah, you don't know, do you? Well, why should you. Federica is so circumspect—in a good way—always respectful. I work for U.S. Treasury, OIG. Office of Inspector General. None of the juicy street stuff Vormittag does. Though yours truly is always packing, since some asinine regulation says I gotta carry a firearm. A pain in the ass at customs. And I'm on a list with Kantonpolizei. See, officially, I'm in the Office of Terrorism and Financial Intelligence. The reality is, my work's a bore. Makes actuarial work look glamorous."

"I thought you were a some kind of hot shot CPA—because of the travel."

"Nope. Although, it's fun to pretend. I do a little of that, too—pretending." Alicia gave his forearm a gentle squeeze and let the hand rest there.

"Vormittag really didn't know Federica was missing?"

"That's my impression. Like I said, he asked me to tell her myself or tell Gregor that he'd like to speak with her. I did see Gregor and he laid it on thick. Said Federica was on holiday in Croatia. He blew me off. If she *is* on a romp—hard to believe—then I hope it's not with Andreas. She dumped him, I thought, but this is the kind of disappearing act they used to pull off.

"You never know. Some women like men that treat them like shit. There was one time—after I found out what the prick had done—I offered to kick his ass."

"She's not run off with anyone."

As though she had not heard him, Alicia continued, "And then she's got that thing about Hitoshi. I don't know his last name."

Surprised and confused, Stonecrop supplied the missing name, "Sato, Hitoshi Sato. Works for New Horizons. They're an investment bank helping Aide Direct on behalf of a client."

"Yeah, well. He's pretty hot I hear. I mean, if Gregor isn't totally full of shit, maybe she and Hitoshi are on a fling. Hell if I know. You'd think she'd tell me, but she can be weird that way."

"Hitoshi works—"

Alicia interrupted, "I gotta tell you this." She laughed as she spoke. "I was chit-chatting with Frau Ott. She said Federica hadn't been around, although she wasn't sure why. So, I asked if any eligible men or women had been by. Frau Ott blushed. She turned bright red." Alicia smiled, a compassionate smile. "So sweet. Then, of course, it hit her that I was asking about Federica. She recovered her composure and said something about Andreas coming by a couple of months back. I guess it was late when he drove up and Rosie went nuts. The noise woke the neighbors, Ferrari vroom-vrooming, and music blasting. The guy's a two-year-old. You met him?"

"Yes, we had a brief but pointed conversation."

Her face drew close to his. "What does she see in him, Max? Other than the movie-star looks, Ferrari, and the fat contribution he made to launch Aide Direct—seven figures. Shit, I wonder if he'd like me! I could make him behave."

"Yeah, doggie's got good taste, right Rosie." Stonecrop glanced at Rosie, whose ears perked up. He'd done it again, speaking to Rosie just like Frau Ott did.

"Federica is so . . ." Alicia searched for the words, "I mean, she's the single brightest person I know, and we are close, but she can be so fucking stupid sometimes. It's not like her to leave me *totally* in the dark. Although she doesn't tell me diddly-shit about some things, like nothing about you. And Hitoshi? Like what's with that guy?"

Stonecrop had the same question regarding Hitoshi and told himself now was not the time. He was hoping Alicia could help find Federica.

"I could ring her neck!" For whatever reason, that warranted another affectionate squeeze. "You were married, right? A couple of kids in the States?"

"No big secrets. I did go through a rough patch. Divorced. I don't dwell on it. Federica and I are friends; she respects my privacy. I respect hers."

Alicia gave Max a full-on hug which lasted long enough for Max to feel pleasantly uncomfortable. His left arm hung over her shoulder. The length of her body pressed against his left side. He told himself the hug was just that, a supportive, friendly hug.

"Thank you, Alicia." He was grateful. "Truth is, Federica is nowhere to be found. Claudia told me Vormittag knew about Federica. You're saying he doesn't. I hate this bullshit."

"A word of advice. Don't get too close to Claudia." Alicia looked upward. "I judge people, Max. She's poison."

He nodded and laughed, "Yeah, well she's a toughie. You familiar with her firm, G24/7?" Stonecrop asked, wondering why Alicia hadn't hit him straight away with a query about Federica's kidnapping. Why were they dancing around it?

Alicia tossed him a knowing smile, "Scuttlebutt is they have a 'who's who' client list and that Claudia is totally phenomenal at her job. Up for gossip?"

"Sure. All ears, Rosie too!" On cue, Rosie's ears perked up.

Years ago, soon after Gregor set up shop in Zürich, there was an incident. Supposedly a Sicilian guy, probably mafia, had threatened some friend of Gregor's. Well, not the friend directly, but the friend's in-laws, their family in Palermo. Next thing, out of the blue, this mafia-type—the one doing the threatening—dies in a boating accident in the Walensee—strangled by a line wrapped around both his neck and the prop." With her fingers, Alicia wrapped an imaginary line around her throat.

"The story goes," she said. "Gregor's people smuggled the in-laws out of Palermo right after this guy dies. Group transported goods all over the place, so this was the kind of thing they could pull off. Then Gregor sends a flower—a single chrysanthemum—to every relative and friend of the guy who died in the boating *accident*." Alicia released him to put air quotes on the "accident."

"The affair had public scandal written all over it. But the entire incident vanished from the radar. No investigation, no exposés. No more bodies and no link to Gregor. The reason? Claudia and 24/7 fixers. They clean it up shit like that."

"So," Stonecrop added, "she's like a consigliere."

"Kantonspolizei must have known something," she continued. "And the Italian authorities. Same with the press, even *Zwanzig Minuten*. Still, nothing. Polizei treated Gregor with kid gloves. No indignant politicians demanded justice. The reporters were mum. No vendetta stirrings from down south. Claudia had her thumb on all of it."

"Did Federica know?" Stonecrop asked.

"We never talked about. You know how people can be friends and still not talk about some things. I wonder, though. She's the top of the class, right? Does the Times crossword in her head in ten-minutes." Alicia squeezed his hand, reflected a few seconds, and then opined on what she had just said. "But that's fluid intelligence; not useful in the real world."

There was more. Stonecrop could feel it.

Alicia obliged. "Between us?"

"Sure."

She looked passed him and toward Uetliberg tower, as if that would somehow lessen the impropriety of what she was about to say.

"Gregor and GR Group were on my docket a few years back, when I was in D.C. Our office had been informed about possible criminal activity. I was under a lot of pressure. The higher-ups at Treasury knew I was close to the daughter. They urged me to use her to dig up incriminating crap on Group. I flat-out refused, told them to go fuck themselves. I used exactly those words. Federica's my best friend. My impertinence about cost me my job. Soon after, I was shunted off to London and the powers that be assigned the case to someone else. Don't know who, or even if it's still hot. I never mentioned it to Federica."

Stonecrop was certain that Fede knew something about what Gregor had done and equally certain that if that knowledge were shared with Alicia, then Alicia would be in an ethical dilemma. And if Claudia was half as good as Alicia implied, Gregor and Federica were likely aware that Alicia had been asked to dig up dirt on Group's doings.

"Does that matter?"

Alicia nodded and continued. "Gregor has enemies. No surprise there. But I don't know who. I can imagine one of them is behind what happened to Federica. It's dumb-fuck obvious she's been kidnapped. Whoever hurt Marion either has Federica, or else our girl got away and is hiding out—from everybody. Can't blame her. I'd get my ass outta here in a New York minute."

"She'd call me," Stonecrop said. "Any particular enemies come to mind?"

"No. But with the shit he was into, plenty folks would pay big to hurt him."

"Why Federica *and* Marion?" Stonecrop asked. "And why not just have at Gregor?"

"Simple," Alicia responded, "Marion wasn't a target. She was in the wrong place at the wrong time and got seriously fucked over. The assholes after Federica need something from Gregor. Could be money, could be anything. They eliminate Gregor, then he can't pay or do what they want.

"In some places, it's tradition. Gangs extort money by kidnapping family members. In Peru, the going rate is five million dollars per family—the kidnappers snatch only one of the kids, usually the oldest boy. Once payment is made, the family's name moves to the do-not-kidnap list. All the gangs honor the do-not-kidnap list, or they can't play anymore. Happened to my cousin. It's a ritual the wealthy take for granted and, believe it or not, laugh about at cocktail parties. Kind of a Peruvian gangster-bar-mitzvah. Nobody gets hurt, the money is always paid. The higher the ransom, the bigger the bragging rights at the party."

"Gregor would pay a shitload."

"Absolutely," she said, "unless he knew the extortion wouldn't end. In Peru, the families are warned to not speak to the police. In fact, that's the last thing they want to do. It puts the kidnapped party at risk. And, of course, enough cops are all on the take so the kidnappers *will* find out. Second, the wealthier families all have business dealings they would rather not bring to the attention of the authorities. The latter is doubly true for Gregor. Has Gregor said anything to you about an ask? I'm not on the inside; but I *can* help—at least, I have friends at Treasury who can."

"I don't know," Stonecrop said. His head hurt. The more he heard, the more concerned he became. "I need to eat. Up for lunch?" It was time to leave the house, or at least time to not be alone with Alicia. The temperature was dropping, and she had nestled closer to him. She was just cold, he told himself.

She took his arm and headed toward the gate. "Did Federica's colleagues notice anything? Like maybe these assholes threatened her at work? Shit, I'm so saddened by what happened to Marion, Christ . . . I hope to crap Federica's okay. She fucking better be . . ." Her tone of voice shifted from sad to angry.

Stonecrop ducked into the apartment to get a sweater and black watch cap. He made sure Rosie was inside and then rejoined Alicia. They squeezed into her rental Ford Focus. She was comfortable driving in Zürich traffic and slalomed down the hill to the Niederdorf, deftly avoiding trams, pedestrians, and cyclists—a trained driver.

Stonecrop restarted their conversation, "I'd like to bounce something off of you. I recently met a man, a business guy. He knows Fede and wants to help. He's a character. Part geeky engineer, into AI, robotics, and he's head of a high-tech DoD supplier—"

Alicia finished the sentence, "—with short hair, pants pulled up to the nipples, thick glasses. Do they still make pocket pen holders?"

Stonecrop went on, "Nope. Try a 300-pound creole-speaking black dude, mostly muscle, bald as an eight-ball, gold canine and gangster chain."

"Yeah, well *that* guy, I met him at a bar in Jamaica. Is Federica sweet on him? The girl *is* attracted to bright minds, like a moth to fire. They ain't gotta be pretty to make the cut." She spoke again before Stonecrop responded. "That's it, right. Bouncer is super smart? We've, ah, kinda known one or two of those."

It struck Stonecrop that he might be a candidate for being known. He wasn't looking and he didn't ask. "Bouncer boy *is* super smart. Speaks this Bahamian Creole, whatever that is."

Alicia offered more, "Yeah, makes sense. Pidgin languages are like her fetish—she collects them. She *loves* pidgin anything, they're *no nonsense*, she says. Practical, good for stuff like prices, weights, and dates. Weird the shit she gets off on, huh?"

That he agreed with but didn't want to digress and was growing tired of gossip. "Alicia, I like this guy. I truly did just meet him. Even his name is colorful. Dante Alexander. He was half the reason for the dinner, where, if you don't already know this, I delivered the kidnapper's note to Ratzow. I thought the note was a birthday card for Gregor." As he said the words Stonecrop reviewed for the thousandth time the circumstances under which he had received and delivered the note.

"It was to be a surprise," he said. "Arrived at my postbox the morning of Marion's accident."

"At Zürich Post or at your place?" Alicia asked.

"My apartment, across from Café Stehli," he answered. "I'm going to check with the family at Stehli today, to see if they saw anything."

After driving up and down Limmatquai a couple of times, Alicia gave up on parking. She dropped Stonecrop off to let him walk to his apartment and get a bite at one of the cafes along the riverside. She issued an invitation as he got out of the car, "I'm here for one night. Text me if you have time for a drink or want to get dinner. Back to London tomorrow. I'll do whatever I can to help. I gotta scoot—call coming up."

Stonecrop declined the dinner invite. He didn't want to socialize. And he sensed the invitation was for more than a drink or dinner. On the other hand, Alicia's suggestion implied that Federica had honored her part of the pact he and Federica had made, namely to not complicate their lives and to present themselves as friends, not lovers —at least until she had sorted out loose ends with Castro.

Had she had made similar pact with Hitoshi? *No, don't be an idiot.*

Stehli

Café Stehli, despite its quintessential Swiss-German name, was owned and managed by a family from Morocco. The Swiss owners had retired and sold the café to the Habibi family. So well had the neighborhood received the Habibi family, and so well had the Habibi family integrated into the neighborhood, that neither the threat of Islamic fundamentalism nor Swiss discontent over immigration detracted from the cozy ambiance and coffee/tea traditions.

The heart and soul of the establishment was Hamdi, a retired Moroccan national-team soccer player who, for thirty years, had been married to a Swiss. Sofia, his wife, was a head taller than Hamdi. Their boys, Michael and Johan, in their early-twenties and strikingly tall, worked at the café and played on local soccer teams. The younger, Johan, at twenty-three, was being wooed by several pro-league teams. His soccer credentials, handsome features, and modest manner were not lost on women who frequented Stehli.

Hamdi had resisted the temptation to make the café into a temple to soccer. Not a single jersey adorned the walls. What truly set Hamdi apart from other people was not soccer, but kindness. If two strangers who happened to have been Stehli customers at one time or another were to meet, the conversation would immediately turn to some act of kindness by Hamdi. Customers loved him, children loved him, and every dog walking by the café got a pat on the head and a treat.

Opposite the café's windows and tables, and across the narrow, cobblestoned Niederdorfstrasse, was the entryway and postboxes of Stonecrop's three-level apartment building. A plaque identified the building as a home of the Manesse family, who, in the early 1300s, had commissioned the creation of the Codex Manesse, a collection of *Minnelieder*—illustrated, lyric love songs. Stonecrop's kitchen window was two meters from where the plaque hung.

When Stonecrop arrived, Hamdi was carrying a silver tray above his shoulder, balancing a steaming, engraved pot of mint tea and two etched Moroccan tea glasses. Hamdi had been aware of Stonecrop well before Stonecrop reached the door—soccer instinct. It was an uncanny skill, and precisely why Stonecrop wanted to speak to him.

Hamdi set the tray on the table for his customers, poured their tea, and turned to Stonecrop. They embraced, and Hamdi spoke, "My friend, you are so serious, let me get you a coffee, not too hot. Do you smell them, fresh fig scones!"

It would be impolite to refuse. "Thank you."

"You are too young to worry. For me, it's another matter!" He tilted his head and looked toward Sofia, who was steaming milk.

Stonecrop extended his arms and held Hamdi's shoulders. "You look well."

"I am old, she works me like I am a beast of burden!" Hamdi held his ample tummy, the gesture intentionally at odds with the words.

"I have a question—" Stonecrop said.

"And I have a question for you! Who goes first? Please, you go." But before Max said a word, Hamdi jumped back in. "Shall I tell you what you are going to ask!"

"Okay," Stonecrop laughed. Hamdi's good nature always put him at ease. "What?"

"Have I seen anything unusual, or anyone watching the door to your building?"

"You *are* reading my mind!" Stonecrop was indeed surprised. And quickly realized what had transpired.

"I can't keep them straight, the people who ask me that question!"

Stonecrop gave Hamdi time to gather his thoughts.

"The first—no, he wasn't the first, he was right after the woman who was here. It was the hunched man from the Kantonspolizei. He eats here sometimes, wears a long black coat, has a white moustache. His hair is smooth like this," Hamdi put his hands to the sides of his head, "next to his ears. He is polite. And he has a funny name. In English, it is 'morning.' It was 'Morgan'—" Hamdi interrupted the dialog with himself. "No, later in the morning. Ah, here it is." He dug a card out of his pocket.

Stonecrop knew the name and said it before being shown the card, "Vormittag. Kommissar Vittore Vormittag, Zürich Kantonspolizei."

"Are you in trouble? He asked about the woman who was here

before him. Just about her. They are chasing each other's tails. You are not in trouble?

"I remember once, a customer was making fun of Johan. It was Ramadan; we were fasting. He was making fun of Johan for not eating. It was in a mean way. That policeman was here and saw the man doing this. Mr. Morning said nothing, but then he took the rude man's arm. He squeezed the arm like this!" Hamdi squeezed his own upper arm to demonstrate how hard the man's arm had been squeezed. "He walked the man out the door and they talked. The man was angry but walked away. He never came back."

Stonecrop waited to make sure Hamdi had finished, then responded to his question. "I am not in trouble, Hamdi," he said, "but, you *can* help me."

"Wait! Listen! Not more than an hour after Mr. Morning, another gentleman comes. I've seen this one before too. He's a dead fish, stiff and thin. His eyes are black. His wears a banker suit. The vest has little pockets, like gills." Hamdi used his fingers to draw lines across along his ribs for the vest pockets. "He had a silk handkerchief, here." A finger went to his chest where there would be a pocket square.

"Hamdi," Max laughed, "Black eyes? C'mon."

"As you say, but I'm the one who saw him." Hamdi paused and looked around, maybe for other people with black eyes, to make the point that people can have black eyes. "He asks me the same question as the woman. And *he* hands me a card. I am so popular now that my wife is suspicious. Johan tells her these people are yacht brokers and I am secretly buying a boat, and naming it Yasamin, after my mistress— which, praise God, I don't have! I don't have either one: a boat or a mistress. Or another wife. One woman is plenty!" Hamdi threw his arms up in the air.

"He gave you a card as well?" Stonecrop asked.

"Yes, I think he is not your friend," Hamdi said.

Stonecrop did indeed know him; it was Geissner's card.

"An associate, I work with him. And the woman?" he inquired, although it was obvious who the woman was.

"Oh, yes. The woman, she was the first. She spoke to Johan, flirted with him. Not the proper way, he is a good boy. Sofia and I were not here. The woman was older, much older, Johan said, and should not be flirting with a younger man."

Stonecrop interrupted, "Claudia."

Hamdi's eyes brightened, "Yes, Claudia, that was her name. Johan said she embarrassed him."

"What did you and Johan say to these people?"

"Would I invite them for tea? No! It is a sin to gossip and spy on each other. They were, except the woman, not your friends. We said nothing. Nothing."

"The woman is my friend?" Stonecrop asked, surprised by Hamdi's comment.

"Maybe, maybe! One man is good but unsure, a judge; one man is bad; but the woman, she is is your friend."

The queue of inquisitors haunted Stonecrop's imagination. Sofia passed by. She put a latte in front of him before attending other customers. Stonecrop thanked her.

"You said nothing to them?" Stonecrop was convinced the garrulous Hamdi had said something.

"Johan saw nothing, he said nothing. He is honest. I told them nothing. Maybe I am not honest; but I am just. I will tell *you* what I think they wanted to know."

"It was none of their business," Stonecrop defended Hamdi.

"Michael. It was Michael who saw something. Last Wednesday—the day the man in the gray suit and woman mentioned, he saw a woman at this table, watching." Hamdi pointed out the window. It offered a direct line of sight to Stonecrop's apartment building. "She watched for an hour. Then, at ten you left, like you do most days, to walk the dog— the one you bring here—for that nice lady. Michael saw you. He waved, but you turned up Napfgasse and didn't see him. After you left, the woman left. She paid for her tea. Green tea. Michael went back to the kitchen to help Sofia. He thinks the woman might have walked towards a man standing outside." Hamdi waited for Stonecrop to react.

"What did she look like, Hamdi?" Stonecrop asked with an unintended edge to his voice.

"Easy, my friend, easy," Hamdi said. "Michael said she was short, like me. And her skin, he said the woman's skin was like flour, never in the sun. Older, but not really old—we are all old to Michael! She wore glasses, with lenses like so," he made circles with his fingers and held them up to his eyes. "Gold. Like a model. The woman had a brown fuzzy coat, good for the cold."

"And the man she met?"

Hamdi tilted his head back, trying to remember something else. "Maybe a Turk? Michael wasn't sure. There are a lot of Turks in the city these days. Tall, dressed nicely, and with long hair, like the hair of a woman."

Stonecrop tried to remember faces, faces he had, for seven months now, been trying to forget. He drew a blank.

They choose the Santa Lucia, a pizza joint a few blocks from Stonecrop's apartment. It had meant another drive down the hill for Alicia, but she had not objected and, if anything, had been pleased by the invite. Stonecrop was restless after his conversation with Hamdi.

"You've known Federica a long time," he said. Maybe they had already exhausted the topic of Federica's abduction and Marion's condition and there were no fresh insights to be had, or maybe not.

"We're like sisters, friends since boarding school in Leysin. We really got close in Chicago—really close—when Federica was at the University, though it bored the hell out of her. She switched to the Royal College of Physicians in Dublin after a year at Chicago. The European systems fast-tracks the doctor path. It's what she wanted.

"Chicago did not challenge that girl, not at all," Alicia shook her head, adding, "Did she ever tell you about our girl-thing there?"

"You mean the two of you?" he asked.

Alicia took her time responding, intimating that if he didn't know what she had referred to, then maybe it would be better to say nothing. After a slug of wine, she waved her free hand back and forth across the top of the glass, signaling No. "Our club."

"Not a word."

Their table was small. Alicia slipped her feet between Stonecrop's. She smiled at whatever mischievous secret she was hiding.

"My legs are cold. Okay?"

"Sure. Mine, too," he said, to be accommodating though his feet were toasty. "About the club? Was it like a fight club?"

"Well, not exactly. You guys are an item, right?"

"Sort of," he said, and then decided she deserved more, a quid pro quo. "We don't broadcast it. To be honest, I'm still a little raw from the divorce. And so is Fede—uncertain, that is. She was, until recently, Andreas' fiancée. When I listen to myself describe our relationship it sounds like we're a mess. It's simpler than that. I love Fede, I really do. Quirks and all."

"Yeah, I thought so . . . Well, I get it, Max. Look, I'm not trying to butt in. He's a sicko creep, by the way. Andreas. He was never a real thing for her." She pressed her legs against his, telegraphing the opposite of what she had said about butting in. Or maybe she really was cold. An impish expression surfaced, and then faded as she concentrated on her pizza, eating it by folding the piece in half lengthwise and attacking it without benefit of fork and knife.

"I'm a Chicago girl, but I like this, even with the thin crust," she spoke the words half-way through the slice and with food in her mouth.

"The Club?" he said.

She finished chewing and drained her glass; the wine was a cheap house red. Stonecrop refilled the glass from the earthenware carafe and then topped off his own glass.

"Fuck it, why not," she said, as if she were placing a bet at the track. "It was a sex club."

"A *what*?" he asked. He must have misunderstood what she had said.

"A sex club."

"Whoa, didn't see that coming," Stonecrop laughed, still not sure if she was kidding or not.

"Federica's gonna kill me—" Alicia stalled, hung up in her own thoughts, the "if she's alive" unstated. "Okay, just the essentials," she smiled, "note please, I omitted 'bare.' "

Stonecrop groaned.

"A few of us girls, all at Chicago, started what I suppose you could call an erotic experiment. We'd pair up with someone we had never met, someone who had been selected by other girls in the group, for an erotic and mostly anonymous rendezvous. Like Tinder with QC."

"That was when her hair was edgy and asymmetric. Yeah, I can see that."

"The encounters followed a protocol. Both participants were blindfolded—I mean really blindfolded so the blindfolds wouldn't fall off. The players were directed to not speak to each other, although some did a little. The room, we called it the 'pit', which sounds gross now, had a futon on the floor, a kind of scuzzy sofa, and cushions and pillows, and a basket with a few sex things, almost never touched. We had a cam in the pit and watched from a comfy settee where two—it was always two of us—acted as monitors. The couple in the pit took it from there. They had one hour. The monitors made sure the couples followed the rules. Basically, nothing too crazy."

"Man, I went to the wrong school! Did you guys do this a lot?"

Alicia responded too quickly. The timber in her voice undermined the outwardly blasé demeanor. "No. Gosh, not at all! The organizational work and planning sucked up hours and hours. All of us, except Federica of course, had to study. Fuck—"

A tear rolled down each of Alicia's cheeks. Like Stonecrop, she'd been holding, or trying to hold back, the wrenching reality of Federica's disappearance.

"Have you watched her . . . with someone?"

"No. She watched me once, I think. I never saw her. After a while, we realized that the format was inherently limiting. I mean, there are people watching everything, and nobody was, like, a professional porn star. Quite the opposite. Nevertheless, I kinda get hot thinking about it." Her legs twitched.

"Yeah, but men are pigs." Stonecrop opined. "Did it get ugly?"

"No, I don't think so." Recovering her composure, she challenged his statement. "Most of the guys, and girls too, were scared shitless. See, that's the thing, they were all these super nerdy tech types. We were terribly, terribly selective—that was the whole point! The club was set up to lure these super-smart, super-shy, hot guys or women. And, they had to be basically good people. You know, the sweet geeky guy at college who never gets any. No jerks allowed. After a few sessions, it was obvious that the encounters were little more than missed-out-on high-school make-outs. We were so keen for a wild erotic adventure . . . and given how damned naïve we were, the make-out sessions qualified. Nothing serious ever happened. It didn't for me. It was a stretch—a tough sell, believe it or not—for most everyone. Eventually we lost interest. And, like I said, the time commitment."

Alicia looked up, smiled, and closed her eyes. More tears came. "Fucking crazy girl. I hope she's okay. I love her too, I really do."

Stonecrop said nothing.

"Well, it was silly fun, and more innocent than it sounds."

"Fede's never said a word," Stonecrop said.

"If you tell her I told you, she'll kill me. But then she'll laugh."

"Are you still in touch with the other women in the club?"

"Only one, other than Federica."

"And the men? They obviously knew some of you. Any happy endings?"

"Hardly!" she laughed. "And nope, none of the men."

"You sure? My very first sort-of-girlfriend found me on Facebook the first day I had an account! Day two I deleted the account." Stonecrop wanted more. He asked Alicia about Fede and their year together when Fede had been a young exchange student in Chicago and had lived with Alicia's family.

It was a way to think about Fede, to think about something in lieu of having a clear plan of action to find her. Before parting, they agreed to update each other the following night. Alicia had an early flight to catch. She unwound her legs from his, gave him a good-bye hug, and left for Susenbergstrasse.

Stonecrop stayed for a second grappa. His thoughts alternated between imagining how he would have reacted had he been one of the chosen—he too had been a naïf, and a late bloomer—and second, how the fuck would he deal with whoever had taken Federica.

The following day Stonecrop canceled all but one delivery, a photograph from a collector in Küsnacht to be transported to a gallery/frame shop in town. He would take advantage of being in Küsnacht to visit Geissner, who, although he rented office space in Zürich, often worked from home. It was the weekend, mid-morning; there was an even chance Geissner would be there. Importantly, Geissner might have an update.

Geissner's home on Conrad-Ferdinand-Meier-Weg was a typical domicile for a well-to-do resident of Küsnacht. The house was cream colored with black shutters that bracketed paned windows. The tiled roof had a Dutch-gabled roofline, a feature that was in vogue in the '50s. The upper floor gave an unobstructed view of the lake.

Stonecrop parked a well-used Audi S6 Avant, a loaner from Ratzow's collection, next to Geissner's spotless, silver Porsche Cayenne. The Porsche was his wife's car; every housewife in Küsnacht had one. He knocked on the door and was greeted by a green, talking plant. The plant was half his height and had long flappy arms and feet.

"Grüezi—hello," the plant said.

The rest of family had gathered beyond the plant and were readying to head out the door.

"Grüezi mittenand—hi everybody," Stonecrop announced, "I'm sorry to barge in. I see you're just leaving."

Geissner approached. He was carrying a box of miscellaneous theater props. He handed the box to Uta, who exited with the giant plant and a smaller child in tow.

"Hello, Max," Geissner greeted him, and then nodded toward the plant walking by. "Little Shop of Horrors dress rehearsal. You have something from Gregor?"

"No. I was picking up a photograph in Küsnacht. Thought I would stop by in case you had anything for Gregor."

Geissner took Max's arm and walked him back toward the S6. He spoke in a quiet voice, "Nothing right now. We'll be busy tomorrow. I'll have to get the cash together; it will be a few days. Probably need a hand then. Two million U.S. is a substantial volume of cash—a couple of suitcases. Who does anything with cash these days? Utterly baffling!" he complained.

Stonecrop played along, angry that he had not been told about the ransom request. It was Gregor's infuriating Modus Operandi, wherein he was the only one who played with a full deck, the only one who had all the information. He'd seen the same behavior with a few CEOs when he'd been a venture capitalist.

Geissner did not mention Federica by name. He was in a hurry, as always.

"Do you need help?" Stonecrop asked.

"Yes, I need help." Geissner spit the words at him. "It's not like the old days, when having a Swiss account meant something."

"I mean with loading up the car," Stonecrop clarified.

"What? No."

Geissner turned to walk away but Stonecrop grabbed his shoulder and spun him around, harder than he had intended. Geissner would have a bruise.

"And Federica, is she alright?" he bore down on Geissner.

"Yes, yes. Fine. Please talk to Gregor, will you? He told me he had spoken to you." His voice cracked. The testiness had been tempered by fear and surprise at Stonecrop's brusque behavior.

Stonecrop got in the car. His body was tense. He forced a smile and waved goodbye to the family. Only the plant waved back at him, cheerfully flapping a long green arm from the half-opened back window of the Porsche Cayenne.

Ein Traum

The owner of the gallery and frame shop, Herr Bachman, spotted Stonecrop standing outside and bearing a flat, square package. The parcel was approximately thirty inches on a side. Leaning on his cane, a late-1800s artifact, he made the journey from the back of the shop to the front door. The shop was closed Sundays. He unlocked the door to let Stonecrop in. Once inside, Stonecrop handed him the parcel.

"Have you seen it?" Bachman asked.

They knew each other reasonably well, or well enough to know each other's routines. Once or twice a month, Bachman hired Stonecrop to make a delivery or pickup, assuming the work was small enough to fit in the back of a van or car or could be carried by hand and was within the city proper. These chores, of all the various chores he did as a one-hundred CHF per hour courier, were among his favorites. In his past life, he had often accompanied Matti when she had been required to personally escort a valuable delivery to a museum or private collector.

Stonecrop was not an artist. He did, however, appreciate art. He'd watched Frau Ott as she painted watercolors of the garden and admired the uncanny ease and economy with which she captured the season, the arc of an iris stem, or the chaos of her out of control magnolia.

Art mattered to Frau Ott. The house was cluttered with paintings and prints, sculptures and textiles, ranging from unknown works by young Zürich artists—including neighborhood children—to museum pieces. In Fede's bedroom, an imposing painting, almost as tall as the ceiling, casually leaned against the wall. The oil, from Dubuffet's *art brut* period, was worth more than the house.

Bachman, a longtime friend of Frau Ott's and her deceased husband, had opined about the Susenbergstrasse house rules to Stonecrop:

Anyone staying at Susenbergstrasse must love and respect art. Frau Ott's vetting process was a mystery. Federica had made the cut, as had Stonecrop.

"Nope, didn't see it." Stonecrop was distracted. He checked his phone again for a return call from Ratzow. He had called right after he left Geissner's. He was furious about not having been included in Ratzow's update about Federica.

"Shall we?" Bachman didn't wait for a response and placed the crate on his work bench. With a utility knife, he carefully slit the duct tape along the seam binding two pieces of protective plywood. He fanned open the top piece of plywood and then removed the protective tissue covering a photo of a woman in an apartment. Part of her face, the midsection of her torso, and her feet and hands were uncovered. The remainder of the naked figure was concealed behind a translucent, stained, and tattered strip of floral wallpaper which, like a cardboard sari, wrapped around her slackened body and expressionless face. Directly behind her, a dilapidated plaster wall separated two double-hung windows. Curled peels of dried paint garlanded the window frames; unidentifiable detritus littered the floor. The vista through the two windows was as void of life as her eyes.

"Thoughts, Max?" Bachman asked.

The wallpaper wrap reminded him of the rug he'd worn in Maputo, its harsh stiffness, and how vulnerable and naked he had felt. Of course, he couldn't explain this association to Bachmann. What else did the photograph say to him?

Stonecrop took a minute before responding. "She *is* the photograph," he said. "It's like there's no separation between the *self* and the work. A longing for something desperate and hopeless."

"Interesting assessment. This is a self-portrait by a brilliant, young photographer. She committed suicide in her early twenties—not long after making this piece. Tragic. I knew her parents," Bachman said and subsequently qualified the statement, "Not well, but we had met."

Bachman and Stonecrop stood next to each other and looked at the photograph. Stonecrop's mobile vibrated.

"Your handy, Max. Your handy just buzzed," Bachman observed.

The vibration of the phone ran through his body.

<GR: 15 minutes at Storchen. F ok>

"Max, what's wrong?" Bachman asked. Stonecrop didn't respond. Bachman put a hand on his shoulders and guided him to the sofa in the studio. "Please, sit. Shall I get some water?"

Stonecrop put his face in his hands. His fingers reached upward and dove into his shaggy hair.

"You want to talk?" Bachman asked.

"She's alive," Stonecrop said to himself. "She's alive." Until this moment, this text from Ratzow, he had been afraid to believe that she was alive.

Bachman limped to the gallery's kitchenette for the water. He returned sans cane and with the water glass full to the brim, having spilled none of it despite his uneven gait. He sat next to Stonecrop.

"Here. Sit here. As long as you'd like."

Stonecrop raised his head, took the glass of water and emptied it in one long drink. He wiped his lips with the back of his hand. The scar tissue on the back of his hand reminded him of Federica. Everything reminded him of Federica.

"Thank you."

Bachman placed his hand on Stonecrop's back. "I'm afraid she's not, Max," he said, thinking of the photographer.

"She is," Stonecrop asserted.

"Whatever you say."

Stonecrop stared into space. "I will find her. Like in Maputo. I found them."

"What's that?" Bachman asked.

This time, when he spoke, he faced Bachman. "I've got a talent for finding people. " An unpleasant laugh accompanied thoughts awash in black vagaries.

In a reassuring voice, Bachman recited a line from a poem:

"Wie Schatten auf den Wogen, schweben und schwinden wir —"

Stonecrop knew the poem by Johann Herder and interrupted. He didn't have the patience for the rest but translated the line as he understood it.

"Like shadows on the waves, we float and disappear—"

The photograph had thrown Stonecrop into the abyss. What had Bachmann intended by quoting Herder? Was it the temporality of our existence and our problems. *Well fuck that! She is not gong to disappear.* He inhaled deeply and forcefully expelled the air through his mouth. He started, as if surprised to find himself sitting on the sofa next to Bachman. "I have to go. Sorry, Herr Bachman. I have to go now. Thank you for the water." The words implied there would be no further inquiry.

"Thank you so much. You're a kind man."

Stonecrop let himself out and looked up and down the street. There were few pedestrians. The trees were mostly bare. A leaf seesawed through the air to a rendezvous with its shadow on the sidewalk. Ἀλλήλων. We are one.

Patio

Ratzow was once again seated at his table at the Storchen patio, an open fur coat over his shoulders. The coat was for show. Ratzow was oblivious to cold. A few dishes on the table displayed the remnants of lunch. A bold sparrow made off with *une frite*.

"Max, better to explain, da, better in person." Ratzow motioned to him to sit in the chair next to him. A blanket was neatly draped over the back of the chair but Stonecrop ignored it. He nursed his vodka, neat, and pushed a tray of nuts to the middle of the table. "Drink?"

"Why not."

Ratzow waved to the waiter and pointed to his drink and then Stonecrop.

"I saw Geissner this morning. He said he was getting the money together. I suppose Claudia mentioned our not so pleasant conversation last night."

"Is nothing, the thing with Claudia. Look! I am busy man!" He pulled a handful of messages on Storchen notepaper; each one contained a time-stamp, name, and telephone number. "Herr Doctor Weller, Rachel, Alicia, Frau Ott . . . I am busy man!"

"Gregor, I don't give a shit about how busy you are. What's happening with Fede!"

Ratzow delivered the words Stonecrop hoped to hear, "I spoke to her."

"Why didn't you call me?"

"They ask for money first. I said only after I talk with her. Later I get this shit recording. Is bad, very bad. After recording, they call second time. We talk. She is okay."

"What's on the recording?" His drink arrived. Stonecrop took a sip and felt better. He realized that he hadn't eaten for hours. That empty pit in his stomach wasn't only anxiety. He grabbed a handful of almonds.

"You want to hear?" Ratzow asked.

"Wait, you recorded the call?"

"Look. I do this," he pointed to an app on his phone, "and last call is still there. Good because sometimes I forget what I say."

"I want to, of course."

"Is bad stuff, okay. Next one is better."

Ratzow put the phone on speaker and scanned the patio area to insure no one was within earshot. "Ready?"

. . . .

The first words were muffled. He couldn't really hear them. She was gagged, drugged, or her head was covered with something. There was an echo; the space had to be relatively small, perhaps with stone walls. Stonecrop worried about her claustrophobia.

"What are you doing?" came through. It *was* her voice, fearful and angry, but it was Federica.

"Let go of me, fuck-face," was followed by a loud thud—her breath stolen by a punch in the gut. A metal chair clanged to the ground. A medley of breaths and grunts accompanied a struggle.

Another scuffle followed. A deep-voiced man grunted from exertion. It sounded like he was trying to flip over Federica's body. Metal chains grated on the floor and rang when they collided with a chair.

"Fuck you, asshole!" she screamed. A second thud elicited a groan, the kind of groan that comes from heaving something heavy.

A man was panting, winded from the struggle. Out of the silence came the sound of a leather belt being whipped out its belt loops, and then air forced out of her lungs from pressure on her torso. The assailant whispered something.

Another slap followed, a moan shrank to a mew and a second period of silence. A new voice barked something unintelligible. Someone racked the slide on an automatic handgun.

. . . .

White hate blinded Stonecrop. He wanted to travel like an electron back through the recorded message, back to its source, and annihilate the person or people tormenting Federica.

"I know, I know," Ratzow said. He was waving his hand in the air, like he was brushing away an mosquito. "They will die," he said matter-of-factly. "But she is okay."

Ratzow took the phone, started a second recorded conversation, and handed it to Stonecrop, once again putting it on speaker. "Listen."

. . . .

"Papà, I love you. Are you there?" The words came slowly, drawn out by drugs, dehydration, or worse.

"Did they hurt you?" Ratzow's voice was tender.

"A little. I miss you, and Max. Is he there? How's Marion."

"No. She is same. I come soon. They want money. I pay. Right away. Soon you come home."

"I want to go home. No police. They said to say that."

"Are they there? You see them."

"Yes, but I can't see their faces. They're listening."

"Good. You shitheads, if you hurt one hair on my daughter's head, I kill you and all your children and their children. Did they hear that?"

"Yes, Papà."

. . . .

"Anything on the phone numbers?"

"Nothing. Calls come from different numbers."

"Fuck. Gregor, what do we do?" Stonecrop asked.

"You do what I tell you, yes, and Federica comes home—how you say—in jiffy."

"Fill me in or I'm heading straight to the Kantonspolizei." The ask and the implied threat were spoken slowly and deliberately. "I want to help."

Ratzow smiled, shaking his head, like a father dealing with an impertinent son. "Good intentions. Lucky for you. Federica likes you. Me too—like you to point, young buck; I like you to point." The repetition was a habit when he wasn't sure what to say.

"Call Polizei right now if you want. Here is phone!" He laughed and held his phone out. Stonecrop thought about grabbing the man by the lapels and dragging him into the Limmat.

Ratzow lowered his voice, their faces close, "You will pay if you fuck this up." He gave Stonecrop time to mull over what he had said, and added, proud of himself, "That is real threat, Max. You understand real threat?"

Stonecrop got the message and was unmoved. "You know how to swim?" Stonecrop said, only half in jest.

Ratzow softened his tone, "Max, I have done things I am not proud of. You, too—you are quiet man, man with regrets. Here, in heart." Gregor put his fist over his heart. "Us two, da."

Stonecrop's response was written in his eyes. *I do, Gregor. You're about to be my next regret.*

Ratzow continued, "Where I come from, my town, it is the way we grow up. Fight with fists. I am *borets*—wrestler! I am old, yes, but I remember everything like yesterday. Now, I am careful. Not—as you say—hot-head."

Ratzow had more and Stonecrop wanted more.

"Federica says you are her special friend—whatever the hell a special friend is. She has said this many times. She is not sharing feelings. She is warning me—can you imagine—to be nice to quiet Max Stonecrop, the man with regrets. The question, Max, is why she is warning me? How would she feel if I wasn't nice to quiet man? What would quiet man do? I never ask. But now, no Federica to answer question. Da, that's why I ask Claudia."

"Does Federica know the truth about your past . . . difficulties?"

Gregor looked toward the river, smiling to himself as he mouthed the word "difficulties."

Stonecrop and Federica intentionally lived in the present. Their relationship was breezy. Effortless was the best word to describe it. *Was that normal? Did it matter? We're happy enough. Why did this shit happen?*

"You are diplomatic Mr. messenger boy. We walk. I have fifteen minutes." They rose and downed the remains of their vodkas in unison, then headed south in the direction of the Münsterbrücke, the bridge crossing the Limmat and linking the Fraumünster and Grossmünster.

Max thought of the two churches in terms of gender: the Fraumünster—built on the remains of a former women's abbey, is identified by the graceful upward sweep of its single, blue-green copper-tiled clock tower. Light passes through slender Chagall-painted windows and suffuses the sparse interior with an insubstantial solemnity. The Grossmünster, by contrast, is a ham-fisted sixteenth-century reformation church, rumored to have been built by

Charlemagne on the patch of earth where his horse fell to its knees above the graves of the city's patron saints, Felix and Regula. Grossmünster's twin towers—two chunky pepper shakers, Richard Wagner called them—lacked grace. On the side of the southern tower, the blank-eyed and grimacing Charlemagne was seated either atop the throne, or, equally believable, a toilet.

Stonecrop and Ratzow resided across the river from each other, like the two churches. Their residences and lives—like the churches—were juxtaposed.

Ratzow guided them through the Roman Bath's passageway and then along the front of St. Peter's, yet another defining church in the city. Its clock face was the largest in Europe after Big Ben, a fact Zürchers were proud of.

"Max, you need story for Polizei? It is true, years ago, maybe I did many bad things. I had—still have—a transport company, AIT, Ltd, All International Transport. Is part of GR Group in Malta. Federica speaks Maltese, you know that? I don't speak word. AIT works all over. Africa, South America, Japan. I did the same thing you do for me. You don't ask your customers what is in the box; you make delivery. You do your job, da. I did mine."

"My packages are documents or art, and I walk a dachshund in the park, Gregor. Hardly the same thing," Stonecrop replied.

Ratzow smiled again, unfazed by Stonecrop's dissent. The fresh air helped their moods. "Dangerous work," he wagged his finger. "The dachshund!" He , "We make deal. Someday you tell me your story," Ratzow's expression was comic, the old one eyebrow up and the other down trick, "and I tell you mine. I asked Claudia to get your story. She finds nothing. Maybe Federica said hands off her quiet man, and Claudia knows best to be on good side of Fede. Or maybe Claudia finds nothing. What do I know! Women are too smart for Gregor!"

If Gregor was speaking the truth, Claudia had, as she had implied at the Rathaus, edited what she had passed on to Ratzow.

"This is what I *can* tell you," Ratzow continued, "Claudia and I know the people who took Federica. I am still worried, but not so much now as before. They want money. I don't know why *now* they want money. We did business together long ago. Claudia has theory that there is unfinished business. Some people are too stupid to move on; they make old problems go in circles. Something to do if bored. We contact old gang—if they are still alive."

"Names?" Stonecrop asked.

"Better I not say."

"Gregor, tell me or I swear—"

"I know, I know, you throw me in river!" Ratzow laughed loudly and shook his head, acting as if he were proud of Stonecrop, "I like you Max, I like you!" It took him a minute to catch his breath.

"They are called Red Monkey. Yakuza—Japanese gang. Red Monkey were once piss-ant group, a branch of Yamaguchi-gumi. A twig. Not now. They own my old neighborhood in Tokyo."

Red Monkey meant nothing to Stonecrop. He had read about Yakuza in articles about organized crime in Japan.

"Uli said two-million U.S., in cash?" Stonecrop was determined to learn the truth.

"That is big worry . . ." Ratzow searched for the right words, "not like Red Monkey I knew. But I am old. Back then, was different—you scratch, I scratch. I don't understand the cash. And I don't understand two million."

"Meaning?"

"Peanuts," Ratzow said, "Chump change, da, chump change." He struggled to pronounce the words. It sounded more like "chimp change." "Maybe I gouge out their eyes—like Kazuo Taoka. I would—for Federica—I would go to war with Red Monkey. A lousy two million bucks." Ratzow spat, indifferent to passersby and city regulations. "Is insult, two million is shit!"

"Suppose it's renegades from Red Monkey who are working on their own?" Stonecrop suggested, shuffling along at Ratzow's maddeningly slow pace. "Would they hurt Federica?"

"Da, is Uli's theory. He's one hundred percent sure that is *exactly* what happens. I don't know. My Red Monkey *kuromaku* fix anything for me. His followers, they are called *kobun*, were loyal to death. He was true boss, *oyabun*. In Japan they say 'If oyabun says passing crow is white, then kobun agree.'

"Clear enough."

"Once Red Monkey, always Red Monkey. Old Yakuza were honorable. Patriots, even religious. Yakuza even have pension plan— better than Switzerland plan!"

Ratzow grinned, then moved his head up and down, like a silent yes to his own comment. "This is *good*: if Red Monkey has Federica, they stick to terms. We pay; she is not harmed. They are professionals. But if it is people pretending to be Red Monkey . . ." Ratzow drew a finger across his throat. The gesture got the attention of a couple who quickly stepped aside to let Ratzow and Stonecrop pass.

"How do you find out?"

"I am a professional, Max. This is how things work. Anyway, do I have choice?"

"The authorities, Kommissar Vormittag. That's a choice," Stonecrop offered.

"This is why I am boss and not you. Talk to police and Federica get hurt. They almost kill Marion. They may still kill Marion. Claudia has people watch her. Is no joke and is over your head and over head of the Kantonspolizei—and *they* know that. I will learn what the kidnappers *really* want. The money is toll to cross bridge. What is on other side of bridge? We find out. Then, Kantonspolizei help, after Fede is home."

Ratzow insisted upon beating the point to death. "Is bad if police swat team tries raid before I fix release." Ratzow warned. "Claudia talked to Vormittag about Marion. Claudia says Polizei have nothing. And Marion—it is sad one way, good another—cannot help."

"Thank you, Gregor," Stonecrop said, genuinely grateful. "I appreciate being in the loop."

"I am not making nice." Ratzow came back at him with an eyebrow raised, a sure sign of trouble.

Not speaking, they crossed the Münsterbrücke and headed back, downriver toward the Rathausbrücke. To the west and on the other side of the Rathaus bridge was the Hotel zum Storchen. Ratzow stopped and faced Stonecrop, who would now head the opposite direction to his apartment. He took Stonecrop's hand in both of his as if he in prayer and faced him.

"I am talking to you, Max, because I will need delivery man. That is what you do. I call soon. Don't go far."

Ratzow did not say goodbye. He released Stonecrop's hand, turned, and—at his slow, heavy pace— walked in the direction of Zum Storchen.

ASVZ

He set the timer on his Suunto watch for thirty-five minutes. An eddy of garnet-colored leaves swirled in the air a few inches above the reddish, rubberized oval at the ASVZ, the Akademischer Sportverband. The difference in color between the leaves and ground created the illusion that a patch of track had separated and lifted off the surface. Stonecrop's concerns gathered at his feet like some viscous resistance through which he had to run. The first mile was a grunt.

A fridged wind dogged him on the upwind half of the oval. He hated running in the mornings. He loathed pushing his stiff-with-sleep body. Yet, here he was, in exercise purgatory, pounding out the laps.

The track was bordered by FIFA headquarters—*Federation International de Football Association*, the Zoo, and the Zürich University athletic facility; all were in a peaceful corner of Zürichberg park. The wooded setting was above the hustle-bustle of the city and only a short distance from Frau Ott's, though a four-kilometer 200-meter climb from Stonecrop's apartment on Münstergasse.

After ten minutes, he dropped into the zone and was no longer consciously training. He became an animal engaged in movement per se.

The frost in the air brought back memories of workouts at the Olympic training center at Lake Placid, New York: pre-season fartlek trail-runs in forested hills, footfalls on frozen dirt, and the crack of brittle-with-cold underbrush. Stonecrop had never taken his conditioning level or good health for granted. He had been born a thoroughbred and he was determined to stay one. He used but did not really need a pulse monitor to know his heart rate or pace.

Like Zen archers performing Kyūdo, competitive biathletes practice and perfect their routines until the routines become rituals and then the rituals become part of their DNA: Approach the shooting stations at 175 beats per minute, drop poles, flip the snow guard, position rifle, insert the five-cartridge magazine and, with an exhale, settle into the bone-on-bone, elbow-to-hip stance that stabilizes the body.

Stonecrop had been conditioned from the contrasting mental states: skate-skiing like a crazed animal and then focusing like a neurosurgeon. Five targets, five shots, sweep them right-to-left. If you shoot from left-to-right and shoot right-handed the weight of the barrel can make the last bullet drop, resulting in a miss. It took total concentration to choreograph the trio of breath, pulse, and trigger pull.

On the first shot, rapid heartbeats cancel each other out and the concentric rings of the target and sights, once aligned, quiver as though suspended in a magnetic field. The next two shots were the hardest, the transition from a continuous heartbeat to discrete heartbeats. The target bobbed up and down at a descending rate and distance with each beat so that the shooter had to anticipate where the target would be. There was a rhythm to it and you were either in the zone or not. Below 140 bpm one had all the time in the world to squeeze the trigger. The bullet left the barrel half-way through the exhale of the third breath and midway between heartbeats. As soon as the fifth round was loosed the rifle and attached harness was slung overhead and dropped into place on the shoulders. Then pick up his poles and skate like your life depended upon it. That was Stonecrop's routine. Every competitor's routine was unique.

Stonecrop had kept and still practiced with one of his rifles, a circa-70s bolt-action 1827 Anschutz with a custom Eberle stock. He'd given his straight-pull-action Fortner to a young biathlete who couldn't afford a rifle.

The beeping from the Suunto ended his reveries. He'd logged five or so kilometers. The fuzz in body and mind was gone. He gathered his things from the visitor's bench and headed toward the tram station.

Dante had sent him a text, <DA: we need to talk>

<MS: call in 1 hr.>

The tram was parked at the station and preparing to depart. He loped the remaining distance and climbed aboard the Number 6 for the seventeen-minute ride to Zürich Central. From there it was a five-minute walk through the Niederdorf to Café Stehli. It was well past latte-o-clock.

He hoped Dante would have something concrete to share.

Potomac

The small table took up much of the kitchen area and the breakfast fare took up much of the table: a triple latte from Stehli; *bircher muesli*—oats, yogurt, and apple; and two still warm *halb-butter gipfeli*, i.e. Swiss croissants.

Alexander called as promised and walked Stonecrop through configuring his laptop connection so they would be able to converse and video and over a secure line.

"Appreciate the security protocol. Gregor rants about the phones being tapped. I think that's all it is, a rant . . ."

"S.O.P." Alexander said, and then, seeing the spread on the table, added, "Whatcha got there?"

"Next visit, we'll go. The bakery is a five-minute walk from here," he said, wondering what the reaction would be from the bakers if Dante walked through the door. Alexander's mass would take up half of the customer floorspace.

"Is Federica aware of Gregor's criminal past?" Alexander dove in.

"No clue. That is, I don't have a clue. We never talk about his business. She must have some idea. She knows Group had to go through a lot of hoops to get Swiss domicile. There was an issue about a tax filing. They don't throw you in jail here if you owe taxes. There's no stigma associated with it. You get a polite letter from the *Steueramt* —the tax office—and pay the penalty. End of story."

Stonecrop's vague response was enough for Alexander. "I've got an agenda for our call. You ready?"

"Fire," Stonecrop said, drowning a piece of croissant with bilberry jam. Even though science had discredited the claim, he chose to believe the old Royal Air Force myth that bilberries were good for night vision. His night vision had always been off the charts good; and he loved bilberry jam.

"Hitoshi Sato, Potomac's lead at New Order, warned me about Gregor and Group when he did background checks required for the guarantee to Aide Direct."

"Interesting. I met him, along with her ex, Andreas—"

"Let me finish," Alexander interjected. Stonecrop wondered why it was that whenever he wanted more about Hitoshi Sato, the conversation was cut off.

"When we met Uli at the airport," Alexander continued, "I didn't get why we were meeting, unless Gregor ordered Uli to smooth over the embarrassment of Federica being a no-show. If that was Gregor's intent, Uli went off-script."

"The reason for our getting together at the airport," Stonecrop clarified, "was me. *I* wanted to talk to you. Gregor and I have this disagreement. I think there's a connection between the kidnapping and Potomac. Gregor doesn't. Uli is Gregor's watchdog. I suspect he was there to keep an eye on *me*. To make sure the errand boy didn't talk out of school."

"You remember Uli mentioning Echo?"

"I do. Why?" Stonecrop picked up a change of tone in Alexander's voice.

"Echo is a hush-hush program. I never once mentioned it to Uli. Hitoshi Sato is in the loop, but Hitoshi also knows it would be a breach of confidentiality to say anything about Echo to Uli."

"You and I are discussing Echo. We don't have a CA. Happy to sign one," Stonecrop offered, the tone of voice making light of the need.

"We are, and I'm trusting you to treat our discussion as confidential."

"Fine," Stonecrop agreed. "And maybe it was that natural for Uli and Sato. I mean, these guys are seasoned business types. Uli probably thought a handshake with Sato was enough. Not unusual, the paperwork to follow. Did you say anything about Echo to Federica?"

"Never," he replied.

"So that means you have a little chat with Sato."

"Point taken," Alexander said, "and I've been trying to find him. He should be here. This is the FAA's drone standards conference. Sato was supposed to be a discussant on one of the panels. Potomac fielded the A-team and brought a demo drone, meaning this is a big deal for us. But our buddy, Hitoshi Sato, is AWOL." Alexander must have expected Stonecrop to ask a question. He waited before continuing.

"Not even a text from Sato. That's not like him. Even in when he's Osaka, anytime day or night, he picks up—"

"Kidnapped?" Stonecrop interrupted, in earnest about the possibility.

"Hell if I know; but probably not. After I got the official bullshit deflection from New Order—they said he needed "personal time"—I called his admin. I know the guy pretty well; he's a no-nonsense type. Anyway, he was teed off with both Sato and his bosses. Said the scuttlebutt was Hitoshi and some rich client were off on lark in the Seychelles. Said Hitoshi winked at him as he left and told him there *was* a family emergency, but it was for some fat client."

"Interesting."

"I hope he wasn't talking about me!" Alexander joked. "Hitoshi had been acting strangely. I mean stranger than his normal strange, which is a couple sigma out. Thrilled about the deal with AD, and then—bang—the next minute, he's talking me out of it. I sort of get it."

"Get what?" Stonecrop asked.

"Hitoshi paints a grim picture of Gregor and Group—transporting arms, drugs, export controlled items, you name it. Federica and Aide Direct are clean . . . he thinks. But, with Group as guarantor, the dirt rubs off. Critically, it rubs off on Potomac."

"But you went ahead anyway," Stonecrop observed. "Or were you planning to spike the deal?"

"I wanted a face-to-face with Gregor, ten minutes to get a read on the man." Stonecrop remembered Ratzow saying the same about Alexander. "The board okayed an arm's length subsidiary to lease and deploy scrubbed drones, so nothing that would make the DoD hot list. Let me tell you, it's a pain in the ass to manage."

"An expensive pain in the ass," Stonecrop added, then circled back to a side question he had had earlier. "Why Brussels? Odd location for a U.S. investment bank."

"Not really," Alexander said. "New Order's aviation defense clients are based there, as well as the FAA, DoD, NSA, and NATO. A hornet's nest of regulatory and defense agencies have set up shop in Brussels."

"What's New Order like?" Stonecrop asked. His VC gray cells were alive and curious. "I get the underlying mission. I'm wondering about the people."

Alexander took a breath. "They're wingnuts—a hodgepodge of ex-generals, bible thumpers, ultra-conservatives, long-jowled politicians, and techies." He waited to let Stonecrop digest what he had described.

"Hitoshi fits right in. He's paranoid about business improprieties and espionage. Claims he's never met a computer he couldn't hack. Takes notes on pen and paper. Claims he's less likely to be mugged than hacked. Probably true when you think about it.

"He's strange. Like you, Max. You're not a criminal, but you work for Gregor. Hell, we're all weird," Alexander laughed, "me included. I'm a bleeding-heart defense contractor."

The statement prodded unpleasant insecurities—the ITA, his own conflicted loyalties, and Mozambique. Was he truly like Sato?

"Dante," Stonecrop lightened up, "you know what *you* are? You're a Cayman Brac kinda guy," he poked fun at Alexander, who indeed reminded him of the bartender at Barracuda's.

"Got that right! Been to the Brac?" Alexander digressed.

"Yup. Good sailing, good climbing, good rum. A short hop to Cuba."

Alexander laughed, "Yeah, well, another conversation." He continued, "How'd you get mixed up with Gregor? Has to be Federica, right?"

"Right again. That too, is another conversation."

"Did you know Gregor from Africa?"

The question bothered Stonecrop. Why did Alexander link *that* to Gregor? It was a question that begged for an answer, like Uli asking about Echo.

With no response from Stonecrop, Alexander resumed his story, "After a month or so of hysteria and Federica persuading, Hitoshi gave in."

"Something else," Alexander continued. "Hitoshi is good about hiding his notes but he's lousy at hiding his feelings. He fell for Federica; hard. I got fed up with his angst and put pressure on senior partners at New Order. Told them my business could go elsewhere if they didn't keep it professional. Sato got booted off the commercial side for a while and was reassigned to scrubbing the technology. He's unbelievably good at it; brilliant."

Stonecrop ate as Alexander spoke. "In the end, Hitoshi's assessment was spot on. He went ballistic after a second due diligence report tarred Gregor. And here we are. We got a situation. One of the Gregor's people, Uli Geissner, knows about something he damned well shouldn't know about; and another party, whoever it was who took Federica, has a shitload of leverage with Gregor and Group, and by extension, Aide Direct and their supplier to be, Potomac Defense. All of which vindicates Hitoshi's rants about the sky falling."

"And it does establish a thin connection between the kidnapping and you guys. Even so, AD doesn't have anything of substance on the technology side, right?" Stonecrop asked.

"At the moment, very little. When we deliver the first drone, we'll see. My real concern, like yours, is that Federica is in the middle of this damned thing. And I pray for her friend—what was her name?"

"Marion Cook. Marion's alive but has serious cognitive problems." Stonecrop answered, and then brought the conversation back to where it had started. "Dante, was that the agenda?"

"Yeah. Three things, Max," Alexander rejoined. "First, how the hell did Echo become something that Geissner knew about? Second, where the hell is Hitoshi Sato? That's on my plate, not yours. And third, I'd like to do whatever I can to help you get Federica back. I'm not sure how I can help but I'd like to try. Just you and me. I will *not* work with Ratzow. I'm not afraid of him either. Remember, I battle bad guys for a living. I'm good at it."

"Fair enough." Stonecrop said, and shared what he knew: "Gregor believes Federica's abduction is an extortion play by a Japanese gang called Red Monkey. He plans to pay. I assume the Swiss police are moving forward with the investigation regarding Marion. I don't know if the police are aware of the kidnapping. They appear to be trying to contact Federica to question her apropos the assault on Marion. Gregor's covered up her absence, but his bullshit will only go so far. I don't believe Claudia, Gregor's henchwoman—is that a word?—has brought up the ransom note or Red Monkey with the Kantonspolizei."

"Red Monkey? I'll talk to neighbors at Meade and Langley. And Uli?"

"The Barracuda—sorry, that's what a friend of mine calls him—I saw him in passing after the meeting with Ratzow. Uli started bugging me for updates, which is backwards. I mean, he's the guy who should be in the know. When I mentioned Red Monkey I swear he turned red himself. He didn't say much, other than that they're Yakuza. He rushed off—some emergency. Uli always has an emergency."

"And what's your role, Max?" Alexander asked.

"Same old, same old. Messenger boy delivers payoff to Red Monkey. Swap's supposed to happen in a couple days. Uli's scrambling to get the cash together without attracting too much attention. He says that's why it's taking a while. He's stalling. I suspect Claudia needs time to work the Red Monkey connection."

"Yakuza. I know the yakuza, of course. Japanese Mafia, self-proclaimed chivalrous organizations—self-glorified thieves, if you ask me. However, their reputation for discipline is well-earned. And it explains Gregor's belief that Federica will not be harmed. If it is yakuza, they're as professional as they are violent. Yakuza are reputed to do what they say they are going to do—no more, no less. For once it may be better to not let police stir the pot."

Stonecrop dissented, "Dante, if they are such goddamned professionals, how the hell does it explain what happened to Marion? Give me a break, she's an old woman! She was not an element of anybody's impeccable plan. She got in the way and they bloody bungled it. Doesn't compute. So *not* professional. Gregor must be blind to the fact. He *wishes* to believe Federica will be safe, but that's not going make her safe."

"It doesn't," he conceded, "compute, that is. Then again, there's more going on than a kidnapping for money. How much?"

"Two million U.S.," Stonecrop replied.

"What! Horsefeathers!" Alexander was incredulous. "It would cost the yakuza double that to snatch somebody in Europe. They are transnational, but doing anything on Swiss soil has got to be a stretch. Unless it's an honor debt or something worth a heck of a lot more than two million." Alexander's voice was imperative. "I am going to see you in person, as soon as possible, before the drop. Stall them. I'll use Potomac's plane."

"Are you the pilot?"

"It is a hoot to fly. I could, but I'd need a co-pilot anyway. I'll use our pilots. It's a cargo Lear—there's a jump-seat. Fits one cheek."

"We'll skip the bakery visit," Stonecrop kidded him.

"I'll be in Zürich in a few hours. Do not," he made sure Stonecrop got the message, "*do not* tell anyone I'm coming to Zürich."

"Wasn't planning to," Stonecrop said.

"Dante," Stonecrop paused, "thank you."

"I'll be at the Airport Radisson. I got an idea." Alexander slipped into Bahamian, "I guh vatchin" duh fishes. It start."

Instructions

A day-and-a-half had gone by before Claudia called. The hiatus in action had given Stonecrop and Alexander time to settle in and run through their own hypothetical scenarios for the swap. Stonecrop had been excluded from discussions within and among Ratzow's team. To them, he was the delivery boy; instructions from Claudia to follow.

Claudia suggested a meeting with Stonecrop at the Lindenhof, once a Roman tax collection site and now a public square poised twenty-five meters above the west shore of the Limmat. To the east of the Lindenhof and along the river lies the Schipfe, the historical core of the city, and the setting for the Waisenhaus—a former orphanage dating back to the late 1700s. Sections of the Waisenhaus had been redesigned in the 1920s by Augusto Giacometti. Its vault and walls, once dull and drab, were transformed by Giacometti into colorful floral patterns. The entry hall is designated as a Swiss national treasure. Today, the building is headquarters of the Zürich Stadtpolizei, and where, on many days, one would find Kommissar Vittore Vormittag.

To be more geographically precise, Claudia wanted to make contact at Lindenhof Hedwig, a modest fountain and statue of a woman-warrior commemorating the legendary 1291 defense of the town by the women of Zürich. Any self-identification Claudia might have made with Hedwig seemed inherently heretical. Had Claudia thought the site propitious—it was an overly public place for a meeting—or simply that the site was convenient to other business she had scheduled. In either event, Stonecrop arrived early and took a seat on a cold iron bench near the fountain. He noted pieces of ice floating in the shadowed corners of the basin and hoped that Federica, wherever she had spent night, had not been cold.

A beaming Claudia arrived at the appointed time. She handed the keys for one of Ratzow's cars, a BMW 7-series, to Stonecrop. She had been drinking, although it was mid-day. She also handed Stonecrop a piece of paper with the directions. "Memorize, love. Then either eat or hand back to mama. Just like in the movies."

"When's the swap?" he asked.

"Tomorrow night, about supper time."

"Good, I think I know what I'm gonna eat for dinner," Stonecrop said, knowing exactly where the sarcasm had come from.

"Down boy," she replied.

It took a minute to review the instructions and visualize the directions. At the proposed time of day, the destination would be less than a half-hour drive followed by a ten-minute hop on the tram. He returned the sheet to Claudia. He knew the area well, as did many people; it was one of the most popular tourist destinations in the city.

Uetliberg is Zürich's own mountain. It rises in the west to 869 meters and commands a view of the city and lake, plus an impressive panorama of the Swiss Alps. Stonecrop had run the peak bottom to top and back once or twice a month since he had been living in Zürich.

His instructions were to drive to Uitikon Waldegg station and from there to take the 19:00 S10 to Uetliberg station. Cars were not allowed to drive to Uetliberg; the only public transport to the summit was by train and foot. A private access road did exist and was used for deliveries, emergencies, and transport of guests unable to use the tram and walk.

"In the trunk," she continued, "is a backpack full of Uncle Sam's finest. The cash is in a Jack Wolfskin pack, the kind used by mountaineers like you, love. The Nasties were quite specific—no idea why."

"Uetliberg is anything but private. I'm supposed to wander around with a backpack full of money and do a hostage exchange?"

"You don't just stand on the deck and gawk at the sunset, dearie. From Uetliberg terminal you cross the tram tracks. There's a playground, and a path marked with yellow signs for Im Sonnenbühl. It's a hippy-dippy spa and retreat, closed for remodeling. A five-minute trundle down the hill. The place should be empty. If not, text me. At an outbuilding under construction, there's supposed to be a large metal dumpster. It should be covered to keep out litter critters. If it's not, close the lid. Place the pack, back strap side up, on top of the dumpster. Got it? Straps up. Those things that go over your shoulders." She touched her shoulders and continued after Stonecrop nodded back to her. "The pack weighs fifty pounds. You, my strong boy, can handle it. To clearly identify the dumpster, our thoughtful Nasties painted a cute, little red spiral mark, like graffiti, on the side of it. Make sure you get the right bloody trash bin, love. Text me after the pack is in place."

"A red spiral, like so?" With his finger, he drew a concentric spiral figure in the air, like the symbol on the note. "Tourists are gonna piss on it—same spiral on the urinals at Sea-Tac."

Claudia batted her eyes. "Dearie, I didn't make this up. And those are black, not red. I've been there."

Stonecrop did not ask the obvious question her statement invited, so Claudia continued, "Love, I know this sounds like amateur hour." The eyes rolled and she sighed. "After the drop, you scurry back to the train station and wait for me to text or call. You're practically sitting on the bloody cell tower; reception will be peachy."

Claudia handed him a phone and charger, a burner model Ratzow preferred, and an attached Post-it note with a short list of code words for any conversation they might have on the phone. "There's one number in favorites—I'm your favorite, in case you didn't know! The Find My Phone app on this thing is activated. Remember, text or call after the drop. Do not linger at the site. No heroics. We don't want Federica to end up in the dumpster."

As an afterthought, she added "Or you, sweetie."

"How do you know Federica will be released. And where? Will I see her? She supposed to pop out of the goddamned dumpster?"

"No, but that would be a nice touch," Claudia waited for a group of tourists to pass by. "We text the Nasties when the drop is done. They say they'll confirm within a half-hour of the drop and give us Federica's location and pick up time. You sit tight. Promise me you won't stuff a 357 in your pants, dearie. The Swiss love their guns and so do you." "Everybody's got a gun here. Defend the Heimat—our sweet home-sweet-homeland."

"No problem, Claudia." He said nothing about the Anschutz biathlon rifle. Mention of a 357 gave Stonecrop second thoughts about what he had planned. The Anschutz uses a puny, low-velocity, twenty-two caliber long-rifle cartridge. At 950 feet per second the bullet is designed to *not* damage steel-plated biathlon targets and has a mere tenth of the stopping power of a common handgun bullet. Still, it was enough to kill.

"We'll call as soon as we have her location. Who knows, love, maybe she's spa-ing at UTO KULM. Whoever is closest will pick her up and zip back to Storchen for the happy reunion."

"And what's the plan B?" Stonecrop asked.

"No Federica, then we're out the money. Maybe. Or you trundle on back to the dumpster in case they don't grab the cash. Schlep it home."

"What'll Gregor do?"

"Hell if I know. Maybe decapitate every Red Monkey he can find and put their heads on stakes in the Tokyo National Garden. No idea, but there'll be hell to pay."

"Home, where home?" he asked.

"Your home, dearie."

"You mean my apartment?"

"Exactly. No running off to the tables." She flashed her curious U-shaped smile again. The act put a period on their conversation. "This is jolly fun. It'll be fine. No fuckups, dearie."

"Forecast?"

She looked at the sky, "Clear now."

Stonecrop shook his head.

"Dearie, I'm not the fuckwit weatherman!"

Matina

The Hauptbahnhof was a short walk from Lindenhof. There was a train every fifteen minutes to the airport. He would be at the Radisson in an hour, giving him and Dante time to map out a backup plan.

En route to the station he considered and for a second time rejected the idea of calling his children. The swap was tomorrow. He would call the kids after Fede's release—it would be eight hours earlier in Colorado. Sarah and Jenny might be ending a day at ski-school. Snow conditions for this early in the season were exceptional and the girls, like Stonecrop, loved to ski. An army of cousins and their parents had probably swept into town to stay with Matti, taking advantage of the good snow and Matti's generosity.

Matina and Federica had never met. Without having ever spoken, the two women seemed to hold each other in high regard, routinely asking about each other. It was a peculiar dynamic and entirely out of Stonecrop's ken. He remembered a recent conversation with Federica about Matti. He and Federica had been riding the tram.

. . . .

"Jenny and Sarah adore Mattie," Federica said. "Me too. She's a good mom. And she works hard. I follow her gallery's blog."

Stonecrop did not; it brought back too many memories.

"She is; kids come first," he said. "Mattie always says the art's not going anywhere and that her clients—they're like a who's who of the art world—can always wait."

"She's not really the snob you say she is." Federica had zero tolerance for snobbery. She was quite sensitive about and embarrassed by any talk about her own linguistic brilliance and uncanny memory.

"Maybe a kind of a reverse snob."

"Meaning?" Federica asked.

"Well, her house is a tasteful palazzo that's been featured in every architecture rag on the planet," Stonecrop answered, and added, "but she tools around in a fifteen-year-old Toyota. Refuses to get a new car. 'It's just sheet metal,' she says."

"Ah, so that's why you love me! For my seen-better-days Alfa! There's a pattern—the man is obsessed with auto Nonitas!" He asked her what in the hell a Nonita was. She tickled him and asked another question: "I read that Mattie lost a Renoir and then found it forgotten in the back of her car. Is that true?"

"Totally!" he laughed. "She tossed it in the back seat. Next day the kids folded the seats down to put ski stuff in the car and covered the painting. It was a while before it turned up."

"I love it!"

"To her credit she never lost the girls."

"Then, why *did* you guys separate, and then divorce? Is there like a dark side, like with Andreas? You've never once spoken disparagingly of her."

"Nothing abusive."

"The divorce was when you were away. Is that why?"

"Yeah, but that was neither here nor there. I mean, the reason we separated wasn't just my shenanigans in Africa, though that's the spin people put on it."

"And the real reason is?"

"It's hard to explain." Her question was something he had asked himself countless times.

"Try me." The tone was sympathetic, not combative.

Stonecrop composed his thoughts before speaking. "There was always something between us, something that needed to be resolved."

"In a marriage, isn't it invariably sex, money, or children?"

"Not at all. Not with us. Did you read that in *Cosmopolitan*?" he chided her. "No, Matti and I had this intangible malaise," he said. "The opposite of you and me."

"How so?"

"An unease. Like always being on eggshells."

"Explain, please. I don't understand."

"At first, we ignored the disconnect. We were busy with kids and work. But it got worse. We gave up trying."

Federica was openly dissatisfied with his explanation. "Romantic claptrap."

'Maybe so. A fairy tale that fizzled."

"Do you still love her?"

"In a way," he answered. "Not as a wife or lover."

"Better not!" she warned.

The pique of jealousy, so unlike Federica, surprised him. Probably feigned, he told himself, but asked anyway: "Are you worried?"

"No," she scoffed playfully. "You're the romantic airhead, not her."

Fede was holding his hand. He realized that he had been looking at passengers who were at stops and waiting for the tram. Was he avoiding Fede's face and the touch of her hand?

"You guys don't talk much. Is that changing?"

"Over time. The tabloids invent drama around anything she does. I don't want to feed the fire."

"Well, I suspect she's a class act," Fede said.

"She is that," he replied. "You aren't really jealous, are you?"

"Only a little," she said, and kissed him on the cheek. "Merde, we missed our stop!"

. . . .

Stonecrop started, suddenly realizing he had been daydreaming. In the here and now he'd missed the stop for the Radisson and would be late for the meeting with Dante. His memories had been so real; it saddened him to let them go.

Uetliberg

He arrived early at Uitikon Waldegg station. His car, one Ratzow's
BMWs, was parked fifty meters from the station at nearby Restaurant
Waldesruh. The restaurant stood between the parking lot and the train
platform, though there was a narrow gap through which the station
could be seen. The Wolfskin pack stuffed with cash was at his side. His
biathlon rifle was sheathed in a USBA rifle cover and attached to one
side of the pack. He waited for the S10 to Uetliberg and began to have
second thoughts about the plan he and Dante Alexander had
concocted.

Five-minutes downhill from the station, if one traveled by foot
along the wooded path of white-crushed stone, was Parkplatz
Feldmoos. There, Alexander had parked a rented, black Mercedes-Benz
Citan Panelvan and set up communications equipment to monitor the
exchange.

"Can you hear me?" Stonecrop tested the earpiece mic.

"Loud and clear," the basso profondo came back. It was followed by
the roar of a passing vehicle. "Shit!"

"What was that? High-pitched, like a V12 Ferrari. Round taillights?"

"Yeah, round. Ritzy neighborhood."

"The S10 is pulling in," Stonecrop reported.

The red/white Swiss flag colored Uetliberg S10 looked a toy train. It
was, of course, on time.

He boarded, took an aisle seat, and put the backpack with the
attached rifle on the adjacent window seat. The rifle bag was Cordura
nylon, a red, white and blue affair, faded from use and emblazoned
with the USBA logo. The assembly did not attract attention. In a
country where military service was required of every eligible young
man, it was not uncommon for passengers with rifles to travel on

public transport. Stonecrop had done training runs before with the covered rifle on his back. No one noticed or cared. Passersby often cheered him on when he was pushing through the steeper sections of a run.

The greater risk posed by the rifle would be when the kidnappers saw that he was armed. The rifle was a threat. Any interference with Federica's release would be costly.

The S10 broke through the clouds. The last light of the day struck the glaciated facets of the Eiger, Mönch and Jungfrau. The peaks shimmered like a three-diamond setting on the arc of the horizon.

Five minutes into the eight-minute ride he took a moment to inventory his co-passengers. Most were in the rear car. In his car there was a Japanese family. They seemed familiar with the tram and its trappings. Two young children, a boy and a girl, scurried up and down the aisle, trying different seats. The babysitter, also Japanese, tried and failed to get them to settle down. The parents ignored the commotion and held on to a baby stroller whose young passenger, bundled up for the chill, was unseen, unmoving and oblivious to the ruckus caused by older siblings. Mother and father, like Stonecrop, admired the sunset. The couple conversed in Japanese and nodded to each other, pointing once or twice to the clouds gathering overhead. Stonecrop mused that if Federica were here with him, she wouldn't be able to resist striking up a conversation with the children in Japanese.

The kids' roughhousing got a little out of control and the boy tripped and hit the floor hard right next to Stonecrop. Stonecrop helped him up and then articulated the boy's knee to make sure it was okay. They exchanged smiles, sure evidence from the boy that a scrape on the knee would not interrupt play. The father nodded to thank Stonecrop.

As the S10 climbed through a thin layer of mist that stretched north and east and through which only random patches of countryside were visible. Stonecrop remembered a run he had made in October when the city had been under a thick canopy of clouds while above the clouds a near-painful clarity filled the sky.

He stepped onto the platform, pulled on his backpack, and adjusted the shoulder straps. The children shot by him, followed by the sitter. The father lagged behind as he spoke on his mobile. Mother gathered up belongings, manhandling the stroller until the father saw she was struggling and gave a hand.

Among people milling around the patio of the Gmüetliberg

restaurant, hidden in the shadows of a yellow awning decorated with icicle lights, he recognized Geissner, who looked like a college theatre student playing Mr. Incognito. Apparently, Claudia did have a plan-B. Stonecrop pretended he didn't see Geissner.

As soon as he was out of earshot from customers at the station café he tested the headset, speaking softly and hoping the mic attached to the earpiece was sensitive enough to pick up his voice. "Still hear me?"

"Loud and clear. Lot of noise on the train. Kids?"

Stonecrop walked around the front of train and headed downhill toward the playground to look for the path to Im Sonnenbühl. He jumped when the boy and girl raced by within a few feet of him.

Horizontal light slashed through gaps in leaf-thin trees and illuminated the gravel path to Im Sonnenbühl. He reached his destination in under three minutes. White river rock traced the borders of pathways to the meditation room, pool, and a two-story residence. In a clearing by the pool he saw a closed dumpster marked with a hand-sized, hand-drawn red spiral. He slipped the pack off, removed the rifle and leaned it upright against the bin, and then heaved the pack on top of the bin, leaving it positioned as directed with shoulder straps skyward. In a well-rehearsed movement, he picked up the rifle and let the harness drop in place over his shoulders.

Stonecrop took a few minutes to explore the site, checking the perimeter first, and then peering in windows of the main house and the studio structure. Inside and out, the buildings suggested a cozy retreat that was unpretentious and inviting. A standalone message board listed yoga classes and massage services from the month before. Ivy had grown over the top and loose strands obscured some of the postings. The outdoor soaking pool was half-full and covered by a skein of leaves and branches held in situ by surface ice.

The resort was situated in a depressed pocket of the hillside opposite the city and the train station. The western elevation guaranteed that Im Sonnenbühl would live up to its claim to be both a quiet and a sunny retreat.

Stonecrop looked for a secluded post with a clear line of sight to the dumpster. *Why did the Nasties—as Claudia called them—pick a location with so few access points and exit options?* Above him on the crest of the hill tourists were making the ten-minute trek back and forth from the station to the UTO KULM summit hotel.

He found a spot slightly uphill from the dumpster and behind a shed filled with pool supplies and maintenance equipment. The rising cloud layer dampen sounds from the woods below. An occasional cry or laugh from one of the children at the playground would interrupt the silence. Fifteen minutes passed.

Something fluttered behind him. He turned sharply and unshouldered his rifle, regretting having forgotten to unfasten the Velcro on the flap of the carrying case. A minute went by. Another rustling in the brush, this time on his left and toward the path back to the station. He scanned where the sound had come from. Nothing. To break the tension—imagined or real—he whispered to Dante. "Still there?"

"Read you loud and clear," the response screamed in his ear. Stonecrop adjusted the earpiece to lower the volume.

"I don't get it. No one's here. I sent a text to Claudia. She said sit tight. Maybe the Nasties are watching."

His ruminations ended abruptly. The whirring of a four-rotor drone broke the silence as it descended and hovered above the dumpster. Had Alexander double-crossed everyone? He couldn't be going after the two million for himself. That would be ridiculous.

"Dante, is that your drone?" he asked.

"Muddo, you see the size of dat baby! Hell no, it's not mine!" came back to him.

"Not yours, copy?" he asked again.

"No, mon, are you crazy? I got a lock on it!" Alexander sounded like a kid with a new toy and excited to follow the drone via his own drone's sensors. "It's an Avio Mark II service drone. Maximum range with the pack will be one-point-five miles, plus-or-minus. I can track it to their front door."

"Alrighty," Stonecrop said loud enough to be heard above the thrum of the drone.

"Hey, you got company! Back to the S10," Alexander ordered. "Move it! Train is still there. I see flashing lights moving up the fire road and headed to the hotel."

"The Avio hooked the pack; it's lifting it, slowly. It's struggling. Can it take the weight?" Stonecrop asked.

"Double that. Go!" Alexander ordered. "I'm on the drone!"

"I'm waiting for Claudia. No sign of Federica."

"No way she's there. Federica won't be released until they see the money. She's in or near the city. Go!"

Stonecrop didn't argue. The Polizei—or maybe an ambulance—could be racing up the hill for any number of reasons. Still, why risk it.

And Alexander was right. Until the kidnappers saw the money, they wouldn't release Federica.

He sprinted for the train. His heart pounded and calves burned. The conductor saw him emerge from the playground area and reopened the doors he had been closing. *Love the Swiss for their small kindnesses.* Gasping for breath, he stepped into the tram car and once again shared it with the same family with which he had ridden before. Geissner was still at the café, seated and reading the paper, oblivious, probably waiting for Claudia to tell him what to do.

The tram car was packed with passengers for the downhill leg, including a Spanish-speaking tour group. This time the two children giggled and huddled together under a blanket. The sun was below the horizon and the alps were afire. In minutes, the temperature had dropped. No one on the tram paid attention to him as he set the encased rifle on the floor under his legs.

Alexander's voice came through the earphones, half-talking to himself and then warning him. "Crap, I can't do both at once. The Avio just passed Uitikon Waldegg. Another police car just parked there—it's parked next to your Beamer. They're sitting in the car."

"Did they see the Avio?" Stonecrop asked.

"No, I'm sure they didn't. Out of earshot, and it's getting dark." Alexander responded.

"Dante, you're still at Parkplatz Feldmoos, right?" Stonecrop spoke calmly, trying to not attract the attention of co-passengers and grateful for the Spanish tourists' animated clamor.

"Roger that. Hard to hear . . ."

"Stay on the Avio." Stonecrop gave up and spoke in a normal tone of voice now. It was obvious he was speaking through an earpiece; he had to press it to his ear to hear anything. "I'm getting off at Waldegg. I'll follow the footpath to Parkplatz Feldmoos. If our curious friends are on the other side of the restaurant, they'll miss me. It's less than a five-minute jog down. And it takes longer to drive from Uitikon Waldegg. Pick me up when I step out of the woods."

"Got it. Junction where the path crosses the highway. I'll be there." Dante confirmed.

Stonecrop massaged his calves. He was fit but was not a sprinter by nature. At least the next one would be downhill.

The children's mother approached him and handed him a paper origami crane. She pointed at her son, now half-asleep under the blanket.

"He made for you," she said.

Stonecrop thanked her, surprised by this second small kindness, and carefully placed the paper crane in the zippered sunglasses pocket of his running suit jacket. She returned to her seat. Stonecrop was grateful for no further conversation.

Within seconds of the tram coming to a halt and the rear doors opening he exited the car and stepped onto the deserted platform. His exit point could not be seen from the parking area.

He circled around the rear of the tram, hopped across the rails, and climbed over a locked gate on the chain link fence separating a small industrial building from the station grounds. Behind the building a driveway led to the trailhead to Parkplatz Feldmoos. A white path wound tunneled into the shadowy overgrowth. Stonecrop jogged. This was not the time to twist an ankle.

Miss Piggy

In the passenger seat Dante tracked the drone from his laptop and gave directions as Stonecrop drove.

"What's with the Polizei?" Alexander asked.

"No clue. Claudia spoke with Vormittag and he was officially unaware of the kidnapping. Could be a different department tracking Gregor."

"Can you see?" Stonecrop asked.

"Quite well."

"No, I meant are you following the drone?"

"We're good as long as the weather doesn't go to shit—which it wants to do. The Avio is blind. Miss Piggy's got night vision, the hottest SDK out there." Alexander was like a parent who couldn't resist talking up the kids.

"Why 'Miss Piggy?' "

"Her snout—a stubby laser/radar jamming snout." He looked up and pointed, "Make a right here." They exited the lighted highway and turned onto a dirt side road. "Pull over. There's a small clearing on the left." The clearing was a wall of black to the naked eye, obviously not to Miss Piggy.

Stonecrop parked the van and killed the lights. He switched off the interior lights to make sure they would stay dark if he opened the door.

"We've been driving only four or five minutes?" Stonecrop questioned.

"The Avio is 100 meters south-southeast, almost exactly one-and-a-half miles from Sonnenbühl." Alexander lowered the window and moved out of the way so Stonecrop could see better. "Follow the bushes. Then beyond the trees, on the left."

The hedge passed and bordered the right side of a farmhouse. A flash of lightning gave Stonecrop a snapshot of the terrain. The building, more a cottage, was surrounded by a thicket of trees. Some distance ahead of where they had parked, he'd seen a driveway that led to the opposite side of the house. He made a mental image of the terrain as the afterimage dissolved. The trees reappeared as two-dimensional silhouettes. To the right and beyond the trees a yellow light lit up the porch at the back of the cottage.

"Closer?" Alexander asked.

"We're not delivering pizza, Dante."

Had he heard the whir of the Avio or had he been hearing things in his head? He waited. The silence continued. No more drone motor. Some distance from the van, muffled guns hots joined in with creaks and groans of the van's engine cooling off. Stonecrop lowered the window on the driver's side. Dante's puzzled expression asked for an explanation.

"Schützenhaus Albisrieden."

"Come again?"

"Shooting house. It's a rifle club. The road ahead turns left and dead ends at Schützenhaus Albisrieden. It's less than a quarter mile north of the copse." Stonecrop pointed into the darkness. "You can just see a couple lights. My shrink recommended I start training again. I go a couple times a week."

"To the shrink?"

"No, I shoot twice a week. Ammo's cheap, therapy's pricey."

"Did you reach Claudia?" Alexander asked.

"Nope," Stonecrop said as he handed his burner phone to Alexander. "But if she calls, you don't have to say anything. Put the phone on speaker, next to your headset."

Stonecrop quietly exited the van. He removed the Anschutz from its case along with three five-round magazines, snapping one into place, inserting the second in a carrier slot built into the stock of the rifle, and pocketing the third. The safety was off. It had never been in the "on" position; biathletes generally remove or release the bolt when they aren't actively shooing.

"Not exactly the right tool for the right job. Unless you plan to clobber 'em over the head. You are not a soldier, my friend. And this is not a sport! Locate Federica and get support only if necessary." Alexander had argued from the start that they should not confront Red Monkey.

"Sorry, Dante. Red Monkey, or whoever the fuck they are, could hurt Federica. Like I said before, I don't buy the gang ethics bullshit."

"You don't want to put her at risk—assuming she's even there." Dante argued.

"Assholes got their money. I want to confirm she's okay. I want a visual. If she's not there, well . . . *We* will talk before I move. Okay?" With that, Stonecrop into the shadows.

"You take care, mon."

Ja, stimmt, Stonecrop whispered to himself. That's true. His life of late had been careful, passive. Well, not tonight. Tonight, every step, every breath, had purpose.

The mist turned to drizzle.

Albisriederstrasse

Alexander was right. What *was* he was going to do with the Anschutz? Probably nothing, which was okay. Little kids have their teddy bears, he had his rifle. That was the real reason, but he wouldn't admit that to Alexander and had only just now admitted it to himself.

The rifle was accurate, but aiming—which consisted of lining up a ring at the diopter peep-sight with another ring atop the muzzle of the barrel—would be a challenge. The rings had to symmetrically wrap the target, which in biathlon is a distinct black circle on a white field. The iron sights were zeroed for fifty meters and blocked out much of the downrange area. That would make it almost impossible to track anything moving, especially if it were moving across a dark field. If he had to aim the Anschutz, Stonecrop had only one advantage: he had shot thousands of rounds with this specific rifle.

He crept along the shadows of the hedgerow bordering the field. With each step the freshly moistened earth released odors of petrichor, joined by the smell of field grass and the bite of pine resin. He intentionally let wet leaves brush his face and ran his tongue across his lips to pick up the moisture.

Should have had something to drink before I took off. Fuck it, then I'd bitch about having to piss.

A heady clarity came from the animal-like movement. Over the backdrop of a steady heartbeat, he listened for anything unusual, breathing with light, even breaths, and calmed by the gentle patter of the rain. His movements melded with the tall, breeze-swished grasses.

Reaching the far side of the cottage he got his first good view of the porch and backyard. At the corners of an equilateral triangle, forty or fifty meters to a side, lay three structures. To the north was the cottage; on the southwest was an old woodshed; a barn was in the southeast corner, a classic Swiss slatted hay storage area with eaves that extended over a ground-level toolshed. The area between the three structures formed a courtyard of sorts, mostly clear except for a few sizable tree stumps. Two vehicles were parked the right side of the house. The vehicles were side-by-side and parked in opposite directions. A newish Audi A6 faced the courtyard. The other car, a nondescript silver sedan, was an Opel that had seen better years.

Stonecrop cautiously traversed a soggy section of ground, carefully placing and extracting each foot to avoid noise created by the sucking of the mud. His strategic objective was the woodshed. The terrain sloped slightly upward and away from the shed but gave a clear view of the back of the cottage. One of the vertical slats on the shed siding was detached at the top and canted to one side. The V-shaped gap provided a well-concealed vantage.

The boxy cottage—maybe a 800 square-feet—had stone walls and a mossy, slate roof. A two-meter-wide eave spanned the south-facing porch. A central door made of hand-hewn planks opened to the courtyard and on each side of the door were two trapezoidal concrete flowerpots that contained withered clumps of flowers decimated by early frosts. In summer, the pots would be bursting with geraniums— no country spends more on geraniums than Switzerland.

Three shallow steps led up to the porch floor. Sconces on either side of the door lit the entry. Four ceiling bulbs gave off an unhealthy, sallow light. At the geometric center of the courtyard the Avio perched atop the Jack Wolfskin pack like a giant mechanical raptor guarding its prey. LEDs on the body of the Avio flashed every few seconds.

Through the paned window right of the door Stonecrop made out a kitchen/living room area with a fireplace, unlit, on the north interior wall. Inside and next to the window a table covered was covered with a Swiss lace tablecloth and on either side of the table were wooden chairs. A man stood with arms extended forward and leaning on the back of one of the chairs. He was standing in front of a laptop and speaking through an earpiece. He made gestures with his face, and then with his hands—either out of habit, as Italians do, or as anyone might to emphasize a point in a face-to-face conversation. *Capo,* Stonecrop christened him. Next to the laptop was a Euro version of an electric hurricane lamp. There was nothing from IKEA . . . the useless thought inserted itself in Stonecrop's methodical cataloging of the surroundings.

Two other men, one Caucasian and the other Asian, exited the house and walked up to the Avio. The Caucasian—he looked Italian—was well-dressed, too well-dressed for the inclement conditions. He was lean, tall and attractive, larger boned than the man at the computer. Stonecrop dubbed him *Romeo*. The Asian was short and stocky, piston-like.

Stonecrop reported to Alexander, "Three men. There might be others. No sign of Federica."

"Hey, another vehicle passed by and went dark. Could've parked up the road. A Subaru, older model."

"Probably Schützenhaus traffic," Stonecrop replied. He thought, briefly, of the round taillights.

The Asian man carried a canvas tarp. The two men knelt beside the pack Stonecrop had hefted atop the dumpster at Im Sonnenbühl. They separated the drone's grappling hook from the pack-straps and carefully slid the backpack out from under the Avio. After untying the drawstring to the backpack's main compartment, they gave each other a high-five. Romeo reached in and came up with a fistful of neatly bundled bills, the fruits of Geissner's labor. He carried the pack inside while the Asian—he looked Japanese—went to work on the drone. The man flipped a switch and the LEDs went dark. Another switch silenced the tinny buzzing the drone had been making. He efficiently removed each rotor propeller unit and slid these into a stuff sack. Satisfied with his work, he spread the square canvas tarp over the drone and its parts. The de-powered and disassembled drone appeared less intimidating than before.

The Asian's hands were nimble, not what one would expect from stubby, cylindrical fingers that grew out of the two-inch thick palms. *I'm calling you Chop-Chop.* With the heel of his hand, Chop-Chop pressed tent stakes into the dirt to secure the four corners of the tarp. The rain picked up and he scurried back to the house.

"Max, Claudia is calling."

"Put her on speaker. Next to our com. Crank up the sensitivity. It's hard to hear. I have to whisper."

"Where have you been?" Claudia asked. Her voice was scratchy. "I miss you, my sweet. Lovely sunset, but you didn't notice, did you? All is well and we are expecting a DHL delivery tomorrow."

'Lovely sunset' meant the kidnappers had acknowledged getting the cash. 'DHL' meant Federica was going to be freed. 'Tomorrow' was simply, tomorrow.

He would like to have had more—specifically where and at what time Federica was to be 'delivered.' The chatting in code felt silly. Nevertheless, he played along.

"Claudia, I had a nice jog. Thanks again for the car. I parked at Waldegg station but it was too dark to run back to the car. The Polizei might give you a ticket tonight. Sorry." He hoped she understood. The police had come to the station; he wasn't there but the car was.

"Did they tell you, say to you it might be ticketed?"

"No, we never spoke."

"Ah, they won't care." She chastised him, "You and your silly runs! Can you find your way home, dearie, or do you need a ride? Getting wet, love?"

"I'm fine. I'll call if I do. *Tschüss.*" He ended the conversation. It was time to attend to the triumvirate in the house.

Alexander disconnected Claudia and came back on the com-link to Stonecrop.

"Max, we got more traffic on the road. Just driving by, I hope. What's up?"

"The three of them are in the house. Chop-Chop, he's the Asian guy, and his sidekick, the one I call Romeo, are taking the money out of the backpack. They're counting and redistributing the cash into green duffels—North Face duffles. Four bags total."

"Any sign of Federica? It's possible she's not with them."

"Could be. Although this would be a perfect place to hold her. She's gotta here. I'm gonna sit tight."

The counting process took forever—forever being about fifteen minutes. Stonecrop had been warm and sweaty from the jog down from Uetliberg. But now, between the approach to the drone's LZ and waiting in the leaky woodshed, the night air and drizzle were stealing warmth from his body. The wind freshened and gusts whipped through gaps in the siding. He tried to cinch up the collar of his jacket and discovered that he had already done so. He made a half-hearted attempt to spread dirt on the reflective stripes on his sneakers. It was futile; the rain would wash the mud away.

His stomach growled. He was hungry, he was cold, and he was, oddly, happy. That self-observation would not be shared with his shrink, who just wouldn't get how alive Stonecrop felt.

Capo concluded his phone conversation along with other tasks on the computer and then closed the lid. A few minutes later he exited the front door with a pile of blankets in his arms. Stonecrop reported to Dante. "The first guy, the boss man, Capo, is carrying blankets to the cars. He's putting them in the trunk of the Opel. There's an Audi parked next to it. Dark color. I can just read the plates. He's spreading the blankets out in the bottom of the trunk. Trunk light's on, I can see well enough. Used to the dark. Good light from the porch."

"Is he armed?" Alexander asked.

"Don't see anything. He's wearing a sweater." Stonecrop said. "The guys inside are done counting. They're going to another room."

"Mon, maybe we get help now. Stay low, mon, stay low. Recon, remember. Three to one, no good," Alexander cautioned.

"Not good for them. I'm going closer. Cover's good from the brush on the left."

The ground was dryer and firmer than the bog he had traversed earlier. Stonecrop cradled his rifle and crawled through the underbrush. He thought of Rosie. *A piece of cake for her! All a game.* He missed Rosie. *A bit of a game for me too, Rosie. I ought to be afraid. I will be, later.*

A backdrop of wind and rain shrouded the noise he made crawling through the brush. He kept to the perimeter of the clearing, finding cover in the vegetation and in the shadows of the tree stumps. He'd moved ten meters closer to the structures west flank. The new position gave him a clearer view of the trunk of the Opel. He had an angled view of the cottage window. Stonecrop waited and watched.

Take the Shot

A quarter hour passed. Then a noise, a hint of movement, imagined or real, from within the cottage. A chain rattling and dragging across uneven floorboards. An ugly duet of sounds followed: the squeal of a rusted door hinge and a muffled, plaintive cry.

Stonecrop parsed the sounds of the procession. A form appeared on the door jam and tilted forward, leading with a ski-mask covered head emerged. The mask was backwards, with the slits for the eyes and mouth at the back. Wisps of flaxen hair floated out of the eye slits; fine hair at the nape of her neck rose through the mouth-hole.

She should be able to see through the loose knitting. Federica's head lolled downward, swaying from side to side as she moved. Metal ankle cuffs restrained the range of motion of her bare feet and limited her shuffles to six or eight inches. *Why no shoes? It's fucking freezing.* A chain ran from the midpoint of the ankle cuffs and attached to the midpoint of the chain connecting her handcuffs. *Fucking barbaric. At least her hands aren't behind her back. They left slack in the chain; she can raise her hands above her head.*

From the handcuffs five feet of chain tethered her to Chop-Chop. He led her on a taunt three-foot leash and held the remaining chain in his other hand like a lariat. Someone else was behind Federica and shoved her through the doorway. *Romeo.* Once clear of the doorway, Chop-Chop handed the chain to Capo. Stonecrop memorized their features. In that moment they became marked men; their fates were sealed.

"Jesus, Max, what's happening?" Alexander's concerned voice blared through the earpiece.

"Quiet," Stonecrop whispered. He waited until the wind and rain, which would vary in intensity from moment to moment, could cover his voice. "She's here."

Capo led Federica across the porch. She shivered in the icy air and stumbled forward each time Capo yanked the chain. She was dressed in filthy scrubs. She had soiled herself. The scrubs were torn. *She must have fought them. Had she been raped?*

Federica tripped and fell as she tried to negotiate the steps, landing hard on one knee. She had been unable to break the fall because chain suspended her hands in the air. Blood seeped through the scrubs where her knee had hit the ground. Capo re-gripped the chain to yank her upright. He was leading her toward the Opel.

When he extended his arm, the Irish cable knit sweater rose above his waist and exposed the handle of an HK nine-millimeter automatic. The unseen barrel of the handgun below the belt-line bulged more than one would expect—a laser sight.

Chop-Chop descended the steps with a flashlight and a large nylon bag for the Avio. Cursing the rain, he scurried to the drone, pulled up two of the stakes, and ducked under the tarp. He put a small flashlight between his teeth and began packing parts of the Avio into the bag. Chop-Chop's nylon wind jacket was unzipped. He too was armed. A handgun of some sort hung from an underarm holster and flapped gill-like against his side.

As if on a theater stage, Romeo made his entrance. With a duffel under each arm he walked the length of the porch to the Audi, tapped the remote to open the trunk, and tossed in the bags. He ferried two more cash-laden duffles, one for the Audi and the last tossed on the back seat of the Opel. *Who the fourth for?*

Although Stonecrop could manipulate the silky bolt of the Anschutz with a flick of one finger to rapidly chamber a round, he moved slowly, using his thumb and three fingers to silently lift and resettle the bolt. He rested his finger on the trigger, grateful that biathlon rifles did not have hair triggers. He felt the familiar resistance of the trigger against his finger and *was* glad that he had brought the rifle.

Clammy fabric of his running suit stuck to his skin. Water from a mop of rain sopped hair trickled down his brow and dripped off eyelashes and his nose. Stonecrop had competed at ten-below Fahrenheit and in blizzard conditions when the targets had appeared for only seconds. The rain was an annoyance which, if anything, helped him focus and relax his breathing.

Capo and Federica reached the Opel. Federica's leg knocked against the bumper and she screamed, "Nein!" It wasn't the knee she had fallen on. Suddenly, he understood the source of her near panic. They were going to put her in the trunk. It was claustrophobia, not the knee. Gauging the revulsion and terror of her scream, he guessed that she must have been transported to the farmhouse in the trunk of the Opel. *You tortured Federica and tried to kill Marion. You guys are amateurs. Yakuza professionals my ass.*

Federica raised her arms, flailing until she bumped against the top of the trunk lid. She stiffened her arms against it, resisting Capo's pushing. He grasped the back of her neck to shove her head and shoulders downward. She arched her back, still resisting him. Her body shook. Suddenly, she dove forward. Capo's hand on the back of her neck slid forward with her. His hand grabbed for her neck and ended up grasping only the back of the ski mask. The movement tore off the mask tore.

Federica ducked backwards and slipped under his arm. She rose behind Capo, raised her arms, and flipped the chain around his throat. She rode him piggy-back and began choking him with the chain, winding the chain around her wrist to take up slack to redouble pressure on Capo's carotid artery. *You got the right target, Fede, but nowhere near the time or strength.*

Capo rose violently and inadvertently rammed his head into the trunk lid. The impact stunned him. He wobbled in place. He was shorter than Federica though much heavier. Like an incensed rodeo bull frantic to shake its rider, her violently flung her from side to side. She was too weak hang on or keep the pressure on his neck. Blood ran down Capo's face from a gash in his skull. He grabbed at the ligature at his neck.

Federica was spent. She let go the chain from Capo's head and yanked the loose tail of the chain out of his wet and bloodied hands. Her knees gave out. She landed on her rear and kept her eyes on Capo as she backed away, having to crawl like crab, slipping on the mud and pushing with her heels and palms.

A lightning strike lit the courtyard and etched the scene in fine-grained relief. The clap of thunder followed and shook the ground. Volleys of rain whipped the courtyard.

Capo came to his senses and made an oafish misstep as he tried to grab the chain. Federica and Capo froze and stared at each other. Blood streamed down his face and formed a pointy red goatee at the chin. *You did a number on him. Well done, girl.*

It must have been the first time she had seen Capo's face. They both seemed to realize that now she would be able to identify him. Capo jerked the gun out of his belt as Federica rolled onto her stomach. Like a wounded animal she clawed at the mud and grass to distance herself from Capo. It was as if the scene unfolding before Stonecrop eyes were in slow-motion, the actors caught in a viscous ether of hyper-perception.

Oh Capo, c'mon, let her go! You were gonna keep your part of bargain. Screw up now and Gregor will rip out your heart. Or I'm gonna fuck with you.

She was crawling at a slight angle toward Stonecrop. Her breath heaved and her eyes searched for cover. She did not see him. Capo pointed the HK at her, roughly in Stonecrop's direction. *She's a flat target, moving fast. He's stunned, blood and water in his eyes. It'd take a lucky shot.*

Capo steadied his gun. Stonecrop watched, as all real shooters do, with both eyes open and relaxed. His right eye maintained the alignment of the sights on the Anschutz as his left eye read the background. The emission point for the red laser sight drifted into the center of Stonecrop's sights and made the decision for him. He acted before he thought about it and squeezed the trigger like he always did when the target floated into sight—gently, no jerks, breathing out, no blinking, almost nonchalant.

The bullet exploded the laser sight on the HK and ripped the pistol out of Capo's hand. The hand was bleeding—his index finger was mutilated. Federica stopped moving. Capo let out a savage curse.

Stonecrop stood and yelled to her, "Keep going. Through the hedge. Then right. Van's on the road!" He repositioned himself opposite the direction he'd sent Federica. He'd keep her out of the line of fire that he was certain to draw.

Chop-Chop burst out from under the tarp, Glock first and less than ten meters away. Stonecrop stepped to the right and crouched, ducking into the shadow of tall bush. Shooters usually steady their weapons to shoot—offering, though briefly, a not-moving target. As Chop-Chop's eyes adjusted to the light, Stonecrop took aim. He put a bullet into the white fingers wrapped around the gun's grip. The weapon flew into the air along with a piece of finger. *Fuck. Needed to disable him and salvage the Glock. Not good, Max, that was not good. Should have gone for a head shot. Did the memory of Mozambique hold him back?*

Stonecrop rose out of the shadows a second time and raised his rifle, aiming it toward the doorway in anticipation of Romeo's appearance. Capo and Chop-Chop gawked at him in disbelief. Had Romeo not heard the shots or Capo's yelp? The rain pounded the roof over the porch.

Romeo stepped into view with a Beretta Cougar nine-millimeter pistol at the ready. He had heard just fine. With no nearby cover Stonecrop simply hoped to distract Romeo long enough for Federica to get out of sight and make it to the road. In classic biathlon off-hand position he let fly three shots—as fast as possible, given limitations of the Anschutz bolt action—and spooked Romeo back into the house.

Two shots hit Romeo's left torso, and another tore a hole in the jacket as he fell back. The hits may or may not have been damaging. Romeo stepped back into sight, finding partial cover behind the stone walls, away from the heavy door—he probably didn't know the door would easily stop a bullet from the Anschutz.

Stonecrop dove and rolled, using Chop-Chop and the tarped drone as cover. He removed his first magazine and replaced it with the second. Force of habit made him put the expended magazine back in its carrier rack in the stock. He made a mental note to pick up brass if he got out of the fray in one piece.

Capo had vanished in the shadows between the Opel and Audi. The interior light lit up the Audi. Capo fumbled for the glove box with his good hand and reappeared holding a second handgun. *If he's well-trained, he can shoot with either hand. I can.*

The rain had muted the gunshots. No one at Schützenhaus would have heard them. Stonecrop reached up to his ear to ping Dante. The earpiece was gone. He'd lost it during the melee. A shot originating from between the cars splattered mud a few feet in front of him. Stonecrop was caught in a crossfire. *At least they're shooting at me, not Federica.* Chop-Chop took advantage of the covering fire and ran toward the house. Stonecrop shadowed Chop-Chop and reached a thigh-high tree stump, a modicum of protection. The underbrush to his left concealed Federica. She was well out of the line of fire.

Romeo came out from behind the door and let fly a salvo of shots at Stonecrop as Chop-Chop dove through the doorway. Pieces of the stump exploded, sending wood shrapnel in the air. Stonecrop had no time to aim, and no place to run. There was an obvious blood stain on Romeo's chest.

The Audi's headlamps came on and blinded Stonecrop. The courtyard lit up. He was both exposed and trapped in the crossfire from which there was no protected exit. He risked exposure and fired a round at the Audi. Glass shattered as one headlamp went dark. In return, a volley of shots from Romeo tore up more of the stump. Any attempt at the other Audi headlamp would be suicide.

Romeo stepped out from behind the door and briefly turned his weapon toward the shed. He had seen something move.

Federica? How could she get there? Stonecrop took advantage of the distraction and put a bullet in Romeo's thigh, counting on Capo to shoot poorly with his non-dominant hand. Romeo groaned but focused well enough to pepper the stump again. A series of wild shots from Capo riddled the trees behind Stonecrop. Stonecrop was afraid to look for Federica, afraid that if they saw him searching they would as well.

He had to stall them. Federica needed time to find Dante. Could Miss Piggy record what was happening? He had no idea. In general, drones don't function well in rain and wind, but Miss Piggy was not your average drone.

Stonecrop was pinned down and had only two rounds left in the loaded magazine. He put his rifle on the ground and, still on his knees, slowly raised his arms. He hoped they would have the good sense to want to question him. It would buy time for Fede. None of them were in condition to chase after her. Capo, standing beside the Audi, held up a bloody hand to tell the others to stop shooting, but Romeo and Chop-Chop missed the signal. Stepping out from behind the wooden door, a bloodied and limping Romeo raised the Beretta and took aim.

Stonecrop was blinded by flashes of light, knocked to the ground, and engulfed by deafening gunfire. Stones dug into his cheekbones; the cold wet ground soothed; the world went dark.

Arigatou Gozaimasu

He opened one eye. Half of his face lay in the mud. The silence had been replaced by ringing in the ears. *Holy fuck, I'm still alive.* He saw the house. No Romeo. At least no standing-at-the-door Romeo.

The current version of Romeo was lying on its back in an awkward sprawl across the porch steps. The back of his head rested on the ground. Standing beside the contorted torso was a slight Japanese man, Stonecrop's fellow passenger, the father from the S10. Father picked up Romeo's Beretta.

Still lying on his stomach and with painful effort, Stonecrop turned his head to the opposite side and faced a pair of mud-splattered pink running shoes. The ankle length socks were pink as well and trimmed in white lace. A woman reached down with one arm and helped him up. In her other arm, she cradled a Heckler & Koch MP7. He got the picture. She had body slammed him from behind. His head nailed the edge of the stump as he fell.

She had come from behind and fired a lethal burst of shots at Capo, who now lay in bloody heap on the ground in front of the remaining Audi headlamp. Steam rose from the barrel of her weapon. *Shit, that's a Swiss military close quarters combat weapon.* Something about her said she knew exactly what was going through his mind. Her headband, soaked from the rain, had fallen at a goofy angle and almost covered one eye. She released Stonecrop and slid the headband back in place. *Annie-fucking-Oakley-san.*

It would have been safer for Mother to fire at Capo from farther away. But instead she had opted for the certainty of a close-range take-down. Stonecrop and the stump had provided a modicum of cover. Mother and Father had saved his life.

A dumb, giddy smile eased across his face, "Thanks, Mom. Ah, there might be a fourth." He held up four fingers. She understood and shook her head in the negative. "Ok, uh, nice shoes," he said, having meant to say *nice shooting*. He rose to hands and knees, still dizzy from the encounter with the stump. Mother smiled back at him. It was a friendly smile, but also kind of said, 'You're full of shit and it's blind luck that I saved your ass.'

A stunned Chop-Chop cautiously stepped through the doorway. He walked to the center of the courtyard, stopped, and stood stiffly at attention. The sleeve of his shirt was pulled down to form a bandage for the injured hand. Father approached him. When Father was a meter away, Chop-Chop spoke—"*Dai mondai*—big problem"—and lowered his gaze to the ground, shook his head back and forth, and mumbled to himself.

Father waited for Chop-Chop. Then he cocked his head to one side. Father's expression was clear, 'Why?' There was no response. It was obvious they knew each other. Father frowned at Chop-Chop's silence; time was up.

"*Mondai nai*—no problem," he said, with sadness in his voice.

He placed the loaded and cocked Beretta in Chop-Chop's good hand with the barrel aimed at Chop-Chop's face. Chop-Chop carefully raised the gun. He asked something from Father, who frowned, but nodded back in agreement to whatever it was Chop-Chop had requested.

An icy rain fell, now less forcefully than before. A shimmering mass of droplets were suspended in the cone of light defined by the Audi headlamp. In its center stood Chop-Chop. Stonecrop watched as Chop-Chop used his shaking but uninjured hand to raise the barrel of the Beretta to the side of his head. He stared at Father as he pulled the trigger.

A clap of thunder marked the ignominy. Chop-Chop lay motionless in a pool of blood-stained the water. Fat droplets of rain dimpled the indifferent flesh and glittered and danced on the surface of the black moat forming around his head.

An animated exchange between Mother and Father ensued as they examined the scene. The subject matter was clearly how best to clean up what had transpired. One or the other pointed to brass on the ground, the tree stump, the bodies and the cars. Mother cupped her hand over a phone, ordering someone to do something.

From behind the woodshed, the place from which Stonecrop had done his reconnaissance, Federica staggered toward them. She had not gone to the road as Stonecrop had commanded. It would have been a challenge with shackled feet. She shivered. Her ankles and wrists were raw.

She stopped in front of Father and bowed. In a quiet voice, she addressed him, *"Arigatou gozaimasu."*

Father reacted with pleasant surprise, not only at the words, a common Japanese expression of thanks, but from what was no doubt her native or near-native accent. Again, Stonecrop wondered what it would be like to have Federica's gift, to so own another language that it was indistinguishable from your own. Did she even have a native language or were they all one and the same to her?

"Itte mo ii yo!" Father tenderly ordered. He spoke as if he were speaking to a child.

Federica translated. Between the rain and ringing in his ears, Stonecrop missed what she said. Federica repeated, "Go!" She half-laughed and half-smiled through painful, cracked, blue-hued lips. She tried to explain Stonecrop's failure to respond by pointing fingers to her own ears. The effort made her dizzy. She zig-zagged a few steps away from Stonecrop.

Stonecrop jumped forward to catch her. He held her shoulders. He could barely hear what she was saying.

"They won't hurt us." She acted as if she had forgotten who he was. Recognition came with a crooked smile. She relaxed into his arms and let him take her weight. He looked for something to cover her wrists and ankles. Mother understood and removed her headscarf. She tore it into several strips and handed them to Stonecrop. The material would at least shield the raw patches of flesh from the metal. As he held her hands, he remembered his own hands having been numb from cold on the jog to the Dolder. Had that been a premonition of her pain?

Carrying too much speed, a vehicle noisily turned into the gravel driveway. It came to a halt only after tagging the rear bumper of the Audi. The impact made the cone of light from the headlamp dive and rise.

Number four?

Father repositioned himself at the west side of the porch, prepared to stop or disable anyone getting out of the vehicle. Mother remained stationary and scanned the perimeter. Her gaze moved in unison with the MP7 cradled in her arm.

The black man exited the vehicle, ignoring the rain and ignorant of Father's MP7 tracking him. The gold chain caught the light as he galumphed toward Stonecrop.

Father glanced at Stonecrop.

Stonecrop shook his head and yelled "No!"

Father acknowledged him but kept the gun trained on Alexander.

"Max, I lost you." Dante stopped dead in his tracks when he saw the carnage. "Whoa, Muddo, you gat plenty trouble here." He stared at Mother and Father. "Friends I hope?"

Federica collapsed against Stonecrop before he had finished the last makeshift bandage. He grasped her shoulders, his forehead leaned against hers. "We're gonna get through this."

He addressed Dante, "Let's get her to the car."

The men put her in a seated carry and carried her to the van. Mother picked up Stonecrop's rifle and followed. Father scurried off to the tool shed.

Dante and Stonecrop eased Federica into the middle of the van's bench seat. The van tipped briefly as Dante hefted himself into the driver's seat. He wrapped his coat around Federica. Stonecrop slipped in next to her on the other side.

Before he had a chance to close the door Mother handed him the Anschutz, the loaded magazine still in place. Her attention went to the barn; she held a hand up. "Wait," she ordered. Father reappeared with a pair of bolt-cutters. He walked up to the van and passed these to Stonecrop. His next move surprised Stonecrop. He held up several phones he had gathered from the house and nodded to Federica to take hers. She did. When Stonecrop reached out for the others Father held them back. He put his face inches from Stonecrop's, a twinkle in his eye, and spoke, "Yu wan kurayji-maza-fakka."

Stonecrop looked to Federica for a translation. She mustered the crooked grin again, "English, silly—you're one crazy mothafucka."

Stonecrop closed the passenger side door and the nightmare abruptly ceased. They sat the surreal silence without speaking.

Dante broke the spell. "Best way to the hospital?"

A bruised and bloodied hand touched his arm. "No! Take me home, Susenbergstrasse." Stonecrop went to work on the chains as Dante backed the van out of the driveway. It started to snow.

The Big Bang

They were barely out of the driveway when Stonecrop signaled to Dante to stop. "Let me out. Go back without me. I'm going that way." He pointed in the direction of the Schützenhaus, less than a quarter mile opposite the direction from which they had come.

Alexander stopped the car, confused by Max's request.

"Polizei know I drove to Uitikon Waldegg. Ratzow's car is there. If I disappear, they'll wonder where I've been. And someone's going to discover the mess at the farmhouse. If I show up at the Schützenhaus —I belong to the club—I can get a lift. Gives me an excuse to be here and looks like I'm not hiding. I've run Uetliberg from the Schützenhaus before, so it's not a big deal if I show up out of the blue. I'll say I had a little mishap on my run, hit my head, and was freezing my ass off." Stonecrop added, "You take Fede."

"No," Federica mumbled. She had bitten her lip. It was probably still numb with cold. She kept feeling it with her tongue and then her fingers. "No, I stay with you. I don't care."

Her skin was waxen. Stonecrop tried again, "Fede, please. No joke, you're hypothermic."

"Really!" The response was testy. "You are *not* leaving my side, Max Stonecrop."

"You sure?" he asked. She nodded back, the look not so brave this time.

"Right. So, here's plan C." Stonecrop gave directions to Alexander: "Head towards the Schützenhaus. There's a small turnout right before the main building. Keep the lights off. Fede and I will get out there. Do you have anything besides your coat?"

"In back, behind the seat," he said. "Moving pads for Miss Piggy."

As they drove, Stonecrop sent a text to Claudia, to make sure she was at her phone. She pinged him back. He toggled on the phone locator and requested immediate pickup. He avoided the *DHL* code-word for Federica. He did suggest using a 'clean' car. Claudia would figure it out and use a car less likely to have a tracking device on it.

<CK: On it>. No wasted words.

At the turnout Alexander pulled over and parked the van.

"This'll help," Alexander handed a thermos to Federica. "I've got to retrieve Miss Piggy. I set her down not far from here. Had to before the optics froze up. Sure you're good?"

"We're good," Max responded. He helped Federica out of the van, then grabbed a blanket from the pile of padding. "Dante, I don't know what to say. Please, please get your ass out of Switzerland."

"We be bon-bon, mon. Flight-plan is filed for 0-dark-thirty. Miss Piggy, me, and Mr. Lear." Alexander reached out and held Stonecrop's arm, saying, "I'm just thinking, Federica would fit in Miss Piggy's crate. No customs to speak of at Checkport."

The terror in Federica's eyes answered for her.

Stonecrop spoke for her: "I don't think that's an option." He unscrewed the thermos cup and then the stopper. The steaming aromas of whisky and tea filled his nostrils. He poured the cup half-full and handed it to Federica, "Achtung! *Heisse*—hot."

She cupped the precious vessel in her hands and raised the brew to her lips. "*Sehr gut*," her voice was a raspy whisper.

Alexander grinned, "Cragganmore and Earl Grey."

Federica perked up. "I love you, Dante." The voice ratcheted up to husky. Whisky laced tea dribbled from a bruised and swollen corner of her mouth.

Stonecrop repeated Alexander's suggestion. "The crate's not a bad idea. Wouldn't be for long—a few minutes. Then you'd be someplace safe. Wait things out."

"It is a bery, *bery* bad idea," Federica said. She fumbled the Vs, but her tone was feistier.

Alexander extended a hand to Stonecrop, holding it upright like he was preparing to arm-wrestle. Stonecrop took it. The man's fist swallowed his own.

"Crap!" Alexander exclaimed.

"What?"

"We forgot the duffles."

"Shit," Stonecrop laughed, "it's just money. I'm not going back."

"Me neither. Be safe," Alexander said. "Let me know when you're clear. If there's trouble, text me something with the word *Redskins* in it." He had one more question: "Hey, how did your friends back there know where you were?"

Max shrugged his shoulders. Federica, standing beside Max for support, gave Alexander a kiss on the cheek. Even with numbed lips she delivered a genuine American kiss, not a wimpy Euro air-kiss. He winked back and flashed the gold-toothed smile.

The pitch of the rain shifted as it turned to sleet and snow. Stonecrop wrapped the padding around Federica. He handed her the phone and headed off for a cameo at the Schützenhaus. Federica was vulnerable, both physically and mentally. He would stay only long enough to say hello to one or two people and make a pretend phone call.

Despite worsening road conditions Claudia arrived in less than twenty-five minutes. She pinged Stonecrop's phone as she rounded the last turn before the Schützenhaus. The distinctive LED headlamps of a Mercedes emerged and followed the curve of the road. He and Federica rose from the brush to flag her down. The car came to a stop beside them and the passenger door flew open. Claudia had come alone. Stonecrop opened the rear door and guided a swaddled-in-padding Federica to the seat. He handed his rifle to her. An arm reached out of the cocoon of blankets to take it. He climbed in the passenger side, hoping for and failing to find respite from the throbbing in his head. The proximity of Claudia added to the pain.

Her lips pursed when she saw the rifle. The hardness in Stonecrop's expression left her with little to say, a first for Claudia. Her hands clenched the steering wheel in a death grip.

"How 'bout I drive?" Stonecrop suggested.

She answered by vacating the seat and running around the front of the car to switch places with him. Stonecrop did the same and took the driver's seat. They buckled in and he swung the car around. They had no alternative but to drive back the way they had come. He hoped the sleet and darkness would cover the presence of Mother and Father. In this, he was to be mistaken.

The blast shook the ground under them. The Mercedes shuddered as the shock wave nudged the car momentarily onto the shoulder of the road. The farmhouse, less than fifty meters behind them, was an inferno. Bits and pieces of the structure were thrown skyward and fell willy-nilly around and upon them. He checked the rearview mirror. There had been several smaller incendiary explosions. *The cars, they got the cars, too.*

Claudia was shaking. Her toad-eyes became impossibly wide. The heavy glasses slipped and sat askew halfway down her nose. Federica turned to watch the transfixing spectacle of destruction and demolition.

Stonecrop grinned. Claudia caught it. He was happy, perversely savoring the finality the explosion brought to the evening. He had been worried about the mountain of evidence at the site. During the firefight, he'd momentarily considered picking up shell casings. Three bodies, what do you do with three bodies? There would be DNA traces from Federica, records on the computer in the house, bullets lodged in the tree stump, and more. How much could Mother and Father cover up? He recalled the image of them methodically pointing and discussing things. *A lot. Maybe not everything, but a lot.*

Claudia, her self-assurance in abeyance, looked to Stonecrop for an explanation.

"Not now," he said. "We'll talk tomorrow. I'm taking Federica home. I'm staying with her and I'm armed. She'll be fine. Here's the deal: No visits tonight, no calls tonight—not even Gregor. Nothing until we call you tomorrow. Understood?"

He had considered asking Ratzow to get someone to stand guard at Susenbergstrasse. Retaliation was a risk. But would it be a risk tonight? Unlikely, he decided. Mother and Father had been sufficiently intimidating to take the brave out of any fourth conspirator.

"Fine," came the dead-pan response. In the rear-view mirror, the reflection of the fireball behind them lit up Claudia's face. Flaming images leapt across the lenses of her glasses. She stared ahead and into the white night.

The sleet turned to snow. The nasty conditions calmed Stonecrop; he absolutely loved driving on snow and ice.

Rösti mit Eier

A too-quiet calm woke Stonecrop. Pre-dawn snow had muffled the strain of the morning tram turning the corner at Krähbühlstrasse as it climbed the hill between Susenbergstrasse and the Zoo. He slid out of bed, grabbed a pair of Levi's and a black tee from the bureau, and carried the clothes to the living room where he dressed without waking Federica.

Beyond the floor-to-ceiling windows the world stood still. A foot of fresh snow covered shrubs and potted plants. Hoarfrost encrusted every blade of grass, every twig or branch not hidden by the snow. The Zürisee had transmuted into lead, its surrounding hills were a rumpled, gray quilt. Overhead, one could touch the colorless sky.

Stonecrop's reflections were interrupted by a torpedo-shaped object under the snow and burrowing at high speed toward him. Said torpedo's front paws furiously scratched at the door. He cracked open the door and Rosie shot inside and left an icy draft in her wake. He reached down to pat her on the head but was too slow. Her cold nose found his hand, the tongue flicked in and out, and off she went. Rosie nudged aside the bedroom door and—thanks to her fitness regime— jumped on the bed and greeted Federica with a snowy shake and nose-to-nose licks.

"Yuck, Rosie, *deine Nase ist eiskalt*! Go away!"

Mission accomplished, Rosie leapt from the bed to retreat to the living room and keep company with Stonecrop. She had missed Federica and was clearly happy that the household was back in order.

A second visitor crunched snow underfoot. The steps were too light to be Ratzow or Claudia. Through a side-window he saw feet clad in gaily colored rubber boots, the kind Venetians wear when Piazza San Marco floods. Stonecrop stepped into the snow barefoot to offer Frau

Ott a supporting arm.

"Thank you," Frau Ott said. She looked at his feet, "Max, your shoes! Where are your shoes!"

"Good morning, Frau Ott. Achtung—watch your step. Are you okay? Fede late with rent?"

Frau Ott did not understand what Stonecrop had said. She chided him, "Your arrival, so late last night. As they say, in English, in the small hours. And today, one must stay indoors, with the weather and all. My . . ." she hesitated and then found an English expression for her thoughts, not exactly the right one, but clear enough. "My kitchen is full of potatoes and eggs. I should like to invite you and Federica, yes, and you, Rosie," she waited for Rosie to wag her tail, "to dine. Breakfast—*Rösti mit Eier*, pressed juice and Kaffee."

A sleepy Federica emerged from the bedroom. She patted Rosie on the head. "Frau Ott, *Morgan*. Absolutely, fabulously super. I'm starved. PJs okay?"

"Of course. We are family." Frau Ott was taken aback by the bruises and scratches on Federica's face. She said nothing as she stepped forward and made a closer inspection of the chafing at Federica's wrists and ankles.

Federica was clean, at least. Max had helped her with a shower. Ignoring her complaints, he had applied antiseptic salve to the cuts and abrasions. She had grown increasingly uncooperative throughout the process. At first, Federica had been ashamed, as if there were something sinful in being unable to care of herself. Then she had argued with him about the bath, but he was worried about hypothermia.

"You can't disinfect me and then bathe me in bacteria! A shower, I'll take a hot shower. Reapply antiseptic." She had refused bandages. Stonecrop had been frustrated and every step of the process had been a battle and an endorsement of the cliché that doctors make the worst patients.

Frau Ott took hold of her own wrist, rubbing it tenderly in an empathetic gesture, as if the act might somehow be soothing to Federica. "Child, what happened?"

"You oughta see the other guy."

"I beg your pardon?"

Federica blushed, embarrassed by her insensitivity. She was grumpy hungry. "An accident, not to worry. I'm fine. Herr Doktor Max did well."

"He is a good boy."

Federica offered a qualified concurrence, "At times, yes." She winked at Stonecrop, "at times, not so much."

Frau Ott turned away out of politeness. "Ah, what have we here?" she asked, picking up the folded paper atop the *Schuhschränk*—shoe cabinet. Stonecrop had emptied his pockets last night and put the contents on the Schuhschränk. Frau Ott picked inspected the damp, flattened origami crane.

"Did you make this? There's a little seed inside. How clever!" She scrutinized the object, holding the crumpled form up to the light. Indeed, there was a small, dark object visible through the paper.

Stonecrop walked up to her. He gently took the wilted crane from her hand and carefully tore it open.

"Yes, a seed. This was a gift from a young Japanese boy who stumbled in the aisle on the tram. I helped him get up. Very clever," Stonecrop said, "putting the seed inside the crane. I was jogging in the rain. Forgot it was in my pocket."

The seed Stonecrop examined was of the electronic variety. A spider-like wire extended into a wing of the crane. *That's how they found me. Dante's gonna love it.*

"Ah, with dispatch! You must not miss the news. I am frightened out of my wits. Can you imagine, a terrorist attack in Zürich last night! Who would attack our peaceful Kanton? I am nonpulsed!"

"Frau Ott, you mean nonplussed. I hope you have a pulse! Shall I take your pulse?" Federica affectionately corrected her.

For a few weeks, Federica had once explained Max, she had tried to tutor Frau Ott. But with each new lesson the last would be forgotten. In the end, Federica convinced Frau Ott to attend classes at the Coop. Frau Ott took the advice, but the lessons didn't last. Most of her classmates, she had reported, were handsome foreign women wearing large engagement rings. She resisted a twofold resentment. It wasn't simply the obvious fact that some of the women were marrying for citizenship—it was also that Frau Ott, try as she might, couldn't otherwise fault the women. As a rule, her female classmates were personable, polite, and well-educated and even helpful!

With Rosie in the lead, the three of them—four with Rosie—tramped a path through the snow and retraced the steps to Frau Ott's door. Max offered an arm.

"I am not one who needs coddling! Help Federica!"

Frau Ott was right. The steps were a challenge for Federica. Her swollen ankles refused to flex. Movement was painful; her balance was shaky. He walked behind her and kept a hand on her hip to steady the ascent. He wasn't so chipper either.

After the women had settled at the kitchen table Max went to work. He knew his way around the well-appointed kitchen. In little time the three of them were digging into the Swiss equivalent of hash-browns and eggs, *Rösti mit Eier*. Max found Sbrinz cheese in the fridge and added a slice to each plate. He scrambled an egg for Rosie who, unlike most house dogs, was not obsessed with food, and who, like most humans, enjoyed company when she ate.

The television news was every bit as dire as Frau Ott had implied. A newswoman at the scene reported that the night before a powerful series of explosions had resulted in the deaths of at least three people at a small cottage in Albisrieden. Kantonspolizei Kommissar Vormittag was quoted as saying that remnants of bomb-making equipment had been found at the site. The reporter elaborated, calling the event a bomb-making exercise gone awry. The victims had been trapped when whatever they were doing had set off an incendiary device. The detonation had triggered a series of fires and explosions and left little for police to use to determine the identity of the victims or the purpose of their presence in Zürich.

A neighbor was interviewed and reported multiple explosions and flashes of light. She described a tower of flames. *"Genau wie Sechseläuten,"* she said, referring to the Zürcher Spring holiday event in which, after the parade of the guilds, a massive ten-meter-tall wood pyre topped with an outsized figure of a snowman, the Böögg, is burned in effigy at Sechseläutenplatz in front of the Zürich Opera House. The head of Böögg is stuffed with firecrackers. The time required for the flame to climb from the base to reach and explode the head indicates what the summer will be like: a short burn means warm and sunny; a lengthy one means cold and rainy. The Swiss version of Punxsutawney Phil.

Stonecrop watched as the newswoman pressed Kommissar Vormittag about the intended target of the terrorists. He responded with *"Kein Kommentar."* Her last snippet referred to reports about the debris, including remains of what may have been blades and battery for a drone aircraft, several small arms, and two charred vehicles, one of which matched the description of a vehicle used in a recent crime in the city. The investigative work is taking more time than usual, the report added, due to the inclement weather. Behind the reporter, a roofless cottage smoldered.

Federica lifted a spoonful of applesauce to Marion's mouth. Like a small child, Marion opened her mouth to accept the food. She was propped up in the bed; an extra cushion had been placed under her knees. The original *Wizard of Oz* movie was playing, muted, on the television across from her bed. Today was the second day she had been able to chew food and swallow. She stared at the television. Her face was blank; the eyes vacant.

By contrast, her room was cheery, with yellow walls and floral-print curtains. Federica had pulled back the curtains. The steel-framed window comprised eight square panels of glass; in the lower-right corner of each pane, snow had accumulated, more on the bottom panes than the upper ones. Other than the variance in snow accumulation, each square of glass offered the same gloomy view. A freezing fog hugged the city. Even now, at midday, visibility was at best a hundred meters.

"Does she recognize you?" Stonecrop asked.

"Can't tell. I thought there was a flicker of recognition in her eyes when I walked in. Now, I'm not sure. She's improving. Eating is a good." Federica lowered her voice. "She hasn't said anything yet, except that sort of plaintive sigh when she exhales. Weller is not optimistic. He gives her a fifty-fifty chance for a normal life. More tests need to be done. It's not just the not talking. She can't pick up an object, like a cup or hairbrush. Patience, Weller says. Be patient."

Federica continued to feed Marion. The cuff of Federica's baggy sweatshirt fell away each time she raised her arm. The movement exposed her discolored wrist. Each cycle of raising and lowering was a reminder of the hell she had gone through and a reminder to Stonecrop of how grateful he was that she was alive. Stonecrop rose and stared out the window: A tree emerged from the fog; it looked like the trunk was stepping toward him.

"Which is the dream, Fede? Last night or now?" he asked.

"*Ein Traum*? None of it, or both!"

Stonecrop tried rolling up Federica's sleeves, but they refused to cooperate. He spoke matter-of-factly. "Did Weller ask where you had been?" Federica had missed a week of work. She had, he had noted, checked in with Dr. Weller when they had arrived.

"No. Claudia had spoken with him. Told him there was a family emergency. When he saw me he ordered me to take two weeks off, more if needed. Gather I don't look the picture of health. Anyway, that's the plan."

Marion drifted off, peacefully sighing. Federica held her hand. Snowflakes held their places in the air like stationary flecks of white on gray wallpaper. A tap at the door interrupted the immobility of the moment.

"Grüezi mittenand." Kommissar Vormittag spoke softly and let himself in. Epaulettes of fresh snow covered his shoulders. His overcoat—a double-breasted, black, woolen affair—accommodated his pear-shaped torso and too-narrow shoulders. The un-tailored sleeves concealed all but the very tips of his fingers. The Kommissar appeared shorter and stockier than he had in the newscast. His coat sleeves, either overly long or his arms overly short, hung flattened against his sides. One wondered if indeed there were arms inside, and if the fingertips were, instead of actual fingers, the ends of madeleines. The burdensome overcoat and its draped sleeves gave the Kommissar the comic aspect of a mustached penguin, wings folded to its flanks.

"*Buongiorno Signore, posso aiutarLa?*" Federica spoke as she looked up from Marion. Vormittag had greeted them in Swiss German; however, Federica had picked up the underlying Italian accent and consequently responded in Italian, asking if she might be able to help him, believing a visitor had entered the wrong room.

Vormittag spotted her first and then saw Stonecrop. He must have doubted Stonecrop spoke Italian or German, as he switched to English to introduce himself. "Yes, good morning. I apologize for the interruption. I am Kommissar Vittore Vormittag, Zürich Canton Police."

"Ah, Kommissar, I sorry I didn't recognize your voice." Federica's tone of voice warmed.

They went through introductions, though it was obvious Vormittag knew who Stonecrop was. It was equally obvious that the Kommissar, like Federica, was being overly formal. They were both hiding behind their professional identities.

"Dr. Ratzow. I've been meaning to speak with you. As you know, your father and I have known each other a long time. You were a child when *we* first met."

"I remember the day well, Kommissar Vormittag."

"What's that? I'm sorry, but my hearing . . ."

Federica raised her voice, enough so he could hear, but not so much as to be inappropriate for the setting. "The first time was in the garden at the Baur au Lac. It was in the spring. You were so handsome in your uniform. You were not a Kommissar, but even then, you had a mustache. You gave me a dish of ice cream, *framboise*—raspberry, from the vendor at Bürkliplatz next to the ferry."

"Remarkable you remember such details. You would be a good investigator!" Vormittag said, openly impressed. "And I remember you. You had pigtails. They were tied with pink ribbons."

"And you had pants," Federica laughed as she spoke.

"I should hope so!" Vormittag said, good-humoredly.

Federica continued the train of remembrances. "They were so short. They were almost to the tops of your socks. I pointed at them and when I did you pulled them up, way above the socks, halfway to your knees! You really made me giggle. Your legs were so skinny and hairy! I never thanked you. Let me thank you now, for the ice cream and that lovely memory. Thinking about it makes me happy."

There was a relaxing lull in the conversation. The initial tension had been dispelled.

"Dr. Ratzow," Vormittag restarted the conversation, "we have a mutual acquaintance: Miss Claudia Knight. I have been speaking with her about what happened to Mrs. Cook. She told me you had been away the last few days, off to Croatia, or someplace with better weather than here, I hope." The pleasantries taken care of, Vormittag still had a job to do. After all, he was Swiss—or partly Swiss—and therefore both capable and responsible.

"Federica, please call me Federica. And you can call Max . . . Max." She spoke in a whisper. Then she repeated what she had said, realizing that Vormittag had probably not heard her the first time. Everyone seemed to believe that speaking loudly would disturb Marion. The quiet added to the tension building inside Stonecrop.

"Sad, isn't it." He first observed Marion and then scanned the room.

"The doctors report that she may, in time, recover. You are close, I understand," Vormittag stated, empathy in his voice.

"Yes, very."

"This is the first time you've been here. What an unfortunate interruption of your vacation." The raised eyebrows made it unclear if the statement intended as a question. Stonecrop, standing behind her, took hold of Federica's shoulders. He was letting her know that he supported her and, in addition, that she should let Vormittag do the talking.

"Well, I didn't . . . I . . ." Federica paused, at a loss. Claudia's parting words last night had been a warning: Offer nothing to the police or Gregor would get in a world of trouble. She, Claudia, would fix things, she had said.

Federica tried again. It was simply not her nature to dissemble, especially to a happy, old penguin. "It's hard for me to speak, I'm sorry."

"*Dimmi*—tell me. You were nearby?"

The comment threatened to commit Federica to being someplace specific. Vormittag's intention was unclear. Did he mean the incident with Cook, or just the last day or two?

"Your father's country house, perhaps?" he asked, offering an answer to the question he had just asked. "I've been there. Once. To see your father." He had either suggested a graceful way out or set a trap. The Italian *tell me* was spoken in a friendly, avuncular manner, like a teacher coaxing his student. Stonecrop's guess was the former.

"Where do you go, that is, when you need to get away?" Vormittag continued, showing—or baiting—the exit path.

"When I need to get away, I do go there," Federica began, the dutiful student repeating the question her teacher had just asked. "And I was there. It's not far, an hour or so. Papà doesn't use it; it's mine now, a summer rental. I mean, I rent it out in the summer and use it the rest of the year. You mean the place in Bäretswil, yes?"

Vormittag, of course, had suggested the cottage. "Not Croatia, then—"

Too late to alter the direction of her response, she continued. "No place exotic I'm afraid. Recently I'd had a slight fever, sore throat, and other symptoms of mononucleosis. I thought it wise to not put others at risk, at home or Spital. Bäretswil is quiet. A good place to rest and read a book."

Fede had, with coaching from Vormittag, artfully evaded a direct answer to Vormittag's own question. She had, in fact, not long ago spent a long weekend in Bäretswil when she had felt unwell and mono truly had been a concern.

"Tell me, did you read anything interesting?" Vormittag asked, giving her time to collect her thoughts.

The answer, however, was immediate. "*Medea*. Euripides's *Medea*."

"A strenuous read. Do you have a preferred translation?" Vormittag asked, continuing the small talk.

"Yes, my own." After she said it, she blushed. The statement could have been interpreted as arrogant, which had not been her intent.

"Impressive. Not something I would not attempt in even the best of health!" Vormittag sensed her embarrassment and understood. She was merely reporting a fact, not boasting. "I like the tragedies," he said. "My Greek is long forgotten, however, a good translation can get to the soul of a play, to what is beyond the words themselves. That, at any rate, is my hope."

Federica was unresponsive, either weary of small talk or lost in the question he had asked. After a minute of silence, he brushed aside the topic, "*Beh*—well, you must be tired. I hope you had someone to care for you in Bäretswil. To cook, do the marketing, that sort of thing." Again, the statement did double-duty as a question.

"No, no need. I'm quite self-sufficient," Federica believed the words. Stonecrop believed her. *I can't read Vormittag, not a bit.*

"And you are feeling better now, I hope?" the Kommissar asked.

"I am better, thank you. Tired, but okay," Federica waited before speaking. "I was very weak, and this . . ." she looked at Marion, although spoke to Vormittag. "I feel terrible I wasn't here for Marion. It's so horrible." Being with Marion gave Federica the strength to reengage. "Can you tell me what happened, or what you think happened?" she asked.

Stonecrop had been naïve. It would be child's play for Vormittag to catch Federica in a lie. She was too honest and the Kommissar was nobody's fool, plenty smart enough to pick up lies by omission. Furthermore, neither Stonecrop nor Federica knew what Vormittag or the Kantonspolizei had learned from Claudia or Ratzow or the inspection of the site at Albisriederstrasse. Was her gambit, oddly suggested by Vormittag, intended to be a trap or not? The Bäretswil house had been empty and was isolated. Had Polizei been tracking her car? Had they been to Bäretswil? Had the road been closed during the storm? The police must have had a transmitter on Ratzow's car to have known it was at Uitikon Waldegg station. Or they followed Stonecrop, and he hadn't noticed.

"Yes." Vormittag complied with her request. "The evidence suggests an attempted abduction," Vormittag began. "We don't know when, or where from, not exactly; nor do we know where her abductor or abductors planned to take her, exactly. It's likely she was released or broke free while crossing Stauffacherbrücke. Her residence is two blocks from the bridge. She had been bound with duct tape—hands, feet and mouth—yet somehow managed to free her hands. From the bridge, she either fell, jumped or was thrown over the guardrail. A person her age and stature would be challenged to simply climb over the guardrail. She landed in the Sihl. The splash alerted two *indigenti* camping on the bank of the river under the bridge. Were it not for them she would have perished. One man pulled her from the water, the other hailed a passerby on the bridge." Vormittag's delivery was methodical.

"Why would someone *do* this? It makes no sense. And who?" Federica asked, at a loss and seeking an answer for the horror both she and Marion had experienced. She was shaking; a tear rolled down her cheek. Vormittag politely gave her time to recover and handed over a handkerchief at the ready in the pocket of his overcoat. A quiet tension settled over Stonecrop. He feared that the details of the assault on Marion would be too much for Federica, that she would crack and fly into a wild rage. He had no plan for how to deal with that possibility.

"Good questions. I regret I don't have good answers. However, the car, the one we suspect was used in the assault, has been recovered. It was one the vehicles found at the recent so-called terrorist incident near Uetliberg. We believe the parties who died in the explosions were also connected with the attack on Mrs. Cook. Claudia Knight and your father have been informed of our progress in the investigation. Have you spoken with them since your return?"

"Not yet. Max has been in touch." Federica was connecting with him. "Any witnesses?"

"None, so far," he replied.

Vormittag did not pretend to not know who Stonecrop was, and having at least fifteen years on him, he was at ease addressing Stonecrop by his first name. "Max, you were at the Schützenhaus the night of the explosion. Peculiar coincidence, isn't it? I questioned staff there. They said you came in to escape the rain and wait for a ride home."

Stonecrop was not as unflappable in social interactions as he was in situations demanding simple, physical confrontation. He wished he were. Vormittag's statement made him nervous, so he said nothing.

"You have quite a reputation. The range director, a friend from military training, told me you were a disciplined shooter. You coached his son a few times—the boy is a junior competitor. He said his son adores you and that the training was fun."

Stonecrop still had nothing to add, so Vormittag went on. "My friend also said you were a complete madman! You run up and down Uetliberg with a backpack full of rocks or a biathlon rifle, and the worse the weather the better! A hard regimen." Vormittag went silent, again giving Stonecrop an opportunity to speak, and again getting silence. He smiled and added, "You're sure you're not a crazy Swiss!"

Stonecrop focused on the gray void beyond the window, searching for an emotional state to match the colorless landscape.

"Last night, did you see anything unusual?" Vormittag asked. "You were at the Schützenhaus at approximately the same time as the fireworks, and the Uetliberg trail is less than a kilometer away. You must have gone near the Albisrieder house—on foot and by auto."

"I must have just missed it," Stonecrop confidently made the partially true declaration. He tried to deflect Vormittag, "For the record, Kommissar, the range officer exaggerates. I don't like suffering. The weather was horrific last night. Lightning, rain, sleet. The forecast had been wrong. I was chilled to the bone. I truly am a softie—*ein weiches Eier*—a soft egg, that's what my ski buddies say. Too soft to jog back for Gregor's car. I had borrowed it earlier and parked at Uetikon Waldegg station."

"Yes, a wise decision, the ride back, that is. You speak German?" Vormittag asked, acknowledging Stonecrop's accurate pronunciation.

"A little, not like Federica," Stonecrop answered, understating his command of German.

"Ah, what is that expression in English—yes, I remember, *a bad egg*? German does not have an equivalent. We say *ein schlechter Kerl*—a bad guy."

The enormity of what Stonecrop and Federica were concealing from Vormittag was daunting. How could they possibly avoid being connected to the conflagration at Albisriederstrasse? And Vormittag wasn't the only one with questions. Stonecrop had a few of his own. Federica had not told him any details about the ordeal she had been through. She had insisted upon visiting Marion first thing today.

"Federica—and Max, same question for you—when did you last see Mrs. Cook?"

Federica responded first, "This happened when?"

"Last Wednesday, Wednesday evening. Perhaps you had left for Bäretswil. Miss Knight mentioned something about missing a business dinner. It was at one of those extraordinary suites at The Dolder Grand, if I remember correctly."

"Yes, I stopped by Marion's on the way home from work. Her place is not out of the way. Probably it was after five, after my shift. I checked in to make sure she didn't need anything. Sometimes I do little chores for her. Or Max does. We had tea together, herbal tea she thought would be good for my upset tummy. We talked a little, plans for the holidays, that sort of thing. Then I headed home. She said she was going to take a walk, which she does every night. I've walked with her before. She strolls up and down the Bahnhofstrasse and, now . . . the holiday displays, they're fun to see. Wednesday night, I don't remember her saying where she was going."

"Did you notice anything unusual?" Vormittag asked, "either in her behavior, or anything out of the ordinary on the way to or from her apartment?"

"She was fine when I started home," Federica said, and then turned away to avoid an exhibition of either sadness or dissimilitude.

Vormittag turned his attention to Max and waited for an answer.

His answer was brief. "I didn't see her. I was working." *Why didn't Vormittag press Fede for more? How she had felt, was she too sick to go to the dinner, what time did she leave for Bäretswil, and the weather that night?*

"You are a courier, correct?" Vormittag asked, making Stonecrop speculate again: How much had Vormittag learned from Claudia and Ratzow?

"Correct," Stonecrop said. "I deliver and pick up documents, sometimes artworks, and I walk Frau Ott's dachshund. A simple life. And, as you already know, I do a little volunteer coaching. Not real work. I just started the coaching." Stonecrop had offered much more than he had been asked. A simple yes or no would have sufficed.

Something in the way Vormittag expressed himself disturbed Stonecrop. Nothing moved except his lips. For someone of Italian descent, it was so *not* Italian. Stonecrop surmised the source of the oddity to be the sleeves of the overcoat. They were heavy and stiff. Had he moved the arms, Vormittag would have looked like a penguin leading an orchestra.

"Do you do courier work for any Asian clients?" Vormittag asked.

The last question, coming out of the blue, froze Stonecrop. He replied as calmly as possible, "No." He debated which would be a normal reaction, to ask why or to ignore the question. He opted for what felt natural, "Why do you ask?"

Vormittag didn't hesitate. It was too facile. "A new bank, Hong Kong based. They have a branch downtown. The manager had asked about bonded courier services."

"Something to consider, thank you," Stonecrop added a line to the performance.

Marion's state and her rhythmic sighing remained unchanged. Throughout their conversation, the sighs conveyed a hypnagogic backdrop to their conversation. A nurse came to the door. She "needed them to leave." The trite expression puts the cause of the dismissal on the patient who needs help, not the caregiver who is keen to get through the rounds.

The entire time during which Vormittag had been in the room he had not removed his overcoat, a carapace within which he was physically suspended. The mass had grown denser; Vormittag stooped more now than when he had arrived. The epaulettes of ice had melted into the shoulders. The three of them walked in silence through hospital halls lined with paintings of Swiss landscapes. They exited to the parking lot and breathed in fresh air. A light dusting of fresh snow covered recently arrived vehicles; ice coated the trees, benches and parking meters. Vormittag offered Federica a ride. She declined, saying she and Max were going for a coffee.

"Might we speak privately, just for a minute?" He addressed Federica, and then turned to Stonecrop. "Do you mind, Max?"

As if Stonecrop had a choice, he answered, "Of course not," and walked away from them, stopping just within earshot and at a junction where he and Federica would have to decide to either walk to the Polybahn or, the opposite direction, to the ETH tram stop. There was little traffic; the air was still, and sounds were muted by the snowfall. He kept his back toward them and listened.

"Federica, I could not help but notice the bruises on your wrists. They are fresh. Is there something more you would like to tell me?" The tone of the words was kind. Hamdi, Stonecrop recalled, had described Vormittag as a kind man.

Federica hesitated, as if she were weighing if she could trust him with the truth. "Kommissar Vormittag, this is personal. Can we keep it personal?"

"You have my word," he answered.

She waited again to speak. Then—as though at confession—she pried out the words, "Rough sex. I like rough sex." She threw her head back and to the side, striking a pose, intentional or not, of defiance and enticement.

Stonecrop doubted Vormittag had expected *that* response. He, Stonecrop, hadn't. It floored him. The statement had been so convincingly delivered. What *had* Vormittag expected? The freshly bruised wrists on Federica, the week-old markings on Marion's wrists —they were connected and they weren't. Vormittag was a detective, and detectives can't let go of such anomalies. Like Stonecrop, he sought causality where others might accept coincidence.

Vormittag did not react emotionally, his words were measured, "If I recall, not long ago there was a problem with a man. I forget where he was from, maybe Mexico. And if I'm not mistaken. He was . . ." he searched for the right expression in English, but preferred the Italian word, "*eccessivo.*" He continued, "Did Max—?

She interrupted him and laughed. She put both hands on one long black sleeve of his coat, pulling downward. Vormittag's fingers—or madeleines, as it were—vanished inside the sleeve, "Whoa! Max! Uh-uh, not at all. Sorry, I just can't imagine."

"Nor, frankly, can I. It would be . . . unlike him." The statement implied, of course, the existence of another man or woman. But Vormittag stayed on Max. "Max is ex-military, yes?"

Federica welcomed the shift in subject matter. "No again, Kommissar. Max and I are friends. I know him as well as anybody. He's never been in the military. Why do you ask, and why ask me?" She was light-headed, almost giddy. The pressure was getting to her.

"Something one of my officers had said. Not the man whose son Max had been helping. This officer also had been at the range. Police practice at Schützenhaus; Max was in the lane next to him. My officer noted that Max routinely shot two and three-centimeter groups at fifty meters, from the bench—that's when the shooter's rifle is resting on a table," he explained. "Oftentimes, the bullets went through the same hole. Quite a remarkable level of skill, a level one would expect from, say, someone with military training."

Federica laughed again. "Kommissar, did you watch the last Olympics?"

"I read, mostly history. I'm afraid I didn't watch—"

"A nineteen-year-old girl won the gold in the air rifle. She's a music student."

"Ah, there you have it! I *can* learn something useful from television." He relaxed, a good-natured and avuncular tone returned to his voice.

Vormittag was never in a hurry. He was quite at ease standing before Federica and saying nothing, as if he were taking time to read her thoughts. His gaze refocused on her hands. "Is there anything else you care to tell me?"

Federica smiled, aware of his gaze, and shook her head, "No." Then quickly recanted, once again taking his arm, though less forcefully than before, "Yes, actually." She took a breath before she spoke, "Mamma once said words are stones, and we don't have to use the same stones to cross the river. She was referring to translation and meaning—her métier."

Vormittag took her free hand in both of his, careful to avoid areas he knew were tender. "Thank you, Federica. I'm feeling less guilty about my dusty lexicon.

"Well, I should let you be on your way. Max begins to look like a snowman." He gave Federica a parting nod and handed her a card. "My handy, a private number. Don't be afraid to call me if anything gets . . ." he struggled a second time for the word, "*eccessivo*. It will be between us, only us."

Vormittag turned and started to walk away. He stopped, having some difficulty remembering or identifying which car was his. He turned again, addressing Federica, "*Fa brutto tempo!* It must have been an unpleasant drive from Bäretswil."

Federica had already headed toward Stonecrop; she kept walking. Vormittag moved on, returning to the search for his auto. It was odd, Stonecrop reflected, that he would have come in a car. The tram was so much easier. Had he been to Bäretswil this morning? What was clear to him was that the three of them shared a common sentiment: Namely, what had gone unsaid about the events in question had vastly dwarfed what had been said.

Federica had put off meeting with her father and Claudia for as long as possible. She and Max had agreed to share a Dante-free version of what had transpired. When asked about how they might explain Stonecrop's knowing the drone's location, Stonecrop had proposed a simple explanation: As he waited at the money pickup site, one of Federica's captors had turned on Federica's phone and before the "Find My Phone" feature had been disabled, Stonecrop had been able to see her phone's coordinates. That data had aligned with the direction of the drone carrying the pack full of cash. Not having an alternative, he had chased after the drone, continuing to the coordinates after losing the visual of the drone. The story would be hard to refute, and the details would be lost in the avalanche of other information related to her capture and release.

Stonecrop stayed by Federica's side. He felt protective and told her so. Her response: "Fuck off, Max. I absolutely cannot stand you hovering over me like a mother hen. I can handle Papà. And Claudia doesn't matter, she'll do whatever Papà says."

"Okay . . . you're welcome," he said. He was pleased to see the feisty Federica back in action. "Rough sex, huh."

"You better rest up," she gave him a faux-seductive wink. "Look, I need family time. I'm better on my own."

"The ransom money. They'll ask about it."

"And I'll tell them. I promise you, Papà could care less."

Stonecrop got the message. "Hiltl for dinner? When you finish up."

The Polybahn's arrival ended the conversation. Federica gave Stonecrop a kiss on the cheek and ducked inside the carriage as the doors were closing. He watched the tram descend, held fast by cables, and wondered if Federica felt confined by the small compartment. He *was* becoming a goddamned mother hen.

Despite the falling snow, Stonecrop opted to skip the shelter of a heated tram car. He realized that his own fear was just as irrational as Federica's, namely, that being easy on himself might weaken him, that he might be unprepared for what came next. There had been no sign of retaliation but the fear lingered.

He set off at slow trot winding up the back streets and alleyways to Frau Ott's. The pedestrian-only pathway was paved with granite cobblestones and gave good purchase even in icy conditions. He made a decision: Whether she liked it or not, he would hover over Federica for at least the next few days.

His body savored movement and the feeling of blood flowing through stiff and bruised muscles. It would take more than a night's rest to erase the wear and tear of the firefight at Albisriederstrasse, an event which he and Federica had dubbed 'The *Buurhuus*,' a concatenation of the Swiss German words for 'farmer' and 'house.' The name distanced them from the experience and made an unreal event even more unreal. Were it not for the physical evidence Stonecrop could have convinced himself that the entire experience had been a shared nightmare. He worked his way up the hill at a robotic pace and was still somewhat chilled when he passed through the gate at Frau Ott's. Rosie, a happy harbinger of his arrival, barked from within the house.

Just inside the gate and in front of the garage door he stopped dead in his tracks at the sight of four bright yellow Swiss Post Dispoboxes—the standardized plastic bins Swiss Post supplied for delivering bulk items. Gauging by the light covering of snow they must have just been delivered in the morning soon after he and Federica had left the house. There were two stacks, each two bins tall. He looked for prints on the ground, but they had been either swept away or covered by the fresh snow. Each box was addressed to Stonecrop. He portaged them two-at-a-time down the stairs to the door to Federica's apartment. Standing on one foot, he balanced the crates on a raised knee and turned the lever door handle to enter the apartment. The weight markings on the boxes were blacked out and the return address was not an actual Zürich address. A band of silver duct tape neatly wrapped around each box. The Dispoboxes could not have been sent via Swiss Post. The Swiss were fussy enough to insist recycled paper be tied with a specific biodegradable twine. It was *unmöglich* for the Swiss Post to permit its perfectly designed yellow plastic boxes to be accessorized with duct tape. As he cut the tape and popped the lid off the first box, he had a premonition that the contents would be a severed head of Chop-Chop, Capo, or Romeo, or that of the unknown kidnapper.

No gore awaited. Only cash, the same cash he had carried in his backpack a lifetime ago to Uetliberg Station and Im Sonnenbühl. *What a bizarre cycle.* Stonecrop inspected the crates. The second and third boxes were the same.

Rosie had exited the doggie door upstairs and tobogganed on her tummy down the stairs. She nosed her way through the door Stonecrop had left ajar and helped him with the fourth Dispobox. With much enthusiasm she sniffed and examined each corner. The last box was different and contained a duffle bag like the one Stonecrop had seen at the Buurhuus. It also contained an envelope. He unzipped the duffle and found another origami crane and, presumably, a quarter of the cash. On the envelope pinned to the duffel, Stonecrop's name was printed by hand in clumsy block letters. *Crap, here we go again.*

To his surprise, the note inside the envelope was in English. He had half-expected Japanese. The directive was neatly typed: *Deliver to Josefstrasse 52 to M Wulf.*

The second message was scrawled above the top of the first message: *Confirm receipt of monies with text. Include <three year on rock> in all texts. +41 79 400 18 28. Destroy note.*

Stonecrop didn't know whether to laugh or cry. He eloquently expressed his feelings, addressing Rosie: "Shit."

Rosie sat. ·

Hiltl

"How was the rest of your day?" Federica asked.

A private table had been reserved thanks to Stonecrop's being a regular and knowing the hostess, Lara. Located at the intersection of Sihlstrasse and St. Annagasse, not far from Bahnhofstrasse, Restaurant Hiltl was an easy stop for passersby and a regular destination for locals. Offering non-meat fare since 1898, Hiltl touted itself as one of oldest continuously operating vegetarian restaurants in Europe. Over the last few years, Hiltl had expanded, opening at locations that attracted a wide range of cliental.

Max had arrived slightly ahead of Fede. He had checked the North Face duffel in the cloakroom, leaving a hundred-franc note with Lara and asking her to keep an eye on the bag. He met Fede at the door just in time for the dinner rush at 19:00. They touched hands and performed the obligatory Zürich greeting, two air kisses, one for each cheek. Like a married couple going through the drill without having to speak, they found plates and lined up for the buffet at the Asian food bar.

At the register, one paid for a meal either per kilo or per a fixed price for all you can eat. Tonight, they would pay by the kilo. Sometimes, when Fede had worked a long shift and not had a chance to eat, she would opt for the prix fixe fare. On those days, even though Max outweighed her by ten kilos, her plate outweighed his.

Fede looked physically and emotionally exhausted. Eating out was a good call. She would have been too hungry to wait for dinner and they both would have been too tired to cook. A common story for couples everywhere.

"The usual," he responded to her question. "Swiss Post dropped off a couple million dollars at your doorstep. I found it; I suppose it's mine."

"Hey, my address. Let's split it and split." She was too exhausted to act surprised.

"There's more."

"Scary or not?"

The buffet line was not an appropriate place for this conversation.

"This time, I swear, I'm not going to overdo it," he said, referring to the likelihood of ending up with a mountain of food on his plate.

"Yeah, right," Fede didn't buy it. Neither did Stonecrop.

The food piled up on their plates—tikka masala, saag tofu, winter dal, eggplant salad, spiced cauliflower, ginger split-pea curry, rice, kale and chickpeas, and curried cashew burgers. Max's plate, as predicted, overflowed. They put their platters on scales, paid the charge, and returned to their table. Max ordered a carafe of house red and they resumed their conversation.

"About scary, I'm not sure. The note's in two parts. I think the first was for Capo and company. They were supposed to deliver one duffle to someone named Wulf. The second part, hand-written, has a contact number which, I'm guessing, is from Mother and Father. Weird, huh? I asked another courier in town—he's got a van—to pick up the other three crates. He'll dump them on Geissner's doorstep late tonight and disappear."

"You trust him?" she asked.

"Very much so. We've worked a couple gallery moves. Valuable art. He's an honest guy—"

"—for a dishonest job," she added.

"Something I don't get," Stonecrop spoke as if he were talking to himself, "is why you, why your doorstep?"

"It is addressed to both of us. It's my money, and you're the designated delivery boy," she unenthusiastically offered.

"I tried to call Ratzow," Stonecrop said. "He's incommunicado. Did he say anything to you?"

"Not really. He just listened. What about this guy, Wulf?" Fede asked casually. They behaved as if they were a couple discussing the kids' homework.

"Must be his cut in a duffel. I'm sure it's the duffle Romeo put in the back seat of the Opel." Federica gave him a puzzled look. She had not been aware of the money transfer. Stonecrop explained, "Ah, you *and* a duffle of money were supposed to be delivered somewhere special last night. I'm guessing Wulf's."

The sassy attitude Federica had had after the meeting with Vormittag had worn off. A nervous twitch made her entire body jump —a muscle spasm, or maybe she was reliving the memory of being blindfolded and trapped in the trunk of the car.

She held her fork in the air and addressed him. "Is it me? Or is the food's not a good as it used to be since they opened Sihlpost and Dachterrasse."

"Wulf's address is just on the other side of the Hauptbahnhof—ten minutes from here on the 13."

Her eyes drifted from one table to the next, unwilling to focus. She was unraveling. Her fork shuffled bits of food around the plate. Fede wasn't eating and she was too disoriented to make sense of what he had said.

Stonecrop closed his eyes and tried to imagine the fear and confusion she must be feeling. The exercise hurt; he berated himself for his tendency to shut down emotionally. He wanted to help, but he felt helpless. And the more helpless he felt, the colder and more distant he became. It was a self-defeating cycle.

Neither spoke until a customer addressed them both, asking if the nearby table was free. They nodded back in unison.

"First Mother and Father," Fede reengaged—the interaction with the customer brought her back. They had gotten in the habit of referring to the Japanese couple as Mother and Father. "And now, a mysterious Herr Sorgen."

"It looks like the money was to be divvied up four ways. Mother and Father dispatched three of the extortionists."

"And Wulf Sorgen is number four," she said, expecting confirmation.

"Hard to say. Hamdi's son Michael described the people who had been casing my apartment as well-dressed. One was tall and *possibly* Turkish, which could be anyone, but the description was different than our deceased friend, Chop-Chop. He didn't exactly look like a dresser. The Caucasian, other guy, was the shorter of the two Michael saw. Capo and Romeo are . . . were tall."

She bowed and closed her eyes as if in prayer. "Poor Chop-Chop."

Stonecrop didn't say what he thought: The son-of-bitch tried to kill you.

Federica looked up again. "Wulf is not exactly a Turkish name, or Italian."

"Nope. Suppose Wulf's got a tall, not Caucasian sidekick—I mean, we've got a report of another person that can't be explained, right?"

Stonecrop's head ached. It wasn't a throb. It was continuous, more like his head was wrapped in barbed wire that was tightening like a Chinese finger trap every time he tried to make sense of their situation. "I want to be done with this business, Fede. And I want number four, or whoever else is involved, to join the other three."

"I don't, Max. And you shouldn't. I'm grateful to be alive, to be here with you. And I'm fed up with trying to pay for others' misdeeds— Papà's or anybody else's. We both do that. You've asked before what we have in common. Well, that's one fucking really bad thing we have in common."

She reached out for his hand. When the sleeve of her sweatshirt rubbed on a patch of raw skin on her wrist she started. Stonecrop helped her roll up the sleeves, baring elbows and wrists to make it easier to eat. Customers who caught sight of her wrists reacted differently, some averted their gaze out of politeness, others stared.

"I had *the talk* with Papà *and* Claudia. Left Dante out the story, like we agreed. Claudia didn't give me the third degree. Papà told her to shut up. You frightened her, Max. You *were* kind of scary. Most people would have been freaked out. You were like one of them, like Mother and Father—"

Max reached out to hold her arm, taking care to avoid the abrasions. "I am not like them, Fede. I swear. And I was scared shitless. I just acted. It's like climbing. If something is flying out of control, you can't worry about it while you're in the middle of it or you fuck up. My focus was for us to make out of there. That's all I wanted."

Their conversation, quiet and intermittent, continued. They took their time, trying to feel normal and from time to time commenting on the food.

"We're arrogant, we Swiss. We have so much. Look at this." She surveyed the room and opened her arms with palms-up hands.

"No," Stonecrop countered, "we're fortunate. And our moral responsibility can only extend so far. Let it go."

With food in her belly, Fede's attitude had improved, "You're right. I *am* fortunate. Yes, my hero—well, you *and* Dante and Miss Piggy! Did you see Miss Piggy? Knock on wood," she tapped the table with her knuckles, "AD will get a few piglets for Mozambique." He nodded. She gave him a peck on the cheek, leaving a drop of raita where she had kissed him. Max felt it, smiled, and used his napkin to wipe his cheek. Her phone vibrated. She read the message and her expression brightened.

"Good news?" he asked. Good news would be welcomed.

"Yay! I texted Alicia and she'll be here tonight! Late flight but she should be at the apartment by the time we're back from dinner."

Max was relieved. He had been on the fence about his plans for the night. It would be best if Federica were with someone. His anxiety over her being out of his sight was something he couldn't put in a box and disregard. But Alicia he trusted.

"Great, super," he said, and then asked the question he'd been putting off. "Fede, what did happen to you and Marion? If you don't want to talk about it, I understand. If you remember and haven't like blocked it all out."

"I remember everything, too well. I was terrified, Max."

"Wine helps!" Stonecrop joked.

Federica sighed, "I've been through the tale once already today, so . . . not too many questions. Okay?"

Max took her hand.

"Marion and I had tea at her place, like I told Vormittag. After tea, we went outside. We walked a few blocks and then went our separate ways. I turned off for the tram stop, which is not far from Stauffacherbrücke. Vormittag thinks I went home. Obviously, that's not what happened. I went maybe fifty meters when a car—it was the Opel —passed by and parked a little ahead of me. After I walked past the car, two men got out and came up behind me. They dropped a hood over my head and wrapped tape across my mouth. Then they taped my wrists and ankles, picked me up, and threw me in the trunk. One of them reached in my pocket and took my phone. It happened so fast. I had an anxiety attack, as much from being put in the trunk as the assault."

"But Marion wasn't with you?"

"No. But she must have heard or seen what had happened. Brave Marion. I can't believe how brave she is. She yelled something and must have run up to the car. I heard scuffling. They subdued her and, I'm guessing, bound her with tape like me. Marion didn't have a hood over her head when she was pulled out of the water. I'm sure they hadn't expect her."

"How did she get away?" Max asked. He had promised to not pester her with questions, yet here he was, asking away.

"I don't know. I was in the trunk, terrified for myself and for her. I heard a scream and heard the man wrestling with her. I felt a thud from Marion being thrown in the back seat. The men got back in the car. Doors closed and men argued. Then we took off." Fede spoke calmly, pausing to eat as she spoke. "I have a theory."

"About?" Stonecrop asked.

"About how she escaped. Marion has atopic dermatitis—eczema—on her hands and feet. I'd just given her a fresh tube of corticosteroid cream. She immediately applied it to her hands and wrists. I'm guessing the abductors were in a panic and did a sloppy job of binding her. She may have been able to free her hands because the tape wouldn't stick to the salve. With hands free, she could have removed or loosened the tape on her ankles.

"The rear door opened right after they started off. She must have rolled out onto the sidewalk. I remember the jerk of car stopping, a man getting out, swearing, and the driver yelling in Italian that people were coming. I heard steps, Marion sort of hobbling and the sharp clap-clap of a man's dress shoes on the pavement. The shoes had hard leather soles and heels. She must have fled toward the railing on Stauffacherbrücke. It's concrete and waist high. And wide . . ." Federica used her the palms of her hands to show the width of the railing. "I can't imagine Marion climbing over it. Maybe, in the scuffle and with people approaching, her assailant decided the most expedient course was to toss her over the side. She weighs nothing.

"The man got back in the car and they took off. They were screaming at each other in Italian. I couldn't make out what they were saying." Her voice was uneven. The front of her sweatshirt fluttered from the trembling of her chest. She spread her fingers wide, flattened them on the tabletop and stared at them. She was willing them to be steady. "Shit, I'm not going to be able to work, not like this."

They ate in silence for a few minutes, then Max resumed questioning her. "At the Buurhuus, Fede. Did they abuse you?" Because she had said nothing about it, and from the recording, Max had assumed the worst.

"They kept their identities from me. Had me face away when they took off the hood. My room was small and cold and damp. No windows. It had a cot and blanket, chamber pot, and pitcher for water. I never saw their faces, at least not until that asshole tried to shove me into the trunk. I could have killed him, Max. I wanted to make him hurt for what he did to me and for what they did to Marion. I was crazed." Fede drank some water and added in a confessional tone, "I had feelings that a doctor—a person dedicated to *not* harming people

—shouldn't feel. I'm not a violent person. You know that, right?"

"I know that, yes. Were you interrogated? They fed you, I hope."

"No interrogation. Random food. Like dog shit on a tray. They would open the door a little, and slip it in. I got sick from it. Diarrhea. Shit in my pants, totally gross."

"I'm sorry, Fede. What a nightmare. A fearful, humiliating nightmare."

"I don't get it. They were Italians and the food should have been better! I, like, really resent that."

"Yeah, you should have asked about the food first."

"I would have, but the tape . . ." Fede shook her head, holding in the smile. A playful moment.

"They were angry. The diarrhea was gross! Maybe it was a good thing. Like you're not so hot when you shit your pants. We didn't exactly hang out." She smiled at Max.

"I love my girl, shitty pants and all."

Federica winked and smiled again. She resumed her story: "It was hard to hear what they were saying in the other room; the walls were thick. I doubt they knew I understood Italian. They spoke a Sicilian dialect. I think Salentino, so I didn't get it all. They spoke to me in poor German and worse English. I picked up a little chatter when they brought food.

"The Japanese man never spoke. He came to my room once. Thank god."

"How so?" he asked.

She looked upward and began twirling the fork on her plate as if there were pasta on the plate. Stonecrop waited.

"Not the Japanese man, but another man, very strong, tried to rape me." Federica leaned forward. She put down the fork. Her hands became fists and rested on top of the table. "I was face down and couldn't see through the hood. He hit me, Max. I was fucked up from the drugs—they put some kind of shit drugs in the shit food. Maybe it was for the diarrhea. I didn't feel much,"

"Were you drugged the whole time?"

"No, it was shortly before this fuck-head showed up."

"You said he *tried* to rape you . . ."

"Yeah. I think Chop-chop walked in on it. He ordered the guy to stop. I was pretty out of it, but before he said stop in English, he might have said *yamero*, which is 'stop' in Japanese. But I didn't pick up on it, not then. I think Chop-chop, if it was him, had a gun. I heard a click like the slide on an automatic. Then the creep backed off. They argued in the other room and then I passed out or something. When I came to, I smelled this weird odor. I didn't remember until later, but the odor was familiar. Smells stick with you.

"I never spoke to Chop-chop. I wish I had. We could have spoken Japanese. He was different than the others. In the end, I felt he was a terribly sad and tragic man."

"I'd be sad too if had been ordered to shoot myself."

"Before this craziness there had to have been something so tragically wrong in his life."

"I find it hard to feel sorry for him."

"I don't."   Federica lifted the wine glass to her lips. Using both hands she steadied it and took several sips before setting the glass down, once again using with both hands.

"The Italians were assholes. They made lewd comments and treated me like," Fede held her fork in the air and skewered the word, "a *puttana*. I was the captured whore they were going to sell to some other guy—no idea who—for his pleasure. Talk about objectifying women, Christ."

"Were you a perk, a reward? In addition to the money and whatever the fuck else they wanted out of Gregor."

"I guess. Unless it was something more."

"Like what?" he asked.

"I really don't know," Fede looked around her, scanning the faces of other diners. "I felt like I was the main attraction."

Stonecrop laughed. "You're always the main attraction," and then realized the levity was out of place. "Sorry."

"They mentioned this weirdo they were going to hand me to. I never got a name. It wasn't a joke or idle threat." Federica continued: "I kept thinking about young women transported to Europe and bought and sold like so much meat. That's what it felt like. Traffickers are sick bastards. The guys who kidnapped me were dumb thugs. I don't know what they had in mind for me. But they weren't supposed to touch the goods. I think they were afraid of what would happen if they did."

Federica slouched in her chair. Disappointed with herself, disgusted with the world. Stonecrop couldn't tell. She hung her head, elbows on the table and hands at her temples. "I'm like this empty vessel." She put the silverware at three o'clock, unable to finish the food on her plate.

A waiter cleared the table and left the wine. Max finished both his and Federica's. When the waiter returned, Federica had closed her eyes. Max excused himself to speak with the hostess, Lara.

He returned and tried to look cheerful. "Fede, time to rest. Sorry about questions." He took her hand. "I just spoke to Johan, Hamdi's son."

"I like him," Fede spoke. The words were sleepy, unengaged. "Handsome young man."

"Well, he's on his way. He's giving you a lift up the hill. I've got a little errand to do. I'll be home in an hour."

The comment snapped her back to attention. "Now? Why aren't you come home with me?" Then it hit her. "*Scheisse!* You're going to Wulf's!"

"Yeah. Hey, won't be long. Text me when you get home, okay?" Max acted like he was going next door to borrow a cup of sugar. She was too emotionally spent to argue.

They sat in silence. Max held her hands and passersby respected their space; even the waiter ignored them. A few minutes later, Lara walked to their table, Johan in tow.

The young man escorted her to the car and helped her in. Max thanked him for being the chauffeur and closed the car door, relieved that Fede was in safe hands and going home. Johan drove a few feet before Max saw Federica grab him by the shoulder and then the car stopped abruptly. She lowered the window and leaned out. Stonecrop was still standing at the curb.

"The smell," she yelled. She didn't care who heard her. "The smell on my body. It was cologne, *his* cologne."

"Whose?" he shouted.

"Andreas! It was Andreas."

"You're sure."

"Dead sure? No. Crap, I don't know. I think so."

The window went back up. Stonecrop watched them drive away. He texted Alicia that Johan was driving Fede home. He also asked if she was armed, and got a thumbs up response.

Federica would be safe. Tension had been building in him since he had read the note from Mother and Father. One option was to return the money and be done with it. Another, to follow the money and determine if indeed it was Andreas who had attempted to rape Federica. Unlikely, he thought.

Stepping back into Hiltl, he asked Lara for a favor. In two minutes he was out the door again, this time with the North Face duffel and something extra weighing it down. He had made a decision.

Wulf

The door at Josefstrasse 52 was answered by a short, thin man in his late thirties and wearing a pair of woven Japanese slippers. His slacks were gray wool and stylishly cut. At the waist, a narrow, Versace alligator-skin belt threaded its way through oversized belt loops. A plain white, high-collared, long-sleeved cotton blouse tucked in at the waist. The ensemble was topped off with a matador-style, three-quarter-sleeved velvet jacket. Elegant gold hoop earrings peeked out from under a curtain of shoulder-length black hair. Reading glasses, the Armani variety, perched atop his nose—or rather, *her* nose.

Stonecrop instantly recalled images of his cross-dressing younger brother, who, at thirteen, had committed suicide. Charley had smiled a lot. He had had a mischievous smile, like he was laughing at some private joke and there was no way he was going to share it with you. Stonecrop had loved him deeply and had always stood up for him—or her, as she preferred.

"Wulf? I'm looking for Wulf Sorgen." Stonecrop said. It was hard to speak. Images and memories of Charley overran the words. Charley had dyed her hair black, like Wulf's. She had tried to straighten it by ironing, but the tangled thicket of hair wouldn't yield. Her hair, like Stonecrop's, had been inherently unmanageable.

"Grüezi, yes, that's me," Wulf said as she stepped forward, close enough for Stonecrop, who was significantly taller than Wulf, to notice hair grafts and smell Wulf's perfume or body wash. It was pleasant odor, not overdone.

"I'm Andreas. Good evening." Stonecrop used Castro's name. He was curious if the name would draw a reaction—a negative one, making Stonecrop out as an imposter, or a positive one, confirming Andreas' involvement in the kidnapping.

"Yes, I'm Wulf, Wulf Sorgen," she repeated, "may I help you?" Wulf squinted above the tops of her reading glasses, obviously also in need of corrective lenses for distance vision. Her gaze fell upon the green North Face duffle in Stonecrop's hands.

"I believe you are expecting this. And I brought a little something to celebrate." Stonecrop put the duffel on the floor just inside the entryway. He unzipped it, revealing the cash, and a bottle wrapped in a Hiltl paper bag. With some fanfare, he removed the bottle of Williams Eau de Vie Poire. "Shall we?"

Wulf grinned. The distinctive grin aligned with a pointed jaw. For some, the angularity would have been unattractive. But in Wulf it suggested a becoming fragility. The alignment and symmetry of her features plus the straight nose and the lack of facial hair evidenced cosmetic surgery. She was vulnerable. Stonecrop felt it; his natural reaction was to protect, not threaten. Wulf lowered her head within inches of the bag. She held her reading glasses so they wouldn't fall off.

"*Fantastisch! Wunderbar!* I am *so* excited! Did *I* get the day wrong? I was *so* worried. Hardly a word! Is tonight *the* night? The deposit can't happen today, obviously. I thought the affair was supposed to be last night. When I got the message to 'wait'—now what does that mean, just *wait*—I thought the transaction was off! Must I leave now? I can. I need ten minutes. I'm packed-up and ready to go."

Stonecrop had no idea why Wulf was offering to leave. She was his source. She had to stay. "No, not at all. No need to go. A drink?"

"I was drinking tea, green tea, if you'd rather?"

Stonecrop held up the Williams to make his preference clear.

"Sure, well, why not," Wulf retreated to the studio kitchen. En route, she retrieved a pair of white hose that had been tossed atop an enormous quilted Moroccan cushion. Sans hose, she returned with two aperitif glasses. One came from the drying rack next to the sink, the other from the cupboard next to and above a modern Gaggenau cooktop and work surface. *She lives alone.*

The apartment, which from the street was indistinguishable from its neighbors, was on the interior a page out of *Architectural Digest.* The main room was a blocky, right-angled affair. The walls had been hand-plastered in a desert-sand color and were ringed with a deep banquette treated in the same manner. The contents of the bookcase displayed an eclectic intellect—poetry, finance, art and anthropology.

Several coffee-table books were stacked atop a round industrial table. Stonecrop read the spines: *Ellsworth Kelly's Plant Drawings, Basquiat,* and *Mapplethorpe.* The focal point of the room was a floor-to ceiling pilaster, a foot deep, with an inset fireplace and wood storage cubby. Discoloration from heat and smoke added texture to the fireplace.

"Who did those?" Stonecrop asked, pointing at a series of large, hand-colored etchings of rocks. The works were hung with intentional irregularity. "I like how you arranged them. Like they're part of the wall."

Wulf answered as she swayed back to the room. "That was the intent, yes. An earthy context to the space. My ex-partner did them. He's quite talented, isn't he?"

"He is. Any shows?"

"Not yet. Not trying. He's young. There's time."

"Well, they're terrific."

"I know! And I know why you're here. Shall we get down to business?"

"Yes, of course."

"But you're not the *One* are you? That's what I call him. I had hoped we'd meet. I've never even spoken to him. Always a friend-of-a-friend thing." Wulf fidgeted. She was trying to conceal her nervousness.

"Correct. Sorry to disappoint," Stonecrop said, doing his best to hide his confusion. "I deliver the cash, make sure *alles ist in Ordnung.*" The trite German expression, he realized after the fact, had been a stupid thing to say.

Wulf handed a glass to Stonecrop, who did the pouring. They toasted, "*Zum Wohl!*" Each had a sip, not downing the shots wholesale. It was an act of wariness on both sides. Wulf set her drink on the top of an early 1900s art deco sideboard.

"Please, sit," Wulf said, and offered a chair. The art deco chair had a narrow, ram-rod-straight back and a velvet cushion. Wulf pulled up a matching chair. Together, they slid the duffel between them. Wulf pursed her lips and petted the duffle—a lazy, green dog sleeping at their feet.

A gilt-framed photo on the sideboard depicted a dapper Wulf, dressed as a man, shaking hands with an equally well-dressed executive in a matching tan overcoat and standing in front of the doorway at Moretti & Cie, Banquiers. Something in the photograph nagged at Stonecrop. Beside the photograph was another pair of glasses—gold wire-rims—which Wulf must have used for distance vision.

Wulf grabbed a packet of bills and held it inches from her face to read the denominations. She peeled off two bundles, one thousand dollars each, and handed one to Stonecrop. "A pourboire! Why not be generous!"

Stonecrop put the money on the floor next to his chair.

"No need really."

"Please, it's yours. One must always share good fortune. I insist!"

"Well, thank you."

"This is magnificent fun," Wulf said, "like the old days, when carriages from France smuggled cash across the Alps to *Genève*. Imagine. What a thrill that must have been!"

Wulf's bankers' hands skillfully assembled a bundle of cash equal to fifty thousand dollars, which she set aside, and proclaimed, "One night's rent!" She zipped the bag shut and leaving a hand on it, announced, "I'll deposit this tomorrow."

They toasted again, downing the rest of the first draught. Stonecrop prepped a second; he didn't push the conversation. Wulf did not come across as a professional crook, she was too nervous, too chatty.

"The thing with that girl is not tonight?" She answered her own question, "Stupid of me. It's not, or she would be here. And the money was to be in the account today. Do you suppose the money is for her? For one night, over 400 thousand U.S. *Mein Gott!* Quite a bundle for one night. Or maybe she's a keeper. Imported goods? Some virgin East-European ingénue?" She thought the remark clever.

Stonecrop didn't react. "Money goes in the account tomorrow," he said, not knowing what else to say and hoping Wulf would say more.

"Yes, yes—that was the deal. First the money, then the girl. It's tomorrow then?"

"So I've been told." To accommodate the flow of conversation, Stonecrop concurred.

"Then I shall be away tomorrow. Out of sight, out of mind. They'll have the place to themselves." The *out* was pronounced with a Canadian raising. "Everything is set. The Champagne is in the . . ." she searched for the word in English, "in the *Kühlschrank*—the fridge. There's cheese, bread, soup, snacks. A picnic, eh! The One, or his little thing, have big appetites."

A picnic? Good grief!

"Yeah, well, they couldn't make it tonight," Stonecrop reported matter-of-factly, not knowing what else to say. He was a lousy liar and hoped it didn't show.

"And those goodies! Hand-delivered yesterday! I had *not* expected *that*!" Wulf laid on the excitement.

Stonecrop nodded, completely in the dark about what Wulf was referring to.

"Our mystery man has expensive tastes; I'll give him that. A lovely Dunhill leather bag. But you're aware—or perhaps you aren't—about the extra item with *my* name on it." She smiled as broadly as the sharp chin allowed. "I *did* peek! Naughty of me, I know," she announced. The mischief of the deed was made clear through the inflexion in her voice. "I wasn't to open *my* gift until after I had made the deposit. But I can't use it, not now."

"Who brought it? We use several people, just curious."

"Handsome man, a brute. I think it was a Max. Yes, Max was his name."

Blood rushed to Stonecrop's head. It had to have been Andreas. And he had used Max's name! He tried to distract Wulf. "I recognize the masks. That is, their origins." He focused on four large masks hanging on the wall. There were two on each side of the fireplace. "The ones on the left are Kabuki. Are the other two—Mali maybe?"

"Very, good, Andreas, *very* good. The Kabuki were a gift from a client. I shouldn't accept gifts, but we made a little exception this time. By the way, lovely stuff in the Dunhill," she said conspiratorially. "It's *abnorm*—not that there's anything *wrong* with kinky. I don't judge. Do you?" She winked at Stonecrop and downed her pear brandy. The way Wulf held the glass, firmly yet lightly, simply aware of what he was doing—reminded Stonecrop of his brother.

"No judgements," Stonecrop said, finding relief again in agreeing to something he at least partially believed.

Their conversation was moving in the direction of a tête-à-tête. Wulf prated on. "Where did you find it all? I thought I saw a choker. Is she a gasper, eh?" It was a Canadian "eh" again. Federica's and Geissner's obsessions with accents was rubbing off on him.

Wulf's eyes twinkled. Beads of sweat formed on her brow. She wiped off the sweat with her finger, lightly flicking aside a forelock of hair. Wulf waxed on, "Oh my goodness, and there's that kit. Let me show you!"

She left for the bedroom and returned with an expensive black leather Dunhill weekender, the size of a small carry-on. She undid the leather fasteners. At the top lay neatly folded masks, ropes, leather bra and panties, and below, a selection of harmless sex toys. Wulf dug through the bag, inspecting and commenting on several articles.

Stonecrop yawned; the brandy and wine from earlier were getting to him. Sex paraphernalia was not his thing.

Another refill. Wulf drank without giving it a second thought, greedily this time, finding what he had been looking for.

"Ah, here it is! *My* kit." She produced a red and gold embroidered silk satchel.

"She must be something else," Stonecrop said. "Are you sure it's just the woman?"

"As far as I know. You see I needed to know to tell my landlady. I'm staying nearby, at my sister's. She's on holiday, spa time. We all love spa time! My place is lovely, don't you think? Ideal for *this* sort of thing, eh. They'll like it, and the fresh flowers in the bedroom. They'll still be fine tomorrow."

The statement confused Stonecrop. At first, he thought Wulf meant that her place was a spa. Of course, that's not what she meant. The brandy was winning.

"When were you supposed to return?" Stonecrop risked another question he should have known the answer to.

"The following night, after nine. I'm not supposed to call or anything. But I told my landlady. She lives next door. She's half-deaf— a blessing, really. And half-blind, like me. I told her my friends would be staying the night. Paid her a little something to make sure she wouldn't notice anything. It's really still on?"

"Yes, tomorrow night," Stonecrop lied again. The liquor helped with lying.

Wulf gracefully knelt on the plush Moroccan area rug. She placed the satchel next to Stonecrop's chair.

"Well, of course, you wouldn't know. But I'll tell you. I don't need this. Well, I do *want* it. But . . . I did HAT."

Stonecrop was familiar with HAT—Zürich's undeniably successful Heroin-assisted Treatment program. *I wish my brother would have had access to a program like HAT.*

"But if *you* would like a taste?" She held up the satchel, and then delicately undid the silk tie-strings and extracted a packaged syringe. "Shame to waste, eh?"

She put her hand on Stonecrop's knee, then slid it up higher, playing with the drawstring hanging half-untied from Stonecrop's running pants.

"Or maybe—"

"Sweet of you," Stonecrop interrupted, "another time."

Stonecrop wanted information, not heroin. He was drunk and tired of the charade. And he was baffled by Wulf's attentiveness.

"You care. I feel it," Wulf said.

Wulf was right. Stonecrop did care, but not quite the way Wulf thought.

"Wait," Stonecrop ordered. He rose from his seat and held Wulf's shoulders. "Here, let me." He smiled at Wulf, and gently pulled her velvet jacket over her shoulders—binding Wulf's arms. He eased Wulf up to her feet and then back onto the chair where she had been sitting. He briefly massaged Wulf's shoulders, and then gently pinned Wulf in place by sliding the velvet jacket over the back of the chair.

Wulf complied as Stonecrop slid the legs of Wulf's slacks halfway up her thighs. Her hands clutched the sides of the chair. There was moisture on the sides of the seat marking where each of Wulf's fingers compressed the cushion.

The veins above the scarecrow ankles were scarred. There were remnants of infection and scarring on the fleshy parts of the thighs— evidence of past intramuscular injections. Nothing recent.

Stonecrop had seen legs like that before, on his brother. The blue streaks and the skin-popping had been fresh. His brother had been ridiculed for being transgender, and heroin had been his escape. The drug use had surprised everybody. The self-abuse had worsened after Stonecrop had left for college and focused on biathlon trials. Stonecrop had believed, and still believed, that he could have prevented his brother's death.

He'd had enough of stringing Wulf along. And he had no desire to make her suffer. "How long have you worked at the bank, at Moretti?"

Confused, Wulf answered, "Five years, why?"

Stonecrop didn't answer. "I need the account number for the deposit. I was told to confirm the number."

"I can't. I respect my clients' anonymity. Surely you have it!" Wulf pleaded.

"I'm sorry," Stonecrop said, meaning it. He stood up and walked slowly to the back of Wulf's chair. "Does the bank know you use?"

"What?"

The answer challenged Stonecrop's failure to recognize the obvious. "I'm clean now, I swear. You can see for yourself."

"Look Wulf, we just need confirmation. The account, please."

Stonecrop undid Wulf's belt and slid it out of the belt loops. She didn't struggle. He took his time doing it. Then, just as patiently, he looped the narrow belt around Wulf's neck and secured it like an oversized twisty.

"I can't," she repeated. Wulf hung her head and sighed. Stonecrop gave the belt a twist.

She tilted her head and tried to swallow. "You're just playing. *Ja*, a little joke, eh?" She begged, hoping this was all make-believe, or elaborate foreplay and not the horror that Stonecrop's actions implied.

Stonecrop cinched the belt tighter. Wulf got the message. When Stonecrop eased the pressure, she squeezed out a response. "If you kill me, you won't have the account."

"True. Just the cash, a nice bottle of Champagne and bag of sex toys, and a dead Wulfie." Stonecrop spoke softly into Wulf's ear, "Consider the alternative. Give me the account number, keep your mouth shut and do your business tomorrow. Say hi to your sister. Forget me and keep the fee. We all live happily ever after, *eh?*"

They looked at each other. Bile rose in Stonecrop's throat. He was sickened by his own behavior. "I promise you," he added, "I do *not* want to hurt you." He meant every word.

Her head bent slightly toward the sideboard. "Under the photo in the picture frame. A yellow Post-it."

Stonecrop put the belt on the sideboard and next to the framed photo. He removed the fold-out easel backing to the frame, revealing, as promised, a yellow Post-it Note with a handwritten account number on it. Holding the note flat on the sideboard, Stonecrop took out his phone. There was a text from Fede. She was at her place with Alicia.

"Your lucky day, Wulf." Stonecrop spoke as he took a photo of the note. "The numbers match. Make the deposit first thing tomorrow. What's your mobile." Her mouth trebled as she recited her mobile number. "There, that wasn't so bad." Stonecrop recorded the number and said thank you. Her teeth, Stonecrop noted, were white, aligned and all there. He'd always associated junkies with horrible teeth. Not so with Wulf. Nor had it been the case with his brother. He had been so young it probably didn't matter.

Wulf was squinting, trying to make out Stonecrop's features. Did she recognize him? Not likely. Unless she had been shown a photo, to know when he had exited his apartment on Münstergasse.

"Oh, and," Stonecrop threatened, "tonight—no calls, no drugs."

Wulf nodded. Stonecrop had no doubt she would comply. He bent forward and pressed his head beside Wulf's. "Look, you're being played. Just do like I say and we'll all be okay. If you fuck this up, you're dead. These people are bad."

Surprising both himself and Wulf, he put his arms around Wulf and gave her a hug. "Take care." Stonecrop said in a calm voice. He picked up the pourboire—his tip—and walked out of the apartment, leaving behind a stunned, obviously confused, and much relieved Wulf Sorgen.

A multitude of concerns nagged at Stonecrop. He was tipsy, emotionally disoriented and making mistakes. There was no way he would have hurt Wulf, a cultivated man—now a woman, a person who, in fact, he admired for having the courage to both be herself and kick her addiction. He was convinced Wulf had nothing to do with the actual abduction.

It was certain that Andreas Castro had delivered the heroin. And that it was Andreas who had used his name. Why two separate deliveries? Sex toys; then drugs?

Shit, I should have grabbed the kit.

Banquiers

The next day, despite the urgency to get on with the hunt for the fourth kidnapper and a new data point about Andreas, Stonecrop slept in. When he awoke, Fede was still dead to the world. He eased out of bed and squished a pillow against the small of her back to fill in where she had been leaning against him.

In the bathroom he rummaged around for Tylenol, popped three tablets in his mouth, downed two glasses of water, and then foraged for something to slip on and ended up in Fede's flowery, silk kimono, feeling silly in it and looking silly in it. A panic-filled but short-lived flashback of the rug-skirt and Maputo came and went. The sleeves of the kimono reached just past the elbows, the hem was at his knees.

Alicia must have been up for some time. She was standing at the kitchen counter and talking on the phone. More important, she had made coffee. Cradling the phone to her ear she poured him a double shot of espresso freshly made in Federica's beloved Bialetti Moka Express. He cradled the cup in one hand. "There is a god."

From behind, Alicia slid an arm around him, being careful not to spill coffee or interrupt her conversation. Her breasts rested against his back as her hand slipped partially under the kimono and the fingertips settled lightly on the flesh of his belly.

A minute later Alicia finished the call, unwound from Stonecrop, and put the phone on the counter. "Interesting," she said. "Interesting."

Stonecrop wasn't sure if the comment was a reference to the call or the kimono or his having slept with Federica. He was doing his level best to not become aroused. Just a morning thing, he told himself. In any case, he was not ready to jump into small talk, or anything else. The coffee monopolized his attention. They skipped the hello-how-did-you-sleep conversation. Alicia ignored Stonecrop's somnolent though quasi-aroused state: "You didn't hear this from me."

He lifted his gaze from the black liquid.

"The scuttlebutt is Gregor is cooperating with both Treasury and Kanton police regarding some investigation. Gregor knows and loathes traffickers. Wouldn't surprise me if he was trading their hides to save his own skin." She reached over and took a sip from his cup. "Am I mixing metaphors?"

The question confused him. Mats of hair rose like solar storms off to one side of his head. And he needed a shave. Teeth could wait.

Alicia continued. "The local police are keeping tabs on Claudia and Gregor. 'Tabs' could mean wiretaps. Although it's hard to imagine getting permission in Zürich. Never did when I was here." Alicia helped herself to a second sip of his coffee. She waited for Stonecrop to speak, assuming the caffeine would do its job.

"Doesn't surprise me." He refilled the demitasse before saying more. "Federica said something about Gregor trying to get his affairs in order. She didn't say de-criminalize, but I hope that's what she meant. I'd like to believe her, but what do I know? Gregor loves Federica; he's been fair to me. I cut the guy a shitload of slack."

"I'll tell you something; she was majorly worried last night. She told me a little about the kidnapping. No details—too wiped out. Said she'd been through the story twice already. You're here and obviously in one piece. Did you meet with the mysterious Wulf or whatever his name was?"

Stonecrop, fortified by caffeine and Tylenol, took a seat at the table. He fished a day-old hard roll out of a bag, broke the roll in two, and patiently slathered both pieces with artery clogging quantities of butter. Alicia sat beside him and watched.

He offered her a piece. She declined.

"Wulf Sorgen. The meeting wasn't exactly what I'd expected." Between sips of coffee and bites of bread, he recounted a version of what had transpired at Wulf's apartment, omitting the threat he had made to Wulf. He also omitted any reference to Wulf's sexual preferences—that was Wulf's business. When he had finished, he presented her with the photo on his phone of the account number and gave her the name of the bank, Moretti & Cie, Banquiers.

Alicia immediately forwarded the number and name to a colleague from Treasury in Zürich. "Jeb Franklin. He's my replacement. He'll run it down." She moved her chair close to his, so their hips touched. He felt the warmth of her body through the silk kimono. "I'm fired, or worse, if they get wind of my pulling favors. I don't know Jeb that well."

Stonecrop nodded. Jeb was her problem.

Alicia rested her fingers on Stonecrop's arm. She was annoyingly touchy-feely. "Did you get the name of the go-between?"

"No," Stonecrop half-lied, "A screw-up on my part. I wasn't thinking and didn't ask. A little schnockered." He should have pressed Wulf more about both Andreas and Wulf's contact.

"Sex toys and syringes, that's out there." She waited, apparently trying to remember something, or debating whether to mention it to Stonecrop. Alicia made a sort of half-laugh, "A few months ago, someone sent a bunch of porn pics to Federica's phone. She blocked the number. At first, the pictures were selfies of this guy's underwear and junk—it went downhill from there. He wasn't circumcised, and almost no hair. Hard to guess the age. Thirties, maybe."

Stonecrop pretended his question was serious. "Pick him out of a line-up?"

Alicia leaned into him, flirtatiously tilting her head and batting her eyes. "Of course!"

Sternen Grill

Federica didn't surface until eleven. With little food in the apartment and the lunch-hour approaching, the three of them piled into Alicia's rental and half-drove and half-slid down Rämistrasse to Theaterstrasse. The snow, though melting fast, had kept drivers off the road. A plus to the weather was that it was no longer impossible to find parking. Stonecrop's plan was to get a bite at Sternen Grill, a casual eatery across the street from Bellevue Station and Sechseläutenplatz.

A famished Federica couldn't wait for table service, so they ordered from the standing-room-only outdoor grill. Federica and Max were regulars. Seeing them, the cooks put two St. Gallen sausage specials on the counter. In addition to the sausage, they grabbed *Bürli* from the help-yourself bread bin. Federica called Sternen bratwurst *bratli*. Bratli isn't a Swiss German word but she claimed it should be. A paper dish of fries, plenty of hot mustard, and *Stangen*—drafts of beer—topped off lunch. Alicia had the same. The trio crowded around a table. There was barely room on the table for their food and drinks. Some years earlier, on snowy days, the outdoor dining area would have had a forest of patio heaters; these days the heaters were banned and diners relied upon their collective warmth.

Boxed in by a wall on one side and the kitchen, grills and bar on the other, the space grew warmer as the on-the-go lunch crowd filled the narrow enclave. "Bratli," bürli, frites, and beer hit the spot. With twelve hours of sleep and full belly, Federica had revived.

Alicia's phone buzzed right after she bit off a sizable chuck of sausage. She fumbled through her handbag for the handy and mumbled hello through a mouthful of food, after which she took a swig of beer and burped directly into the phone. "Jeb, hi. Apologize.

Having a bite. Literally."

Stonecrop turned to Federica. "No wonder you guys get along!"

She poked him in the ribs and apologized too late. Stonecrop didn't jump, but they both knew that his bruised rib cage wasn't happy.

"Okay . . . Let me know when you've got something . . . Text is fine, I don't care how late. I might not respond right away, back to London in the a.m." There was a long pause and Alicia's interest in lunch seemed forgotten. "You gotta be fucking kidding me . . . Dates for the transfers?" She was practically standing at attention when Jeb, ten minutes later, had finished whatever he had been telling her. She wrapped up the conversation, "Thanks. Appreciate it. I owe you."

Alicia spoke before they had a chance to ask. "Not here." She took a last bite of sausage. "My feet are fucking freezing."

Back on Theaterstrasse, Alicia picked up where she had left off. "You guys got to talk to Gregor. ASAP. This is not coming from me. Make up some bullshit. I'll explain when we get to the car."

"About Wulf?" Stonecrop asked.

"No. Not Banquiers either. I'll drop you off at the Rathaus bridge. You can walk to Storchen."

Fireplace

Ratzow had responded to Federica's text, giving her the room number, a new one. He was "home" at Zum Storchen.

"Two wet dogs! Come, sit by fire." He greeted them at the door, giving Federica a kiss on the forehead and Max a bear hug that produced another shot of pain in the ribs. "Thank you, Max. For rescue my *milichka*, my little girl. You are hard man. I am grateful beyond words. Especially English words! Ah, life is good to Gregor. My darling is here, and Claudia tells me Uli has all but a half-million of my money. Like magic, da! And the bastards, they burn in hell. Life is good, da!"

Papà Ratzow took Fede's hand with his left hand and held it as if he were once again traipsing the world with his little girl at his side and assuring her the world was a safe and wonderful place.

Fede responded to his touch. The tension was wiped clean from her face and body.

With his other arm, Ratzow made a grand sweeping gesture. "You like? My new suite. I move in this morning. The old room was too cold. What did they think, I was Russian? Here I have bar and fireplace! It is new suite this winter, first one with fireplace!" He picked up a remote from the living room table and punched a button. The fireplace ignited, radiating heat from the gas burners tucked behind the faux logs. Ratzow touched another button and above the fireplace, a framed photograph of the Matterhorn transformed magically into the local news channel. Ratzow usually left the TV on, the theory being it would interfere with audio bugs. And he tracked various exchanges.

Stonecrop was not so sanguine. He had not sent the *three year on rock* text to Mother and Father. And, there was an ongoing debate in his mind. Should he mention the account number he had gotten from

Wulf? It was a death warrant for Wulf and whoever the account holder was. He had decided to call Wulf first, to give her time if need be, to disappear. Andreas was another matter he had decided to postpone. Right now, Geissner's greed ranked number one on the list.

He sat on the floor, cross-legged in front of the fire, and turned his palms to face the flames. The heat did feel good, "Gregor, are we okay talking here?"

"Is fine. Claudia did sweep."

"Can you turn off the TV."

Ratzow hit the mute button. The TV went silent; the audible portion now streamed as a banner at the bottom of the screen.

"Does it seem odd, Uli getting the money back?" Stonecrop asked.

"You worry too much." Ratzow walked to the bar, getting a water for himself. "Drink?"

Federica asked for a water. Stonecrop wanted coffee. Ratzow's Nespresso machine was on. "Coffee. I'll get it," Stonecrop offered. He jumped up, first getting a water for Federica and then finding a coffee pod.

While Stonecrop busied himself with the machine, Ratzow spoke, "Claudia, she is good."

Stonecrop resettled in front of the fire. Federica joined him. "True," Stonecrop said. "She was also scared shitless when the farmhouse blew. And she had nothing to do with the money. It turned up on Federica's doorstep. Red Monkey, or whoever they are, left a note to deliver it to Uli."

Ratzow waited a moment and then responded, "Geissner knew it was not Red Monkey. Da, he is smart. He talks to real Red Monkey, and they fix everything. Save you from being martyr. He is business genius, and" he added, "you, delivery boy, you bring money. You return money." Irritated slightly by Stonecrop's impertinence, Ratzow swiped his hands together like cymbals. "Done!"

The attempt to draw out Geissner's involvement had stalled. Stonecrop looked to Federica for a non-verbal okay to introduce what they had learned from Alicia. Federica originally had wanted Stonecrop to be the one to inform her father. She changed her mind. "And the twenty million, Papà? How about the twenty million you owe?"

Ratzow had been working his way through a package of almonds. He stopped mid-chew. "What twenty million? I don't owe any twenty million. Twenty million what? Pesos, clams, Swiss, nuts?" He took another handful, forgetting he hadn't made much progress on the first. His cheeks bulged.

Federica shot out something in Bulgarian. Both she and Gregor smiled.

Gregor chewed slowly and swallowed. He turned to Stonecrop first, "She tells me I should not talk and eat nuts. It could kill me and I'm being rude. And worse, I look like chipmunk!" Then to Federica, "Your mother said the same thing. Da, here I am—"

"Dollars, Papà. From Group's UBS account. An advance made to Uli, personally. It's past due. Group's the guarantor," she said.

Ratzow got out of his chair and started pacing behind Stonecrop, at first suspecting he was source of Federica's claim. "Did you do this? Who says so?"

"Call UBS," Federica answered.

Stonecrop added a last bit. "And we have the number of the account where the remaining 500k went."

Ratzow looked to Federica for an explanation. "What is errand boy talking about?"

Federica spoke softly, trying to calm her father. "It's true, Papà. Max has a friend at the bank."

"Is good explanation. I show you," Ratzow said this as he walked to the door to leave. He stepped out, and then, remembering his coat, reached in the doorway to pluck it off the rack. "Wait here. I have short meeting. I call Uli. When he comes, we talk. Your 'friend' at the bank is full of shit. You, too, errand boy." Ratzow took one step out of the room and then leaned back in and grinned. "And I know who she is." Ratzow left without closing the door.

Federica lay on the floor with her head resting on Stonecrop's leg, watching the muted TV. "He smiled but he's angry. I hope Alicia's not mistaken. He knows, of course, that she's the source. And Andreas—" she added.

His unpleasant presence always popped up.

Federica continued after the pause. "He wasn't there when Mother and Father showed up."

"Anything from him? Or Hitoshi? A text, a call?" he asked.

"Nada."

"Yeah. But this is starting to make sense to me. We should talk to Dante." He started to text Alexander.

"Oh, fuck!" Fede grabbed Stonecrop's ankle and squeezed. A news clip showed footage of ambulance EMTs carrying a body down a flight of stairs at what might be described as a Zürcher version of a New York brownstone. The sub-titled dialogue moved too fast for Stonecrop to translate, but he clearly made out the words *Herr Doktor Wulf Sorgen* and *tot*—dead.

Fede filled in the details. "At his sister's house, this afternoon. The housecleaner found him. Drug overdose. Sister returning from abroad. No foul play. In the morning, he had gone to work at the bank."

"I think we just heard from Andreas," a stunned Stonecrop flatly announced.

His phone vibrated. Alexander wanted to talk. They switched to speaker. Stonecrop handed the phone to Federica; he was too upset to speak.

"Max, I was going to call. Crazy mon, real crazy. Where are you? Can we talk?" Alexander's voice was tense.

"Yes," Frederica answered for him, "just Max and me. We're at

Gregor's, zum Storchen." She put the phone against her leg and quietly asked Stonecrop if she should mention Wulf.

"Wait," Stonecrop whispered. "Give me a minute." He felt like he was falling.

"What's that?" Alexander asked. "I can't hear you."

Stonecrop punched through the emotion. "Gregor's not here. We're warming up by the fire. Cozier than the last one." The attempt at humor didn't take.

Federica pulled Stonecrop close. "I'm sorry," she whispered.

Alexander exhaled, then spoke, "Mon, I told you, I guh vatchin" duh fishes. Duh fishes come home now. Lookee, mon, lookee."

Alexander had flipped the view setting on his phone. The screen displayed a nondescript IKEA desk, an Apple computer with multiple displays, miscellaneous office supplies, and a thumb drive. A second desk was littered with tools and bits and pieces of electronics parts. Alexander panned above the desk, to the wall behind it.

Pinned and taped to the wall was a collage of photos of Federica— leaving her apartment at Susenbergstrasse, meeting Stonecrop at Stehli, entering the Aide Direct office at Löwenstrasse . . . One photograph depicted a forlorn Federica, alone, at some bar, not one Stonecrop recognized. The architecture and the signage suggested Brussels. The most disconcerting picture was from years earlier, of Federica in Chicago. Stonecrop recognized the ratty University of Chicago hoodie. A second cluster of photos showed her adjusting her hair and straightening a skirt. These had been cropped to enlarge suggestive details. On a bookshelf and to the right sat a pile of Auto World magazines, a collection of well-used moleskin notebooks, and a large photo of a car dealership with a red Ferrari in the foreground.

Stonecrop steadied the phone as Alexander spoke, "Don't show this stuff to Federica. Sick, mon."

"Too late," Stonecrop said.

"I'm not a child." The words were sharp and projected anger about both the man-speak and the photos. She had been stalked and she was pissed. "*And* they're lousy photos. You boys want titty-pics, you shouldda asked."

Dante streamed the image of his hand removing a thick binder from the bookshelf. He placed it on the desk and opened it. Each page in the binder was a transparent pocket envelope and contained a passport photo of a woman or girl, plus additional information, much of which was hand-written in either Japanese or English.

"Where the *hell* are you?" Federica asked.

"There's more. This is different." The display showed an armoire; the upper half was shelving that framed a narrow, vertical mirror. On the shelves were several framed photos of shrines and monk-like figures, more stacks of magazines and books, mostly in Japanese. A porcelain crucifix was centered on the bottom shelf and in front of the mirror. Beside the crucifix was a Bible and a folded white headscarf upon which several hand-written kanji characters were inscribed. The phone's lens wandered the room as Alexander spread out the headscarf and took a photo.

Then, a man's voice warned Alexander to stop touching things. The voice—the words in English—declared it was time to go.

Alexander's hand covered the mic on the phone. The conversation was muffled until its end, when Stonecrop clearly heard an intimidating Alexander speak: "Hold your horses, buddy."

Alexander reappeared on the screen and addressed Stonecrop and Federica. "I'm with the landlord. I explained to him that a colleague I work with has been missing for several days. I was worried about him. His office was unhelpful. Which is why I'm here at his apartment." His little speech—recited in deliberately slow and clear English—was intended to be overheard and to calm the landlord. Alexander seemed reluctant to say the renter's name.

Stonecrop caught a reflection in the mirror of a photograph of two men—a tall Asian man with his arm around the shoulders of another man, a Caucasian with long, black hair and wire rim glasses. The men had similar hair and both wore tan, expensive-looking overcoats. The short one held a Gucci bag in the air. The Asian was too slender to be Chop-Chop.

It was Wulf. The same two men were in the photo at Wulf's. The revelation was immediate. He had missed it at Wulf's. The man with his arm around Wulf was Hitoshi Sato.

"Name," Stonecrop wanted confirmation—he wanted to be sure he wasn't imagining what he had so briefly seen. Dante stalled. "Give it up, Dante," Stonecrop ordered.

The camera drifted by several other objects on the desk, including a rather elaborate silk mask rimmed in black fringe. Federica said the name in her pitch perfect Japanese, "Hitoshi Sato." And then in a clear voice and loud enough for all to hear, "This is my fault."

"I'm sorry," Alexander either apologized or misunderstood what she had said. He had switched the camera back to himself.

Federica stiffened and spoke as if she were addressing the missing Hitoshi Sato: "You son of a bitch, Hitoshi. I never realized. Shit."

Stonecrop hoped the landlord had not overheard. He sent a text, <MS: get thumb drive?>

<DA: will try. Echo?>

"If he's not in Brussels, any idea where Sato might be? Is he here?" Stonecrop asked.

"Don't know. He's been missing for over a week."

The landlord had had enough of Alexander rummaging around in the apartment and threatened to call the authorities.

"Look, I'll call later." Alexander's heavy steps indicated he was leaving. A door closed. Then silence.

A text message with a photo of the headscarf appeared.

"Can you read it?" he asked Fede.

She took his phone and zoomed in on the kanji characters, 善行団の兵士, studying them. *"zenkodan no heishi.* I'd translate it as 'Soldier of the Good,' or maybe 'Soldier of Good Deeds'."

Lucy

He had to do something physical to release the tension in his body. Plus he wanted to get Federica out of the oppressive confines of the suite at zum Storchen.

"I can't sit any more. Up for a walk?"

He took her hand. She groaned, moving stiffly as she rose. "It'll be cold; sun's gone down." Stonecrop helped her with her coat. "Wulf," she said, "poor Wulf? Any—"

"No idea. Not right now, anyway."

"I'm never going to watch the telly again. Text Papà?"

"We'll come back," Stonecrop said. "Let's get some air." He found the remote, shut off the fireplace, and started toward the door.

"Hang on—" She left him standing in the doorway and ran to the bathroom adjoining Ratzow's bedroom. Stonecrop heard her gag and throw up. He waited as she rinsed and watched through the open door to the bedroom. Federica drank some water, then stopped to rummage around a drawer in her father's bedside table. She extracted a phone and a SIM card.

"You okay?" he asked.

She nodded, "Yeah," and held up the phone. "One of Papà's burners." She inserted the card into the cheap, clamshell phone. "They're pre-programmed with apps he uses." The determined movement reminded Stonecrop of a shooter pulling back the slide on an automatic. The act was her antidote to tension they both felt. "I have an idea," she said, "a couple, actually."

They left the room at zum Storchen and took the stairs to street level. Stonecrop led the way to In Gassen, a narrow alleyway that connected with Bahnhofstrasse.

At Bahnhofstrasse they stepped into a fairytale. Shops were open and storefronts decorated for Christmas. A light snowfall notwithstanding, people walked and shopped. Cinnamon flavored *glühwein*, a mulled wine, warmed in vendors' iron vats. Chestnuts roasted on charcoal grills. Hand-painted signs advertised them—*heissi marroni*. Overhead a net of red, white, and blue lights—like low-hanging stars—covered the length of Bahnhofstrasse. The corridor of lights brightened faces and brightened moods. Fede and Max bought glühwein. The warm drink beat back the damp cold and damper spirits.

"*Lucy!*" Fede exclaimed.

Lucy is the name Zürchers use to describe their holiday lights. Stonecrop had no clue as to its origin. Federica looked upward and Stonecrop watched her expression change. The dark circles under her eyes unweighted as the eyes filled with points of light.

I love this woman.

From Paradeplatz they turned north on Bahnhofstrasse in the direction of the Haptbahnhof and walked among window shopping pedestrians. It was a refreshingly normal moment.

"Give me Uli's mobile number," Fede ordered. Stonecrop found it on his phone's contacts. With some difficulty she cradled the glühwein in her arm and then extracted the burner, put in the number, and tapped compose.

<XX: What is status of Echo?>

She showed the text to Stonecrop. He shrugged his shoulders, "Why not, I don't know what else to do."

She hit send.

"And, what's your other idea?" Max asked.

Fede stopped in front of the Zegna display. "Do you ever wear your Zegna suit? Remember, when we met. You looked terribly handsome. I did have a crush on you, you know. I would have slept with you. I mean, well, I did sleep with you, but, you know, the other kind of sleep with you." Fede gave him a coquettish half-smile, "Advance sleeping."

"A lucky Goodwill customer got a fine suit at a good price." Max laughed heartily. "I have no regrets, not over the suit and not over the night."

"Would've been naughty fun!"

"Yeah. And Papà dear would have had me drawn and quartered." The sobering comment had implied fear of personal physical harm and not moral reservation. Either was sufficient reason for his decision.

"Been a while since we read Greek," he suggested. "Tonight?"

Fede didn't respond. She was once again lost in her own thoughts. Clearly, neither of them wanted to deal with the realities at hand.

"I think we'd met before the train. Do you ever feel that? I'm sure of it." Her brow furrowed as she searched for a particular memory in that preternaturally accessible repository of almost anything she'd ever experienced, seen, heard, read, or spoken. "It's in a drawer in my brainbox. I can almost open it. Someday, I will. I saw you, I think, in Africa."

She went back to the fantasy tryst on the train, "It would have been okay, Max. I was so cute then. Now, fuck, I'm like this old babushka."

He laughed, pulled her close and did a lousy imitation of Gregor's Bulgarian accent, "I *adorrre* Babushka!"

"I like the navy one," she pointed to a suit on a white, faceless mannequin, "Double-breasted power suit."

He replied with a shrug as indifferent as the mannequin's. Federica didn't let him off the hook, "It's not like you grew up milking cows. You're getting a wardrobe upgrade for Christmas!" She took his arm and marched them in the direction of the Hauptbahnhof. They walked on without speaking.

After a few minutes Federica broke the silence. "Hitoshi Sato . . . Hitoshi Sato," she gazed at the lights overhead, repeating the name, pronouncing it clearly and distinctly each time she said it.

"Are you a believer? We never talk about religion."

The question reminded Stonecrop of a peculiarity of their relationship. They both had serious academic credentials, but generally kept the conversation light. Hell, he thought, less than light, it was downright shallow.

"Where did that come from?"

"Hitoshi—the cross."

"Yeah, well, the guy's weird. Are you?" he asked. "A believer, not weird!"

Federica gave him one of those looks that said he couldn't get away with flipping the question. He stepped up and answered, "I accept the awesome and enduring indifference of nature."

"And miracles?"

"You can't deny personal miracles, although you can challenge the credulity of the one reporting the miracle."

"Hitoshi Sato, do you suppose he could have experienced a miracle, some kind of epiphany?" Fede asked.

Stonecrop suspected the topic was something she and Hitoshi had once visited. "Doubtful. Have you?"

Fede was quiet. Stonecrop filled the space. "Hell, I see no reason why he couldn't have, if we allow for miracles. But a Soldier of the Good—what is a Soldier of the Good? Give me a break, the guy's a pervert."

"Such an enlightened and unbiased assessment! He once told me he'd had a vision, a kind of miracle."

"Could be." Stonecrop reflected for a minute and then qualified his response. "And it could be it's all intellectual bullshit to rationalize deviant behavior."

"Hitoshi is complicated. We worked together—quite a bit, actually—on the AD agreement. He's a prodigy and product of Japanese pressure cooker education. He comes from a Christian family. Doing the lord's work is part of who he is. And he's an idealist, but not like you and Papà. And he's a serious gamer. A lot of hours in the fantasy world. But very sweet. We played a bunch."

Stonecrop's raised eyebrows said *C'mon!*

"Hey, it was fun! He's quixotic. You're both quixotic."

The comparison did not please him. "Different windmills," Stonecrop said in his defense.

"Don't be so stuffy. I don't know if Hitoshi has a single friend. He's lonely, intense, with an artist's imagination. Brilliant man."

"And Hitoshi's friend is very dead."

Federica ignored the sideswipe. ". . . sensitive and emotional."

"I'm emotional," Stonecrop reacted.

"Max, emotions are more than hungry, horny, and honey I want to work out!"

"Huh?"

"You want to know if I've slept with him?" She squeezed his arm and gave him a kiss on the shoulder.

Stonecrop said nothing.

"The answer's no. Tempting intellectually, but no fire in the belly." Fede batted her eyelashes and tilted her head toward him. All that was missing was the bubble gum. "I'm a brawn over brains kind of girl! People don't think that, but it's true!"

Stonecrop specifically recalled Alicia saying the exact opposite. *What the hell do I know?*

She continued, apparently processing the call from Alexander. "I'm trying to imagine what's going on inside Hitoshi."

She laughed to herself and gave her head a vigorous shake to discard the snow. They walked slowly, pressed against each other, kicking up snow in unison.

"Dante said Hitoshi flip-flopped on the deal. Is that how you saw it?" he asked.

"At the point when Group was engaged and after Hitoshi had completed his due diligence, he became afraid Group would use Potomac drones for criminal purposes. Hitoshi was angry. He told me his conscience would not let him close the deal. He didn't want to hurt me, he said. We argued. I told him Group was not a threat and that Papà didn't care, and even smart-phone technology overwhelmed Papà. Hitoshi had real dirt on Group, he said. Some was old news to me, some not.

"Papà has done truly regrettable things, worse than I'd thought. I'm convinced Papà's different now or that he is trying anyway, to be better. I hope so. I'm tired of paying for his sins. I'm tired of the guilt I feel over what he has done. I'm really having a go at accepting Papà actions. In a weird way that makes it easier to accept Hitoshi."

"How about the Clerk?"

"Who?" she asked, and then answered when she remembered. "Oh, you mean Francis. In the Malta office, in Valetta?"

Stonecrop nodded.

"He's nice," she said

"Nice! Give me a break! He's a totally scary guy. I had a couple beers with him last month. First time we'd spent time together. We talked about combat pistol—the sport. I competed at our local gun club. His competitions were in deserts and jungles with targets that shot back. He's ex-military, South African, worked as a mercenary in Angola, Congo and DRC, and the Middle East. Why the fuck does Gregor keep someone like that on the payroll?"

"Maybe he's the world's best accountant? Only the best for Papà! Why are you on the payroll? You're kind of scary, too."

"Fede, I am so *not* scary!"

"Well, that's true for me! You're more cuddly than scary." The words were breezy; she swayed into him as they walked.

In front of Ferragamo she changed the subject. "Do you even own a pair of dress shoes?"

"Sorry," Max shrugged. "What happened next, with Hitoshi?"

Federica had a swig of glühwein before speaking: "Well, Hitoshi begged me to withdraw AD from any arrangement with Potomac."

She stopped and wiped wine off her chin. "And he said he had no choice but to walk from the deal. I told him he was making much ado about nothing. Then I returned to Zürich."

"But the deal did go forward," Max said. "And, according to Dante, with newfound support from Hitoshi."

"Yeah, there was a turning point, I guess when Hitoshi decided to . . . do something desperate." Fede struggled for the words. "With a kidnapping in play Hitoshi could pretend to support the deal because he knew a any serious wrongdoing would give him an acceptable excuse to kill the arrangement with Potomac. And Andreas must have helped."

"Explain, please."

"Well, Hitoshi knew that Potomac's investors would freak out when they heard about the kidnapping. And he could make sure that happened. The whole thing was timed for maximum effect—that night, when you were at the Carezza Suite."

Stonecrop's silence asked for more. She had a story that fit with what had transpired; he wanted to hear it.

Federica obliged. "Hitoshi presumed that after the ersatz Red Monkey gang had abducted me, I would be delivered—unharmed—to Wulf's. Hitoshi would take credit for my release to, you know, super impress me. Voilà, my hero!"   She frowned and looked up into the falling snow. "What I don't get is Andreas' role."

Stonecrop restated and added to her explanation. "So Hitoshi would have been the good guy who had negotiated your release *and* he would have torpedoed the deal, actualizing his crazy, fucked-up version of saving the world and getting laid. And there's that half-million walking around money."

"*Genau!*" Fede said.

Stonecrop embellished, "The grateful damsel would fall into his arms and he'd have his way with her."

"Not exactly. I know Hitoshi. He would have wanted it to go the other way, for me to have my way with him!"

"C'mon. You didn't see Wulf's." Max was happy she hadn't.

"I knew something was off with Hitoshi. I can see it now. Hitoshi has an obsession . . . about me. He believes that he loves me—it's really a fantasy version of me that he desires. I suppose he imagines that I love him, or will love him if he's richer, more important, smarter, whatever. And of course, nothing will ever be enough because the feelings aren't real.

"I could have managed Hitoshi—if he hadn't gotten in so deep—and maybe gotten professional help for him. But there was nothing I could do about those thugs at the Buurhuus. Or Andreas."

She was defending Sato again. A little common sense appeared, however, when she asked, "Should I talk to the Kantonspolizei? To Kommissar Vormittag?"

He wanted to yell at her that defending Hitoshi was effectively defending a crazy, criminal pervert. Stonecrop bottled the anger.

"It's too late for Vormittag," he said. "Thanks to Hitoshi, Marion's near braindead. Thanks to Hitoshi, Wulf *is* dead. Thanks to Hitoshi, three carcasses are smoldering at the Albisrieder cottage. These are or were real people, Federica. Fuck, I don't know why Vormittag isn't all over you and Gregor."

"He is protecting me. Or using Papà. Or he owes Papà." Federica took a minute to compose her words. "I don't mean to defend Hitoshi's actions, just understand them. Do *I* talk to Hitoshi and Andreas?" she said.

"Talk?" Stonecrop was incredulous. "They did this together. Don't forget that. One way or another, they're gonna pay. They're both gonna pay."

She shuddered at Stonecrop's threat, a harsher threat than the hardening winter wind. "Back to Storchen?"

The tension was interrupted as both of Fede's phones buzzed. A text from Alicia appeared on her personal mobile.

<AG: Moretti account is trust FBO a Nassau shell. Money went in and out in a day. No names. A soft violation of Swiss banking law.>

Fede showed him the message and then sent a reply,

<FR: Can you get info on Hitoshi Sato accounts at Banquiers and Nassau?>

<AG: OK. will try>

Federica put away her personal phone and pulled out the burner.

There was a response from Geissner. <UG: Who is this?>

She texted back. <XX: three year on rock>

The response was immediate, <UG: Need 30 days.>

Fede held up the phone for Stonecrop to read the message.

"That's why Gregor wasn't surprised by Red Monkey," Stonecrop said. "He made the call."

"Not quite," Fede countered. "Uli contacted Red Monkey, not Papà. Papà had nothing to do with Father and Mother. Papà was aware of the exchange at Uetliberg, but Uli's the one who contacted the real Red

Monkey. Uli *knew* the abductors weren't the real thing. He'd said as much. Papà gave Uli credit."

Federica was shivering. Her lips were bluish.

"Hitoshi's here, in Zürich," she asserted. "He's compulsive. I don't think he can let go of me. I feel it under my skin."

"Andreas is the guy I'm worried about. There were two packages given to Wulf. One was the sex toys, probably from Hitoshi. Did you and Andreas ever play with any of that shit?"

"Never."

"The other was the drug kit. That's what killed Wulf."

"The heroin," Federica added, "could have been cut in a way that would kill him. Or he ODed."

"I imagine the police will do a toxicology report."

"Wait," Fede said. She put the burner in her pocket and took out her own phone to find Hitoshi's mobile number. She typed a text addressed to him but did not tap the send button.

<FR: Call me.>

Stonecrop read it. "Are you sure? I'm inclined to let Mother and Father take over."

"Executing him is not the answer. I can't face him alone."

"He's sick in the head and he's dangerous. He let Andreas beat you and try to rape you."

"I doubt Hitoshi knew what Andreas was going to do. You got to believe me. It's not in Hitoshi to do something like that. Andreas found out where I was being held. And Chop-chop stopped him from raping me. I've got to settle this." Fede scanned the lights overhead, took a deep breath in and out. She faced the icy breeze, breathed in and out again, staring into space as her breath dissipated in the cold air.

"Do it," Stonecrop said, tabling his own thoughts about how to best deal with Hitoshi. She hit send.

They turned right on Augustinergasse and walked back toward zum Storchen, once again kicking snow in unison.

"You never answered," Stonecrop said.

"Answered what?"

"What you believe in—religion . . ."

Her face softened, as if she had swept away all the worries of the world. She gave Stonecrop a wink, "At Spital we resurrect people every day. That's a real miracle!"

The Put

Ratzow welcomed Federica and Stonecrop in outwardly cheerful spirits and with the usual hyperbole. "Uli, are you impressed? Messenger boy rescues my lovely daughter! Is super-hero, da!"

Geissner mustered a modicum of warmth. "Hello Federica. I can't tell you how relieved we are. What a horrible ordeal." Generally, Geissner barely acknowledged Stonecrop's presence but tonight he offered praise. "Well done, Max. Truly extraordinary!" Praise did not come naturally to Geissner; he looked uncomfortable.

Ratzow continued. "They join our little parley. Is good?"

Geissner acquiesced—as if he had had a choice. Ratzow guided Geissner to a spot in front of the reignited fire. "I know you are busy man—hah, I make busy!" Ratzow laughed at his own joke though no one else found it funny. "I go to point! Please, Uli," Now Ratzow spoke as though he were asking a favor, "why do I owe twenty million dollars for loan I never see one fucking piece of paper about?"

He turned to Federica, to apologize. "I am sorry for bad language." He paused for dramatic effect. Ratzow was being a showman but genuinely struggling to control his anger. "This is loan to you, Uli, only *you*, but my company guarantees! Why is that?" Ratzow repeatedly thumped his fat wrestler's finger on Geissner's chest and forced him a step closer to the fire with each thump.

Geissner fidgeted. He used his pocket square to wipe his hands and brow and delivered a carefully worded explanation. "What you say is technically correct, Gregor. But the purpose was administrative, to facilitate a transaction that might require executory action in a near but indeterminate period. We didn't want to bother you with having to be on call. I accepted the responsibility personally. Regardless, the loan is secured."

"*We* are so thoughtful." Ratzow made no attempt to hide the sarcasm. "You are my chief financial officer, yes, Uli?"

"Yes, of course."

"Then, what is my net worth?" Ratzow was subject jumping, an interrogation technique used to distract the interviewee from focusing on a explanation for a prior question.

"Gregor, this discussion, perhaps for another time, a more private —"

The reddening of Gregor's face was a barometer of his temper. "My daughter is here, Uli. She can hear anything that comes out of your mouth about my money. As for errand boy, he's deaf and dumb!" Ratzow glared at Stonecrop, "Is right, da?"

"Yes, sir," Stonecrop played along, puzzled about whether he should or shouldn't speak. *I shouldn't laugh. Don't laugh, Max.* Federica flashed a quick smile his way. They were both tipsy from the glühwein and were enjoying Ratzow holding Geissner's feet to the fire, damned near literally. It was a moment of shared schadenfreude.

Geissner played along. "Do you mean, you personally, or including the trusts and GR Group? Offshore assets as well as domestic?"

"Just do it," Ratzow ordered.

"Dollars or euros?"

"Uli, I break one of your fingers for every more question?"

Uli forced a smile, the implication being that Ratzow wasn't really as upset as his words implied. "I'll go by business unit, then country exposure, if that's okay."

Geissner spent the next ten minutes giving an expert and succinct summary of Group's various enterprises around the globe. It was Stonecrop's first overview of Ratzow's mini-empire. Group was a boutique shipping and distribution business with strong representation in Southern and Eastern Europe, Japan, and parts of Africa—not surprisingly, all places where Federica had lived and traveled. Group assets exceeded a hundred-fifty million U.S. Gregor had salted away eighteen million in a couple of offshore trusts. Personal balances held in Swiss and Maltese accounts—ignoring real property like land, boats, cars, and so forth—came to another ten million U.S.

As Geissner finished, Claudia walked into the room. She had been on the phone in Ratzow's bedroom.

"My dear," she said, "What about those pesky little loans. "Haven't we a few of those?"

Geissner had not noticed Claudia, ever the watchful cat lying in wait. In lieu of claws she clutched notepad and pen. On the notepad she had scribbled numbers and doodles.

"The Group figures are net of liabilities, excluding taxes."

Uli was wearing his trademark gray, tailor-made, wool suit. Either due to the heat from the fireplace or the grilling by Ratzow, a crescent of sweat had formed at the the armpits.

"To be explicit, current liabilities in personal balances are nominal, say 500 thousand. Trustee fees this year will be two-and-a-half to three million. Long-term debt totals approximately thirteen million, mostly for remaining work on the Therme Tavate, and small amount due for the marina project in Kalymnos."

Claudia scribbled in her notebook as Geissner ticked off a list of miscellaneous liabilities. At times, she would underscore number, others she would circle. Without looking up she raised her hand. "*Ç'est tout*—that's all?"

Geissner came back at her. "That is, yes."

Ratzow interjected, "You forget the office."

"Yes, sorry, a little is still owed, a hundred-and-fifty thousand euros, give or take, for the office security system upgrade."

"My, my, where's the twenty million smackers again, love?"

"It's footnoted in Group—Japan, as I described."

Claudia raised her glasses higher on the bridge of her nose. She focused on Geissner. "Imagine that footnote, love, like a concrete block and your foot in it." She was warming up. "A few minutes ago, I hauled our Swiss banker out of bed with his mistress. Nice thing about Swiss bankers is they're available twenty-four-seven. He told me the number was closer to twenty-five million U.S. A two-week bridge loan is now several weeks past due. He fessed up—the Swiss are painfully forthright about money—and reported that you exceeded your fiduciary power of attorney by a shitload—am I right, dearie—on a promise of authorization to be provided by Gregor any day now. He said that twice, the 'Any day now'."

"I haven't looked at the documents recently. But, as I said, the investment, and hence the loan related to the investment, is secured by shares of a company constructing a hotel in Osaka."

"Being a bit dodgy about the authorization, aren't we?" Claudia flipped the page on her notebook. She rose, circled him and then flopped into an overstuffed settee. The action amplified her already ample proportions. "The hotel shares are yours, right dear? Or are they booked in Group's assets?"

"Correct, I'm the nominal holder of the shares. However, as I said, I'm doing the transaction for the benefit of group. In essence, as a trustee."

"Yes, you've said that. Got it papered someplace we don't know about?" She grilled.

"No. But some things we don't paper, Claudia. You damned-well know that!" Geissner was not about to roll over.

"You never said a word to Gregor, did you?"

Gregor was within arms-reach; she dutifully tapped his arm to make the point. "Gregor, sweet, what's the largest, most gigantic-est transaction our Uli has permission to make under his own name?"

"Maybe a few million. A year ago. I am sick—gout." Ratzow kept the response short to let Claudia run the the interrogation. That's what it had become, an interrogation.

Geissner became defensive, "I had planned to mention it. I didn't have a chance. You were busy. We've all been worried sick about Federica and Marion. In any event, this is a short-term transaction, and I *will* cover the exposure. I need thirty days."

A bit of saliva crept out of the corner of Claudia's mouth. "Uli dear, for our edification, please. Do you have a partner in the hotel deal?"

"Yes, a Japanese company. Allied Bank, Osaka."

"Owned by whom, sweet? The real owners?" She held her finger in the air, indicating Geissner should wait for her to finish. The pause added suspense to the question and it gave Geissner time to think, or alternatively, to cook in front of fire. "But you probably think I already know, don't you?"

Geissner's pocket square was soaked from repeated brow-mopping. "May I sit down?"

Claudia was neither bored with their game nor sympathetic. "In a minute, dear, and let me save you the embarrassment of answering. Allied is owned by affiliates of those feisty Red Monkey people. The rub is this: the hotel shares are worthless." She smiled as she made the point. "The site is contaminated, and uninsured. You boys—you and Allied—bought a pig in a poke. And potentially a mountain of liabilities! You put into escrow a non-refundable deposit for the property. Then, Uli, you planned to flip your share of the deal to Allied's umbrella company in two weeks for a seven million U.S. gain, riding—I should point out—on Group's coattails. The deal went south fast when the partnership failed to bury a damning environmental report which, I believe, is now public and in the nervous hands of our UBS analysts."

"Allied still must buy my shares—at cost, our cost. That's the minimum they are required to pay," Geissner shot back.

"Your worthless shares? Now why on earth would they do such a silly thing?" she asked. "They're already in the hole! Same as you."

Geissner was defiant. "They'll have to; I have a put option."

Claudia peered at each person in turn. "Any takers for Uli's put? Do I hear five cents on the dollar? Come now. Is there any dearie here with the cojones to force our simian colleagues to double-down on a deal they already pissed away twenty-five big ones on? A deal stuck in the ice at the south pole. The put, my sweet, was for show-and-tell. *I* know it's worthless. The *bank* knows it's worthless. And *you* know it's worthless."

Federica looked to Stonecrop for an explanation. He said, "The put is an instrument that would allow Uli to force Allied to buy his shares. The price and date are agreed to in advance. If it chooses to, UBS can use the put as collateral for the loan to Uli."

Stonecrop approached Claudia. He took her pen and wrote one word on the pad in front of her: "Echo."

Claudia glanced at what he had written and then redirected her attention to Geissner.

"Love, I'm to ask you about 'Echo.' Can you bring poor, ignorant Claudia up to speed?"

Geissner gave up. The sigh was involuntary. He looked relieved, confident even.

"Yes, as a backup, to ensure Allied would buy back my shares, although it's not documented in the put option. I—or rather Group— promise to give them Echo."

"For the record, who is 'them'?"

"Allied."

"Again?"

"Red Monkey, Osaka."

"And what the fuck *is* Echo, love, a yodel in a can?" For dramatic effect, Claudia lowered her glasses and glared at Geissner, although she could not see the features of his face any better without them.

"A state-of-the-art stealth drone system," came the dead-pan reply from Geissner.

"And it's worth that much to Red Monkey! Well holy shit! And do you, or is it 'we' now, our cozy little team here, do we have this Echo thing? You got one in the garage parked next to that Porsche?"

Ratzow had had enough. "Fede, is this what AD is getting from Dante Alexander?"

Federica had been standing apart from Stonecrop but decided to walk up to him and wrap an arm around his waist. She spoke clearly and choose her words carefully. "I have no idea what Echo is. But it seems highly unlikely that Dante would give Aide Direct any sort of secret military grade hardware. Anyway, Aide Direct will never get anything from Potomac. The deal is dead. Dante's investors might have been persuaded before. But after I was kidnapped—and now that they are aware of Papà's past business dealings—any association with me or Group would be too big a risk for Potomac. They have multiple contracts with DoD. They don't want to lose them. So I guess," she repeated the words, "the deal is dead."

She walked up to Geissner and stood face-to-face with him. She was the same height. "You were already working with Red Monkey, weren't you? And when those bastards took me, you knew it couldn't be the real Red Monkey. Right? Why would they want to wreck their own deal and make it impossible for you to get Echo technology for them?"

Geissner, seeking an out, responded in a confessional tone. "At first, Federica, I was afraid it *was* Red Monkey and that they took you as leverage with Group. They assured me that that was not the case. They were incensed, though not at me. First, someone or some organization was posing as Red Monkey; and second, the interlopers were interfering with Red Monkey potentially getting Echo technology, or something similar. Reverse-engineering the AD drones was a start."

Federica expanded on what Geissner had said. The words were tinged with sadness. "The person who did the real damage was Hitoshi Sato. He arranged and directed my kidnapping. Ironically, he was trying to protect me and save the world. He figured if AD had access to Potomac military technology, then someone—the 'bad guys'—would come after the technology and me. He had done his homework and knew Group was deeply corrupt, or at least it had been. He knew people like Papà—I'm sorry, Papà—or Uli would misuse the technology. Turns out Hitoshi got it fucking exactly right!" Her comments and demeanor argued in favor of Sato's insightfulness while still condemning him.

Ratzow could not tear his eyes away from his daughter. Nor could anyone else in the room.

"Hitoshi's plan failed for good reason," she went on. "Uli had the means to utterly squash it. Plus, that pretend Red Monkey crew turned out to be totally incompetent at what they had been tasked—to kidnap me, and not hurt anyone. The operation was supposed to be a scary farce, a harmless piece of theater! But the scheme went wildly awry. Marion was an unintended and unfortunate consequence of their bumbling—collateral damage. And the people Sato had hired to help him—all of them—are dead. They're dead, in part, thanks to you."

Geissner raised a hand. The sweat had by now dampened the collar of his coat. The wet arcs had grown.

Ratzow denied him the privilege of speaking. "Shut up, Uli." Then Ratzow addressed Federica, "Where did Sato find these jokers?"

"I don't know," she said. "One of them, Max dubbed him Chop-Chop, used to be Red Monkey. The other Japanese recognized him—or one of them did. I'd guess Hitoshi found Chop-Chop online. Maybe he was working in Italy as an ex-yakuza thug for hire. Hitoshi can be brilliant, but he can also be incredibly naïve. It's the sort of dumb thing he would do."

She stopped and eyed each person in the room.

"What he would *not* do," she paused to let the point sink in, "is kill anyone." No one reacted to her statement, so she continued. "And what I will not do is add one more body to the cycle of violence. I am not that kind of person."

Ratzow looked as if he had just eaten something sour. He looked not at his daughter, but to Stonecrop. He spoke slowly, "I am. My child, I am that kind of person. And I am not alone."

At a loss about how to reconcile the impasse between Federica and her father, and equally uncomfortable with Ratzow enjoining him in violence, Stonecrop turned to Claudia. "Suggestions?"

She came to Stonecrop's defense. "My sweet, *I* know revenge is not your cup of tea—*these days*. Nor should it be." Claudia slyly slipped in a wink that Stonecrop caught and hopefully others missed.

Federica spoke again. 'Red Monkey is looking for Hitoshi and they will kill him. We have a link to them, to the Red Monkey people here in Zürich. A code and a phone number, same as Uli."

"We don't know where Mr. Sato is, dearie," Claudia stated, then reconsidered the statement. "Or do we?"

Ratzow, rarely the realist, became one. "Federica, I am sorry. He is dead man." Ratzow ticked off the alternatives with his fingers. "I kill him, Red Monkey kills him, or, what do you call him—Chop-Chop, da

—Chop-Chop's friends kill him. And if Vormittag finds him first, it won't be long before we all are in jail. Is not best alternative."

"No." She faced her father.

Stonecrop rejoined her and addressed Ratzow, "Let me talk to Red Monkey."

"Why?" he scoffed.

"Well, I'm," he held his arms in the air to make the point, "still here." Stonecrop kept his eyes fixed on Ratzow. He thought about bringing up Andreas, but because Federica had volunteered nothing about the attempted rape, he held back. Probably Ratzow assumed any rapist would have to have been one of the kidnappers who had been killed.

Ratzow considered what Stonecrop had said. "You have good point, Max. You were . . ." he hunted for the word, "a leftover. When Red Monkey took out trash, you should have been in trash! Da." As was his habit, he clapped his hands like cymbals to emphasize the point.

Stonecrop noted that Federica sometimes did the same. For her, the mannerism was light and playful. With Ratzow, it was like an executioner who had satisfactorily beheaded a prisoner.

Ratzow went on: "But maybe, just maybe, they leave you alone for reason. You and Federica—they would not touch Federica—will lead them to Hitoshi. Just like you led them to Chop-Chop. Do not flatter yourself." Ratzow sighed, "Hitoshi Sato is on their list. Maybe you come next. Better to leave Zürich tonight. Go somewhere! The States. Go see your daughters. I give you money."

Claudia and Geissner started speaking at once. Federica put her arms up. She addressed them like an Italian schoolteacher addressing an unruly class, "Zitti, zitti!" She had felt a buzz from her phone. An app on her phone notified her when a previously blocked call sent a text or called. "Blocked caller," she announced. "I remember this one."

Stonecrop glanced at her phone and saw the notification. "Private?"

"Yup." Fede selected the option to unblock the call.

<FR: resend>

<TT: RUOK>

The message was from Hitoshi, although the name shown with the number was *Toshi Taisho*. Federica recognized and immediately decoded the alias for the others: "An anagram of 'Hitoshi Sato.' In Japanese, that name could be translated as 'intelligent' and 'cope.'"

<FR: What a tacky name! Can't believe I missed it.>

<TT: Ez2 >

<FR: fuck you>
<TT: Urgr8>
<FR: no thanks to you. where are you?>
<TT: Sos>
<FR: Sorry my ass. I'm gonna break yr neck!!>
<TT: Lol>
<FR: Leave Zurich. NOW.>
<TT: W / u>
<FR: Andreas—>

The call disconnected and reconnected. Stonecrop continued to read their exchange.

<TT: Tomorrow noon. Susenbergstr. Pack bag & pass..>
<FR: go fuck yourself>
<TT: Noon. Be there.>

The connection broke off. Federica tried to call, but Hitoshi didn't pick up.

Claudia's high-pitched voice sliced the air. "Federica. *Hell-ooo!*"

"Crap!" Federica ignored her and swore at the phone. "Answer you son-of-a-bitch!"

She stared at the silent and inert object in her hand. Something was bothering her.

"My, dearie," Claudia took back command, "what did he say? I presume that was Mr. Sato?"

"Noon tomorrow. At home. He wants me to . . ." She regretted the words as she was saying them and dwindled off. Federica turned to Stonecrop for help.

"What?" The clipped reply had been whispered. The others missed it.

Her head twitched in confirmation. Yes, something is wrong.

Federica took Stonecrop aside. She closed her eyes as she put her lips to his neck. The intimacy of the act made others turn aside.

"Max. Something's off. I'm remembering texts from Hitoshi, the ones in English—I can see them in my head and I can't remember one text with punctuation in it."

She showed her phone to him again; he got it.

Stonecrop pulled out his phone and texted Alexander. <MS: How about those Redskins. Talk tomorrow early.>

Between Geissner's shenanigans, the call from Sato, and the silent treatment from Federica, Ratzow had reached his flash point. "Claudia, stay. The rest of you, get out!" he ordered. "Do nothing. Wait. I call."

He went to the bar and poured himself a vodka, no ice.

Stonecrop approached Claudia, out of earshot of Ratzow, and made a request: "A favor?"

"Of course, love."

"Wulf Sorgen is dead. The news said he died this afternoon from a drug overdose. Can you get the toxicology details?"

"I'll try, no promises."

Tzum

The mobile bleated from atop the bedside table. Stonecrop had been having a dream in which he had been frantically searching for the phone. Federica groaned and rolled over to snuggle against him as he answered the WhatsApp video call.

"Dante, what time is it?"

"Midnight here, six there."

Losing her snuggle buddy, Federica eased out of the covers and headed to the kitchen.

Stonecrop fumbled the phone, then repositioned himself and flipped on the wall-mounted bedside lamp. "Still there?"

"Yeah. You first," Alexander ordered.

"Sure. Hitoshi will be here at noon. We're at Federica's." Stonecrop yawned at the phone. "He told her to pack a bag and passport."

"Did he say where they were going?"

"Nope."

"What's the plan?"

"We're working on it. I'll keep you in the loop. And your end?" Stonecrop asked. He wasn't awake enough to spell out what he and Federica had discussed last night.

"I've become very popular! You want creepy or creepier?"

"It's pre-crank. Hit me with creepy," Stonecrop mumbled.

"You guys know Harry Chum?" Alexander was drinking a glass of milk. Oreos were piled like poker chips on a plate next to the milk.

"Minister of Fiestas, right? That's what Gregor calls him. Yeah, he's the resident spook at the U.S. embassy in Bern. A real character, likes motorcycles and never shuts up. He met with Gregor about arrangements for Marion's family."

Federica carefully slid back into the bed beside Stonecrop. She was

265

wearing undies and a loose-fitting white camisole and was bearing two bitter ristretto coffees. The coffees had been made the quick and lazy way, with capsules.

"Morning, Dante. You're so cute! Milk and cookies. Like a cozy bear." She blew a kiss his way. The chipper behavior was an act. She was so *not* a morning person.

"Back to Chum," Alexander recaptured center stage from the ristretti. "He called me yesterday. Potomac and New Order popped up on his radar in connection to an unnamed, foreign criminal organization. Our conversation was more gossip than an agency interrogation. Been there, done that, so I know the difference. What got my attention was that Chum knew that *I* had been to Sato's place. I explained how Sato had not been at work and I was worried. Not sure if Chum bought it. He acted like he did, and told me Sato had been a person of interest for some time and that I should be circumspect in my business dealings with him. Group got a pass, which was a surprise. I asked if he knew Hitoshi Sato's whereabouts. Chum effectively told me that his people—whoever the hell they are—had the same question. He did say that Sato had not, to the best of his knowledge, left Europe."

"Doesn't surprise me," Stonecrop said.

"Chum tzum," Federica yawned and almost spilled her coffee.

Neither of the men responded.

"Chinook word—salmon or maybe fish bait. Is Harry fishy smelly?" She drank her coffee in one swallow, handed the cup to Stonecrop, and rolled over to go back to sleep. The act left him with a cup in each hand and the phone on his lap.

"How 'bout creepier," Stonecrop said.

"We're still on creepy, mon!"

"Proceed, sir." Their conversation verged on the surreal. Stonecrop would have pinched himself to see if he was awake if—that is—he'd had a free hand.

"I figured since Chum knew Hitoshi Sato, I'd ask him about the Soldier of the Good stuff."

"And?" Stonecrop asked. Federica rolled her head to the side to listen.

"I felt like Chum didn't want to say anything, not at first. But then, the cat was out of the bag. The Soldiers of the Good—he calls them Good Warriors—are a hybrid 'terrorist-trending' sect that split off from something called *Yom Shinryo*—"

Federica interrupted, *"Aum Shinrikyo.* Sarin attacks in the Tokyo subway in the 90s."

"That's it," Alexander said, and continued. "I looked it up. The Warriors' philosophy is some nut-bag mix of Buddhism, Christianity, and MENSA. They're ultra-elitist and super-smart, out to expunge evil from the world."

"Did you get the secret handshake?" Fede chimed in.

"I asked him if they were Yakuza. I didn't mention your friends."

"And?" Stonecrop asked, surprised that he felt protective of Mother and Father and concerned that Dante had compromised them.

"He said, 'yes and no.' For example, the Warriors don't have something he called an *oyabun-kobun* structure, whatever that is, but, like Yakuza, they have a public front and a political affiliation—"

Fede jumped in again, "Mentor-follower." She was too sleepy to care that she was being an obnoxious smarty-pants. "Hitoshi's oyabun," she said flatly. "Chum is full of chum. I tell you the guy's fishy—"

Thick-skinned and unbothered by the interruption, Alexander continued, "I asked if there were women Yakuza."

"Not smart, Dante," Fede snapped, instantly on the same page as Stonecrop in not wanting to draw Chum's attention to the Buurhuus incident.

"He said no." Alexander went on to defend his position, "I don't think he read anything into it."

"Wrong on both counts," Federica lectured. "He's CIA, not much slips by. Even so, 'fish-man' is only mostly correct. In feudal times, gambler Yakuza were called *Bakuto.* Female Bakuto controlled waterfront gambling houses between Edo and Kyoto. And when we lived in Tokyo, I remember Papà mentioning a female *Tekiya*—those are peddler Yakuza. She took over her husband's *kobun* when he passed away. Women are gaining stature in business in modern Japan. And all business in Japan is connected to Yakuza, ergo—"

"Dante," Stonecrop interrupted to apologize. "Fede needs to eat!"

"Creepier?" Alexander reminded them.

"Shit, I already forgot about creepier," Stonecrop said. Fede shoved her butt against Stonecrop's side. It felt like she'd farted. She flipped him a Mona Lisa smile that said "Hungry."

Alexander went on, "Mon, it's weird alright. A woman called me on my cell, the one I use *only* for DoD communications, and, in so-so English, very calmly threatened me."

"Not good," Stonecrop said. By now he was more than awake.

"Hey, threats happen. I don't spook easy," Alexander said. "This one hit a nerve. She said that if I tell anyone about the 'man with the fancy rifle' or 'the woman in chains,' we have big problem. She said that twice, the 'we have big problem' part. Now, I don't know if she meant that *she* would be the problem or *I*—as in me—would be the problem."

"Mother knows best! It's both!" Fede had resurfaced.

Alexander devoured a couple of Oreos and drank the rest of the milk. "Clear enough it was that little-old-lady with the MP7."

"*Dai mondai,*" Fede chirped in, twisting to her side so she could see Dante. Her camisole had also twisted, revealing one breast. "That's what Chop-Chop said to Father, 'Big problem.'"

Stonecrop and Alexander looked at each other but said nothing. Alexander politely lowered his gaze.

"What's more," Federica rejoined. Her tone of voice turned serious. "My fucked-up ex-fiancé is somehow connected with Hitoshi, that brilliant idiot Hitoshi. Andreas is no idealist. I introduced the two of them—not smart, Federica—and I think Hitoshi told Andreas about the kidnapping, maybe when they went for a joy ride in Andreas' Ferrari. Not that anyone would fuck in a Ferrari—no room. I mean—"

"Fede," Stonecrop killed the digression.

"Andreas," she pressed on, "turned Hitoshi's scheme, which was intended to be a harmless caper, into something twisted, vicious, and ugly."

"Why?" Alexander asked.

"He's egotistical, jealous, vain, violent . . . Want more? Maybe to prove to Papà he's really badass. Papà called him a wimp, right to his face. Or maybe Andreas wants to get back at me for humiliating him when I returned the engagement ring. It was stupid to do that right in front of Hitoshi and Max. Or, just maybe, he's angry that Hitoshi loves me. Or a bruised ego from when Max put him down. He lost it."

Alexander was hanging on every word. "What happened?"

She dropped the lunch encounter and switched to Albisrieder. "At the Buurhuus, the farmhouse, Andreas beat me and tried to rape me. He didn't speak. They had put a hood over my head so I couldn't see. But I knew his smell, his cologne. Chop-chop stopped him from hurting me. Max thinks Andreas killed Wulf. Hitoshi's next."

Alexander's serious tone matched Federica's. "Any idea where the son-of-a-bitch is now? Or Hitoshi?"

"We'll find out soon enough," Stonecrop said.

The Föhn

Vormittag checked his watch for the tenth time in as many minutes. "He's late." Then he checked the time on the phone Federica held in her hand. "*Spät,*" he repeated.

They stood behind the gate at Susenbergstrasse, waiting. The only message Federica had received this morning had been from Alicia. She had texted from the Zürich Flughafen where she was waiting for a flight back to London. She did have information for Federica and Stonecrop. Apparently, Hitoshi Sato had recently gotten a loan for 500 thousand SF from Banquiers. No other significant deposits or withdrawals had been made to his account.

Overnight the föhn, a dry, warm, down-slope wind, had descended from the alps south of Zürich, rolled northward across the lake, and spilled across the city. The snow on the lowlands had all but disappeared; the warming sun was doing its best to melt snow off the roads. The evaporating moisture shimmered above the asphalt on Susenbergstrasse; snowmelt flowed into the ditches beside the road and trimmed the black asphalt on either side with a streamer of reflective silver. It was a glorious day.

At their morning meeting, Ratzow, Claudia, and Stonecrop had worked out a compromise with Federica. Ratzow had agreed to Federica's desire to prevent as much as possible a summary execution of Hitoshi. She demanded closure, however, and had insisted upon a face-to-face with him.

With some misgivings they had left it to her to orchestrate the confrontation. That was the only way, she had told them, to get Hitoshi out of her mind and out of her life. Other than Alexander, she and Stonecrop had told no one about Andreas.

Claudia suggested engaging Vormittag and was eager to to mediate the arrangement. "Best case," she had said, "Vormittag arranges for Sato to be legally expelled from Switzerland. If our target behaves himself, he gets a pass. Worst case, Vormittag arrests Hitoshi for stalking Federica and links him to Wulf, the kidnapping, and Marion. Then we're all in the shitter." If this happened, Claudia suggested giving Father and Mother Hitoshi's whereabouts. Her opinion was that Red Monkey would swiftly dispatch Hitoshi. The latter option worried everybody—the cure could be worse than the cold.

Stonecrop had objected, but in the end capitulated. He'd replayed the scenario at the Buurhuus and argued that there was a good chance Mother and Father would do absolutely nothing. First, Chop-chop had been the Red Monkey rogue, not Sato. Second, another bloody execution by Red Monkey, upon review, might link them to the Buurhuus affair, an event Mother and Father had done their best to erase. No one listened to Stonecrop.

Ratzow had been busy. He had conferred with his lawyers and formally removed Geissner, Pfaff, and Reeb from any position of authority over Ratzow's and Group's enterprises. Ratzow had lamented to Stonecrop: In the good-old-days, he would have had a more colorful fix to Geissner's self-dealing. Today, and for Federica's sake, he would dismiss Geissner with balls attached.

That did not mean that Ratzow would forget and forgive Red Monkey and Geissner. Twenty-five million was at risk. Geissner had misappropriated the funds and the put option, though nearly impossible to enforce, existed on paper.

But now was a time to focus on other matters, Ratzow had insisted and had set the threats aside. He had accepted the reality that neither he nor Geissner would ever deliver Echo to Red Monkey. Separately, Stonecrop and Federica feared Ratzow would get creative and hunt for a substitute technology, a concern because any action in that direction would undermine Ratzow's ever-slimming odds of avoiding prison.

Federica left Vormittag at his position at the gate. She descended the stairs to speak with Stonecrop, who was in the side-garden sitting on the stone bench, scratching Rosie on the tummy, and speaking on the phone with Gregor. The sun had not touched the garden; patches of snow hid in the shadows. Federica shivered through her black Patagonia hoody and flannel shirt. She sidled up to Stonecrop as he slipped the still-on phone into his pants pocket. From the side pockets of her hoody she withdrew two phones, the burner from last night and her own.

He put an arm around her shoulder. "Gregor's staying on the line. I told him I'd give updates."

"I'm freezing," she said.

"It's fifteen degrees warmer today!" Stonecrop snuggled closer.

"I hate the föhn. We get more patients when there's a föhn. And more suicides."

"Same with a full moon?" he kidded.

"You laugh, but it's true." Federica let the weather chatter die out. "Did Father and Mother know about Hitoshi?" she asked.

"Doubt it. When I sent Father and Mother a *three year on rock* message this morning, saying we had identified number four and wanted to talk tomorrow, they expressed no interest in number four. Just the same, I want to get together with them. The plan is we meet them at the Zoo tomorrow morning when it opens. They were very clear: only the two of us." Stonecrop added an unrelated thought. "I'm curious what Chop-Chop said to Father right before . . ."

"I couldn't hear very well. Just a few words. He was squaring up his affairs, something about his family, I think."

"Would he have told Father if another Red Monkey defector were involved?"

"Probably. He'd already broken the kobun code of behavior. He would speak the truth. Certainly, if he wanted to keep his family safe from retribution. Chop-Chop looked relieved—as relieved as anyone seconds away from death can look—when Father agreed to whatever he'd asked for. It was so surreal, Max."

Stonecrop had given up on not worrying. The upcoming meeting with Hitoshi Sato was a disaster in the making. When so many things *can* go wrong, they will. He fatalistically accepted that he would have to improvise an outcome to minimize the damage—but damage there would be.

Hitoshi was unpredictable. Federica was unpredictable. She would have to use all the dissimilitude she could muster to not sway from the fiction Claudia had fed to Vormittag. The story Claudia had concocted named Hitoshi as the party responsible for Federica's bruised and raw wrists. Coordinating the 'when' of the abuse would have to be done on-the-fly between Federica and Hitoshi. Federica had told Vormittag that her objective was to never see Hitoshi Sato again. That, hopefully, was not a lie. Nor did she want him to go to jail. It was unclear to Stonecrop how much of her concern was about incriminating the lot of them and how much was about a fear that confinement would kill

Hitoshi.

Vormittag had promised to do his diplomatic best to deal with Sato. He would order Sato to be out of the country within thirty-six hours or face charges. Stonecrop doubted Vormittag had the actual authority to issue the directive and further believed that there would be push-back from Sato. The Kommissar could accommodate Ratzow only to a point. *It's gonna to be a shit-show.*

"Will Hitoshi blabber to Vormittag?" Stonecrop asked. "To show off, out of pure arrogance?"

"No," Federica replied. "He doesn't 'blabber'." She seemed offended by his remark. "And I implored Kommissar Vormittag to limit their conversation to the abuse and ignore anything else Hitoshi might say. He asked why. I just said there was more but it was too personal and involved a lot of people. I wasn't ready. He didn't argue with me. He and Papà—and Claudia—are closer than they let on. I have a feeling they talked this whole thing through again after my conversation this morning."

Rosso Corsa

Federica heard and recognized the sound before anyone else. "Merde, Andreas!"

"No, it's Hitoshi," Stonecrop said.

She hadn't seen the car, but she recognized the slapping whine of the engine. The sound echoed off garage doors, fences, and planted embankments along Susenbergstrasse. Stonecrop and Federica took the stairs two at a time and gained the top as Vormittag stepped out from behind the gate and onto the sidewalk. The Ferrari came to a stop in front of the house, passenger side to the curb. At idle the engine beat irregularly.

The driver revved the motor a few times. The act cheered up the car and distracted Stonecrop. The sound reminded him of his dad's garage and endless hours his father had spent in a never-ending quest to coax more horsepower out of engines already stretched to the limit. The distraction didn't end when the driver turned off the ignition. The carbon-fiber and aluminum bodied machine, a ravishing Italian red, screamed "look at me!" The driver's face was obscured by tinted glass, a feature which required a specific permit from the Zürich *Verkehrsamt*.

Stonecrop assumed the car was Hitoshi's five-hundred-K toy, the one in the photo in his apartment . . .

Like a satellite maintaining a fixed distance from the earth, Kommissar Vormittag kept his distance from the front of the car. His steps were tentative. He seemed afraid to re-awaken the beast as he walked toward the driver's side door. En route, he extended a hand and without touching the car scribed the exquisite sweep of the sculpted hood.

The driver's window lowered. Vormittag's movements were awkward, either from the heavy overcoat or a stiff back. He looked like a monk pronouncing a benediction. One hand rested on the roof of the car, directly above the driver's head.

Stonecrop speculated that one way or another the cash in the North Face duffle had provided security for a loan to buy the car. Hitoshi would have been too smart to directly deposit the money into his account. Or maybe the money was nothing to Hitoshi. Hell, he was an investment banker. None of the investment bankers Stonecrop had known were exactly poor.

Federica and Stonecrop stood near the gate; then stepped forward of the Ferrari to get a glimpse of the driver through the less-tinted front windshield. Federica clenched her hands into fists. Stonecrop said nothing, equally surprised and not sure how to react. He was wrong about the car. He was wrong about the driver. He'd seen the Ferrari before and should have recognized it.

"Mr. Sato, I presume," Vormittag politely began, not looking at the driver and handing his card through the window as it opened. A large hand with wrist bedecked with a Patek Philippe plucked the card from Vormittag; the driver's other hand raised his sunglasses and set them atop a nest of short, curly black hair. He glanced at the card and Vormittag for only a second before zeroing in on Federica and Stonecrop.

Vormittag quickly realized his mistake. "Ah, who have we here? Certainly not Herr Sato." He didn't drop a beat. "But I *do* recognize you, Mr. Castro. You were warned to stay away from Fräulein Ratzow. That was what, a year ago?"

"Good memory, old man. Yes, a while ago. Relax, Kommissar. You see, we're engaged. Everybody's happy!" Andreas Castro was unfazed by Vormittag's presence; his tone of voice suggested he was the authority, not Vormittag.

Vormittag, surprising both Federica and Stonecrop, improvised on his suspicions and in precise English continued as if Hitoshi and Castro were one and the same. His statement sounded rehearsed. "Frau Doktor Ratzow asked me to speak to you about a personal matter, a matter which concerns her very much, and one which I have offered to address on her behalf. Per her request—which I will abide, but only agree with in part—I've been asked to limit our conversation to her report of stalking and physical abuse."

The Kommissar must have presumed that the issue with Hitoshi had been intended for Castro and that somehow there had a been a miscommunication. He looked to Stonecrop and Federica for confirmation or a look that suggested he do something other than what had been scripted.

Andreas smiled and started to speak. Vormittag cut him off by putting his finger to his own lips. The effect, as always, was somewhat comical, as if the Kommissar were balancing his moustache on top of his finger. The words, however, were serious. "I must advise you: You will be held accountable for anything you say to me."

An arrogant Andreas waited, impatient and disdainful, changing their roles and treating Vormittag as if the Kommissar were a supplicant. "Are you finished *Kommissar* Vormittag?" His demeaned the word "Kommissar" and didn't wait for Vormittag to respond. "You are confused, *Kommissar*. Federica and I are leaving together, today. Holiday, you see." He repeated the words so the Kommissar would not fail to understand them: "Together, holiday, today. *Verstehen Sie*?"

Vormittag, in general a patient man, had had enough. "Mr. Castro, you are the one who is confused. Dr. Ratzow has filed a fresh complaint with our department. You have thirty-six hours to leave Switzerland. I am notifying the Mexican consulate. Were it not for Frau Doctor Ratzow's advocacy, I would arrest you. Let me be clear: You are not to call, text, or communicate with her, either directly or indirectly. Call, text, or communicate. *Capisce*?" Vormittag hissed the word. He was angry, though also embarrassed by his anger. "Keep your distance, or you will find yourself in much trouble."

Castro's response was the epitome of self-control. "No. That won't be necessary. Look, there she stands? Is she harmed? No, and it is *because* of my intervention. You've got it all backwards, Kommissar!"

Stonecrop and Federica were on tenterhooks. Stonecrop eyed a fist-sized rock, a piece of the landscaping along the fence. *If Andreas starts in about the Buurhuus, I'll smash the goddamned windshield.*

Vormittag was incredulous. "No. You are responsible for *this*, yes?" Vormittag raised the sleeve of his coat, a signal to Federica to do the same. She complied, unsure of herself, and revealed the purple and red bruises ringing her wrists. In a way, Castro was responsible. At least he had had the option to do something about her abduction.

Castro's voice didn't waver. "Yes, a little discomfort is sometimes what a woman wants, what she needs. It's complicated. You wouldn't understand."

Stonecrop had forewarned Federica: If Hitoshi lost it or if Vormittag went deep, he would derail the confrontation. This far along, that it was Castro and not Hitoshi, mattered little. When he reached down for the rock, Federica instantly understood what Max was thinking. She touched his arm, telling him to stop. Her look accused him of being an idiot.

Vormittag turned to Federica and silently asked for some indication of what she would like him to do. No doubt he remembered her comment about "rough sex." If the injuries were consensual, would that matter?

Federica walked to the driver's side door to join Vormittag. Castro's eyes followed her like an osprey stalking a fish.

She addressed the Kommissar: "May I speak to him in private?"

Vormittag consented and took a step or two back toward the rear of the car, stealing a peek at the engine through its plexiglass cover. Stonecrop ignored Federica's request for privacy and followed close enough to hear their conversation.

She too had to bend forward to speak. *It's like a confessional.* Her pigtail fell in the window and brushed against Castro's shoulder as he looked up to face her. He let Vormittag's card drop to the floor and lightly ran his fingers along the cord of hair. His touch was too assured. Stonecrop immediately wanted to hurt him.

Her voice quavered. "You disappoint me, Andreas. You hurt me and others. Where's Hitoshi? You were with him last night. When we texted."

Castro dipped his head and bowed. He was mocking her like he had mocked Vormittag. When he raised his head, the eyes radiated something wanton and evil.

"You let *him* have his way with you?" he said. "That little shit. Why him? Why not me?"

"What the fuck are you talking about?"

"Don't play dumb, *chica*, it doesn't become you."

"I'm not."

"He's wanted you ever since. Did you know that? He told me all about it, so fantastical, magical. I really thought he had made it up. But he didn't. The detail, he remembered every little detail. Even blindfolded, on your knees, you gave him everything. You're going to do that with me!"

Federica burst out laughing. "You jealous prick! Oh my god, I had no idea that was Hitoshi. You're talking about when I was at University in Chicago? Really? That's what you want? You want to hold hands? A blindfolded French kiss? I can't tell you how innocent we were. That's a Hitoshi made-up fantasy—that's why it sounded like one, you dipshit. God, we were kids. And so what, asshole, so what if I fucked his brains out."

Federica threw her head back and laughed again. She tossed a quick glance at Stonecrop before returning to face Andreas. Her pigtail, once again, lay against him.

"You know what?" she said.

He tilted his head to listen.

"You're a total fucking loser."

It suddenly made sense to Stonecrop: Hitoshi and Federica's attendance at University of Chicago had overlapped. He'd been a perfect candidate for the sex club that Alicia had described. Obviously, he had discovered that Federica had been his erotic playmate and had invented, maybe even believed, what had transpired between them. He had followed her for years. The revelation triggered another question: Who were the other women in Hitoshi's album, the album Dante had showed him?

"Here's the deal, Andreas," Federica continued, "you will never speak to me again." She lightly flicked her head to free her pigtail, but Andreas closed his fingers around it. Federica let it slide, her tone was confident. "You want to make me happy? Leave me the fuck alone. Hitoshi too." Federica added something in Spanish. Whatever the last bit was, it did not go over well.

With his left-hand Andreas pulled Federica's pigtail downward and pinned her head against the sill of the window. Her head, lying on its side, faced up and out the windshield at an awkward angle. Her body froze.

She said nothing and stared forward at nothing. Castro turned and slid his right hand toward her crouch. He pressed his face against hers, "Puta, you like it, don't you!"

Vormittag was closest and got there first. He grabbed Castro by the windpipe, forcing him to release Federica. But then the younger and stronger Castro bent Vormittag's wrist in a manner that forced the contorted hand out of the window. Vormittag went to his knee. Stonecrop stepped forward to help but Vormittag waved his other hand to warn Stonecrop to stay put.

The only thing keeping Castro in one piece was that hand wave.

The rage reached its apex and then quickly settled. Stonecrop took hold of Federica's shoulders. He gently put one hand around the nape of her neck and then brushed aside a loose wisp of hair. She returned his worried look with a game smile that said I'm tougher than you think. Out of fear that Stonecrop would do something he would regret, she seized his wrists and held them so firmly that he could not break her grip without hurting her.

In a calm voice that belied the anger he felt, Stonecrop expressed his intentions, "I'm gonna hurt him."

She leaned against him and stated just a calmly. "No, you are not, not if you love me."

They had reached a détente. She reduced the intensity of her grip in increments as the tension in his body diminished.

"*Basta!*" Vormittag shouted. "Out of the car." Castro had let go the paralyzing twist he had had on Vormittag's hand. With his good hand the Kommissar fumbled for something under his coat—a weapon, a phone, handcuffs?

Federica stepped between them and walked Vormittag a few steps back and next to Stonecrop. She took the hand out of his pocket. "Settle down. Over there," she pointed, commanding with the same voice she would use with Rosie. "Max, both of you. Please, let me handle this my way."

Stonecrop backed away, but not so far that he couldn't hear them. The conversation was out of range for Vormittag.

"Where is he? Where's Hitoshi?" she asked.

"Get in. Or Hitoshi ends up like his pretty friend. And this shithead and your Papà will spend the rest of their lives behind bars. Hitoshi told me everything. He was insane to think he could get away with it. He is insane!"

"No."

"Your choice, Frau Doktor. A little talk, that's all I'm asking."

"You touch me and you're a dead man."

"Call off the dogs."

"Someplace public?"

"Yes."

Stonecrop noticed Frau Ott watching from her bedroom window. Rosie was just able to reach the bottom of the diamond-paned window. Her nose left wet marks on the glass. Frau Ott and Rosie appeared totally confused by the comings and goings with the driver of the Ferrari. In chorus and as the drama unfolded their heads turned toward each other, Frau Ott looking down and Rosie looking up.

Stonecrop's gaze swung back to Federica. The passenger door opened and Federica got in, raising her hand up and willing both Vormittag and Stonecrop to stop after they both had begun to move forward.

She was putting Hitoshi's safety and well-being ahead of her own.

"Alright," she said to the driver. Turning away from Castro, she winked at Max and pointed to the pocket of her hoody. Stonecrop understood. He would track her phone.

Castro gripped the wheel with one hand and lowered his sunglasses with the other. He grunted, "*Pendejos*—fucking idiots!"

The Ferrari's five-hundred-plus-horsepower engine came to life. Castro's invective was lost in the engine noise and tires spinning on the wet pavement as the car accelerated away from them. Vormittag had had last minute second thoughts but had moved too slowly to block the car's passage. Stonecrop, in spite of the rage he felt and fear for Fede, respected her imprecation to not interfere. As the car approached the corner, like a fledging bird ejected from its nest, one of Federica's phones flew out of the driver's side window.

The Ferrari's high-pitched whine melded with Castro's words and lingered in Stonecrop's ears as the car crested the hill on Susenbergstrasse and then sank below view.

The dramatic departure launched a cacophony of yelping by neighborhood dogs, Rosie among them. Frau Ott's eyes met Stonecrop's. She raised a veined, shaking hand in the air, questioning the meaning of it all.

Stonecrop realized Gregor was still on the line. He took the phone out of his pocket.

"It was Castro, not Hitoshi. He can't control himself. Vormittag intervened."

Stonecrop paused, unsure how to explain what had transpired.

"Andreas has something on Hitoshi. They're gone."

"Who's gone?"

"Castro and Fede."

"I'm at Zürichberg. Wait there."

The Sorell Hotel Zürichberg, next to the Zoo and an entrance to the Zürichberg park, was at most two minutes by car from the house on Susenbergstrasse. The morning plan had included Ratzow being stationed nearby as backup.

Vormittag took the phone from Stonecrop.

"Gregor. I can do only so much. I am a Swiss policeman. This abusive man is a danger to your daughter and others. . . . I need to notify . . . An hour, no more . . . Aviation authorities as well . . . I don't see what you can do in an hour."

Vormittag stared at the blank asphalt which, despite the Kommissar's intense scrutiny, refused to give up Castro's destination. The Kommissar looked a broken man.

Marmorerasee

The pavement-gray Audi R8 10 crawled to a stop in front of Stonecrop. Ratzow, like many business types, favored Audis and BMWs. He had a garage full of them but hardly ever drove, and, when he did, he drove like the proverbial little old lady.

Claudia was in the passenger's seat. She opened the door before the car rolled to a stop.

Stonecrop extended his hand toward Ratzow. "Give me the fob. I'll follow him."

Claudia spoke: "To where, dearie? Some Gstaad chalet? There's no place for him to hide."

"I can track Fede's phone—"

"Not possible, I saw Andreas toss her phone out the window," Vormittag said. "The department can track the car with photo radar. A Ferrari is not inconspicuous—except downtown."

"She had two phones," Stonecrop informed them, "a burner and her own. That was the burner. The discarded phone was silver; hers is black."

"What can you do, love? That is, what can you do that won't put Federica at risk?" Claudia was keen to manage the conversation, to ensure there would be no mention of the Yakuza or the kidnapping.

Claudia and Vormittag were correct, of course. But Stonecrop could not accept Federica being under Castro's control. Also unacceptable was the idea of waiting for Kantonspolizei to locate the car, arrest Castro, and risk his incriminating the lot of them. And Castro would get off scot-free. The only thing that pinned him to the Buurhuus was a drugged Federica's claim that it was Castro she had smelled—a report that would be child's play for Castro's lawyers to discredit.

"I've got an idea," said the man without a plan. He turned to

Ratzow: "The fob, Gregor."

Ratzow ignored Claudia and handed it over. "You know what to do," Ratzow said. "One hour." Stonecrop nodded back; there was no need for Ratzow to spell it out.

Stonecrop, with phone on the console and set to track Federica's phone, drove off in the same direction that Castro had, leaving the others to ruminate, conspire, and lie as need be.

Contrary to his expectation Castro had not gone far. Within five minutes the Ferrari pulled up at the entrance of the Dolder Grand Hotel. Stonecrop was close behind and gave them a minute to exit the vehicle and then parked the R8 directly behind Castro's car. He watched Fede and Castro in the lobby.

He was still without a plan when the phone vibrated with a text from Alexander.

<DA: Chum called. Hitoshi Sato just boarded a plane for Osaka.>

<MS: In one piece? Alone.>

<DA: Roger.>

<MS: That's all I need! Gotta go.>

Castro had been bluffing. Hitoshi was safe.

Stonecrop, buoyed by the update from Alexander, strode into the Dolder's grand foyer. Standing at the reception desk, physically a foot apart from each other and worlds apart emotionally, were Federica and Castro. Federica appeared prepared to keep her word and acquiesce to Castro's abuse in order to protect Hitoshi and her family.

The Patek Philippe announced itself on the marble counter as Castro signed the guest registration. Federica turned around and saw Stonecrop jogging toward them. The concierge, seeing him approach, looked up as well and smiled.

"Hi Lenz! How you doing?" Stonecrop said.

The concierge, a poised professional, nodded back. He was a fellow shooter from the Schützenhaus. His expression sought a reason for the sudden intrusion in the transaction with Castro.

Stonecrop beamed and Castro glared back at him.

"Lenz," Stonecrop repeated the name to pull rank on Castro and piss him off, "they don't need a room. This guy's a jerk and Federica ain't interested."

"I'm warning you. Get out of here," Castro's lips quivered when he spoke. His face reddened and breath shortened like it had in Bruxelles. The macho man did not take public humiliation well.

Lenz had been a concierge for twenty years, mostly at the Dolder.

He had managed movie stars, business magnates, and Russian mafia bosses. As such, he was unruffled by Castro's threat and Stonecrop's interruption. Lenz calmly walked around the reception counter and took Castro and Stonecrop each by the elbow.

"Gentlemen, if you please, you are free to continue your discussion outside. I have other guests to attend to. You are, of course, most welcome to rejoin us after you've sorted things out."

No one wanted a row in the lobby of the Dolder. "Frau Doktor Ratzow, I have a car available for you." Lenz, of course, knew Federica and her father.

Stonecrop twisted his head and leaned over the concierge's shoulder to speak to Federica. "Hitoshi's fine. He's on a plane to Osaka."

Fede's eyes teared up; her face softened and she half-smiled. Castro's power over her was gone. The threat that Castro would speak to Kantonspolizei was still present.

The valets had been following the fuss in foyer. They worked for Lenz for years; he didn't have to tell them what to do. A valet stood at attention by each car and held the driver's side door open. There was something festive about the scene, the formally attired valets and the dozen or so vehicles, all extraordinarily expensive and poised for their owners or chauffeurs to return. Stonecrop felt the urge to sprint to his car Le Mans style.

"Hey, a little talk, that's all I'm asking!" Stonecrop yelled to Castro, repeating the words Castro had said to Federica. He followed the request with "Asshole!"

The Ferrari's high pitched *VRRP, VRRP* was followed by the rumble of the R8. The dueling sounds rattled the cantilevered roof over the parking reception area.

Stonecrop still didn't have a real plan. *Maybe I will talk to Andreas,* he told himself. *That's sort of a plan. Try to make a deal.* But first, of course, he had to pin him down someplace private.

The F-series left streaks of rubber on the pavement. Stonecrop eased the R8 down the drive. He kept within two hundred yards of Castro.

One hour, that's all you get with Andreas, until Vormittag green-lights the Keystone Cops. Except they're not Keystone Cops, they're Swiss Police and damned good at their jobs.

Having no idea where Castro was heading, Stonecrop decided to follow him until there was an isolated place to force him to pull over. He also decided to stay far enough behind Castro so that both cars wouldn't appear in the same photo radar shots. He wouldn't hurt

Castro. He had promised Fede, and he had made that promise to himself. But he did want Castro out of Fede's life. *There's the rub.*

At first Stonecrop figured Castro would head north to Schaffhausen. In less than an hour from Zürich he could be out of Switzerland. Of course, Castro was unaware of Vormittag's threat so maybe the time didn't matter. When Castro turned south on Katzenschwanzstrasse and then continued toward Chur, Stonecrop recalibrated his expectations. Castro was driving fast, gathering tickets no doubt, though not fast enough to warrant being pulled over. He was on en route to the Engadine, to St. Moritz and his private jet. A couple hours at the rate they were going.

Stonecrop drifted back, as if he were unable to keep up with Castro. They were still on highly trafficked roads. He called Gregor.

"Gregor, I need another hour. Castro's heading to St. Moritz, his plane. I want to intercept him someplace less populated."

Gregor, a mind-reader at these sorts of things, didn't waste a breath.

"Marmorerasee. Try there. Or high, at quarry before Julier Pass. Roads will be wet. Better for you. I get you extra hour. Will cost me something with Polizei, something real—information they can use."

Stonecrop pressed on at a measured pace, enjoying the R8's superb handling. The car had not enough ground clearance for pro rally but was awfully good otherwise. Every so often Castro's car came into view and incited mixed feelings. If he could see Andreas, then Andreas could see him. On the other hand, each siting confirmed that Andreas had not changed course.

Marmorerasee was a reservoir, not a lake. A dam was built in the 50s after the village of Marmorera had flooded. The artificial lake had become a popular diving destination. The road to Julier Pass followed the west shore of the reservoir. Stonecrop had stopped once at the restaurant on the north end, the dam side of the reservoir. He remembered that there were often spotty patches of ice on the road from weather or moisture rising from the reservoir.

The Ferrari popped into view right after the village of Albula, the last point at which Castro could have turned off before Julier Pass and twenty or so kilometers from Marmorerasee. The road was empty of traffic. A light snow activated the wipers. Now, with no reason to hold back, Stonecrop closed the gap.

Castro must have thought Stonecrop had given up the pursuit. The gray R8 was a mere two hundred meters from his tail before he noticed. Castro twitched and his car veered across the centerline. The

Ferrari dropped a gear and accelerated. Stonecrop did the same. The Ferrari was the faster car, however the last five hundred meters before the lake included a sharp S-curve. The snow was starting to stick. They would have to slow down.

At the end of the last turn, Castro drifted wide and Stonecrop was able to execute a late apex dive to the inside of the curve, both passing Castro and for the first time since the Dolder seeing him eye to eye. Castro had a death grip on the wheel and a face to match it. Stonecrop, quite used to rubbing elbows with other cars at high speeds, was enjoying himself and relishing the R8's sticky grip on the wet.

Both cars blew by the Kiosk/café at the north end of the reservoir. They were inches apart and carrying too much speed. The man without a plan, slowed. Each time the Ferrari tried to pass, the R8 blocked it.

Stonecrop had been looking in the mirror when the road narrowed and pavement turned to gravel. The Audi swerved toward the embankment and drop-off. The guard rail was anything but: a scalloped fence of wooden stakes and orange-flagged polypropylene rope. The entire length of the road beside the reservoir was under repair. There must have been warning signs but he'd missed them.

In the mirror, Stonecrop saw the Ferrari repeat the same figures as the R8 but with less control. Stonecrop slowed, thinking Castro would do the same. He looked again at the driver's side rear mirror. The Ferrari had vanished. The car reappeared on his right, wildly accelerating on the gravel, inches from the R8 on one side and on the other inches from a ten-meter plunge into the reservoir.

It would be so easy, Stonecrop reflected. One flick of the wheel, a love-tap. That's all it would take. Problem solved. But he couldn't do it. Not because it would make Federica hate him and her father gloat; not for revenge over Castro's abusing Federica and taking advantage of Hitoshi. None of those things. He wanted to talk sense into Castro, not kill him. He'd had enough of killing.

He slowed as Castro roared by and shook a fist at Stonecrop. White gravel kicked up by the Ferrari's rear tires pelted the R8's hood and windshield. Dandelions-gone-to-seed sized snowflakes splattered the windshield. A crack snaked through the glass.

Castro raised his fist again. The gesture was cut short as the Ferrari fishtailed. Stonecrop felt the same patch of ice under the Audi and braked. The cars were now nose-to-nose and traveling at a hundred kilometers per hour. Through snow and mud-splattered windshields the wide-eyed drivers stared at each other.

The flip was sudden. The tail of the Ferrari dipped into a depression in the road and the vehicle reared up like its iconic emblem and exposed its naked underbelly. Stonecrop relaxed his grip on the wheel as the Audi's anti-lock braking did its hard-wired best to keep the R8 in a straight line. In a violent twist the Ferrari pirouetted toward the embankment and slipped tail-first into the reservoir. The splash was minimal—a perfect ten. Water quickly refilled the surface cavity. The bubbling eddy quickly dissipated, and the reservoir returned to its former serenity.

Stonecrop eased the Audi to a stop. He turned off the engine and watched and waited. There was nothing but the silence and falling snow. He had thought the car wouldn't sink, at least not like that, so suddenly; and he had hoped that Andreas would exit the vehicle and swim to the surface, arms flailing and mouth gasping for air. But none of that happened; nothing but silence and an isolated bubble or two. The reservoir was too deep and too cold for heroics. With a hand raised to cover his eyes from the snowfall he peered into the water. It was impenetrable. The car could under twenty feet of water or a hundred. He waited and shivered—though not from cold. He felt afraid and alone.

After restarting the Audi, he made a few passes over the tracks leading to where the Ferrari had dropped from sight. He got out of the Audi and replanted a toppled wooden stake. The flagged rope on either side was still attached. If the snowfall continued, other drivers would need the road markers.

Stonecrop had been unthinking and unhurried as he completed these tasks. He felt numb to what he had witnessed and numb to the consequences of being found in the act of covering up the incident.

The Audi, like a warm carapace, took him in. He headed home. En route he remembered a story about a child that had survived for twenty minutes underwater in an ice-covered lake.

Der Zoo

Stonecrop paid entry fees for everyone—himself, Federica, Mother and Father and their two children. After a cursory greeting, Mother put an arm around Federica's shoulder and took her aside. Stonecrop held the hand of Father's son. The boy had recognized him the minute they had met at the Zoo's entrance. He had run up to Stonecrop and thrown his arms around Stonecrop's legs.

Children adored Stonecrop. He never understood why. He thought of Sarah and Jenny, his daughters; he had missed his weekly call to them. Mother and Father's daughter, maybe seven years old, was shy. She clung to her mother's coat. When his girls were that age they were tyrants. The memory made him smile and miss them.

They ambled along in two groups, men behind, women ahead. Federica's sadness was unclothed; her gestures were strained, distracted, and separated from her surroundings. She had slept alone last night, shunting Stonecrop to the guest bedroom.

Mother took out her phone and flipped through photos, sharing them with Federica, who then reached over and swiped through pictures herself.

She put a closed fist to her lips. Her chest heaved as she exhaled. She covered the face of the phone with her hand, "Enough."

The groups broke up. Father and children took the lead. Enthralled with the exhibits and animals, the boy was oblivious to the ensemble's somber mood. He chattered in both Japanese and English to himself and anyone who would listen. He kept his younger sister in tow, unmindful of her shyness. They followed the footpath through the Masoala Rainforest exhibition and experienced a world as unfamiliar and unlike Zürich as one could imagine—warm, humid, verdant, populated with unfamiliar animals and unfamiliar sounds. The exhibition, a fifty-million Swiss franc addition to the Zoo, was a reproduction of a wooded peninsula in north-east Madagascar. The region was home to a plethora of indigenous species of plants and animals. Federica interpreted and translated as they strolled through the greenhouse.

"Father says one does not stand under a bat hanging by its hands," she translated.

"Japanese omen?" Stonecrop asked. She relayed his question in Japanese. Father squatted, hands held high, and bounced up and down like an aerobics instructor. He laughed so hard he lost his balance and did a pratfall. Everyone laughed and the children leapt forward to help Father get back to his feet.

"No, silly! That's how bats poop!" She smiled and laughed, and punched Stonecrop in the shoulder.

"Hey, I get it," Stonecrop was late to avoid the hit. He was pleased to experience a human side of Father, who, up to now, had seemed a mythic caricature of a humorless Japanese Yakuza.

Less than two meters in front of Stonecrop, as if on cue, a bat hanging by its hands, technically its thumbs, let'er rip. Stonecrop was curious now that he knew what was going on.

"Federica," he asked, "what did Mother show you?"

"Other women, some very young. The implication was that Hitoshi Sato had been tracking them. I'm not sure I buy it. She said they were part of his dream life. It was some expression I didn't get. Hitoshi may have had those pictures, but I doubt they were for the purpose she assumed."

"I'm sorry."

"She speaks decent English." Federica changed the subject. "Understands everything. And she's the boss, not Father." Federica looked at Mother as she spoke to Stonecrop. She wanted Mother to understand what she had just said.

Mother didn't react at first. A few steps later, she stopped and got Federica's attention.

"Yes, true. But you speak lovely Japanese." After a few steps, during which she lowered her eyes to the ground, she spoke again. "The photographs. You are correct. I don't know for sure."

Another conversation between Federica and Mother ensued, this one in Japanese. Federica relayed the content to Stonecrop. "Mother won't tell me her real name. She says she loves being called Mother. Anyway, Mother claims she is affiliated with the *koanchosa-cho*—that's the Public Security Intelligence Agency. It's the organization that went after the religious terrorist cults in Japan in the 90s. Apparently, these cults still exist and still make trouble. Father is Yakuza, through and through."

"A criminal and a cop?"

Stonecrop tried to speak to Mother, but she ignored him. With Federica's help, he questioned Father. First, about Wulf. Father was forthcoming and what he had to say was surprising. When Father and Mother had not heard from Stonecrop they had searched for and found Wulf's name online, including a photo of him—dressed as a man—and information describing his position at Banquiers Moretti.

They had followed Wulf to his sister's. Wulf had gone there after a brief visit to the bank, presumably having deposited the cash that was in the North Face duffle. They intercepted Wulf at the sister's house— she was away—and collected the same information Stonecrop had gotten from Wulf. In addition, Wulf had described the interrogation by Stonecrop. He had been distraught over the affair. Stonecrop's using Castro's name had complicated Wulf's story. When they left, Father said, Wulf was upset, but very much alive. Mother and Father had not touched or threatened him.

After Father related this history to Stonecrop, he made a side comment that Stonecrop had good *operational* potential. Father could use him now and then. The suggestion upset Federica. She squeezed his hand in a not so friendly way. Father reached up and awkwardly patted Stonecrop on the top of the head.

Two questions remained: How had Wulf died? Again, he queried Father, who responded in clipped English, "Not know."

The second question was about what was going to happen to Hitoshi Sato; it got the same treatment: "Not know."

It might be the case, Stonecrop reflected, that that was the extent of Father's English and it didn't matter what questions he asked.

Father stopped in place, absorbed in the setting. He recounted, through Federica, the experience of being in the actual Masoala rainforest in Madagascar. The replica in Zürich was much like the rainforest he remembered.

It was time to leave. They would not be back, Mother said.

The Zoo visit ended in silence. The group stood outdoors outside the ZooCafè. Father helped the children put on their coats. It was fifteen degrees Celsius cooler outside than in the greenhouse. Federica, in rapid Japanese, said something to the children and they ran up to her.

Father took Stonecrop aside and handed him a card with a phone number—Japan country code, but no name—only the expression "three year on rock" in English and Japanese. Stonecrop accepted the card, doing so without the Japanese formality of taking it in two hands and making a small bow.

Federica had disappeared in the ZooCafè with the children. When she returned, she and children had ice cream cones. The boy ran to Stonecrop and the sister followed and stood beside her brother. Stonecrop knelt and reached into his pocket and brought out two origami cranes. He gave one to each of them. They accepted the gifts and politely thanked him in English. No further farewells ensued. The silence was awkward, as if the cover of a book had closed unexpectedly and the reader was still a few pages from the end. It was time to get on with normal life.

Father and family climbed into a nondescript Subaru; it didn't look like a rental. Father started to back out of the parking space, and then stopped and lowered his window.

Stonecrop turned to Federica and whispered, "They probably forgot to shoot us."

Father said something to Federica, who, like the children, was preoccupied with her ice cream. She translated, "Father used the term *ashikase*—it means something like a thorn in the side. He forgot to ask about the twenty-five million—the put. That was the reason for meeting today."

"Oh. Yeah." Stonecrop thought a moment before replying. "We'll annul the put," he said. "I'll take care of it."

Federica struggled with the translation.

Mother leaned across Father and spoke in English, "I will explain." She tapped Father on the shoulder and nodded at him: Time to go.

Father smiled and held eye contact with Stonecrop, approving of what he had understood. He raised the window, backed the car out of its parking space, and drove off. The children looked out the rear window. They held their ice cream cones in one hand and in the other held the cranes so the cranes too could look out the window.

Stonecrop waved. Federica attempted a smile; it only half-happened. He speculated that she was trying to reconcile the Father and Mother who had treated her with kindness and undoubtedly had saved her life, with the man and woman who had ruthlessly taken the lives of Capo, Romeo, and Chop-Chop.

Her hand tightened on his forearm. Unknowingly, she was gripping a bruise on his arm. He ignored the pain and felt the tension in her body. That tension was possibly the only thing keeping her upright. She remained in a rigid state until the Subaru disappeared. Then, suddenly, she doubled over as if to vomit. He held her hair back as she crouched down. Her ice cream cone was squashed between her hand and the ground. The other hand clung to his leg for support. Tears struck the dirt.

The deaths of her captors had given her physical freedom. Freedom from the memories of their horrible deaths would take time.

"What a waste of life," she addressed the ground.

Stonecrop had not told Federica or anyone else about Marmorerasee. He's said only that he had turned around because of the weather. He knelt beside her and used his sleeve to wipe the ice cream and dirt from her hand.

Capuns

Stonecrop was in his element—icy roads and snow. The winter traction tires had stick. He worked the throttle through one set of hairpin turns after another. It was a familiar rhythm: set a line, brake hard, turn hard, and just as the rear end of the car starts to cut loose, accelerate to transfer weight to the rear wheels to gain sufficient traction to hold the line. Late apex maneuvers were second nature.

The car touched gravel on the shoulder of the road and shuddered. The disturbance woke Federica.

"Where are we?"

"Oberalp Pass, less than an hour to Dardin. We'll be there by midnight," Stonecrop welcomed the conversation, to pass the time and to help stay awake. They were on the southern flank of the alps, the side responsible for the föhn in Zürich. This windward side was colder and had wrung moisture out of the rising air. The road east from Zürich would have been a dryer and faster route, but the tragedy from the previous day was too fresh. Stonecrop hadn't wanted to relive it.

"Another forty kilometers or so. Not too far."

Fede stared into the onslaught of white. "Can you see anything in this shit?"

"X-ray vision. No worry." He was tired but having fun. Stonecrop's father had been an amateur pro-rally driver and young Max had been drifting through corners on snow and ice since he could reach the gas pedal.

"This is Andreas's cousin we're visiting? The family from Chihuahua?"

"It is. She's rarely there. I mean rarely in Chihuahua. Lupita's married and has made a life for herself in Dardin."

"Interesting. How did an industrial heiress end up in a backwoods hamlet in the Graubünden? Do they speak Romansh?"

"They do indeed. Lovely language. Like Italian, sprinkled with Latin."

"You speak Romansh?"

"Not like Lupita."

"What's hubby's name?"

"Casanova. Riccardo Casanova. The population of Dardin is maybe two hundred. Half of them are named Casanova. He teaches elementary school. They met in a Coop class in Zürich. I forget why Lupita was there. Something to do with the family business. Riccardo was taking his education certification and brushing up on French."

"Love at first sight?"

"Absolutely. C'mon, he's a Casanova. And he's *muy guapo*. She beat me to him!"

"Kiddos?"

"Twins. Boys, a real handful, two handfuls! It's a lot, managing the household—you'll see. Lupita works too. She tutors Spanish and French."

"And why are we going there?"

Fede and Max had hardly spoken since parting ways with Mother and Father at the Zoo. She had given a statement to Vormittag at the Canton police station and met with Dr. Weller. Weller announced he would personally take charge of caring for Marion. He very directly and wisely ordered Federica to not come back to work until well after the New Year. Second, he had insisted she join a support group at the clinic. Attendance was a requirement if she intended to continue working at the Spital.

When Fede returned to Susenbergstrasse she announced that she was going to Dardin for a few days. Stonecrop could come or not. He said yes, packed a bag and purloin an Audi RS7 from Gregor. Fede had been ready to go. She punched directions into the GPS, downed a mini-bottle of Stolichnaya, and put on headphones, a baseball cap pulled low over the eyes, and a hoody over that. "Drive," she ordered. She had not said a word for two hours, not until awakened by the sound of tires scraping the gravel.

"I need to be someplace normal," she volunteered, speaking more to herself than Stonecrop.

"Lupita knows we're coming?"

"I sent a text. She didn't respond. But it'll be okay."

Without a GPS, Stonecrop would never have found the place.

Knowing the location, however, didn't guarantee one could get there. The Audi, even with four-wheel drive and Blizzak snow tires, barely had the ground clearance for the last uphill into Dardin proper. He drove around a corner at speed, expecting they would high-center the Audi and have to walk the rest of the way. To his surprise they came upon a freshly plowed road and, in another 250 meters, a man who could only be described as tall, dark, and handsome. He was wearing a headlamp and was shoveling the driveway in front Casa Casanova.

The snow was a foot-and-a-half deep around the freshly cleared thirty-square-meter path to the carport. Stonecrop added strong as an ox to Casanova's attributes.

"*Buna sera*, Federica. And you are Max!" Riccardo's English was excellent, a fact which, for no good reason, surprised Stonecrop. Riccardo took Federica's pack and led the party through a second garage. Splits of wood two and three layers deep were stacked against every available wall. They exited the wood room via a stairway to the living room and the largest wood stove Stonecrop had ever seen in a private residence. Riccardo, knowing Stonecrop would ask, gave a short explanation.

"This one is less than ten years old. And yes, they are common in the Sedrun and Disentis regions of Graubünden. Ours is made from green Surselva soapstone and comes from the quarry here. The stone is high density. It holds the heat, which is good because the stove has to heat the whole house, all three levels. It's our only heat, except propane for cooking and electricity for hot water."

The stove was a floor-to-ceiling affair, a hexagonal edifice two meters in diameter. Surrounding the stove and made of the same soapstone was a floating bench covered with colorful throw pillows. There were canvas cubbies underneath to store slippers, or, in the case of Casa Casanova, a menagerie of stuffed animals, including a giraffe, a dolphin, and a floppy bunny with only one ear.

Lupita came flying down the steps from the bedroom. She and Federica screamed and greeted each other like college sorority girls— arms wide, hugs, and innumerable kisses.

"Yikes, we'll wake the boys! Sorry!" Federica tried to whisper.

"Not a chance. They're down for the night, thank God!" Lupita beamed back. "Food. Did you eat? Jesus, chica, you are *flaca*! I made *capuns*. I put two plates in the oven for you. And, we have our own Pinot—Riccardo made it! It's medicine. The twins drive me to drink!" Lupita turned her attention to Max and embraced and smothered him with kisses. "I like your hair. So you are the wild man?" Using both hands, she ruffled his hair like one would a child's. "*Que rico*, Federica! Let me keep him for a while! Riccardo, you won't mind, will you?"

Federica and Lupita kept up a continuous and animated conversation throughout dinner. The kitchen and living area were illuminated by candles on the table and glass slits built into the stove. Riccardo excused himself, arguing for a few hours of sleep before an early start in the morning. "*C'est l'histoire de* ma *vie*—the story of *my* life," he translated, referencing the work by Casanova, the infamous lover and writer—and poking fun at himself.

The only somber moment in the evening occurred when Lupita asked about Andreas. Federica simply replied that they had broken up, and that was the end of it.

Lupita took Federica's arm. "He is my cousin. But chica, trust me, it's for the best. I shouldn't say, but he is a pig. I'm happy for you."

Max relaxed, happy to be quiet, happy to enjoy a scrumptious meal and homemade wine, and listen to Fede and Lupita talk about nothing and everything.

He had asked about Capuns and learned that the dish is a local dumpling-like specialty made from spätzle dough mixed with meat and wrapped in Swiss chard. The dumplings are boiled and served in a milky broth, with cheese and bread on the side. Lupita promised a cooking lesson.

"How long do you visit? Longer than last time, I hope!"

"Not sure," Federica said, "Maybe tonight and tomorrow. We don't know, but I'm hoping a day or two, and a visit to Vals. Zumthor is like, so brilliant. Or maybe Papà's new place in Davos, the Therme Tavate— if the construction is mostly finished. Can you go? Spa-time for girls! I'd love it."

"Unlikely. But we'll see. Tomorrow you get to pull the stinkers around in a sled. Max can split wood. We're stockpiling. Already, there's so much snow!" Lupita took Federica's hands in her own. "Alicia, have you seen Alicia?"

"I have," Federica said. "Last week. She had to return to London."

"She's good? Next time bring her. Tell her *besos* from me!"

"She's super. Yes, I promise!"

Lupita took Federica by the shoulders, "You know what tomorrow is, right? I'm so happy you decided to come *here*!"

"No," Federica answered, thinking it might be a local holiday.

"*Tu cumpleaños!* Silly, it's your birthday!" Lupita screamed at Fede.

"Holy shit! I forgot!"

Stonecrop had already left the table and stretched out on the thick rug next to the stove. He removed his phone from his pocket and debated whether or not to look at it.

There was a note from Dante referencing the thumb drive, the one from Hitoshi's apartment. That was followed by a long piece about the girls in Hitoshi's album being part of a program to provide support for women victims of human trafficking.

Stonecrop didn't finish it, relieved though to learn that Hitoshi hadn't been trafficking the women, he'd been helping them. Both notes vanished after Stonecrop closed them.

The next text, this from Gregor, told him to prepare to travel to Japan after the holiday. He was to meet with Allied and work on a joint plan to salvage value from Geissner's failed real estate play. Gregor would call when he returned from Malta. A second text, marked with multiple exclamation points, informed Stonecrop that Gregor had accumulated several thousand Swiss francs in photo-radar tickets and that Gregor planned to deduct the sum from Stonecrop's pay!

Claudia texted him to call. She had information about "snow conditions." He did want to know if the drugs Hitoshi had given to Wulf were tainted but had no will to speak with her tonight or to revisit the pain and guilt he felt about Wulf's death.

Stonecrop let a dozen or so other texts go unread, until he saw one from Frau Ott asking if he could walk Rosie next week. He replied that he was away and that he and Federica were fine—knowing that that was the real reason she had contacted him. He turned off the phone and placed it on the bench that wrapped around the stove.

Snow accumulated on the windowsills and filled in the darkness on the other side of the glass. The wonderfully normal conversation at the kitchen table, like the soft light and radiant warmth from the soapstone stove, lulled him into a dreamy calm. He tucked a cushion and the one-eared bunny under his head for a pillow and immediately fell asleep.

The End

Author Bio

Wayne and his wonderful wife share a modest home a block from the beach in Manzanita, Oregon. He writes, climbs, and skis. His background includes long stretches of work in venture capital and project finance, and equally long stretches of study in philosophy, ancient Greek, and mathematics. He enjoys reading Shakespeare before bed, dancing salsa, cooking, and playing congas. He dearly wishes he knew a dozen languages but struggles mightily with the few with which he is familiar.

Other works:

How I Learned French or Certain Events in the Life of Otto Pulaski

Clave

Website: wwgoss.com